Flight of the Golden Harpy III

SONS OF SHAIL

NOVELS BY SUSAN KLAUS

Fantasy, the Golden Harpy Trilogy

Flight of the Golden Harpy

Flight of the Golden Harpy II, Waylaid

Flight of the Golden Harpy III, Sons of Shail

THRILLERS, the Christian Roberts Series

Secretariat Reborn

Shark Fin Soup

Wolf in the Crosshairs

Flight of the Golden Harpy III

SONS OF SHAIL

SUSAN KLAUS

CLAY
GULLEY
Publishing

Myakka City, Florida

© 2020 Susan Klaus

All rights reserved. No part of this book may be used or reproduced, stored in or introduced into a retrieval system, or transmitted in any form or by any means without the express written consent of the Publisher of this book.

This is a work of fiction. Names, characters, places, and incidents either are the product of the author's imagination or are used fictitiously. Any resemblance to actual persons living or dead, events, or locales is entirely coincidental.

ISBN 978-0-9979064-6-2

First Edition December 2020

Clay Gulley Publishing
Myakka City, Florida

Printed in the United States of America

Dedication

To Bill Carrigan, a great editor
who taught me to write.

ACKNOWLEDGEMENTS

To Jane Crick for the beautiful art and cover design, Mark Mathes, editing, Maryann Burchell, formatting. My critique boys, Pat Gray, Bill Carrigan, and Ray Ryder, and. my family, friends, and readers for their support.

CHAPTER ONE

In a hospital room on planet Oden, Monica Carlton sighed and gazed at her unconscious son. Alexander rested face down on the gurney with his bound yellow wings covering his lanky frame from shoulder to toe. His long blond hair partially hung over his flawless face. By all appearances, he looked an angel, but for her, it was camouflage, cloaking a demon.

Monica was a large unattractive woman and was grateful he resembled his beautiful harpy father, but at one-year-old displayed the feral nature of the half-bird, half-human creatures. Now approaching eighteen, he was out of control and lethal.

"You've given me no choice," she whispered, stroking his feathers. She pushed aside his hair and kissed his cheek. Strapped down and sedated, he was powerless to resist. "After the surgery, you'll be human, and we'll have a decent relationship."

She lowered her wide frame into the only chair and pressed a tissue to her nose, not for tears but to suppress the hospital smells, which made her queasy. She checked the time and, with irritation, fingered a gemstone pendant at her neck. The doctor should have arrived ten minutes ago.

She considered finding a pathetic nurse to unleash a tirade, but the door opened, and the balding, middle-aged doctor stepped into the room. “Miss Carlton, I didn’t know you were here,” he said with a weak grin. “I was told you’d left the hospital.”

“I did, Dr. Potter, but changed my mind and came back.” To leave while her son was in surgery might raise eyebrows. She rose and placed a hand on Alexander’s wings. “Dr. Potter, I’m having second thoughts about the amputation.”

“His wings are extraordinary, but you came to me asking for a normal son. I assured you he could be altered with surgery, but if the wings remain, he’ll hardly integrate with society.” Potter walked past her and checked the monitors. “We could forego the wing amputation and just do the lobotomy. At least he’ll lose the telepathy and his hypnotic ability.”

She stroked the pendant. “I definitely want that done, but without the wings, he’ll be grounded and might resent me. We already don’t get along.”

Potter chuckled. “After today, he’ll be too docile to care. My advice: remove the wings. He’ll soon adjust and be like other boys. Actually, these surgeries should have been done when he was little so the transformation was less traumatic. With the delayed abstraction, he’ll have more difficulty going from a harpy to a man. But it’s your decision.”

“I suppose you’re right.” For a keepsake, she plucked a large feather from his wing, held it to her nose, and inhaled the sweet scent. Father and son smelled alike, and a whiff from the plume reminded her of the passion with the fiery male harpy when her son was conceived.

“Don’t worry, Miss Carlton,” Potter said, patting her arm. “Alexander will walk out of my hospital as a well-adjusted young man.”

Three nurses wearing scrubs entered the room, and they fixed their stares on Alexander. Even out cold, he was mesmerizingly seductive.

Monica frowned at the women, and said to Potter, "Go ahead. Take off his wings. I'm sick of gawkers."

"Move him to room four," Potter ordered the nurses. "We'll prep him there." The nurses detached the monitors and pushed the levitating gurney into the corridor. Monica and Potter followed.

"Why don't you go to the waiting room," he said. "The best physicians on Oden will perform the surgery, and we should be done in a few hours."

Monica nodded and walked down the hallway to a large room with rows of chairs. A bay window had a panoramic view of the red desert and distant purple mountains. In searing heat, the barren terrain was treeless with little life. She wondered if raising a jungle-dwelling harpy on this miserable planet had contributed to her son's insolent behavior.

She stepped past a seated man with a small child on his lap and a toddler playing at his feet. Preferring grievers to brats, she sat down near two older women engaged in whispers and tears. She removed a small communicator from her purse and checked the messages.

A familiar female voice addressed her backside. "Miss Carlton?"

Monica turned to her son's nanny. The mousey, fifty-something woman pushed back the salt-and-pepper bangs, revealing moist eyes. Monica snarled, "What are you doing here, Mollie?"

"I learned what you planned to do to Alex. Please, Miss Carlton, it's wrong. Cutting open his head and removing part of his brain and taking off his wings won't make him human. Harpies might resemble humans, but their temperament is as fragile as a bird's. If he's disfigured, the stress will kill him. He'll curl up into a ball and lose the will to live."

"That's bullshit, Mollie. He's too willful, and those wings are socially unacceptable. Dr. Potter assures me he'll adapt and be fine."

"That man knows nothing about harpies. I'm telling you, you're making a huge mistake."

"I hired you because of your expertise with harpies, but what has it gotten me? I have a son who hates me and uses his telepathy to terrify people. I'm done listening to you. He's my son and it's my decision to have him fixed."

Mollie lowered her head and stared at the floor. "Alex doesn't hate you, Miss Carlton," she said quietly. "He lashes out because he can't sense your love. It confuses and hurts him."

* * *

The nurses moved Alex into room four and placed him on a stainless steel table. Lying on his stomach, they strapped down his arms and legs. His wings were freed and hung off the table, his feathers covering the surrounding floor. As the nurses began the surgery prep, Dr. Potter and three physicians entered and stood over their patient.

"He's a pretty thing," the anesthesiologist said. "I looked up 'harpy.' According to an Earth dictionary he doesn't fit the definition of an ugly female monster with wings." On Alex's body, he attached the patches with wires leading to monitors that would record his breathing and heart rate.

Potter pulled on surgical gloves. "His species is from a small jungle planet, and they're called harpies, but don't let his elegant looks fool you. He is a monster. His mother is scared to death of him."

Another doctor examined the wings. "Gorgeous wings, shame they have to go. This A.J. should be interesting without robotics."

"His composition is unique, and robots would be risky," Potter said.

"I see an irregularity now," said the anesthesiologist. "He has an enormous heart, twice the size of a man's."

A nurse applied a cool surgical scrub to the wing joints, and Alex flinched. She stopped and said, "Dr. Potter, he moved."

"Impossible," said Potter. "He's heavily sedated. It's your imagination."

A second nurse grasped a clump of the patient's hair and turned on a hair clipper to shave the head for the brain surgery.

Alex shuddered, hearing the buzzing near his ear.

"He just moved again!" the second nurse said, releasing the hair and stepping back. "I think he's coming around."

The anesthesiologist looked up at the monitor board. "She might be right. There is a surge in his heart rate, and his breathing is elevated. Something is upsetting him. Oh my God, his heart just stopped!"

"Get the restraints off," yelled Potter. "Flip him over so we can revive him." The nurses and doctors hurriedly unfastened the straps, folded up the wings, and rolled Alex onto his back.

"Wait," the anesthesiologist said, staring at the monitors. "His heart rate is normal again. Maybe this is an apparatus malfunction."

Alex opened his eyes and stared up at the four men and three women surrounding him on the table. He quickly surmised he was in a hospital amid doctors and nurses.

"He's awake!" one nurse voiced.

"Secure the straps and get me a sedative," Potter shouted. A nurse rummaged through a drawer and handed him a syringe. Two doctors held Alex down while the nurses tried frantically to re-buckle the restraints.

Alex lifted his head and stared at the two doctors pinning down his arms. "Let go," he said, and they immediately released him and froze in a trance.

The nurse dropped the restraints and stepped away from Alex. "Dr. Potter, look at them."

Seeing the doctors, the little balding man yelled to a nurse. "Lidia, call Security! And get his mother in here."

A nurse ran to a wall communicator and hit the keys. "Code Red, operating room four. Send guards," she cried and fled the room.

The two dazed doctors took up medical scalpels from a tray and pressed them against their own jugulars. A nurse screamed, "They are going to kill themselves."

"Alexander, stop this!" said Potter.

Alex sat up and swung around while pulling his wings to his back. "Dr. Potter, I'm sure you've been informed I can read and control minds. Yours tells me how you and my plotting mother drugged my food and brought me here to…" He shuddered with the revelation. "You intended to amputate my wings and give me a lobotomy?"

"I was trying to help you, Alexander," said Potter.

"Lies," Alex seethed and hopped off the table. Grabbing a towel, he wrapped it around his waist to cover his nude body. "You were only interested in my mother's money, not my welfare. Perhaps you should learn how it feels to lose your limbs. I'll give you a choice; legs or arms?"

With a glance, Alex put the two doctors into motion. They lowered the scalpels from their throats, thrust out the blades, and marched zombie-like toward Potter. The anesthesiologist and two nurses scurried to a wall and crouched behind the medical equipment.

"Please, Alexander, stop them. Don't make them hurt me," Potter wailed, stumbling away from his spellbound colleagues. Trapped in a corner, he broke down and blubbered, "I'm sorry, Alexander, I'm so sorry."

Alex flung the hair from his cold blue eyes. "Terrifying, isn't it? Now you know how it feels."

"But your mother hired me to do it."

"Yes," Alex said, and rubbed his forehead. "What to do with her?"

Three security guards burst into the room with drawn laser guns and fired at the two doctors on the verge of slashing Potter. The stunned doctors fell to the floor.

"Not them, him," Potter yelled, pointing at Alex. "Shoot him!" The guards swung their weapons toward Alex, but immediately halted and stood like statues.

Alex chuckled. "They can't shoot me. No one can." With a nod, he brought the guards to life, and they aimed their weapons at Potter.

Alex's mother along with Mollie and a nurse rushed into the operating room and stared at the two unconscious doctors on the floor, the three disorientated guards pointing their weapons toward Potter as others hid behind monitors. Alex stood in the center of the chaos.

"He wants to kill me, Miss Carlson," Potter shrieked. "Stop him."

"Alexander, what have you done?" Monica rasped.

Alex instinctively arched his wings and ruffled his feathers, displaying harpy anger. "What have *I* done?" He stepped to his mother, who was triple his weight and girth, but the same in height. He aimed his piercing stare directly into her eyes. "What have you done, my loving mother? Perhaps I should have these doctors operate on you and insert a heart."

Seeing his raised wings, his mother lowered her brazen gaze and her stance wilted. Without a word, she sheepishly moved away from him. "Good idea, Mom. We'll talk later." He tossed the hair from his eyes and refocused on Potter.

"That's enough, Alex," Mollie said. "You've made your point and given them a good scare."

"But, Mollie, this Potter guy was going to chop off my wings and open up my head to make me a vegetable. He must be punished."

"Alex, you are a golden harpy, superior to humans, and should behave with grace, not wrath," Mollie said, moving next to him. "Let this go."

Mollie was right, Alex thought. She was always right. With drooped wings and a weary glance at the guards, he telepathically ordered them to lower their weapons.

Mollie turned to Potter. “Alex is young, still learning, but you were in no danger, Doctor. Harpies are gentle, and he would have calmed down before shedding blood.” She grasped Alex’s hand. “Come on. I’ll take you home.”

Alex followed her, but hesitated at the doorway and looked back at his mother and the hospital staff. “I probably wouldn’t have harmed you, but don’t press your luck and try this again.”

In silence, Alex and Mollie walked down the corridor and exited the hospital. In the vast parking lot, Alex leaned against the door of Mollie’s vehicle and gazed up at the dome that covered the city. “I still can’t believe it. My own mother tried to destroy me.”

Mollie stroked his head. “People destroy what they fear and don’t understand. She tried to change you because she’s afraid.”

He turned toward the hospital. “That’s the first time I’ve been truly afraid. It was like a nightmare, Mollie. I could hear and smell them, but couldn’t move. Even worse, my mind was too groggy from the drugs to use my telepathy. The panic helped stop my heart, and that gave me time to get control of the situation.”

“I’m sorry you had that bad experience.”

“You told them I wouldn’t have hurt them, but I’m not so sure. I wanted revenge. That proves I’m not a real harpy and am more like my mother.” He dropped his head and his bare foot kicked a pebble across the pavement.

“Alex, you are a true harpy with the nature to protect, not harm. Never doubt it.” She lifted his chin. “Have I ever lied to you?”

He bit his lip and shook his head. “I’ve missed you, Mollie.” Taking the small woman in his arms, he nuzzled her cheek.

“Missed you, too.” With a smile, she ruffled his long hair and opened the back door. “Now hop in.”

“I could fly home.”

“In broad daylight, I don’t think so. People will see you, and you’ve caused enough commotion for one day.”

Alex tightly folded in his wings and climbed into the backseat. Mollie drove out of the parking lot merged with the bumper-to-bumper traffic of Mirage. After several miles, she turned into the winding driveway of his mother's mansion. They stopped at the front door and entered the large white house.

Sally, the elderly, plump housekeeper, met them in the foyer. "Alexander, thank heavens you're home, and you still have your wings. I've been worried sick. I'm so glad your mother didn't go through with the surgery."

"You knew about it?"

"Only after you ate breakfast and passed out," Sally said. "That's when Miss Carlton explained she'd drugged your food and planned to transform you at the hospital. As soon as those men took you away, I called Mollie."

"I'm glad you did," Mollie said, "Miss Carlton didn't change her mind. Alex stopped the doctors."

"Alex, I'm so sorry," Sally said, tearing up. "I never would've given you that food if I'd known."

"If you had known, my telepathy would've have sensed your thoughts and warned me," Alex said, placing his hand on her shoulder. "None of this was your fault."

Lilly, his mother's skinny, red-headed secretary, stepped out of her office into the foyer. Her jaw dropped when she saw Alex.

"You look surprised, Lilly," Alex said, "not expecting me here and still in one piece."

"You...you should be at the hospital," Lilly muttered.

Alex smiled. "I didn't approve of you and my mother's plans. Sorry to spoil your day."

Lilly backed against a wall, knocking a hanging painting askew. "Alexander, don't you do anything to me."

"Lilly, you're a snake. Maybe you should slither around on your belly for a week."

"Leave her alone," said Mollie. "The bitch isn't worth the effort."

Lilly scurried to her office doorway and turned. "Mollie, you were fired. You're not supposed to be in this house," she screeched before slamming the door.

"Miss Carlton fired you?" asked Sally. "She said you went on vacation and to tell Alex."

Alex sighed. "My mother's getting smart. She can't deceive me, so she uses others." He took Mollie's hand. "You'll be reinstated. I promise."

Mollie grinned. "I could use the job, but you don't need a nanny anymore."

"But I need a friend."

Alex stood alone in the foyer and watched Mollie drive away. The hospital events left him unsettled. His relationship with his mother had gone from difficult to nonexistent. The smidgen of trust was gone. He searched his feelings for her, trying to find affection and forgiveness. It was unfathomable.

Sally had fetched a white cotton sash and handed it to him. "I thought you might want this instead of that towel."

"Thanks," he said, wrapping it about his hips. Edgy and still troubled over his mother's betrayal, he needed to settle down and consider his future. He walked across the cool marble floor in the lavish house and approached his safe place, a large solarium. Through the glass walls, he saw Jerry, the old black gardener, raking around the plants.

As Alex entered, Jerry grinned through his white beard, "Praise the Lord, you still got wings."

"So you heard about my mother's scheme?"

Jerry leaned the rake against a tree. "Yes, sir, I came to work after you'd gone, and your mom said that she was turning you into a man and planned to cut down your tree and getting rid of this here solarium. And I should find another job."

Alex sucked in a breath, feeling dismal. "I guess I disappoint her."

Jerry scowled. "Come on, Mr. Alex, don't be like that. I'd be darn proud if you was my son, wings, and all. You're smarter than people and as handsome as they come, but more important, you got a gift, boy. You can see right through people. You're gonna do great things." He picked up the rake and chuckled. "Yes, sir, another Alexander the Great, conquering the world, and what I read about that young blond Greek, he had troubles with his mom, too."

Alex smiled at the gardener's common sense and wisdom. He respected Jerry far more than the professors and his first-class tutors.

He flapped his wings and landed in the gigantic oak, the first tree imported to Oden and planted in a city park. Stretching out on a moss-covered limb, he relived an old memory as a fledgling. When initially seeing the tree, he had become so excited that he flew into its branches and refused to leave. The authorities had to be called to get him down. His mother was embarrassed and scowled him, but a year later she purchased the park and built the mansion and solarium around the oak. She told people that it would keep her rowdy youngster off the curtain rods and out of the chandeliers. He knew better. She wanted him happy because she loved him back then.

"But not now," he whispered. Stroking the rough bark, he inhaled the woody aroma and closed his eyes, feeling a knot in his stomach. Besides her attempt to remove his telepathy and wings, she'd intended to eliminate all he loved: Mollie, Jerry, this tree. He gripped his mouth and covered himself with a wing. For the first time since very young, he buried his face in his wing feathers and wept.

After some time, he collected himself. Shaking off the tears, he climbed to the treetop and stood on the highest limb. He lifted his wings to the two suns and gazed out at the scorched landscape beyond the solarium glass and the city dome. The restless longing swelled, the desire to escape the barriers and fly across the desert until his wings gave out or he died of heatstroke.

Humans were content in their confining homes and cities, so his harpy roots and psyche must cause this reoccurring daydream, a suicidal willingness for freedom and flight. As he approached adulthood, the sentiment grew, and after the misery of today, it was stronger.

CHAPTER TWO

After the calamity in the operation room, Monica watched her son and Molly stroll down the corridor to disappear around a corner. She looked upward and shook her head. Without lifting a wing, Alexander had destroyed her plans and made a mockery of the hospital staff. The three guards under his hypnotic spell regained awareness as the doctors and nurses, breathing sighs of relief with his departure, collected themselves.

"Should we go after him?" a guard asked Dr. Potter.

"No, he's too powerful," said Potter, wiping the nervous sweat from his forehead. "Before you could neutralize him, he'd control your minds again." He took a deep weary breath and turned to Monica. "Miss Carlton, we need to talk."

Several hours later, a secretary directed Monica into Dr. Potter's office. Besides Potter, a short, mustached man was present. Potter rose from his desk and introduced him. "Miss Carlton, this is Dr. Collins, the leading physiatrist on Oden and the administrator of Mirage Mental Institution. I've asked him to join us for this consultation."

"It's a pleasure to meet the granddaughter of the founding father of our planet," Collins said, smiling and extended a hand, but Monica snubbed the handshake, in no mood for little social-climbing doctors.

"A mental facility," Monica said, settling into a chair. "Has it come to that?"

"I'm afraid so," Potter said. "Alexander endangered the lives of ten people this morning. If not for his nanny, I believe he would have maimed or killed me. Either you place him in Dr. Collins's institution or the hospital is pressing charges for attempted murder. He's dangerous. Confinement in a mental facility run by robots is the best solution and preferable to prison."

Monica sprang up and leaned over the desk, face to face with Potter. "How dare you threaten me with ultimatums," she thundered. "If you press charges, my lawyers will have a field day with your hospital. You and your incompetent, ill-equipped people caused the problem. As for attempted murder, my son didn't touch anyone. No judge and jury would convict him. "

Potter backpedaled. "Please, Miss Carlton, I had no intention of threatening you, but something must be done. By your own admission, Alexander is a threat. Next time he's angry, someone might be seriously injured. It could be you."

Monica stepped back from the desk, struck by Potter's last words. Alexander was furious about the intended surgeries, but would he harm her? The tigress defending her cub diminished to a worried woman. She sat down and reconsidered. "Maybe a mental institution is the answer."

"That's a wise decision," said Dr. Collins with an eager grin. "I promise your boy will receive the best of care. From Dr. Potter's account, his psychic abilities are extraordinary. There's nothing on record like him. He can be safely studied, and I might help him. I could teach him to harness his powers."

Monica did a sideward glance. "I'm no fool, Collins. You don't care about him. You're only interested in having a fancy lab rat in your nuthouse."

"Institutionalizing him is a valid alternative to surgery," said Collins.

Monica's eyes watered. "Is it? Removing his telepathy and wings seems kinder than a lifetime in a cage." She sniffled and brushed away a tear. "I can't believe it's come to this. I was in my late forties and had gone through the change when I became pregnant and gave birth to a beautiful winged baby. I later learned that no woman and male harpy had ever produced a baby, so I called Alexander my miracle child. Now my precious miracle has grown into a terrible beast."

"Even by today's standards, we still consider harpies feral," Collins said. "It must have crossed your mind that besides wings and looks, your son could inherit his father's undesirable personality."

Monica harshly wiped away the tear. "Of course, I considered it," she snapped. "But the damn experts assured me that if I raised him in a civilized environment he'd behave like a human."

Collins opened a file resting in a briefcase. "Since Alexander might become my patient, I researched harpies. Unfortunately, we know little about them." He looked at the papers. "They're part human and part loca eagle, and inhabit a tropical planet called Dora. Until eighteen years ago, they were listed as wild animals and hunted like game, but the courts changed their status. They're now recognized as mortals with human rights. They use their telepathy to communicate silently with one another, but nothing in here suggests they abuse it or have Alexander's capabilities. Miss Carlton, tell me more about his father? How did you meet him?"

She fluffed her hair and reclined a little. "The harpy was mute, never made a sound, so I never really knew him. I met him on a voyage to Earth. A prostitute approached me and several women friends and said she owned a harpy. She claimed he was gorgeous and an excellent lover. For a fee, we could use him."

Monica glanced uncomfortably at the doctors. "It's rather embarrassing, paying for sex, but those long voyages grow boring. The harpy proved gorgeous and extraordinary in bed because he could sense our secret desires, but he didn't have psychic powers like

Alexander. The creature was chained to a bed and fed drugs that kept him aroused for the customers. It was pathetic, but he was just an animal. Later, the prostitute was arrested, and I don't know what became of her harpy. I never saw either of them again."

"How was his temperament?" asked Collins.

"For a slender male, he was strong and the sex was a little rough. I later learned on the ship that he carried a red tag, listing him as dangerous for killing several men on his home planet." She looked up anxiously.

"My God," said Potter. "I wish you'd told me about his murdering father. I would have taken extra precautions before subjecting my staff to Alexander."

"But Alexander is educated, cultured, and grew up with people," Monica said. "He's nothing like his father, a wild beast that was captured in a jungle."

Potter sighed, "He is civilized, but at the hospital, he revealed his aggression. His nanny said he's young and still learning, but obviously not for the better. Miss Carlton, for the safety of others and your son, he must immediately be placed Dr. Collins's care."

"And how do you purpose that?" asked Monica.

"Perhaps we can stun him while asleep?" said Collins.

"Impossible," said Monica. "His instincts are phenomenal compared to us. He can hear the slightest footstep and smells anyone entering the house. He's a light sleeper and sees like a cat in the dark. No one can sneak up on him. An even bigger problem is his ability to read your thoughts. If I got near him, he'd know your plans. He also learns quickly and would never be tricked again with drugged food."

"Is there a chance you could convince him to come in?" asked Collins.

Monica frowned. "I hope you're kidding. Mollie is the only person who can make him do anything, but she devoted to him. She'd never lead him into a trap."

Collins looked down at Alexander's file. "This says she's been his nanny for twelve years, since he was five. How did you come to hire her?"

"Initially, I didn't need help. Alexander was a delightful baby, never cried, but when he reached the terrible twos and learned to fly, he became impossible. He'd rip off his clothing and run around nude, urinating on everything. If I tried to stop him, he'd fly out of reach. His wings broke lamps, vases, you name it. Child caregivers were no help. I was at my wit's end and placed a web ad for a harpy handler. Mollie showed up. She walked in and ordered him off the top of a bookcase. He flew into her arms, and from then on, they became inseparable. I never cared for her. She's a menial woman with no education, but she's the only one who could manage him."

"Can she still control him?" asked Collins.

"She doesn't try," said Monica, "In fact she's encouraged Alexander's outrageous behavior, telling him he's a superior golden harpy and should embrace his heritage and develop his animal instincts and telepathy. That's why I fired her."

"All right, Miss Carlton," said Collins. "I believe I have enough information on Alexander for now. I'll figure out a way to bring him in so no one gets hurt." He held out a paper. "I'll need you to sign for his commitment, putting me in total charge of him."

Monica snatched the paper out of Collins's hand. Without even reading it, she scribbled her signature on the bottom line. "At least he'll be out of my hair."

* * *

At the Carlton home, Lilly remained at her secretarial desk in the study, avoiding contact with Alexander. The spoiled winged brat was pissed at her and his mother for the hospital stunt this morning, and he could dish out some humiliating revenge. At 5 pm she collected her purse to leave for home when the communicator buzzed. Miss Carlton appeared on the screen.

"How is he?" Monica asked.

"Not happy," said Lilly. "He's up in his tree sulking. Agatha said he refused to come down for lunch so he might start one of his hunger strikes. Are you coming home to deal with him?"

"No, I don't dare. It'll take him some time to get over this hospital fiasco. Tonight I'm staying at a Desert Sands hotel, but tomorrow morning I'm catching a shuttle to the space station for a weeklong vacation, planning to relax and do some shopping. By the time I return, maybe Alexander will have cooled off."

"Do you want Agatha to pack a bag for you and have it sent to the hotel?"

"Yes, but just the essentials. I can buy extra clothing or anything else I need there. Also tell Agatha that in my absences, some workers are coming to the house and add more sprinklers to the solarium. I don't want Alexander to read a lot into these repairmen. You understand?"

"Perfectly," Lilly said, grinning about the so-called repairmen.

"You should also take a week off. If you bump into Alexander, he might get ideas."

In Dr. Collin's office at the mental facility, Monica ended her call with Lilly and leaned back on the plush sofa. "I've done my part. It's up to you now to get him in here."

"Don't worry," said Collins. "My staff can handle him,"

She chuckled. "That is exactly what Dr. Potter said." Rising, she gazed out the window at the institution's manicured grounds. The peaceful setting hardly appeared like a prison. "I'm washing my hands of the whole affair, but remember I warned you. If Alexander senses your repairmen have really come to take him, there will be trouble. His patience with clinic employees is probably gone."

Dr. Collins twisted his thin, greasy mustache. "I have a backup plan."

* * *

Alex lay on the tree limb with his chin resting on his arms. Jerry had gone home, so the solarium was quiet. He closed his eyes and listened to the haunting desert wind outside the city dome. The front door closed with Lilly leaving for the night. He lifted his head when Agatha tapped on the glass and entered the solarium with a tray of food.

"I have your dinner." She placed the small baskets of fruits and nuts on a rock slab that served as a table. Like the tree he slept in, the rock brought him comfort. The peculiarity of longing for the natural world had manifested with age. He attributed to his harpy blood.

"Alexander, stop daydreaming and come here," said Agatha.

He smiled and glided down to her. "I haven't heard my mother's vehicle. Has she's chosen not to come home?"

"She knows you're angry," said Agatha. "Lilly said she's gone to the space station for a week to give you time to calm down."

"After what she tried, she'd better stay a month."

Agatha's eyes darkened with concern. "Alex, you wouldn't hurt your mother, would you?"

Alex took a deep breath. "No, not physically, but she might start attending her club luncheons with the lipstick applied to her nose. She deserves to look like a clown."

"Oh, my word, she'd be mortified." She pulled a leaf out of his shoulder-length hair. "You better behave and stop those gags. They have brought on your troubles." She looked down at the berries and nuts. "Now, are you going to eat for me, or do I have to worry?"

The old housekeeper's scowling brightened his mood. "For you," he said and popped a few nuts in his mouth before flying back to the limb.

Over the next few days, the house remained quiet with Lilly and his mother gone. Although Alex had a spacious bedroom and luxurious bathroom, he washed in the cold waterfall and doused his feathers in the solarium pond. Since becoming a teenager, these daily habits further upset his mother, who complained to Mollie that he was turning into an animal. Mollie had replied, "Miss Carlton, your son is a harpy, and part animal. It's like raising a lion cub and expecting it to grow up into a domesticated cat. The older Alex becomes, the more he will reject his human side."

Mollie always spoke the truth, even when his mother didn't like it. She was also the only one who understood Alex, knew he would embrace his harpy blood with maturity. It had been gradually building. As a small fledgling, he could detect human feelings and had learned to probe a person's deepest thoughts. As a teenager, he fine-tuned his instincts and bolstered the telepathy. Then he had read a book about hypnosis and discovered he could invade the human subconscious and force a response, manipulating the weak-minded humans. He spared those he loved, like Mollie, Agatha, and Jerry, but others bearing ill-will toward him were fair game. His callous mother topped the list.

She had never shown him much love, treating him like a prized possession to show off to her wealthy friends. At five-years-old, he gave up nuzzling her and seeking a gentle, stroking hand. Longing for affection, he had turned to Mollie.

His paltry relationship with his mother completely deteriorated into a clash of wills. Mollie had explained that his rebellious, wild nature, intelligence, and telepathy came from his father, a golden harpy. The yellow-winged species were considered more aggressive, intelligent, and braver than the brown-winged harpies so they were the alphas and dominated the flocks. Alex had probed his mother's mind, hoping to learn more about his father, but she didn't know much, not even his name.

With an uncaring, spiteful mother and no fatherly guidance, Alex found himself at odds with the world. Increasingly, he disliked humans after probing their minds. They thought his human frame was attractive and were fascinated with his wings, but people also considered him a freak, part animal and beneath them. He had never known another harpy, so Alex approached adulthood frustrated and bitter. With the capacity to kill and his growing aggravation, he thought of himself a ticking time-bomb. He had to get out of here before exploding.

Alex stepped from the shallow pond and ruffled his wet feathers. He bent over, retrieved his sash from the grass, and tied it around his waist. Mollie had told him that male harpies wore a hip sash. He proudly accepted the custom, trying to conform to who or what he was. His mother, of course, disapproved of the sparse clothing.

He stretched out on the soft grass and extended his wings to dry them and thought about his mother. His telepathy revealed her deep, dark secrets, and perhaps that was why he forgave her shortcomings.

She was born into the wealthy Carlton family, the founders of Oden, and the owners of mineral and mining rights on a dozen other planets. She had anything she wanted, except for one thing; the love of a man. Her appearance didn't help, being tall, heavy-boned, and overweight. Cosmetic surgeries added little to improve her horse face. Her snobbish attitude was also a turnoff. The result, she never married. As a young woman, she had two relationships that quickly ended. The first man was unfaithful and the second stole her jewelry.

By the time she met Alex's father on the spaceship, she was a resentful, middle-aged woman. She told Alex that the harpy was a horrible beast, but searching her memories of the encounter, he learned the truth. His father was the victim, tied up and drugged. His mother was the true beast, brutalizing, and ravaging him to satisfy her anger with men. Finally, having his fill of the abuse, his father attacked her. His dominance earned her respect. The brief ship fling was the happiest time in her life. Knowing she loved his dad gave Alex some peace. Inside his coldhearted mother was a sad woman who had longed for the loving companionship with a man.

Alex heard footsteps in the house and sat up as Agatha walked into the solarium.

"The house sure is empty," she said. "Even Jerry is off today. I'm done cleaning and thought I'd come out, so you won't be lonely."

Alex wrapped his wings around his body. “You are one of my favorites, Agatha, and appreciate the concern, but I’ve grown used to being by myself.”

She sighed and sat down on the rock. “You’re still young. Someday, you’ll have someone to share your life. Are you still upset with your mother?”

Alex looked skyward. “I’m more upset that I failed to sense she’d harm me. And I believe it isn’t over. I’ve been thinking that perhaps I should leave this planet and find my people, the harpies.”

“You’re nearly eighteen, and your mother couldn’t stop you, but I’d miss you.”

Alex cocked his head. “A vehicle just pulled up out front.”

Agatha smiled. “Your hearing always amazes me. Lilly told me to expect some repairmen today. They’re supposed to install more sprinklers in the solarium. I better let them in.”

“Jerry said my mother was tearing down the solarium. So why would she order sprinklers, especially when they’re not needed? It sounds like a lame excuse to get in here with me.”

“Oh, Alex, do you think they’re up to no good?”

“I’m coming with you.”

The doorbell rang as they walked through the house. Agatha opened the front door while Alex stood back in the foyer.

Two men in work uniforms stood in the doorway, and one said, “We’ve got a work order to install sprinklers in your solarium.”

“Can I see the order,” Agatha asked, and the man handed her a paper. She turned to Alex. “This looks legitimate.”

Alex crossed his arms, “Come in, gentlemen.”

The two men seemed surprised to see Alex. They stepped into the foyer and simultaneously reached for something under their jackets.

Alex leered at the men, and they froze. They turned to face one another and violently head butted each other. They collapsed on the floor, one man moaning in pain with the other out cold.

"My God, Alexander," Agatha screamed, staring at the blood from the men's head wounds that pooled at her feet. "They were just repairmen."

Alex reached under the jacket of the semi-conscious man and pulled out a laser gun. "Since when do repairmen need weapons? I read their thoughts. They planned to stun me and take me to a mental facility." He shook his head, "This is more of my mother's doing."

"Regardless, you shouldn't have forced them to hurt themselves. They're seriously injured. I better call an ambulance."

"Screw them. My mother and those doctors were warned not to try this again." He suddenly got a whiff of something toxic. "Agatha, something bad is in the air." He sniffed again and located the source. "It's coming from the house vents. Get out of the house now."

"I don't smell it but believe you." She stepped toward the door, but weaved and leaned against a door jamb. "I don't feel so well." As she fainted, he caught her in his arms.

Gently placing Agatha on the floor, he felt the lightheaded effect from gas odorless to humans. He staggered through the door and crumbled outside. Softly panting with fear, his drowsy eyes glimpsed several more men running up the drive toward him before falling into a deep sleep.

* * *

Alexander woke in a small room and gazed at the padded floor, walls, and ceiling. Except for a mirror on a high wall, the room was empty. He stood and yelled at the mirror. "You can't keep me in here." He tried to detect a human subconscious, but sensed nothing. They were elsewhere and safely beyond his telepathic reach. He paced around the twelve-by-twelve foot room; so confining he couldn't completely extend his wings. He stopped in the center and shivered with helplessness. "Mother, why are you doing this to me?"

The mirror turned into a screen, and a man appeared. "Alexander, your mother is not here. My name is Dr. Collins, and I'll be treating you. Don't be afraid. We won't hurt you."

"How long…." Alex swallowed his throat lump. "How long will you keep me in here?"

"That depends. Right now, this is the safest place for you. You're a danger to people and yourself. The two men who came to your home had to be hospitalized. Once you're evaluated, treated with the right drugs and therapy, we may let you out. Your telepathy must be nullified or controlled."

"I don't need telepathy to know a lie. You'll never let me go. The only way you'll control me is when I'm dead." He curled up on the floor and covered himself with his wings. Concentrating on endless captivity, he felt the stress and despair take over. His heart beat faster, but stayed at a safe rhythm.

A woman's voice conveyed the monitor readings to Dr. Collins. "Alexander, I know what you're trying to do. I've studied harpies and learned how they stop their hearts in captivity. We have given you a drug that prevents suicide. If you refuse to eat, robots will force-feed you."

Alex rose and focused on the screen. "Dr. Collins, those studies were about brown-winged harpies, but I am a golden and cannot yield." He partially spread his wings and flew up to the screen. Using his head, he hit the screen with full force. The blow nearly knocked him out, and he fell to the floor. He wobbled slightly when rising. Again he soared up, crashed against the hard plastic screen, and plummeted to the padding. His light body and head couldn't shatter it to escape, but that wasn't his intent.

"Stop, Alexander," shouted Collins. "You can't break the screen and get out. You'll only hurt yourself."

Alex lifted his head and shook it. He staggered to his feet, reeling from dizziness. His head hurt, and blood ran down his face. He glared at the doctor and spread his wings.

"Jesus, he's trying to break his neck," Collins yelled. "Gas him, gas him."

Through small vents, gas entered the room. Alex detected it and held his breath. In a third attempt, he fluttered, slammed into the screen, and collapsed on the floor. Breathing hard, he clawed at the padding until the gas rendered him unconscious.

When Alex woke in the same room, his head ached and the nerve endings in his feathers also stung. He extended a wing and saw his long flight feathers had been clipped in half. The mutilation of severing the veins inside the quills left his yellow wings smeared and spattered with dry blood. With short plumes, he couldn't fly into the screen and kill himself.

He coiled up and covered his head with a wing to hide his moist eyes. His feathers quivered in terror. For the first time, he was helpless.

CHAPTER THREE

In her small apartment, Mollie sat on a worn couch with a computer on her lap. Lying alongside her leg was Frankie, a domesticated trit, a little weasel-type species from the mountain caves of Oden. Mollie read the advertisements on the screen while stroking her pet's red fur. "No jobs, Frankie," she said with a sigh. "No one needs an animal handler on this godforsaken planet."

The communicator buzzed on her desk. She rose, and Frankie jumped to the floor and followed her. Agatha was on the screen. Mollie tapped the connect key and said, "Hi, Agatha, how's our boy today?"

Agatha's eyes welled with tears. "He's gone, Mollie. They took him yesterday. I'm afraid I'll never see Alexander again."

"Wait a minute. Who took him?"

Agatha brushed away a tear, and said, "It was some horrible little doctor and his men."

"How could they possibly subdue Alex? He's capable of defending himself."

"They gassed the house and knocked us out. They revived me, and I watched them load our poor boy into a van. When I threatened to call the police, Dr. Collins showed me Alexander's commitment papers to Mirage Mental Institution. Miss Carlton had signed it."

"That bitch!"

"I didn't call you because I thought Alexander would overpower them and come home, like before, but he hasn't. Is there anything you can do?"

Mollie slumped into the desk chair. "I doubt it. I'm not Alex's guardian, and it would take a lot of money to fight it in court— money I don't have."

Agatha bit her lip. "Mollie, there's something else you should know. Before the gas, two men came to the door. Alexander sensed their intentions and forced the men to hurt themselves. One was in bad shape and had to be rushed to the hospital."

"Idiots! They pushed him too far." Mollie bit her knuckle in thought. "This changes everything. They might charge him with attempted murder and lock him up for a long time in the institution or prison. Even Miss Carlton and her money might be unable to release him."

"What can we do?"

"I'll go to the institution and try to see him."

After Agatha's call, Mollie walked into the bedroom to dress for her trip to the mental institution. Staring at the clothes in her closet, she couldn't focus on what to wear. Her thoughts were of Alex and how to free him. The anxiety brought back the memory of a similar experience.

Over two decades earlier, another golden harpy had been caught and caged, and Mollie was powerless to help him. It was déjà vu all over again. She compared a golden harpy to a yellow rose, beautiful but with menacing thorns, and like the plant shut up without sunlight, a harpy withered and died. That could be Alex's fate.

She put on her best dress and drove to the institution. After parking in the visitor garage, she walked into the silver high-rise and approached the receptionist. "I'm here to see a patient, Alexander Carlton."

"Are you a relative?"

"No, but I'm his nanny."

The receptionist tapped the computer while reading the screen. "I'm sorry, but Mr. Carlton is in isolation and not allowed visitors."

"I'd like to speak to his doctor, then."

The woman studied the information and lifted her eyebrows. "It appears Dr. Collins, our administrator, is personally handling his case. You will need an appointment to see him."

"Can you tell his office I'm here? I'm Mollie Harris, Alex's nanny. It's important I speak to Dr. Collins about Alex's care."

The receptionist contacted the administration office and conveyed Mollie's request to a secretary. A minute later the receptionist looked up and smiled. "You're in luck, Miss Harris. Dr. Collins will see you. Just follow the yellow lights."

Mollie walked down the corridor, sticking with the strip of lights. She knew luck had nothing to do with Collins's agreeing to see her. Alex was likely throwing a fit, lashing out at his captors, and Collins probably needed advice or someone who could control him. As the only harpy expert on Oden, she was that person. She strolled into the reception area of the administrator's office and approached the secretary. "I'm Mollie Harris."

"Take a seat, Miss Harris," said the secretary. "Dr. Collins will be with you momentarily."

Mollie sat down in a plush chair, thinking "momentarily" could mean hours with a doctor. She glanced at the oil paintings, lavish furnishings, and hand-woven rug. The mental hospital spared no expense to conceal it was a nuthouse. After half an hour, a skinny man with black hair plugs and a mustache entered the waiting room.

"Miss Harris, I'm Dr. Collins, please come into my office."

"How's Alex?" Mollie asked, following him.

"He's fine, just fine," Collins said, sitting down behind his desk. "Please have a seat."

"I imagine he's been less than cooperative," she said, facing him.

"It's nothing we can't handle, but I'm glad you came in." He grinned and tapped his computer keys. "Miss Carlton gave me information about her son, but according to his file, you took care of him for twelve years. Maybe you can fill in some blanks."

"Dr. Collins, let me be clear. I'm here to help Alex, not you. I'm concerned because you and his mother don't seem to understand that harpies have fragile natures, and if locked up, they can die."

"I'm aware of a harpy's mindset. I did a preliminary study and learned that feral harpies can go into shock or suffer a fatal heart attack when caged. As a precaution, we gave a preventive drug to Alexander, although he's hardly fragile or feral. He was raised in civilization and lived inside a house all his life."

"Where he grew up is not a factor," Mollie argued. "It's about Alex's age. Fledglings and young harpies can endure confinement, but not the adults. They become overwhelmed with hopelessness and will go to any length to end the claustrophobic depression. Alex is approaching maturity, and shut up in that house, he was experiencing the suicidal tendencies. In another year he'd have flown the coop, so to speak, but you have accelerated those destructive inclinations by putting him in your fancy institution."

Collins chuckled. "You seem to forget that Alexander is half-human, and not likely to have a full-blooded harpy's psyche."

Mollie's eyes narrowed. "The African Masai and Australian aborigines were ancient human races on Earth, and when imprisoned, they suffered from despair and died like the harpies, so don't count on Alex's human side to protect him."

"For a nanny, you're quite knowledgeable."

"I'm not a nanny. Miss Carlton gave me the title because she was ashamed that an animal handler had to be hired to deal with her son. And it's my job to know everything about the creatures in my care."

"Still, you don't hold a degree in animal behavior and training, especially one that specializes in harpies."

"Experience is more effective than a classroom." Mollie crossed her arms and took a breath to control her irritation. "Doctor, have you ever taken care of a captive harpy, tried to keep it alive only to watch it take its last breath? I have. I lived on Dora when harpy hunting was legal and watched dozens of caged harpies pass away. It was very sad, and I never want to see it again—which brings me to Alex. I need to see him."

"That's impossible. No one is allowed in his room. Once Alexander adjusts, he can have visitors."

Mollie glared at him. "You don't get it," she snapped. "Alex will never adjust. He'll just die." She stood and stepped toward the door.

"Wait a minute, Miss Harris." With a weighty breath, he said, "To be honest, he has been difficult. He flew into the viewing screen several times in an obvious attempt to crack his skull or break his neck. We were forced to clip his wings. Since then he has slipped into a comatose state. We've tried to bring him around with drugs, but nothing has worked."

"You want him stable? Turn him loose."

"He put two men in the hospital. One has a serious concussion and is on a ventilator. He might not live. Alexander is too dangerous to go free."

Mollie grimaced. "It was your fault those men were injured. You misdiagnosed your patient and treated Alex like a human. He's not. He's a golden harpy, the most dangerous of the species, and when threatened, they strike back. But I'm sure Miss Carlton forewarned you that detaining Alex was risky."

Collins twisted his mustache and nodded. "All right, I'll let you see him. Maybe you can give us some suggestions on how to treat him."

They left his office, walked down a hallway, and entered an elevator. On the fifth floor, they stepped out and strolled down a corridor.

"I'm not a cold-hearted person," Collins said, walking. "I really want to help Alexander."

"Spare me. You find Alex and his mental skills intriguing and want to pick his brain."

"You're not very fond of doctors."

"I don't mind doctors," said Mollie, "but I dislike men who harm others for their own gain."

Collins stopped midway and gazed at her. "Who hurt you, Miss Harris? Were you rejected or abused?"

His remark caught her off guard. The administrator was not only a doctor but also a shrink, and was right about her on both accounts. "My life is none of your business."

They entered a room and stopped beside the duty nurse stationed in front of numerous screens that monitored the patient rooms. "Enlarge room four," Collins said to her. A full screen displayed Alex, who lay on the floor with his shortened wings awkwardly spread. He resembled a gun-downed fowl.

"Any change?" Collins asked the nurse.

"No, Doctor," she answered. "He hasn't moved, even when tube fed."

Mollie covered her mouth, appalled at Alex's pathetic state. "How could you do this to him, chop off his wings and seal him up in that tiny room?"

"I explained we had to ground him for his welfare," said Collins. "And his telepathic powers hospitalized two men, so I'm not about to jeopardize more of my staff. Robots are maintaining him."

"Maintained? You're turning him into a vegetable. I have to go in there."

"That room is off-limits to everyone. He's too treacherous."

"He'd never hurt me. If you don't let me in, he'll stay in that coma until it's irreversible and his brain is mush."

Collins held his chin and finally nodded. He turned to the nurse. "Pull up the waiver that exonerates the institution if Miss Harris is injured. Also, prepare to gas the harpy if he threatens her."

After signing the waiver, Mollie trailed Collins down another corridor lined with numbered doors, and they stopped at room 4. He tapped a series of numbers on the keyboard on the wall and the room door opened. “He’s all yours,” Collin said. “See what you can do.”

Mollie stepped onto the padded flooring and went to the limp frame. She rolled Alex to his side and folded his wings in place against his back. Kneeling beside him, she stroked his silky blond hair and said, “Alex, it’s me. It’s Mollie.” She placed her hand to his nose. “Smell me, Alex.”

There was no response. The only sign of life was Alex’s shallow breathing. Mollie sat down beside him, and as she had done when he was a small fledgling, she cradled his head in her lap and spoke in a soothing tone. “Come on, prince, my sweet, sweet prince. Come back to me. You are a golden harpy, the bravest and most honorable living thing in the universe. Don’t let the bad people beat you.” For nearly an hour, she caressed his head and spoke quietly to him.

Eventually, Alex reacted. He wrinkled his nose, sniffed her, and slowly opened his eyes. “Is it really you, Mollie,” he whispered, “or is this a dream?”

“It’s me. I’m really here.”

With both arms, he clutched her and buried his face in her side. “Please take me out of here,” he muttered. “I promise I’ll be good.”

Tears ran down Mollie’s cheeks. The mental institution had broken him. She lifted his chin. “Listen to me, Alex. I can’t get you out of here right now, but you mustn’t give up.”

His deep blue eyes widened. “You don’t understand. If I stay here, I’ll be lost in my dreams and won’t be able to get out.”

Mollie grasped both sides of his face and gave him a little shake. “Damn it, Alexander, don’t go into the coma,” she said sternly. “Somehow I’ll figure out a way to free you.”

“You promise? You won’t desert me?” he asked with the terrified voice of a child.

“Promise. I’ll never leave you.”

He nodded, seeming reassured. He glanced upward at the viewing screen. “I hate them, Mollie.”

"Hate is a human emotion, and you're better than that." She pulled away from him and stood. "I'll be back tomorrow."

"Okay." He pulled his legs to his chest and hugged them. Using his sheared wings, he covered his coiled body. He had never known another harpy, but instinctively rested like one.

The harpy's physical and mental damage made Mollie want to throttle Collins, but she had to control her anger. Otherwise, she'd never see Alex again. She stepped to the hidden door, and it opened. She walked into the hallway, and Collins was waiting.

"Very good, Miss Harris," he said. "He responds to you."

"If you want to keep him awake and healthy, I must see him daily. Harpies are social creatures that live in flocks and don't do well alone. Another thing, harpies have a human body, but they are not mortals. They're extremely intelligent animals with the same mentality and nature. They live in the present and have trouble foreseeing their future. Alex is no different. He doesn't believe he'll ever escape that room. Without contact and me giving him hope, he'll trigger another blackout. Next time he won't recover."

"How does he induce a coma?"

"All harpies have the concentration to control their organs. That's how they can cause the fatal heart attack when depressed. Alex, though, is exceptional. He hasn't led an active life, flying through a jungle, so he's had time to develop his mental abilities. He's beyond controlling his organs, but can alter the state of his mind and bring about a coma."

"That's fascinating."

"Yes, isn't it," she said with a jaded tone. "I'll be here tomorrow."

Mollie strolled to the elevator and left the building, pleased to have impressed Collins enough to grant her visits with Alex. Still, it was a temporary fix. Alex would eventually lose faith and end his life. She climbed into her vehicle and thought, "But maybe there is one who could save him."

CHAPTER FOUR

On planet Dora, Windy meandered out to the wide veranda, her white harpy gown sweeping the wooden planks. Holding two glasses of nectar, she paused to view the scarlet sky with ribbons of orange and pink clouds. Below the horizon, the multicolored jungle trees grew dark. "I think it will be a good one tonight," she said to Jim, her human husband.

"All the sunsets are nice, but in a few months, the wet season will ruin them," Jim said, and took a glass from her.

She joined him on the porch swing. "It is strange. I always detect depression in humans with the rains, but harpies celebrate because the water brings life."

Jim chuckled. "Harpies don't have to sludge through muddy with wet clothes." He placed an arm over her shoulder, wingless in most female harpies. "So how was your day, babe?"

She rested her head against his chest. "Quiet, but I welcomed a new family into Terrance. The man is a fine artist, and his wife loves to garden. They will blend well, but so many humans want to live here. When turning them away, I sense their disappointment. It is unpleasant."

"Windy, you had to close the outback borders. Too many people would destroy the wilderness. Look at Hampton. It's become a big modern city surrounded by farms, groves, and timber mills. The eastern jungle is fast disappearing."

The com buzzed inside the large Victorian house. "I'll get it," Jim said, rising, "Probably police business." He left the deck and disappeared in the house, but returned a minute later. "Windy, you'd better take this call. It's long-distance from some woman on Oden. She's asking for Shail and says it concerns a captive golden harpy. I got the impression she thinks your son still rules."

"Did you tell her he does not?" Windy asked.

"I thought I'd let you straighten her out."

Windy walked into the house and sat down at the com on the desk. On the screen was a middle-aged woman with short-cropped hair. "I am Windy, the ruler of the harpies."

"I recognize you. You're Shail's mother. What happened to him? Shail is all right, isn't he? He's not…not dead?"

Windy heard the stress in the woman's voice and saw the concern in her eyes. She not only knew Shail, but cared deeply about him. "My son ended his rule and now seeks a quiet life in the jungle. I govern the Outback until his oldest son is of age."

"Oh, thank God," the woman said. "Shail deserves some peace."

"You said you were calling about a captive golden harpy."

The woman rubbed her jaw. "I had hoped Shail could help me, but maybe you can. My name is Mollie Harris. I was the caretaker of a young golden harpy on Oden. He is now going on eighteen and has become a handful for his mother. She locked him up in a mental institution. He's fighting depression, and I'm afraid it will kill him. I didn't know who else to call."

"Miss Harris, you are mistaken. All golden harpies live on Dora."

"I know a golden harpy when I see one. Hold on, I'll prove it. I have a recent photo of Alex. That's his name." The woman placed a picture up to the screen.

Windy stared at a young male standing next to Harris on the screen. He had a tall, trim humanoid frame and wore only a hip sash. His blond hair hung shoulder-length, and one of his large wings was partially extended and enclosing Harris in yellow feathers. She smiled in the photo, but he did not. He was, no doubt, a golden harpy. "How can this harpy be on Oden?"

Harris removed the photo and said, "From my understanding, Alex's mother, a Miss Monica Carlton, was traveling from Oden to Earth. A male harpy was on board the ship, and Miss Carlton had sex with him and became pregnant. I'd never heard of a male harpy sleeping with a woman, much less producing a fledgling, but Alex is living proof that it happened."

"You say this golden is seventeen?"

"Yes, nearly eighteen."

Windy did the math and sighed. "I know how it might have occurred. Nearly two decades ago, Dora law changed and harpies became game animals again. It created a great conflict, so Shail was captured and shipped to Earth. Your young golden could be Shail's son."

Harris nodded. "I suspected. When Alex hit his teens, he looked a lot like Shail. He definitely inherited his dad's temperament. Can you help him?"

"Golden harpies are few, and the brown-winged flocks treasure them. The harpies shall save Alex or die trying."

Windy disconnected the com after talking to Mollie Harris. Once a solid plan was in place, she'd call Harris back.

Jim had listened to the call from the veranda doorway. Shaking his head, he stepped inside. "Windy, the woman's a crackpot. She's probably working an angle to live in the Outback."

"I saw the picture, Jim. The young male is a golden harpy."

"Babe, I do this stuff for a living. The photo is doctored. It's a scam. Ignore her so-called harpy."

"I believe her. Few people know that Shail was forced to breed women passengers on the voyage to Earth. Rachel was one of those women, and she became pregnant with Summer, my son's first daughter. The same thing could have taken place with this other woman, and she gave birth to the male harpy. He is the right age, seventeen like Summer. Given the possibility, I will not ignore the young male."

"Fine, but before you organize a hell of a long space trip for this boy, you'd better have more proof than a picture."

Windy smiled. "Are all Earth policemen so skeptical?"

"I was a detective, not a policeman, but yeah, good cops are suspicious."

Her focus shifted from the banter with her mate to verifying Miss Harris's story. She pressed the com keys, and Rachel, Shail's second mate, appeared on the screen.

"Miss Windy, it's so good to see you."

"How are you and my lovely granddaughters?"

"The three young ones are fine, but Summer is driving me crazy. She's become so defiant, doesn't listen to anything I say. Kari and Lea have no trouble with their boys."

"Summer is like her father and needs his guidance. Perhaps Shail—" She stopped, her suggestion infeasible. "She requires the sterner hand of a golden harpy. She must learn control and wisdom, but her spirit should be encouraged, not crushed. Send her to me. I might be able to help."

"It would be wonderful if she stayed with you in Terrance."

"The reason I called: On the spaceship to Earth, do you remember a woman named Carlton? She might have had contact with Shail."

"Monica, Monica Carlton," Rachel said with disgust. "It'd be impossible to forget that fat, rich wench."

Windy glanced up at Jim. "Was she intimate with my son?"

"More like she raped him," Rachel seethed. "Poor Shail, Every time that bitch used him he had choke bruises and his back was raked and bloody from her nails. The prostitute who owned Shail allowed the abuse because Monica paid a small fortune for him. She said that he performed better when goaded with pain, and the torture made her climax. She was a twisted, disgusting woman."

Windy's mind turned from the cruelty that Shail endured to thinking about Alex, his son. Raised by a heartless mother, he likely had issues, but had he been ruined? Was he a troubled man with wings, or did he have a harpy's soul? Windy collected herself and said, "Thank you, Rachel. That is all I need to know."

"If Monica has applied to move here, don't let her," said Rachel. "She's the nastiest female I've ever met."

"I sense all who come here, but her name will be put on the undesirable list."

The call ended, and with a lifted eyebrow, Windy looked to Jim.

"Okay, okay," Jim said. "The Oden harpy is most likely Shail's boy, but we need to think this through." He paused and ran his fingers through his grey-streaked blondish hair. "From a legal standpoint, you can't touch the harpy. He's underage, and his mother had every right to commit him to a mental hospital. DNA testing could prove that Shail is his father, but Shail would have to go to Oden and fight for custody in a court. It could take a long time, and if the mother can afford rich lawyers, she'd probably win."

"You know Shail cannot go. I fear we will lose him soon."

Jim took a deep breath. "Sorry, I was just tossing out thoughts."

Windy rose and walked past him to the outside. She crossed the lawn to the edge of the jungle and called telepathically. A harpy swooped down from the trees and landed before her. Folding his mahogany-colored wings, he knelt on one knee and lowered his head.

Bring Aron to me, Windy relayed telepathically.

With a nod, the harpy leaped into the orange dusk sky to begin the journey. He would fly half the night across the continent to reach the west coast and Aron, her son's best friend. Aron would then make the same trek back. At the earliest, he would arrive at the riverside city of Terrance and her home tomorrow afternoon or later.

During the war, Aron had used a small, portable communicator to easily contact Windy, but after the fighting, he refused the man-made device. Like his adopted brother Shail, the brown-winged harpy lived in torment and was through with humans and civilization, longing to spend his remaining days in the calming jungle with his family. She disliked disturbing Aron, but was in need of his good judgment. She returned to the house and walked past Jim to the communicator.

"What are you doing?" Jim asked.

"Saving my grandson," she said, then placed a call to Ted, the supervisor of the Terrance airport.

The forty-something, easygoing Ted appeared on the screen. "Hey, Miss Windy," he said with a smile. "What can I do for you this evening?"

"Ted, I need a pilot with a small, fast spaceship for a voyage."

"Sure thing, I'll contact Hampton and should have a bead on one within a day or two. I'll need the itinerary, destination, cargo, and a list of the passengers, if any."

"All that information must remain unknown."

"Miss Windy, perhaps you don't understand. No ship can take off from Hampton Port without a flight plan and the names of the people on board. Without that, it's illegal."

"I'm sure it is, but the ship will leave from Terrance, not Hampton, and secrecy must surround this journey."

Ted's grin vanished. "You're…you're looking for a smuggler?"

"That is correct."

"Okay, then," Ted said with wide eyes. "I have to warn you. Using a smuggler is risky. They're criminals. Some will take your money, kill their passengers, and dump the bodies in space. Even if I find a halfway honest one, he'll still rob you and overcharge for the trip."

"The cargo is precious, the cost and risk for the pilot are unimportant."

"I'll still need the destination. No space jock will take the job unless he knows where he's going."

"Oden."

Ted whistled. "Wow, that planet is a long way off. I'll call back as soon as I have something."

She switched off the com.

"Windy, you're not serious," said Jim. "Ted is right about smugglers. They're lowlifes, and even if you found a decent pilot, you can't just zip over to Oden and grab the harpy. Traveling without the proper documents is only the start of lawbreaking. There's also the illicit landing on Oden, busting into the mental hospital, and even if this underage harpy wants to go, it's still kidnapping. We're talking about serious crimes. You're the harpy ruler, but that doesn't give you immunity from our laws."

"Human laws don't concern harpies. The greater crime for us is imprisoning this harpy."

"When you face a judge, he's unlikely to agree with you," said Jim. "Jesus, I'm the chief of police in Terrance. I can't let you go through with this."

She glared at him. "You are a mate, Jim, not a master. Either help or stay out of my way."

He stepped back and grumbled, "Obvious where Shail got his stubborn streak." He sighed. "All right. I want to help before things are botched up, and my wife ends up in jail. Who are you sending on this rescue mission?"

"Will is the most capable and would gladly go to save his half-brother, but I cannot allow it. His destiny is to rule soon, and he is vital to the harpies."

"He would have been my first choice. He's a smart, gutsy boy. Nothing scares that harpy. So, no goldens. Does that mean you're relying on browns?"

"I sent for Aron. He knows the flocks, and the bravest and most qualified harpies who would wish to go on the trip."

"Speaking of wishes, I wish I hadn't given up drinking. I could use a stiff one about now." Jim collapsed into a nearby chair. "Windy, let's be realistic. From what I've seen, no brown-winged harpy is up to the task. They're skittish of people and avoid cities. Heck, just getting them to Oden might be a problem. They'll be shut up in a little ship for a month. With their claustrophobic issues, they probably won't survive the journey."

"Jim, you were not on Dora during the war when the flocks fought men to save us. As then, they will find the courage now. The life of a golden harpy is very dear to them."

"I'm glad you got faith in your flyboys, but I see a disaster in the making." Jim stood, seeming to gaze upward at the ceiling for answers. "When I settled here, I thought I was done with space travel, but looks like I'm off again. If I don't go on your mission, it will fail."

"No, Jim, you must not." Windy stepped to her tall, rugged husband and pushed back his thick locks. "I have lost two mates. I cannot lose a third."

Jim wrapped his arms around her and kissed her forehead. "You won't lose me, babe, and to make this work, you'll need more than nervy harpies. Someone has to have street smarts, know how to break into the Oden hospital for the kid, and leave without getting caught. I've spent my life solving crimes; I should know how to commit them."

Windy sensed Jim's unswayable resolve. He was going. The rescue she had put in motion had become personal. Risking her harpies was of great concern, but the life of the man she loved was crucial. She returned to the desk to call Mollie Harris. A strategy was in place. Tapping the com keys, she thought about Alex. She knew little about him but was taking a huge gamble to save him.

* * *

The harpy nest in the enormous fan tree swayed in the cool night ocean breeze. Aron lay in the moss with one of his chocolate-colored wings draped over his sleeping mate, Starla. Five of their six young also dozed, snuggled around them for warmth and security. Their oldest son had reached adulthood and left the family nest last spring.

Aron shut his eyes but couldn't sleep. Like other harpies who survived the war, he suffered restless nights with dreams of bloodshed and killing. He thought about this son, Freely, born during the conflict and given his name when the harpies won their freedom. Currently, Freely lived a bachelor's life and roamed the continent with Will, Shail's eldest son. The two males, one yellow-winged, one brown, were comparable to Aron and Shail in their youth. They enjoyed the independence, adventures, the camaraderie of watching each other's backs while sharing a nest. Unlike when Aron was their age, the jungle was a safe place.

Aron and Shail had depended on their speed and wits to survive because human hunters invaded the Outback and killed harpies for sport. The atrocity ended with the war, but it came at a price. Both of them were left shattered.

Every few weeks Aron flew several hundred miles south and visited his lifelong friend, but on the return, he fought tears. Shail, who had never taken a backward step, was a shadow of the bold golden ruler he had been. The men had beaten him. He saved his harpies, but not himself.

On his last visit, Aron had tried to instill confidence, but discovered Shail's mind was nearly gone. He had lost his telepathy and couldn't comprehend vocal words. The local doctor had explained to his mates that Shail suffered from post-traumatic stress disorder. Aron could only nuzzle his neck and wrap him in his wings while Shail shivered with paranoia and nervously stared at a threat that wasn't there. It broke Aron's heart.

Aron's sniffle woke Starla. She relayed, *Aron, my love, you must stop dwelling on Shail.*

I long to help him.

You cannot. He does not know you anymore. You struggle with your own demons, and after seeing Shail, you are worse. We spoke of moving to the western islands. Perhaps it is time.

No, not while he lives. Aron lifted his head, sensing another harpy. At this late hour, the visit caused concern. *A harpy approaches.* He removed his wing from Starla and stood. Gazing into the dark jungle, he saw the shadow of wings weaving through the jungle trees. The harpy neared the fan tree and landed on a branch below the nest.

Aron fluttered down to him. The harpy, covered with sweat, panted hard. He had traveled far and fast. He was not a member of the coastal flocks, so he must be a river harpy serving their ruler. *What does she wish?*

Our golden queen asks you to come to her.

Aron nodded to the male and returned to his nest. *I must go to Terrance,* he relayed to Starla. *Windy needs me. The flock shall see to your needs.*

Starla sat up. *You have done enough for her and the harpies, and Windy knows you are unwell and should not be disturbed.*

Aron found his protective mate amusing. *My duty to the harpies and her ends with my last heartbeat.* He leaned down and kissed Starla's cheek. Spreading his wings, he leaped into the star-filled sky and flew east, with the river harpy gliding beside him.

They soared above the jungle as dawn broke on the horizon. Harpies normally travelled at night or glided in the shade under the vegetation during the day. Flight in an open, cloudless sky was too hot, but Aron endured the heat to reach Terrance faster. By midday his hair and body dripped with sweat, his wings were spent, and his throat was parched. Though younger, his flying companion was also drained. When spotting the river that divided the continent, Aron relayed, *We shall stop and rest.* He sensed the relief in his companion.

They landed on the riverbank and plunged into the flowing clear water. After cooling off and drinking his fill, Aron stepped onto the sandy bank. Downriver, half-submerged near the shore, was the bloated corpse of a fifteen-foot long reptile. The smell of the carcass had attracted two red dragons that gorged on the rotten flesh, stopping only to occasionally hiss and snap at each other.

Standing in waist-deep water, the river harpy gazed at the dead reptile. *It drowned crossing the river during the rains. The water is deadly then, very fast and deep.* He hadn't conversed with Aron since the start of their journey.

Yes, but its death gives life to others. Aron shook his wet hair and ruffled his feathers.

Terrance is near, the harpy relayed, stepping from the river and facing Aron. *Before we part, I must say it has been a great honor to fly with you. My father told me the stories of how you rallied the flocks and fought the humans on this very river.*

Shail deserves the credit. He instilled courage in harpies to fight the threat. I only followed him.

He is the greatest of all golden rulers, but of the brown-winged, you are the best of us. No other has ever been so fearless. My father and all river harpies call you a hero.

The praise should have uplifted Aron, but he felt dismal. He had grown up in a nest with a golden fledgling, and Shail's attributes had brushed off on him. All Aron was and became, he owed to his adopted blond brother. *We should go now.*

They took flight and followed the winding waterway south, tilting their wings around the bends. Terrance, the capital and largest city in the harpy land, was a hundred miles away. Before harpies were granted half the continent west of the river, the region had been known as the Outback, and many still referred to it by the old name.

During the war, Aron had spent a great deal of time in Terrance when he led the harpy flocks and outback people against the invading mercenary army. After the conflict, Shail returned to Dora. Aron, no longer needed, moved his family to the remote northwestern mountains. He had not been back to Terrance since those turbulent times.

In the distance, he saw the city rise from the riverbank. The numerous tall buildings surprised him. Terrance had grown over the years. He and the young harpy left the river and flew across the town toward Windy's home.

Aron gazed down at the many humans that roamed the streets lined with hotels, restaurants, and shops. Excited people spotted them overhead and called, pointed, and waved.

These humans act strangely, Aron said.

They are called tourists, his companion explained. *They travel here, hoping to see a harpy, but we stay away from them. To go among them, a harpy is surrounded and must endure their touches, talk, and cameras.*

Why does Windy allow them?

She says they are a nuisance, but harmless. Their money helps the humans that live here and protects the jungle from those wishing to cut trees.

Aron huffed. Humans, unlike harpies and other creatures that lived in harmony with nature, were greedy and destructive, destroying the jungle for their buildings and farms. Also, many were pathetic, aggravating, and lacked honor. If up to him, he would run most of them out of the harpy land.

Aron and the river harpy winged past the populated area and arrived at the large white home on the outskirts of town. Windy and Jim sat at a table on the veranda, eating lunch.

Windy rose to greet them. "I am pleased to see you, Aron," she said from the porch steps. "I miss your counsel."

Aron dropped to one knee and bowed his head. "And I have missed you, my queen."

She nodded to the young harpy, and he flew into the trees. "Come, eat with us. You must be hungry after the long flight." She sat down at the table and offered Aron some fruit. "Kari tells me you frequently visit Shail. I am grateful my son has such a loyal friend."

Aron stood at the table, but had no appetite. "I visit him, but—." He gazed at the floor. "Shail did not know me this last time."

Windy sighed. "I have heard he loses his memory and sometimes does not recognize his sons and daughters. He seems to only know Kari."

"It is because he loved her more than life," Aron said. "A feeling that strong cannot die."

Windy covered her mouth, and tears filled her eyes.

Aron had never seen her cry. Windy was a golden female, a mix of dignity and strength, but instead of a ruler, he saw a mother on the threshold of losing her only son. Aron placed his hand on her shoulder and relayed telepathically. *Like some birds, harpies fly in flocks, but Shail was an eagle that soared alone through many stormy skies. He shall soon find a peaceful horizon.*

Windy nodded and dried her face with a napkin. *Thank you, Aron.*

Jim saw his wife's distress and changed the sad subject. He held up a bread basket. "Have some nut bread, Aron. I doubt you get it in the jungle."

Aron took a piece of bread and sat on the railing with his long brown wings hanging outside.

Windy collected herself. "I did not ask you here to discuss Shail." She poured some juice into a glass and handed it to Aron. "It's about one of his sons. Yesterday I learned of a golden harpy on another planet. Like Rachel, his mother had sex with Shail on the spaceship to Earth and became pregnant. The young male has been imprisoned, but I intend to free him and bring him to Dora."

"Shail has another son?" Aron said, amazed. Only two decades earlier, the golden harpies nearly went extinct with Shail being the last of the males. Since then Shail's seven sons and four daughters had increased the offspring numbers, and now there was an eighth son among the stars. Sentiment played no part in Aron's reasoning. The young male was crucial to reviving the golden bloodline. "Yes, he must be saved."

"Yeah," Jim said, "but it won't be easy. First it's a long voyage on a little ship, a month to reach the desert planet and a month back. The harpy is in domed city and held inside a secure mental hospital. That means getting into the dome and busting him out of the building. It's dangerous. If it fails, those involved could be jailed or killed."

Aron finished the drink in one swallow and said, "The difficulties and threats do not matter."

"Windy said you'd say that."

Aron looked to Windy. "I shall go, my queen."

"No, you have done enough," said Windy. "You are here because you know the harpies and the ones who can carry out the task."

"All harpies love Shail and would gladly go for his son, but I understand the strongest and bravest are needed. They must endure the journey and be daring and cunning in the city. How many harpies do you wish?"

"Two," Jim said. "That's four total, counting me and the pilot. A small number can sneak in and out more easily. And, Aron, this is a hush-hush operation. No one except us and Ted knows about it."

Windy breathed deeply. "I especially do not want Will to learn of the undertaking. He would insist on retrieving his half-brother."

"My son, Freely, too," said Aron. "He and Will have the passion and courage of youth, but lack the caution and experience of age." He hopped off the railing. "I know who would serve." He spread his wings to leave when a vehicle pulled up to the house.

Ted climbed out and called, "I have your ship, Miss Windy." Approaching the veranda, his eyes lit up. "Oh my God, is that you, Aron? The last time I saw you, Freely was knee-high."

Aron refolded his wings. "He is now taller than me, and I have five others."

Ted stepped onto the porch and grasped Aron's shoulders. "Darn! Six kids and you haven't aged. Still a handsome devil. I sure have missed your ribbing about us inferior humans."

"And I have missed your smile," Aron said.

Jim broke up the reunion. "What did you find, Ted?"

Ted strolled to Windy and Jim at the table. "I called a buddy at Hampton Port, and he told me about a pilot with his own ship that had recently arrived on Dora. Said the guy was a little shady, but not a hardcore felon. For the right money, he'd do the job, and his ship is small enough to take off from Terrance, eluding the satellites. I contacted the space jock. He's a real character. Anyway, he's wrapping up some Hampton business and should be here tomorrow."

Jim said, "I guess we're really going through with this."

* * *

Mollie woke in her bed and grinned. She couldn't wait to tell Alex the good news: the harpies were coming for him. Hope would drive off depression and keep him alive.

The com buzzed, and she left the bed and strolled to the living room desk.

On the com screen, Dr. Collins spoke with urgency. "Miss Harris, I need you here immediately. We have a major problem with Alexander."

"Is he all right?"

"Just get here."

Mollie threw on clothes and hurried out of the apartment to her vehicle. Racing through traffic, she arrived at the Mirage Mental Institution and ran inside to Collins's office.

Standing outside the office, the secretary said, "Hurry, it's an emergency. I'll take you to the isolation ward."

They jogged down the hallway to the elevator and rode it up to the fifth floor. Down the corridor, Dr. Collins and a team of medics and nurses stood outside of Alex's room.

Collins spoke into the monitor com on the door. "Alexander, she's here. Mollie is walking toward me right now. I'll send her in." He turned off the com and wiped the sweat from his forehead.

"What's happened?" Mollie asked.

"He's threatening to kill himself." Collins pushed back his false hair. "This morning he appeared to be in another coma. The robots were sent in to administer drugs. He jumped up and attacked them, kicking them to pieces. Before he could be stopped, he grabbed a strip of sharp metal and held it to his throat. He says he'll slice his jugular if he smells gas. He's demanding to be released, but I can't allow it. Do you think he'd go through with it and kill himself?"

"Of course," said Mollie. "I warned you harpies are suicidal when caged."

"Christ!" said Collins. "If he severs the jugular, we're ready to save him, but we'd have only seconds to stop the bleeding."

"Let me in there," Mollie said. Collins unlocked the door, and she entered the small room.

Alex squatted in a corner and held the shiny object to his throat. The robot rubble of metal, plastic parts, and wires covered the floor.

She stepped over the pieces. "I see you've been busy this morning."

"I'm going to kill myself, Mollie, but I wanted to say goodbye to you."

"Alex, there's an army of people outside and they're ready to patch you up if you try it."

"Let them come," said Alex. "They'll die before I do."

Mollie sat down next to him. "Maybe I can negotiate some terms. No more drugs, gas, or robots, and I'll be here every day to see you."

He looked around the claustrophobic room and shuddered. "I don't care about damn robots. I want out." He lowered his head so his long hair hid his face. "It's probably better if I die," he murmured. "All my life I've heard people's thoughts and know what they think. No one wants to be around a freak."

She lifted his chin and smiled. "Alex, you're not a freak. You're a harpy in the wrong place without your kind. You'll soon learn you're loved. Let's play our little game, so focus on me."

Alex frowned. "This is hardly the time, Mollie."

"It is." So that Collins and the hospital wouldn't know about the planned rescue, Mollie concentrated and projected her thoughts to

Alex. *I have good news. I found your harpy family and spoke to your grandmother. The harpies are coming to take you home to Dora, but it's a month-long journey, so you must be patient.*

Alex's eyes widened with astonishment, and he lowered the sharp metal from his throat. His telepathy allowed him to understand Mollie, but she couldn't comprehend his mind, so he whispered, "You found my father?"

I know who he is. Mollie relayed.

"He is the harpy who has always been in your memories."

Mollie nodded. *He saved my life.*

"Tell me of it."

Mollie reflected on the incident twenty years earlier. She had lived on Dora and worked at a hunting range, maintaining its game animals. A young golden harpy had been caught and brought in. The range planned to auction him off so the high bidder could hunt and kill him. To make the harpy more aggressive and a pricier trophy, the range owner and his two men raped him. The sexual assault worked. When the same men molested and intended to murder Mollie, the harpy killed them. Never before had a gentle harpy slain a human. Mollie glanced at Alex. *The harpy was Shail, and he is your father.*

Alex took her hand. "You loved him and still do after all these years."

She cleared her throat. "Yes." She gripped his hand. "But, Alex, you're like my son, and I also love you."

"I have always felt it. Okay, we shall play the charade." Alex stood and spoke out. "Negotiate the terms, but if they break them—" He held up the blade. "I will use this." With a glimpse, he gave Mollie a subtle wink.

Going along with his idle threat, she said seriously, "I'll tell them." She rose and her insides tingled with joy. Alex was back. The anticipation of being freed and united with harpies drove off his despair. She left the room and stood before Dr. Collins and his staff.

"Terms?" said Dr. Collins. "What terms is he talking about?"

"You heard them; no more drugs, gas, or robots."

"I can't promise that," said Collins. "He has to sleep sometime. We'll immobilize him with gas and take away his crude knife. Tell him we accept the terms."

Mollie chuckled. "I tell him, and he'll sense it's a lie. Do you want to chance that he smells gas and wakes up? He'll immediately cut his throat. Even if you got his weapon, he'll force the coma. Doctor, you might have caged him, but he has you by your balls."

"Ridiculous," said Collins. "That winged creature has nothing over on me."

Mollie shook her head. "How soon you forget your panic call to me this morning. You weren't concerned about Alex, but you are afraid of his mother. Miss Carlton might have differences with her son, but deep down she cares about him. If Alex is mishandled or dies, you be cleaning bedpans for a living. I'll also tell Miss Carlton's lawyers that I warned you about harpies, and you had options."

Collins chewed the end of his mustache. "You and that harpy are a resourceful pair. I'll concede to the terms, but he has to cooperate with my tests."

"I might convince him to work with you," said Mollie.

"What about the mess in that room?"

"Send in your cleaning crew. If I'm there, Alex won't hurt them." Mollie stepped back into the room and said to Alex, "All right, you got your demands, but you must behave. Some people are coming in to clean up the trash. Don't harm them, Alex."

Alex extended one of his hacked up wings. "I should. Look what they did to me."

"Let's not screw this up."

He folded the wing with a grumble. "Fine, send in the clowns."

Two maintenance men walked into the room with garbage bags and quickly cleaned up the smashed robot parts. Throughout, they fixed their worried stares on Alex. After they left, a nurse entered with a tray of food.

"His lunch," she said, setting the tray down and hustling out.

Alex tossed back his hair. "They're scared of me, and they ought to be."

"Yes, yes, everyone's afraid of the big, bad harpy." Mollie ignored his boosts. He had been wronged and was venting. She examined the items on the tray. "For hospital food, it looks good." She handed him a slice of orange.

Alex took a bite and turned up his nose. "It has the bitter taste of submission."

Mollie laughed. "That's something your dad would say. You're becoming like him."

"Really, Mollie?" he said with a little smile.

CHAPTER FIVE

On planet Dora, Aron listened as Windy, Jim, and Ted discussed the voyage to Oden—the cost and supplies they would need. Aron then left Terrance to find two harpies for the journey. He needed brown-winged males with a golden's tenacity, but he sought neither a brown or yellow-winged harpy.

Although tired from his earlier flight, he winged rapidly toward the west coast. He reached a valley nestled in the mountain foothills and descended into a forest of red trees. He landed on a limb and gazed down at the group of playful fledglings. Like their father, they were the rarest of harpies, having black hair, and the males, ebony wings. The oldest, a preteen male, sniffed the air and looked upward. He took flight and landed beside Aron.

Bowing, the young male relayed, *Aron, father shall be pleased to see you.*

Is Bloom here? Aron asked. Four other small males able of flight also set down on the branch and muscled with their wings to get closer to Aron.

He is not far. I shall seek him, relayed the oldest fledgling. He turned to his younger siblings and, with raised wings and a hiss, he growled, *Show him respect or I shall break your feathers.*

The fledglings backed off, giving Aron space.

Aron approved of Bloom's rough and tumble clutch. Most harpies feared Aron, and their fledglings were too timid to approach him. He watched the oldest male sail into the trees to bring his father. This next generation of black-winged harpies might grow to be as tough as goldens.

Aron fluttered to the forest floor, and the male fledglings followed. Petite wingless females with long, shimmering black hair stepped to him. *Master, can we bring you food or drink?* One asked.

I need nothing, Aron relayed. *How many make Bloom's clutch?*

The little female held up all ten fingers. *This many, but my mother and second mother carry two more.*

Bloom must stay busy feeding and protecting all of you.

Several little female giggled and the one said, *His flock does much of the work.*

Bloom appeared and glided downward. He landed before Aron, fell to a knee, and lowered his head. *Master, I am honored with your presence.*

Do not bow, Bloom, Aron said. *I am no longer your flock leader.*

You shall always be my leader and more. When I lost my father, you took me under your wings, mentored me, and saved my life. Bloom rose and embraced Aron. In a male harpy greeting, they nuzzled each other's necks. *I have so ached to see you.*

It has been too long.

Bloom then turned to his brood. *This is Aron, the bravest of all dark-winged harpies. He deserves reverence.*

The little harpies dropped at Aron's feet, but kept their anxious eyes on their father, obviously more concerned with him than Aron.

Your seed must be strong, said Aron. *All have inherited your black hair, wings, boldness*— He grinned. *And good looks.*

Yes, like I, none shall want for mates. Bloom flexed his wing muscles and sighed. *But I failed to instill obedience in them. Before the peace, an unruly fledgling was a dead one. Mine do not know this fear.*

The shoots become the tree. You were unruly, and the cost was a broken wing and nearly your life.

Bloom addressed his youngsters, *Leave us now. Aron and I must talk.* They scampered away and he focused on Aron. *I sense your solemn mood. You did not come to visit. What brings you?*

A dangerous challenge, Aron relayed. *It begins with a long journey through the stars, a possible fight, and rescue. One of Shail's sons is held captive on another planet and must be brought home.*

Bloom's emerald-green eyes brightened. *When do I go?*

Aron studied the mid-thirty-year-old harpy. He had the wisdom, combat experience, attitude, and nerve to undertake mission, but he also had the responsibility of a large family. *You seem eager to leave but you might die and not return. What of your many fledglings?*

If fatherless, they shall know self-reliant and become stronger, sooner than later. I love them and, when gone, shall miss them. Bloom shook his shoulder-length hair. *But my soul stirs for one last adventure, the freedom and excitement.*

This adventure shall be more than exciting. Facing death does not concern you?

Bloom's lips curled with a slight smile. *We all die. I prefer to leave the living while fighting rather than curled up in a nest and covered with worn-out, old wings. Allow me to go, Aron.*

Aron nodded. *The spaceship arrives in Terrance tomorrow, but another harpy is needed for the journey. You decide who he shall be.*

Bloom summoned his eldest son. *Find Ribot and bring him here to our nest.* After the fledgling took flight, he smirked. *You know Ribot and dislike him, but he is the best of the browns.*

Aron shuffled his feathers. *I remember him. He was a brash adolescent, and I nearly took him out with my wing, but Shail was fond of him and admired his insolence.*

And he worships Shail like no other, said Bloom. *His devotion has brought him much torment because he cannot end the golden's suffering. He shall welcome this chance to help Shail's son.*

Then it is fitting he should go.

Bloom flew off to inform his three mates of his trip and to say goodbye. His brood chased after him.

With a flutter, Aron landed on a large log from a downed tree blown over during the wet-season storms. While waiting alone for Bloom and Ribot, he sat down and let his wings droop and recover from the exhausting flights.

After half an hour Bloom returned, with Ribot soaring alongside. They landed before Aron, and Ribot bowed low and long.

I have told Ribot of the star journey, said Bloom. *He longs to go.*

Still bowing, Ribot relayed, *Master, my life is yours*.

Aron hopped from the log and raised his head. Instead of harpy telepathy, he spoke the human language to be more forceful. “Bloom trusts you, but I have doubts.”

Ribot straightened and said with an emphatic voice, “Master, I am not what I was. I no longer am the foolish, young male who questioned your judgment during the war. Please I must do this for Shail. He…he is….” His gaze shifted to the ground. “I have no words worthy of him.”

“You found Shail in the hunting range, and later he chose you as his messenger,” Aron said. “He believed in you and so shall I, but you must obey Bloom.”

“I shall fly into flames if asked.”

“Do not disappoint me, Ribot.”

Although Aron was forty-seven-seasons-old and a retired leader, he had a fierce reputation. No harpy disputed or challenged him. Ribot, however, didn’t care about disappointing Aron. His motivation was a constant, life-altering love for Shail. Bloom was right to choose him.

“Our queen awaits us.” Aron spread his wings and leaped into the air. The two males followed him on the eastern trek. They arrived at the river city in the middle of the night and curled up in tree branches to sleep until dawn.

* * *

Jim woke early, but as usual, the bed was empty. Like all harpies, Windy was up before dawn. He showered, dressed, and packed some clothes for his trip. With Oden in mind, he headed for the computer to study the planet. Before long, Windy approached with coffee and placed his mug on the desk.

"Thanks, babe," he said, never taking his eyes off the screen. He leaned back in the chair, took a sip of coffee, and sighed. "Getting this boy will be tricky."

"You see problems?" she asked.

"Plenty. Oden was colonized centuries before Dora was even discovered. Means its surveillance and technology are superior to ours. The harpy is in Mirage, a domed city, and its port is outside in the desert with a connecting tunnel. The only way in is through port security with the proper papers." He looked up. "Which we won't have."

"Must you land in the port?"

"I thought about that. Trouble is, Oden has two suns, with only two hours of darkness when the temperature is under two-hundred degrees. Doesn't give us much time to land, grab the kid, and get out before we're fried. Even if we take that route, we still have to break into the dome. Nabbing the harpy from the mental institution is the least of our worries. I hope this pilot is a decent smuggler and has some ideas. Otherwise, the mission is a nonstarter."

Windy stood behind Jim's chair and massaged his shoulders. "I have faith. All will end well."

"Glad you're confident." Jim glanced out the window at the jungle. "Shouldn't Aron and his two harpies be here by now?"

"They await me in the trees." Windy strolled to the veranda.

Jim turned off the computer. By the time he joined her, he saw three harpies fly out of the jungle. Two had brown wings, but the third resembled a giant raven. They soared closer and Jim recognized Aron, Shail's old buddy, but not the other brown or the harpy with jet-black hair and wings. He nudged Windy. "I didn't know harpies had black wings."

"They are rarer than goldens. That one is Bloom. He and Aron are very close."

The three harpies landed on the lawn and bowed to Windy. They rose and Aron spoke. "These two shall make the journey with Jim."

Windy smiled and walked down the porch steps to Bloom. "I have not seen you, Bloom, since a teenager and slept here with your broken wing."

Bloom returned a smile. "I was reckless in my youth."

"Not reckless— brave," said Windy. "You tormented the enemy so they would chase you into our trap on the river. Your feat helped us win the war."

Bloom glanced at Aron. "He disapproved of my feat."

"Aron would," said Windy. "Brown-winged harpies place caution over courage, and that is why they outnumber the yellow- and black-winged." She turned to Aron. "I should have known you would seek Bloom."

"He is an adult now but still a risk-taker," said Aron. "The other harpy is Ribot. They shall serve your needs, my queen."

Windy placed her hands on Bloom's and Ribot's shoulders. "Thank you for accepting this challenge to save my grandson."

Jim strolled over and introduced himself to his traveling companions. They gathered on the veranda and discussed the voyage, planet, and city. Windy's assistant, a young female harpy, arrived and placed a fruit-and-biscuit breakfast on the table.

"Getting in," Jim said, "has its share of problems, but getting out might be worse. Once we take the golden, the authorities will be looking for him. Alarms, locking exits, and who knows what else might be an issue. The timing has to be perfect."

"Shall we need weapons?" Bloom asked.

"I'm bringing several," Jim said, "but hopefully we won't have to use them."

Windy sniffed the air and tilted her head. She looked to Aron with a question.

"I, too, sense her," said Aron.

Windy stood up from the table and ordered, "Summer, come here."

Rachel's eldest daughter tiptoed from the side of the house. She tossed back her waist-length blond hair and ruffled the pale-yellow feathers on her back. The genetic cross of a harpy father and human mother had created the first female harpy with wings, surprising everyone on Dora. "It's not fair being around harpies," she muttered.

"You can sneak around your mother but not us," Windy said. "Now how much have you heard?"

Summer fluttered her wings and landed on the deck. Her white-linen cloth hung off one shoulder and covered her breasts and barely her thighs. The petite female was seventeen but had a woman's seductive curves. "Enough." She smiled and her big blue eyes twinkled with mischief. "I apparently have another brother on a planet, and he needs to be rescued."

"Great, just great," Jim said with disgust. "This venture was supposed to be top secret."

Summer sashayed to the table and said, "Hi, Aron."

"Summer," Aron said as he and the two harpy males lowered their heads to the golden female.

"What's the big deal?" Summer said. She picked up a piece of fruit, placed it to her plum lips, and sucked out the juice.

Windy caught Summer's wrist and twisted it. "This is serious, Summer. No one must know, especially Will. Do you understand?"

Summer dropped the fruit and winced at the painful grip. "Grandma, that hurts." When she wasn't released, she said, "Yes, yes, I understand." Once freed, she backed away, holding her sore wrist, and looked teary-eyed at Windy.

Jim scratched the back of his head. Harpies looked like delicate, graceful beings, but under the I they were tough. Windy, his little wife, was no exception. "All right," he said. "Let's calm down. Summer, what we're doing is against the law. Your grandmother, me, the harpies, we could all be jailed if it became known. If that happens, your half-brother will probably die. He's caged and not doing well. You see why this mustn't leak out?"

"I get it, but Will should be told," Summer said. "When it comes to a fight, he's better than all of you put together."

Windy said, "He rules soon and is needed here, I do not want to argue with him about it."

"Okay, but a golden harpy belongs on this rescue," Summer said. "If Will isn't going, I'll do it. My Oden brother would expect the support of his family."

"Absolutely not," said Windy.

"Consider me the family member," said Jim. "This attempt will be dangerous. It isn't child's play and no place for a girl. You'd only be in the way."

Summer lifted her head, eyes filled with fire. "I'm not a child or a girl." Arching her wings in a challenge, she said, "Would you like me to show you, Jim?"

"Summer!" Windy growled and rose from her seat.

Jim realized that his comments had insulted her, and she was mad. "Summer, I don't believe in fighting females," he said with an uneasy chuckle, wondering if the impish harpy could whip him. Jim was a big strapping guy, six-two, and over two hundred pounds, but on Earth, he had fought Summer's dad. Shail was eighty pounds of attitude, more agile than a man, and had six limbs that hit hard and fast. Even tethered down, the harpy had knocked him senseless. Jim learned never to underestimate slight golden scrappers. They were lethal.

Summer, looking at her angry grandmother, deflated and lowered her head and wings. "I am sorry, Jim. You know I'd never hurt you, but don't call me a girl."

"It won't happen again," Jim said, "but the fact is, I couldn't live with myself if you came and something bad happened to you. Plus, your grandmother would kill me."

Ted's vehicle pulled up alongside the house, and he and another man climbed out. "Miss Windy," Ted called. "I want you to meet your pilot." They stepped onto the porch, and he said with an eye roll, "This is Matt. He's the best I could find on short notice."

The young man's shaggy, light-brown hair hung over the collar of his worn army jacket. He swaggered toward them in faded jeans. "Howdy, folks," he said with a poker grin, but his hazel eyes focused on Summer.

"You arrived early," said Windy.

"Yes, ma'am," said Matt. "I fly fast, known to vanish in thin air."

Jim frowned. "How old are you?"

"That's none of your business, old man," said Matt.

"Look, boy," Jim snarled. "It's my goddamn business if I use your ship."

"Twenty-four, but I got experience," Matt said. "I'm as sly as a fox in a chicken coop when it comes to slipping on and off a planet."

Jim glanced at Ted with a scowl. "Where did you find this joker?"

Ted shrugged. "He checks out."

Matt moved beside Summer. "Hey, doll, I've heard about Dora's winged harpies, but didn't know they're so hot, and sweetheart, you're hotter than a burning phoenix."

"Back off, human." Summer sneered. "Besides hot, I can sense your mind, and yours is full of smut."

"Ain't smut, doll. It's wishful thinking." Matt turned to Jim. "So what's the cargo?"

"No, cargo, just passengers; me and these two male harpies," said Jim. "The return flight will hold another harpy. He's being held in a mental hospital on Mirage. We're to take him out and leave Oden illegally."

Matt eased into a chair and stretched out, resting his knee-high leather boots on the railing. "Knew the destination was Oden, but what you're planning…gonna have to be as slippery as a snake. There's a lot of security because of Oden's black-diamond mines." He helped himself to some fruit. "You can't sneak a mouse out of Mirage's closed port, and outside the city the desert's hotter than a witch's tit in a brass bra. It'll fry your brains. Plus, it's monitored with heavy-duty satellites."

"Are you saying that stealing the harpy is impossible?" asked Jim.

"Nope, never said that, old man," Matt said. "I can get fake landing papers for Mirage port so you and your harpies are in the city, but leaving is tricky. After I drop you off, I'll fly to the mountain range about forty miles off. The mining caves there are big enough to hide my ship. You'll have to break into the hospital, grab your harpy, and haul ass, but you'll only have a few hours of night to do it. If cops don't nail you, you gotta outrun the sunrise. Caught in that desert under Oden's twin suns, you'll burn crisp as bacon."

At first impressions, Jim didn't like the cocky young pilot who spoke in idiotism and clichés to sound cool, but the guy seemed to know everything about Oden and how to get around the problems. "So the landing has been solved. After we have the harpy, it's a matter of getting from Mirage to the mountain cave."

"Yep," Matt said, and glanced up at the harpies. "How fast can these boys fly?"

"Faster than your hovers," said Bloom.

"Wow, that works," Matt said. "They should make the desert cross in under half an hour."

"But how do they get out of the dome?" Jim asked.

"Money," Matt said, rubbing fingers against his thumb. "Ya know, the root of all evil. I got a good-old-boy who works the exhaust systems. For the right price, he'll look the other way and let your harpies out. I used him for swiping contraband stones when I landed in the desert at night."

“If you can land in the desert, why bother setting down inside a cave miles away?” Jim asked.

Matt plopped his boots on the deck and sat upright. “Shit, that’s one mistake you don’t make twice. I got back to my ship with the package of stones. As soon as I climbed aboard, the feds were all over me. The bastards were waiting to catch me with the goods.”

Summer stepped to the pilot, and her eyes were big with fascination. “How did you get away, Matt?”

Matt smiled, eyeing Summer. “Doll, it was a matter of guts and quick thinking. I fired her up and took off before my ship was boarded. Had to fly into an asteroid field to shake ’em, and those asteroids are hairy. No one in their right mind follows you.” He turned to Jim. “That’s when I learned about Oden’s satellites. They monitor everything outside that’s electronic but don’t bother with life forms because Oden has critters and probably figure that a man couldn’t survive the desert. The good thing for us, they don’t bother with surveillance in the mountains.”

Jim strolled to the railing. With Matt’s knowhow, the venture was feasible. “What’s your little smuggling operation going to cost us?”

“Getting you there and back in one piece,” Matt said. “Two million credits upfront.”

Ted broke in, “That’s ridiculous. For that kind of money, we could almost buy a new ship.”

“Yeah, but can this old guy or his harpies fly it?”

“Even if we agreed to the price,” said Jim. “You’re not getting one credit upfront. You could take the money and run.”

Matt stood and was face to face with Jim. “And if you’re busted in Mirage or croak in the desert, I get zip. Two mil for gambling with my ship and ass. Otherwise, find yourself another boy.”

“Half,” said Jim, “half upfront and the rest when we return.”

Matt looked down, rubbed his eye, and grinned. “You drive a hard bargain, but okay. You gotta deal. When do you want to leave?”

“Today,” said Windy.

"I'll need a few hours to charge my ship," Matt said. "Lady, just make darn sure my million is in cash vouchers."

Aron lunged, grabbed the front of Matt's collar, and snatched him off the floor. "Show respect to our queen."

Matt jerked a laser gun from under his jacket and pressed the barrel against Aron's temple. "Let go, birdman, or your feathers will cover the deck."

Bloom jumped behind Matt and wrapped an arm around his throat. "Hurt him, and I shall snap your neck before one feather falls."

"Easy, fellas," Jim said. "Aron, Bloom, let him go. We need him."

Bloom released Matt and stepped back. Unclasping Matt's jacket, Aron gave him a shove.

Matt stumbled slightly and collected himself. "Damn, those harpies are as mean as hornets when you poke their nest," he mumbled and holstered his weapon. He straightened his jacket and faced Windy. "Sorry, ma'am. Didn't mean no disrespect."

Windy nodded.

Matt placed one hand on the railing and leaped over it to the grass. "Let's go, Ted."

Jim stepped to the edge of the porch. "Matt, keep this little incident in mind. Men hunted harpies for decades, so their patience is thin."

"No shit."

"Another thing, I'm the chief of police here and don't like being called an old man."

Matt lifted his eyebrows and cackled. "Looks like I'm in for a pleasant trip."

After Matt and Ted left for the airport, Aron came up to Jim. "That man holds no honor."

"I don't need your instincts to know that, but we're about to commit a crime and need a criminal."

Overhearing them, Summer piped in. "I think you are wrong about Matt. He's charming and a good guy."

Jim agreed that Matt was probably good at charming the pants off a girl, or a gullible teenage harpy. “Summer, Matt’s a heartbreaker. He seduces females with his looks and charisma, but he has no morals and would never make a commitment. He’d use you and move on.”

“I don’t believe that,” Summer said, flipping back her hair. She spread her wings and flew into the forest.

Jim said to Windy, “It’s a good thing we’re leaving. I believe your granddaughter was smitten with that pilot.”

“Yes, she likes him, and Summer nears the age to choose a mate. After you go, I shall have a long talk with her about bonding with a devoted harpy.”

“You can tell her.” Jim grinned. “But I doubt she’ll listen. She’s rather willful.”

Windy breathed a sigh. “I know.”

“I guess we need to get moving. I’ll load up the gear and weapons, and then we’ll hit the bank for the pilot’s vouchers and then the store for supplies before going to the airport.” He turned to Bloom and Ribot. “Sorry, guys, but you’ll be on a nut and dried fruit diet for some time.”

“We shall gather fresh for the beginning of the journey,” said Aron. “We shall meet you at the star vehicle.”

After running the errands, Jim and Windy drove to Terrance airport and maneuvered around the local hovercrafts on the open lot. They parked alongside the only spaceship, a tired, banged up ship that was shaped like a gray dagger. Ted, Aron, and the two male harpies stood on the pavement in its shade.

Climbing out of his vehicle, Jim said, “You gotta be kidding me…two million for this heap. The damn thing’s an antique, at least a hundred years old.”

Matt emerged from the ship’s doorway. “She’s got some age on her, but she’ll get the job done.”

“I’m just hoping it clears the atmosphere.”

Matt grinned. "When we take off, she'll have your hair standing on end."

Jim shook his head and opened the back of his vehicle. He, Ted, and the harpies unloaded the gear and weapons, placing them in the rear of the ship. The store-bought food crates and harpy bags of fresh fruit were put below in the cargo hold. They came back out for final farewells.

Jim stepped to Windy and glanced at the smug pilot and two edgy harpies. "They're liable to kill each other before we make Oden." He put his arms around her. "I'll sure miss you, babe."

Windy hugged him. "Be careful, my lover. Without you, life is not worth living."

Jim knew this wasn't idle talk. Harpies took bonding seriously. "Don't worry. I promise I'll come back to you."

Aron clasped Bloom's shoulders. "Make me proud." Bloom nodded, and Aron turned to Ribot. "You represent the browns. Do not fail us."

"I shall not," said Ribot.

Jim walked to Ted and Aron and shook their hands. "Larry is in charge of the police department while I'm gone. He's a capable man." He breathed a long, heavy sigh. "Wish us luck."

"Luck," said Aron.

"Good luck," Ted said, and turned his gaze to Windy. "Jim, I'll check on her often and make sure she's okay."

"I'd appreciate that," Jim said. Ted also knew that harpies suffered from separation and could even die if they lost their mate. "See you in a few months."

Matt took a last look under the ship and then boarded. Jim, Bloom, and Ribot trailed him up the ramp. Inside, the pilot pushed a lever, and the door shut with a hiss, confirming the seal. "Strap in. She bucks like a bronco on takeoff."

With large frightened eyes, Bloom asked, "What is a bronco?"

"He means it'll be a little bumpy when we leave." Jim helped the harpies buckle up, pulling the straps over their wings. Confined and tied down, both males quivered. "It'll be okay, fellas," he said and patted their shoulders. "Once we clear the clouds, you can move around." He stepped to the cockpit, sat down in the co-pilot seat, and fastened his seat belt. Out the window, he spotted Windy, Ted, and Aron. They had moved to the port building to avoid the blast of the ship on takeoff.

"How are your harpy boys doing?" Matt asked while adjusting the instruments.

"They're nervous as hell, and so am I."

Matt laughed. "I haven't lost anyone yet." He flipped several switches, and the engines fired with a thunderous roar. "Here we go." He pushed the throttle forward.

The ship lifted off, creating a huge dust cloud at the port. "Jesus Christ!" Jim said as the thrust shoved him hard against the seat. The vessel shuddered violently in its race through the grayish-green clouds. Several minutes later, the gravitational pull, the loud rumbling, and intense quaking became a slight hum and vibration. Dora was soon a multicolored ball suspended in a dark, starry sky.

"Told ya she bucked," said Matt.

"Yeah, right," Jim huffed. "I'd better check on those poor harpies." Unbuckling his seatbelt, he wondered about another harpy, the reason for this long trip ahead and their dangerous mission. His wife believed the young male on Oden was worth it, but Jim was skeptical. There was more to a golden harpy than yellow wings.

CHAPTER SIX

After Monica's vacation on the enormous Oden space station, she returned to Mirage but didn't go straight home. Instead, her limo took her to the mental institution. She wanted to check on Alexander, and an unannounced visit had advantages. Catching his doctor and the staff off guard would more accurately reveal her son's care.

She strolled into the administrator's office and asked the secretary, "Is Dr. Collins in?"

The secretary jumped to attention. "Miss, Carlton, umm, did you, did you have an appointment?"

"I don't need one, dear," she said, and marched toward the doctor's office.

"Wait a minute, Dr. Collins is consulting with a patient. You can't go in."

"*Can't* is a term that doesn't apply to me." She opened the door and saw Dr. Collins at his desk. A mousy woman with puffy red eyes sat before him. "How's my son?" Monica demanded.

Collins gaped, appearing as stunned as his secretary. "Miss Carlton," he said with a swallow. Drumming up a fake grin, he rose and addressed his woman patient, "Can we reschedule, Charlotte? My secretary will arrange another time."

With a vapid nod, the woman left the room. Monica took her seat.

"Give me a minute while I pull up his file," Collins said, sitting back down and hitting the computer keys. "If I'd known you were back in town, I could have been better prepared for your visit."

"I'm not interested in preparation or files, just answers. Is Alexander well or isn't he?"

Turning from the computer, Collins took a deep breath. "He has been difficult. Have you spoken to your housekeeper? She was at your house when we removed Alexander."

"I haven't heard a word, but everyone knows not to bother me. I go on vacation to relax and don't want to be stressed with Alexander's pranks."

"I'm afraid this is more serious than pranks. Two of my custodians tried to subdue him with stun guns, and he put them in the hospital. One is still in a critical condition."

"I'm sorry about your men, but I warned that he'd retaliate."

Collins nodded with a sigh. "You did, but there's more. Since arriving at our facility, Alexander has attempted suicide several times. First, he flew into the viewing screen to break his neck. For his safety, we clipped his feathers. He then became comatose. When he recovered, he went on a rampage, demolishing the robots that cared for him. He placed a piece of sharp metal to his throat and threatened to kill himself if not released. Luckily, Miss Harris arrived and talked him out of it. She had also brought him out of the coma, and her daily visits have kept him stable."

"Those visits are over," she growled. "I don't want Mollie near him. She ruined him, filled his head with grandeur, that he's a golden harpy and above humans. I want her out."

"Miss Carlton, I don't think Miss Harris is to blame for your son's behavior. Alexander is a harpy and has animal DNA. He doesn't reason like a human. Serial killers are easier to treat. I hoped to learn how his telepathic powers work, then to nullify it with the right drugs or teach him control, but he's so bent on self-destruction, it's a chore to keep him alive. Removing Miss Harris is a mistake."

"I'll take her place. Now I'd like to see him."

"He's upstairs in Isolation." They took the elevator up several floors and went into a monitoring room, where several screens showed the precarious patients. A nurse stood by, observing the confined. "Enlarge Alexander Carlton's cubicle," the doctor instructed her.

Monica stared at the ball of yellow feathers resting on the floor. "Can he use his telepathy on me?"

"No, we're safe. He can't project it through the electronics. I learned that harpies can't translate their thoughts to one another over a communicator. I'll turn on the speaker so you can talk to him."

"Alexander, it's Mommy," Monica said sweetly.

A blond head emerged from the feathers, and Alexander gazed at the screen but remained silent.

"Alexander, I know you've given these people trouble, but if you behave, you'll soon come home."

Alex uncurled his body and stood. "These people have yet to see trouble, and I don't need telepathy to know you lie," he said, shaking his feathers. "I will not get out soon, if ever."

"That's not true. I can bring you home whenever I please. I am your mother."

"You are not, not anymore. A mother cares about her son. You don't." He dropped to the padded floor, coiled up, and covered his lean frame with wings.

"Alexander, I do care about you. I…I love you. Please, this is only temporary. You'll soon be back in your tree." Monica kept talking, but he wouldn't respond.

"Miss Carlton, this isn't helping," Collins said, and turned off the speaker. "He needs to be quiet, and you're only upsetting him."

"Of course, he's upset. He's confined and not happy about it, but he'll get over it and forgive me. He always does."

Collins lifted a skeptical eyebrow. "I'm not so sure, but regardless, he's correct about his release. He's not going anywhere soon. His suicide attempts were in earnest, and when one doesn't value his own life, he values other lives even less. If he's freed, he won't just hurt people but might kill them."

Monica staggered back from Collins, feeling alarmed and outraged. "This is your fault. Instead of fixing him, you and your lousy clinic have made him worse. He's become more dangerous and is so angry that he's rejected his mother. I'm sending him to an Earth sanitarium. Perhaps a competent doctor can repair the damage you've done."

"That's your decision, but in the meantime, I'll keep treating him. With Miss Harris's help, maybe we can lower his hostility and bring him around."

"Whatever, he'll be on the next voyage to Earth." Monica stomped out of the room. Outside the Mirage Mental Institution, she climbed into the limo and ordered the driver to take her home.

At her mansion, she found her secretary working at her desk. "They're idiots, Lilly. Dr. Collins and his moronic staff have turned Alexander into a psychotic killer. Find me the best mental clinics on Earth and make arrangements for Alexander to be on the first available ship to Earth. My son will be on it."

"The first ship arrives at the end of the month," Lilly said. "Miss Carlton, do you want to tell me what happened at the clinic?"

Monica's riled state had overridden the hurt, but her anguish burst out in a flood of tears. "The doctor promised to change him, and he did. Alexander hates me. My darling harpy child hates me and says I'm not his mother anymore. What have I done?"

* * *

With Dora far behind and out of sight, the ship traveled through the deep void of space. Matt put his ship, *Dream Weaver,* on autopilot and left the cockpit to check on his passengers. Jim sat in the dining booth while the two harpies explored their small living quarters. Before today, Matt had never seen a harpy. They were lanky, handsome creatures with long, flowing wings and humanoid frames.

They wore only a hip sash for clothing. He'd learned quickly that their graceful looks were deceptive. They were strong with nasty tempers. He realized he'd have to watch his himself. Forced to shoot one, he probably wouldn't get the rest of his money. He smiled and trying to be friendly, he asked the black-winged harpy, "You guys okay? Departure is always a little rough."

The harpy didn't answer but glared at Matt with his penetrating green eyes.

"They survived," Jim said. "But on lift off, I knew how the ancient astronauts felt."

"Most small ships kick like mules," said Matt. "They're not like these big shuttles. We're approaching the wormhole, and we'll come out on the white end in two weeks. Then it's another week and a half to the Oden spaceport. I'll dock and register a false flight plan so I can land on Oden. If I don't, the law will be on our butts before we even reach the planet. Mirage is a skip and a jump away from the spaceport."

The black-winged harpy tilted his head. "There are worms in the stars?"

Jim grinned. "No, Bloom, not real worms."

"It is a hole in space that speeds up time, a time capsule so to speak," Matt said. "Without it, we'd travel for years to get where we're going." He shook his head. It was like trying to explain ship propulsion to a bird. "Never mind, you won't understand."

"I am of the jungle," Bloom said, "but I understand this race for time. If I fly very fast toward the sunset, I keep the light and stop the time."

Matt blinked in amazement. "Yeah, it's something like that. You birdmen are smarter than you seem."

Bloom raised his head. "I am no bird or man. I am a harpy."

"Okay, Bloom," Matt said, and eased into the booth across from Jim. He placed his elbows on a table. "So tell me about this harpy we're fetching. For two million, he must be important."

"I don't know much about him," Jim said. "Only that he's a seventeen-year-old and my wife's grandson."

"He is a golden," said Bloom. "The yellow-winged are rare and valued for their courage and wisdom. They are the monarchs of our flocks."

"How'd this one end up on Oden? And why the need to sneak him out?" asked Matt.

"The kid is half harpy," Jim said. "His mother is a woman, Monica Carlton, and she's placed him in a mental institution, but locking up a harpy is a death sentence. This is a rescue mission."

Matt frowned. "Wait a minute. Did you say Carlton?"

"Do you know her?" Jim asked.

Matt stood and paced the small area. "Not her, but I sure as hell know the damn name. Shit, I should have charged double for this gig." He turned to Jim. "Don't you backward people on Dora know anything?"

"We heard Miss Carlton has money," said Jim.

"The damn Carlton family is filthy rich. They own the mining industry on Oden and a few other planets. Their power is unlimited. Stealing her harpy kid is like jumpin' from the frying pan into the fire. Every federation ship will be hot on our ass. Even if we make it back to Dora with this boy, he won't stay long. The feds will come after him and drag him back to his mom."

"Not if he hides in the Dora jungle until he's eighteen. His mother will lose parental rights, and her only alternative is questioning his competency and fighting him in court."

Matt sat back down and massaged his jaw. "Yeah, that might work. Sometimes having a lawman around who knows the laws is a help. What's this harpy boy's name?"

"Alexander Carlton," Jim said.

Matt chuckled. "You know little Alex will probably inherit the Carlton fortune someday. That's a pretty good incentive to save him and become his buddy."

"Only one problem, Matt," Jim said. "The youngster is a harpy and can sense your motives. So far, your intentions haven't impressed Bloom and Ribot. They know what you're all about."

Matt had noticed the harpies rarely showed emotions with a smile or frown, but Bloom's hateful stare conveyed plenty. The harpy didn't like him. "You got a point. I'll work on that one." A beeping in the cockpit made him rise. "We're nearing the wormhole. I'll need to guide her into the center."

Matt grabbed the controls and maneuvered the ship into the cavity of brilliant, swirling white and yellow clouds created from dust and debris.

Jim sat down in the co-pilot seat and said, "Amazing, just amazingly beautiful."

Jim's comment had Matt appreciating the phenomena that he normally took for granted. "Yeah, these holes are pretty awesome," he said, plotting the course through the wormhole. "Here we go." The ship picked up speed, entering the abyss. He throttled back and killed the engines to save energy. The result was utter silence. "All set. I won't have to reengage until we reach the other end."

A few minutes later Bloom stepped into the cockpit and said softly, "Jim, there is a problem."

Jim stood. "What?"

"Ribot and I feel a presence on the star vehicle. We would have known sooner, but the shaking and noise frightened us and affected our senses."

"Don't get excited," Matt said. "Some little varmint probably slipped aboard for the food. It's happened before."

"It is not an animal, but a harpy," said Bloom.

"Are you sure?" Matt asked.

"Matt, it's not wise to question him," Jim said. "But how could a harpy get aboard?"

"The hatch door was open all morning," Matt said. "One could've flown in while I was at your house or under the ship, recharging the turbine."

"We better find him," said Jim. They returned to the main cabin and began the search. Jim and the harpies looked in the closets and cupboards of the back berths, galley, and head. Matt opened a hatch to the bowels of the ship and descended the ladder into cargo. He opened the many compartments, holding food, equipment, and extra ship parts. The last one was full of yellow feathers.

"Come on out, doll."

In the cramped space, the little harpy poked her pretty head out of her wings and sighed. "Please, Matt, don't tell them I'm here."

"They already know. Your harpy boys sensed you," Matt called to the others. "Found the harpy."

Summer uncurled her body and crawled out over the duffle bags. They mounted the stairs, and Jim was waiting in the cabin.

"Summer, what the devil are you doing here?" Jim said.

"I am needed on this mission."

"Your grandmother said no, and she's the ruler. Matt, get up in that cockpit and turn the ship around. We're taking her back."

"No can do," said Matt. "The wormhole is a one-way trip. It's impossible to reverse course and fight the pull. She's with us until Oden spaceport. From there, she can catch a shuttle in the return wormhole to Dora."

"Terrific, just what I need," Jim stormed. "Young lady, when we reach the spaceport, you're going home. Matt, put in a call to Dora before everyone panics looking for her."

"Sure." Matt grinned. He had expected a miserable voyage, considering that his male passengers wanted to throttle him, but now the trip was looking sweet. In the cockpit doorway, he smiled at Summer, "Welcome aboard, doll."

* * *

After the ship's departure, Windy returned home. Without her mate of sixteen years, the empty house seemed unbearable. Jim's booming laugh, affectionate touch, and encouraging words would be absent for two months. He had a way of making every day seem like their first. She fought the regret of letting him go.

She meandered into the bedroom, crawled onto the bed, and inhaled Jim's scent from the sheets. "You must come back to me," she whispered. If he did not, she knew the possible results. She had lost two prior mates, but the death of her first, her harpy mate, had nearly killed her.

Her thoughts drifted to Shail's father. Like his son, he was a majestic golden, the monarch of the flocks, but his reign was short. A man shot him down in his prime. She, consumed with grief and the deadly depression, had placed her five-year-old son in the care of Aron's father and wandered into the jungle to die.

Her second mate, a kindly older man, had saved her. He found her under a tree, unconscious and suffering from shock. He nursed her back to health and, more important, returned her hope. She married him because he was a wealthy politician and could help her harpies. He planned to change laws and end harpy hunting, but died of heart failure before succeeding.

Widowed twice, Windy determined not to bond again. She then met the rugged ex-cop from Earth, who accompanied Shail back to Dora. Jim too had known heartbreak. His wife and son were killed in a hover crash, and to numb the pain he turned to alcohol and lost his job. When he and Shail crossed paths, Jim found a reason to live by helping Shail. The attraction between her and Jim was immediate. They felt like kids again, madly in love, and starting out fresh. But he was now gone on a perilous quest.

She shuddered and climbed off the bed. Dwelling on worry and fear would make the months feel like an eternity. Jim had questioned if the Oden harpy was worth the trouble, but went anyway. He was doing it for her. Windy also now wondered. Who was this Alex?

Windy walked to the living room, sat down at the desk, and pressed the com keys for a connection to Oden. "Hello, Mollie," she said when the woman appeared on the screen. "I am letting you know that several hours ago my husband and two harpies left for Oden."

"That's wonderful," said Mollie. "Alex will be ecstatic."

"Yes, about Alex. I know how he came to be, and I saw his picture. He is handsome, but I do not know much else about him."

Mollie's wide grin disappeared. "What do you want to know?"

"To start, is Alex a harpy or a human with feathers on his back?"

"He's a harpy—has the same nature and instincts, and he's like his dad, brave and very smart. The best tutors in the galaxy taught him. He received a college degree at thirteen. He'll blend easily with his kind when he arrives on Dora." Mollie's gaze shifted downward from the screen.

"You are not telling me everything."

"You must understand that Alex has had a difficult childhood. His mother is a cold woman and never gave him much love. As a teenager, he stopped trying to please her and rebelled. There have been some incidents."

"When you say incidents, I assume they were serious. Why else would his mother have him locked up?"

"If I tell you, I'm afraid you'll abandon him."

"Miss Harris, my husband is risking his life for this young male," Windy said harshly. "You had better explain everything. If not, I shall order the ship back and leave Alex to his fate."

"All right," Mollie said sadly. "Alex is different from other harpies, but he's not human either. He's gifted, special. He's taken his harpy telepathy a step further. He can not only sense feelings and thoughts, but is able to invade a mind and control people, coercing them to act. He had a lot of time on his hands and learned this form of hypnotism."

"And he used this power to hurt people."

"He's not to blame. A doctor wanted to cut off his wings and operate on his head. He stopped them. They came for him a second time and two men had to be hospitalized with self-inflicted injuries. Alex was only defending himself. He's like his father. Shail killed the three men in the hunting range. Please, Miss Windy, Alex is a good boy. He's just confused and needs love and acceptance. He'll be fine on Dora with his harpies."

Windy leaned back in the chair. "That is your hope, but not a guarantee. Just so you know, Shail killed far more than three men, and it destroyed his mind. Alex could end up like his father."

"Please don't prejudge him. He's very loyal and affectionate with the people he loves."

"Affection is easy when bad behavior is not punished. From what you tell me, Alex sounds spoiled and has not learned to respect others. He treats humans like toys and misuses his dangerous telepathy. The harpies would not tolerate such conduct."

"It's my fault. I was lenient with him and tried to instill a golden's confidence."

"Miss Harris, golden harpies are born confident but must be taught when to be fearless or rational. It is a narrow branch they walk." Windy paused and swept back her hair. "The abuse of his psychic powers is a concern. All harpies have telepathy, but we are discreet and honorable beings. We rarely expose the frailty of the weak. Alex apparently lacks these principles, but he is young and can possibly be re-taught. He shall know love, but also the hard smack of an older male's wing."

Mollie smiled. "You're still taking him then?"

"It was never a question. He is Shail's son and belongs with us."

***

As evening approached Windy strolled out on the veranda and thought about Jim. He would have enjoyed the vivid pink and pale-green sky. The com buzzed, and she stepped inside. Seeing Jim on the screen, she smiled and said, "I was looking at the sunset and thinking of you." His aggravated expression had her ask, "What is it, Jim?"

"Your granddaughter is here," Jim said. "Summer snuck aboard the ship. We're already in the wormhole and can't turn back. We're stuck with her until we reach Oden spaceport in two weeks. I'll put her on the first shuttle to Dora."

Windy heard Summer's voice in the background. "Put her on!" Summer appeared on the screen, and Windy raged, "Summer, you disobeyed me. You will be disciplined severely upon your return."

"I know. I'm sorry, Grandma, but I had to come. I can help Jim and the others, but I was also thinking about my half-brother. We're both goldens and the same age. He'll connect better with me, and he is likely to be lonely and uncomfortable."

"Consoling your lost brother is not the reason you are there. You seek adventure."

Summer dropped her head and didn't argue.

Windy reflected on the com call with Mollie Harris. Alex had been coddled and could be treacherous. If they gave him orders, he might resist and use his telepathy on those aboard the ship. However, his pretty, willful sister could probably control him. "If I let you remain on the voyage, you must obey Jim."

"I promise, Grandmother."

Jim appeared, looking more aggravated than before. "You're not serious about letting her stay?"

"I spoke to Miss Harris about Alex. He is not a typical harpy, but has learned to use his telepathy as a weapon. He can harm you, Jim. That is why he was locked up. He also approaches the age when male harpies spar with one another for dominance. Five males confined on a small ship for a long time is risky, but males do not challenge female harpies. Summer will captivate him, and he will want to please her. She can make him behave."

"Stupid me." Jim chuckled sarcastically. "I thought once we got this boy, my worries were over. Instead I'll be dealing with a winged powder keg on the return trip. All right, Windy. Summer stays. You know your harpies best."

CHAPTER SEVEN

In the Dora jungle, Will stood knee-high in a clear stream and doused and ruffled his yellow wings. He shook the water from his blond locks and gazed at his brown-winged companion, who still slept curled up in orange moss on the bank. “Freely, get up. We waste the light and need to go.”

Freely opened his drowsy green eyes and relayed, *We flew all night. Are you not tired, Will?*

“Speak to me. We are not old harpies talking silently for fear of hunters.”

“Habit,” Freely said, “My father hates speaking like a human.” He snuggled back into his feathers.

Will fanned his wing across the stream and the water landed on Freely. “Rise, I have already bathed and have places to be.” Oil in harpy feathers made his wings waterproof and kept Freely dry so Will tossed water, aiming to soak Freely’s head.

“Stop it, Will,” Freely growled, but was ignored. A splash hit his face, and he jumped up, shook his wet hair, and arched his wings.

“Seriously?” Will asked. “You are challenging me?”

“It has been a long time, and I am bigger and stronger now,” said Freely, keeping his fighting stance.

Will shrugged. “Okay if you prefer bruises to a little water.”

Will started to step from the stream but in a blink, opened his wings, and flew into Freely, hitting his gut with a shoulder blow. Freely fell back against a tree trunk and scrambled to regain his footing. Will was ready for him. He fluttered off the ground and kicked Freely's face. Freely went down, blood dripping from his nose. Even in a mock fight between eighteen-year-olds, they expected some injuries.

Will set down on the bank and asked, "Have you had enough?"

"Not nearly," Freely grunted.

The two faced off, fluttered a few feet in the air, and struck each other with their feet like clashing waterfowl. Freely, heavier and a few inches taller than his rival, should have had the advantage but lacked Will's golden tenacity and aggression that blocked out pain and doubt.

Freely tried to hold his ground, but Will fiercely threw life and limb into the fight. His pounding fists, feet, and striking wings overwhelmed Freely, who was finally knocked down and sent tumbling into thick blue ferns.

"All right, all right, I am done," Freely said, lying in the brush, panting.

Will landed and offered his hand. Pulling Freely to his feet, he gave his brown-winged companion a friendly slap on the shoulder. "You did well. Perhaps the irritation from little sleep helped."

Freely shook his head. "My father wanted us to be friends, like he and your father were. I am supposed to protect you."

"Tell Aron I do not require a bodyguard."

"No, not from any living creature, but you need protection from yourself. Rather than yield, you were willing to break your wings. I do not understand goldens."

"Wash the blood off your face and we shall go." Nor did Will understand his golden nature, the innate drive to dominate or die.

Freely knelt by the stream and splashed water on his face, grumbling to himself. "I must take care of him, but I am the one losing blood."

"You whine like a fledgling. Go home or pair with a brown-winged male. Despite Aron's wishes, you do not have to be with me."

Freely rose and stepped to Will. "I know. I am here because you inspire and fill me with awe. I am honored to share the sky with you."

Will cloaked Freely in yellow feathers. "I love you too, and am sorry I hurt you."

Rubbing his bruised face, Freely said, "I shall live. Where do you wish to go that is so important?"

"For two full moons, we have traveled the coast and mountains. I am sick of it. We shall follow the old road into Terrance."

"Terrance is full of gawking humans. Why go there?"

"Unfortunately, I shall soon rule those gawkers. My grandmother longs to retire and wishes to prepare me. I must see her."

Freely wrinkled his nose and sniffed. "I sense your fear. You who fear nothing are afraid of your coming reign."

"It is dread, not fear. My father felt the same way, saying that to rule is work, worry, and no freedom. It is worse than a cage."

"Then let one of your younger brothers rule the harpy land."

"I was chosen, Freely. On the day of my birth, my father held me up before a large crowd of humans and harpies and said I was the future monarch. I cannot dishonor my father's wishes." Will spread his wings. "Shall we go or waste the day yapping?"

They took flight and headed south to pick up the old dirt highway that ran east to west, connecting Terrance in the middle of the continent to the western ocean.

After traveling several miles, Freely said, "When you rule, I shall always be there for you."

"Do not make vows you cannot keep. A mate and fledglings shall soon have your loyalty."

Freely glided alongside and said, "You too have the urge to bond and make a nest."

"My body longs for a female, but my mind resists. Suppose I disappoint her, and she stares at me unsatisfied."

Freely smirked. "I have seen you without your sash. You shall not disappoint a female."

"You are an idiot, Freely. I spoke of effort and control, not size. What if I am too eager and release my seed before she is pleased?"

"You worry about the strangest things."

Sensing Freely's amusement, Will became irritated and picked up speed, leaving his friend behind. They would normally talk about the jungle, animals, humans, and combat, but nearing maturity, Will's mind was on mating and rule. Expressing his secretive concerns, he received no advice or empathy.

"Slow down, Will," Freely called. "I cannot keep up."

Will stopped his vigorous flapping and glided over the colorful treetops, realizing Freely wasn't to blame. He was not a mentor, just another young, inexperienced male.

Freely caught up with him. "I did not mean to offend you. I was just surprised. You are always so confident."

"Now you know I am not. I have anxieties and doubts."

"I shall give you my father's advice about the bond. He said that I and my mate shall be virgins, not knowing what to expect. I should follow my instincts, and even if I am nervous and make mistakes, she shall love me and I should not worry."

"It is good advice. You are lucky Aron is your father. When I became a teenager, mine could not tell me of courtship or much else."

The discussion ended on a somber note. Will longed for a relationship with his father, but Shail was incapable of fulfilling the role.

When they reached the old highway seldom used by ground transports, they turned east. The road went directly into Terrance, and flying above it, their wings avoided trees and vines. An hour later they saw a vehicle ahead traveling in the same direction.

"Tourists, they are in a rented vehicle," said Will. "The human law says they must remain within ten miles of Terrance, and these sightseers should not be this deep in the jungle."

"They are hoping to see a harpy. Should we overtake them and give them a thrill?"

"It would only encourage others. We shall go into the trees and fly around them unseen."

Farther up the road, Will saw a cabo. The sluggish tree dweller which resembled a teddy bear had wandered into the path of the speeding vehicle. "Why does he not slow for the cabo?" he said with panic, and batted his wings to intercede, stop the vehicle or save the cabo, but it was too late. He cringed. The driver struck the cabo and had not reduced his speed or swerved.

Will landed beside the injured animal in the stirred up dust and glared at the departing vehicle. He picked up the ball of fur and stroked its fussy head, then swallowed the lump in his throat when he detected the small animal's terror and pain from a broken spine. The cabo gasped and seemed to look to a harpy for help. *I cannot fix you, only end your suffering.* Will snapped the cabo's neck, stepped off the road, and set the limp body under a tree. He sprang into the air and chased after the tourists.

In hot pursuit, Freely raced after him. "Will, stop. I know you are angry, but you are forbidden to harm humans."

"They harm our wildlife. This shall not go unpunished."

"Your grandmother would not want you to confront them."

Ignoring his friend, Will sailed into the trees and snatched a basketball size fruit from a limb. Without missing a wing beat, he caught up with the vehicle and threw the fruit against the windshield. The glass shattered and chunks of red pulp and thick syrup blinded the driver. The vehicle veered off the road, plowed through a ditch, and crashed into a tree.

Will lit on a branch and stared down at the damaged vehicle. Still fuming, he was unconcerned about the occupants.

Freely set down beside him. “Are they hurt or dead?”

“I do not know or care.” He then heard voices below in the vehicle. “They live.”

The door opened and the hefty, shaken driver stumbled out. He examined the smashed front end of the vehicle, picked up some pulp from the windshield, and called to his passenger. “Where the hell did this come from?”

Will fluttered down and said, “From me.”

The man’s mouth opened with surprise. “Silvia, there’s a harpy here. He’s saying he threw the fruit at us.”

A woman stuck her head out the window. “Dick, the brochure says harpies can be dangerous. Stay away from him.”

The man huffed. “He’s a skinny fucker. I could squash him like a fly.” He touched a gash on his forehead, looked at the blood on his fingers, and growled at Will. “You might’ve killed us.”

“And that would have been justice, a life for a life.” Will glanced back down the road. “You could have avoided the animal in the road, but you ran it over without a thought. I value that animal’s life more than yours.”

The woman said, “I told you to slow down when we saw it.”

The man trudged through the mucky ditch and stood on the roadside. “I should wring this little bastard’s neck for what he’s done.”

Will arched his wings, tossed his hair, and baited him. “Come try, fat man.”

“Dick, harpies are protected,” the woman called. “If you hurt him, you could be arrested.”

“Bullshit; it would be self-defense. He attacked us first.” The man clutched his fists and marched toward Will.

Will placed his hands on his hips and didn’t budge. “You are too pathetic to hurt me.” The man’s eyes narrowed and his face turned red with anger. He swung his fist, but Will ducked, fluttered, and kicked the man's face.

The blow sent the guy staggering backward. "Shit," he cursed, wiping his bloody lip with a sleeve.

Will landed. "Try again."

The man charged at Will with flaying arms, but his fists failed to connect. Will lifted a few feet off the ground and hit the guy's gut and face with numerous foot blows. With the onslaught, the man fell to his knees, clutched his stomach, and coughed. "I'm gonna get you yet," he said, puffing.

"I am waiting."

As the man attempted to rise, the woman stepped out of the vehicle. "Oh, for heaven's sake, Dick," she said, and hurried to her husband, who stood. "Can't you see he's playing with you? If you don't leave him alone, he'll put you in a hospital."

The man nodded and took a wobbly step back to lean against the vehicle.

The woman turned to Will. "I'm so sorry about the little animal. My husband is an oaf."

"Perhaps the painful lesson shall make him wiser." Will flapped his wings and was quickly airborne. Freely who had witnessed the fight from a branch was soon flying beside him.

"A good ruler does not beat up tourists, Will. You must control your temper."

"Had I lost control, the man would be dead."

At dusk, they soared over Terrance and landed at his grandmother's home. Will stepped onto the veranda and called into the house. "Grandma, are you here?" He opened the screen door and called again while Freely waited on the porch.

His grandmother walked down the staircase from the bedrooms. "Will, what a nice surprise." She went to him and kissed his cheek.

"It was time I visit."

"Yes, we must talk about your duties as a ruler. The time approaches." She noticed Will's buddy on the porch. "Come in, Freely. I am not worried about your wings knocking things over."

"I shall be careful." Freely folded his wings tightly and stepped inside. Going down on one knee, he lowered head and said, "My queen."

Windy stroked Freely's head. "I have honey cake. I know your weakness for it."

Freely rose with a smile, and they strolled into the kitchen. As his grandmother removed two plates from a cupboard and cut the cake, Will leaned against a counter and said, "We traveled here on the old highway, and I saw many dead animals killed by vehicles. Grandmother, there should be a law, a punishment for slaughtering our wildlife."

"Those are accidents, not intentional," Windy said, and placed the cake plates on the table. Freely didn't lose time devouring the treat.

Will shook the hair from his eyes. "You call them accidents. I say they are crimes."

Windy studied him for a moment. "What have you done, Will?" When he didn't answer, she turned to Freely and, in a demanding tone, asked, "Freely, what did my grandson do?"

He stared at the table, obviously struggling with his loyalty to Will and obeying his monarch.

Will spoke up. "I attacked a man, a tourist, after he deliberately ran over a cabo. His act was no different than the cruel hunter's who kills for pleasure."

"Is he all right?"

"His aches will heal quicker than his pride." Will looked out the window at Jim's vehicle. "I wish to speak with Jim about a penalty for harming our animals. Humans must learn to be careful."

"Jim is not here." Windy eased into a chair and pushed the plate toward him. "Eat your cake."

Will tilted his head. Mentioning her mate, he felt her nervous sadness brought on by true loss. "Where is he, Grandma?"

"He is on a spaceship. Three days ago he left with Bloom, another male, and Summer." She then explained about the golden harpy on Oden, and how Jim and the others had gone to free him and bring him to Dora.

Fuming, Will ruffled his wings so hard that few feathers drifted to the floor. "How could you do this?" he ranted. "You sent a man, two dark-winged harpies, and a female to save this brother when the rescue should have been mine."

Windy stood with burning eyes. "How dare you question me? I still rule, not you. And I did not send your sister. Summer sneaked aboard the ship. You could not go because cool heads were needed, and you are too impulsive."

"I disagree."

"You just assaulted a man over road kill."

Will was surprised at his grandmother's anger, never having experienced it. He stepped away from her and placed his hands on the kitchen sink, and gazed at the faucet. "If you feel I was unfit for this rescue, perhaps I am also not fit to rule."

Windy stepped to him, cupped his cheeks, and forced him to look at her. "The pressure and responsibility of ruling shall temper your impulses. You are fair-minded, with a tender heart, but brave. You shall be a good leader, but that is also why you could not go. The harpies and humans cannot afford to lose you."

With her touch, he felt her emotions. She was frazzled, worried that her mate might not return. The additional aggravation from a grandson didn't help. "I am sorry I upset you," he whispered, and hugged her. "Jim is a worthy man. He shall succeed and come home to you."

Windy forced a smile. "I am sure you are right."

They drew apart, and Will took a bite of the honey cake. His thoughts returned to the mission. "I am glad Summer is with them. Her nerve and determination match mine. She shall save this Alex."

* * *

Jim sat in the main cabin of the ship and studied a city map of Mirage. Nearby, Bloom was curled up on a small couch with his chin against a port window as he gazed at the yellow and orange clouds drifting past. Ribot slept on the floor in the back berths, flustered with the confining space. Matt and Summer sat in the dining booth with a chessboard between them.

"Doggone it, girl," said Matt. "You're as smart as a whip. I just taught you chess, and you've beaten me twice."

Jim chuckled. "Matt, you'll never win that game against a harpy. She's reading your mind and anticipating your moves."

"Is that right, Summer?" Matt asked, but only got a lifted eyebrow and a smile.

"Damn, that's foul play," Matt said. "Get it, Jim, *fowl* play—ya know their feathers and all."

"I got it," Jim muttered.

"That's okay," Matt said. "We can play another game that only requires luck. It's called spin the bottle."

"That sounds like fun," said Summer.

Jim looked up. Summer wore only hip-high dress. He loudly cleared his throat.

Matt winced. "Maybe that's not a good idea."

For the last ten days, Matt and Summer had been cozy, joking, flirting, and rarely leaving each other's side. They were clearly infatuated. If not for Jim and the two male harpies, their relationship might have become sexual.

After they had discovered the pretty stowaway, Jim had pulled Matt aside and given him a harsh warning. If he fooled around with the impressionable teenager, Jim would beat him bloody and the male harpies would tear him apart. Jim further reminded him that Bloom and Ribot had razor-sharp instincts and would sense if he messed with their little princess.

Matt had responded. "You don't beat around the bush. I won't lay a hand on the doll."

Jim also had a heart-to-heart with Summer. As a middle-aged man, he was hardly qualified to advise a headstrong golden harpy. If he criticized Matt and called him a no-good jerk, she'd only defend him, so he appealed to her feelings. "For Matt's safety, keep your distance," he had said. "If things go too far with that young man, Bloom and Ribot will kill him." She agreed, knowing it was true.

So far, the chats and threats had kept the couple apart, but Jim was sure that once the supervision ended, the hanky-panky would start. Preoccupied with the map, he didn't pay attention to the couple now in plain view—unlike the black-winged harpy on the couch.

With a low hiss, Bloom rose, shook his feathers, and stepped to Matt. "Do not touch her."

Matt sat upright. "I only kissed her hand and said her skin was soft as butter."

"Do not do it again," said Bloom.

Summer leaped out of the booth and arched her wings. "Stop threatening him, Bloom."

"Summer, you are a golden," Bloom said. "I dare not tell you what to do, but him, I tell." He looked down at Matt. "She is royalty. You are unworthy of her, so stay away."

"Gee whiz, we weren't doing anything," Matt said, staring up at the leering harpy. "Besides, if you kill me, you'd be up a creek without a paddle—no one to steer the ship."

"You would not die," said Bloom, "but your days as a stud shall be over." He returned to the couch, curled up, and glared at Matt.

Jim had watched the exchange and chuckled under his breath. That kind of threat would keep Matt in line.

"Jesus Christ, your harpies are worse than junkyard dogs," Matt said.

Summer returned to the booth and sighed. “Male harpies are overly protective, and Bloom and Ribot sense your desires. This causes their hostility.”

Matt mumbled, “They’re not much different from people. I seem to rub everyone the wrong way.”

“But I like you,” said Summer.

“Doll, you don’t know me. Your birdman has me figured right. I’ve lied, cheated, and stolen all my life and don’t have the commitment to settle down with a girl. I don’t deserve you.”

“Give me your hand. Contact allows a harpy to look deeper into a mind.” Summer clasped Matt’s hand and shut her eyes.

Matt worriedly glanced at Bloom. “She took my hand. Okay?”

After a long silent moment, Summer opened her eyes. “You believe you are bad, so you projected this image to others, but you are mistaken. Your heart is good.”

Matt shrugged. “Whatever you say, Summer.”

“You do not believe me. I will tell you what I saw. You have had a hard life. Your mother abandoned you when small, and your father, a cruel, drunken man with a beard, beat you. Before a teenager, you ran away and traveled—”

“Stop.” Matt jerked his hand from her, “I don’t want you to know the rest.”

“Too late,” said Summer. “Matt, you have grown into a man, but deep down you are still the hurt and betrayed little boy who buried his honor to survive. Someday, love will heal you, and the smuggler will become a loyal nobleman.”

“A nobleman?” Matt laughed. “You got more faith in me than I do.”

Summer frowned. “It is not faith, but instincts, and they do not lie.”

Jim shut down the map and slid the computer under his seat. Was Summer right about the young pilot?

CHAPTER EIGHT

Matt had guided the ship out of the wormhole and now recalculated navigation to the Oden Spaceport. A few days later the ship approached the station, which resembled an enormous clear spider with docking bays for legs. Within the body was a huge city holding millions. Matt sat at the helm, and Jim and Summer stood behind him, watching. "I'm docking in freight," Matt said.

"It is so big," Summer said. "Half the city is upside down, like looking at a town in the reflection of a lake."

"Yeah," Matt said, "but the upper half lives on cloud nine in fancy condos. It's a tourist trap with swanky restaurants, shops, nightclubs, and hotels. The luxury liners and private ships dock there. We're going to the bottom half, basically a slum with warehouses, sleazy bars, and flophouses. That's where cargo comes and goes on freighters. It's a lively place, but has a tough crowd. You don't want to bark up the wrong tree, and especially need to go when the lights shut down to simulate night. The human trash crawls out of the garbage and preys on visitors."

"If it's dangerous, why dock in the freighter section?" Jim asked.

"Less trouble," said Matt. "The long arm of the law doesn't reach down there, and no one asks questions. Besides, I know a guy who can provide false registration papers, saying we're going to Oden for legit reasons. Once we're in the Mirage port, I'll get with the exhaust system guy and find out when he can let you and the harpies out of the dome, and how much it'll cost."

Jim nodded. "While you're with him, I'll contact the woman who's helping Alex and get the mental hospital layout for the kidnapping. We'll rendezvous at her place and iron everything out."

"Sounds like a plan," Matt said. "Once I have the lowdown, I'll take off from the port and hide the ship in a mountain cave while ya'all do the deed and grab this harpy boy."

Matt maneuvered the ship through a space hangar and entered the docking bay below the station. He parked between two giant freighters that dwarfed and concealed his small ship. A clanking sound against the ship's hull confirmed that the magnet hold had secured the vessel.

Matt slid out of the seat and grinned at Summer. "Too bad we're not staying longer, doll. We could paint the town red."

Summer frowned. "Paint?"

"Yeah, it's too bad," Jim said. "Let's get this registry over so we can get back underway."

Matt went to the cabin and opened the door hatch. A loud shush released the ship's compression. He stepped onto the clear plastic platform of the loading dock. Jim, Summer, and the two male harpies followed him.

At the end of the platform, Matt recognized the gorilla of a man with hairy arms hanging from a greasy tank-top who hollered at him, "Matt, I hope you're here with my fucking money."

"It's good to see you too, Rog," Matt called back "and don't get your balls is a knot. I got your money." He turned to Jim. "Wait here while I deal with this guy." He strolled down the long dock while pulling a roll of credits from his jacket pocket.

While Matt waited, Rog puffed on a half-smoked cigar and counted the money. Stuffing the credits in a pant pocket, he said, "Okay, we're square, but you can't stay."

"Don't plan to," Matt said. "I only need paperwork so my ship can land at Mirage."

"That'll cost another five hundred." Taking the cigar from his mouth, Rog squinted at Matt's passengers. "What the hell are those winged things?"

"They're called harpies, come from the little jungle planet on the other end of the James wormhole."

"Huh, never seen one before," Rog grunted, "They're pretty."

"Yeah, pretty but temperamental as all get out," Matt said. "Put on the papers, our purpose in Mirage is to buy black stones for their queen."

"Knowing you, that's bullshit. The paperwork will be done in a few hours, but this time no fake vouchers, I want cash."

"So we've got time to hit a bar for a drink. When does the bottom lose light?"

"Four hours, but take some advice, Matt. Stay on your ship. After your last visit, the Heath brothers came gunning for you, claimed you swindled them in a card game. Bump into them and you're dead."

"I'm not afraid of those pricks, and I won that money fair and square."

"Whatever," Rog said. With a headshake, he lumbered to his office.

Matt walked back to Jim and the harpies standing by his docked ship. "Okay, we're all set, but we got a couple of hours to kill. There's a bar a few blocks away. Let's get drunk as skunks."

"Harpies don't drink," said Jim, "And I gave it up years ago. Maybe you should listen to your friend and stay here."

Matt frowned and scratched his head. He glanced back down the long dock to where he and Rog had talked. Jim and the harpies couldn't have overheard them.

Jim grinned. "Guess I forgot to mention that harpies have excellent hearing."

"Damn, I guess so," Matt said. "I'd better watch my yapping, but regardless of what they heard, I'm going, with or without you guys."

"Please, Jim, can we go?" said Summer. "I've never seen a spaceport."

"You're seeing it," Jim said.

Bloom stepped to Jim. "I shall go and protect Matt. He is needed."

"All right, Bloom," Matt said happily, and gave the harpy a friendly pat on the arm. Bloom released a low hiss, obviously disliking the hands-on contact. Matt disregarded the creature's sour disposition and considered the advantage of having a harpy watch his back. "Okay, let's hit that bar."

He and Bloom started down the dock. In the open space, Matt noticed that the barefoot harpy had a tip-toe gait, more like a bird's than the heel-to-toe stroll of a man. More and more he realized that despite their humanoid bodies, harpies were very different from people.

"Hold up," Jim called. "We're coming. It might take all of us to keep you alive."

"Great," Matt said while he and Bloom waited for them. The small group passed the freight building and reached the trash-covered street lined with dilapidated buildings. People stopped and stared at the three scantily-dressed harpies with long wings nearly touching the ground.

The harpies ignored the gapers and seemed fascinated with the millions of twinkling lights on the colossal mushroom-shaped buildings.

"I could never imagine such a place," Summer said, "but humans did and made it."

"Yeah, that's the lavish upper half," Matt said, "Maybe on our next trip I'll take you there." He led the small group down a back street to the shabby tavern with silver tin walls scavenged from old ships. A blinking sign above the door said The Starlight Lounge.

An unconscious man lay in the tavern doorway. Bloom bent over and felt his forehead. "He is alive but unaware."

"Forget him, Bloom," said Matt. "He's only drunk,"

Bloom straightened. "I have seen this drunk in Terrance. Men act foolish and have false courage."

"Isn't that the truth," Jim said. "Back on Earth, I became an alcoholic after my family died." He smiled at Summer. "I'd probably be dead now if Shail hadn't saved me."

"My father saved many," Summer said. They stepped over the man and entered the tavern.

"What do you think?" Matt grinned while Jim and the harpies looked around the dark room dimly lit with small ceiling lights. A loud, scruffy crowd filled the mismatched crude tables and chairs. Most of the patrons were on shore leave from the docked freighters.

Jim turned to Matt. "You're asking what I think of this dump."

"So it ain't classy, but it's a lively, fun place," Matt said, "Just relax."

The noisy chatter turned to whispers when the crowd noticed the harpies.

"Let's get a drink," Matt said. Disregarding the stares, he stepped to the bar. "Hey, Brian," he called to the bartender. "Can I get some drinks here?"

At the end of the bar, a skinny brunette in a sleazy purple dress called out, "Miracles never cease. It's Matt." She sashayed to him and slung her pale arms around his neck, pulling him close. "I heard the Heath brothers killed you, but apparently heard wrong." After planting a wet kiss on his lips, she said, "I'm available right now. We could go upstairs and renew our friendship."

Matt glanced at Summer. "Maybe another time, Patty. I want you to meet my friends." Before he could introduce them, Patty sidestepped him, her sights on the tall black-winged harpy.

"Aren't you a gorgeous thing," Patty said, caressing Bloom's bare chest while feeling under his sash. "Nice package, baby. I'll do you for free."

Stunned, Bloom stood motionless with startled eyes and helplessly endured the hooker's groping.

Matt grinned, enjoying that the bad-ass harpy who had threatened him with castration, was being fondled and molested.

However, Summer didn't find it amusing. Coming to Bloom's defense, she stepped to Patty and shoved her away from Bloom. "Back off, wench," she snapped. "He's not your type."

Patty stumbled and fell against the counter. "Jesus, what a little bitch," she said, righting herself.

Summer arched her wings, the signs of harpy aggression, and started toward Patty. But Matt grabbed Summer's waist and pulled her back. "That's enough. You got your lick in. Now let it lie." When she turned and glared at him, Matt said sweetly, "Come on, doll, for me."

With a nod, Summer lowered her wings as Patty retreated down the bar.

Jim stepped to Matt. "Glad you jumped in. Goldens are stubborn little buggers. She wouldn't have backed down for me."

Matt shrugged. "Heck, Jim, I just want a drink and have a good time, not get kicked out. So, what do you all want?"

"Virgin screwdrivers for us," Jim said, and with a nod towards Patty, he added, "Then I think we should drink up and go. I'm getting bad vibes."

After ordering their orange juice and a whiskey on the rocks for himself, Matt glanced down the bar. Patty was ranting to five big guys and pointing at the harpies. Scowling, the men rose and strolled toward them.

Matt, hoping to avoid a fight, intercepted them. "Hey, fellas, can I buy you a round of drinks? The girls had a little misunderstanding over a guy, but it's over now."

"One of those winged parasites pushed Patty," said a bearded man with a ponytail.

Matt chuckled, "But no harm done, right?" Suddenly blindsided with a punch to his jaw, he hit the floor, but then glanced up to a canopy of yellow feathers.

Summer hovered several feet above him. The blustery air current from her elongated, flapping wings sent napkins, drinks, and debris flying. She kicked the man who had struck Matt, and he doubled over holding his groin. She next took out the second and third men with foot strikes to the face, throat, and gut. Whirling around, she struck the fourth with her outstretched wing, and he flew backward over a table. In seconds she had leveled four men.

The fifth man hustled out of her range and stammered, "I don't want any trouble, lady."

Summer landed, folded her wings, and looked down at Matt. "Are you okay?"

"Holy shit, Summer," he said, astonished at her performance. He struggled to his feet and rubbed his jaw, hurting from the sucker punch. "Remind me to never piss *you* off," he said, gazing at the petite female harpy. At that moment it hit him. He was in love.

"We're leaving," Jim announced to the crowd and pulled back his jacket to expose the hand-clasped blaster on his belt. The two male harpies arching wings further intimidated the patrons, who scrambled away from Matt's party, overturning tables and chairs. Jim looked at the chaotic scene and said to Matt, "Time to go."

"Agreed," Matt said and downed his whiskey in one gulp. He tossed some credits on the bar and said to the barkeep. "This should cover the drinks and damage." He took Summer's hand, and Matt's small party exited the place. Bloom lingered in the doorway, daring anyone to follow them out.

On the street they regrouped and headed back to the ship. Summer and Jim led the way and talked. Matt was several paces behind them, still amazed with Summer's attack and his own revelation. He wanted to be with her forever, but how?

Bloom came alongside him and said, "Thank you for showing us your star city."

Matt was unsure if the harpy was sincere or being sarcastic. "Anytime." He gazed ahead at Summer. "I still can't get over her. She's as light as a feather, but took out those boys with one fell swoop."

"Summer is a golden, born to defend family and flock," said Bloom. "She is also a daughter of Shail."

The group returned to the docking bay. Jim and the harpies proceeded to the ship while Matt strolled into Rog's office for the illicit paperwork.

Rog glanced up from his desk. "I see you're still alive."

"Yeah, sorry about that," Matt said, and tossed five hundred credits in front of him. "I'm sure you had plans to sell my ship."

"I had a buyer in mind." Rog laughed and handed him the papers. Matt tucked them in his jacket and turned to leave. "Matt, be careful out there. You're a swindling asshole, but I like you."

"I must be losing my touch. You're the second one to say they liked me. See ya next go-around, buddy."

Matt soon sat in the cockpit and plotted a course to the large orange planet of Oden. Jim joined him in the co-pilot seat. "It won't take long to clear the station and be underway."

"Good," Jim said. "It's possible Summer injured one of those guys in the bar. We don't need to stick around for that kind of trouble."

Matt glanced back into the cabin at Summer. "Yeah, she really creamed those boys. I still can't believe it."

"Well, the four were drunk, and she caught them off guard, not expecting a little female to knock them silly. Still, I wouldn't tangle with her. She's too much like her father, and he kicked my ass."

Matt flipped several switches. "I keep hearing about him. Was this Shail some kind of hero?"

"More than a hero, he's a living legend. He saved every living thing on Dora. including the people and his harpies."

"Summer won't talk about him. Says it makes her too sad. But you know him. What's he like?"

Jim leaned back and sighed. "There is no one I admire more than Shail. He once was the bravest, smartest, and most honorable soul I've ever met, a true one-of-a-kind. His enemies hated him, but they sure as hell respected that harpy. Unfortunately, he suffered unimaginable abuse in the hands of men, and he's now mentally burned out. He lives in isolation on the west coast, hiding in the jungle. My wife is his mother, and even she doesn't see him anymore. It's a damn shame."

"That's a bummer. No wonder Summer doesn't want to tell me about him." Matt backed the ship out of the docking bay, with his thought on Summer and her notorious father. The ship left the spaceport and headed toward Oden.

Matt adjusted the controls and said, "Okay. We'll be there in a few days." Jim rose and turned toward the cabin. "Wait a minute, Jim. Can we talk?"

"Sure." Jim settled back into the seat.

Matt chewed his lip. Over the weeks, he had grown to look up to the cop. Jim was a man's man, bold, trustworthy, and likable. Matt wished that his father had been like Jim. "I need some advice about Summer. I might as well let the cat out of the bag. I'm head over heels for her, and I've never felt like this about anyone."

"It's obvious, and I'm afraid she feels the same about you. I suggest you end it and save yourselves the heartbreak. The harpies would kill you rather than allow the relationship."

"It's because I'm a no-good, piece of shit, and have no honor like her dad. You all are right about me." Irritated with himself, he banged the buttons that put the ship on autopilot.

"Summer seems to think that down deep you're a good guy," said Jim. "Is she right?"

"I don't know, but for her, I'm willing to turn over a new leaf and clean up my act. Do you think there's any hope?"

"I feel for you, kid, but the odds are against you. Over my career I've seen my share of junkies, thieves, wife-beaters, you name it—all claiming they'll make amends to their loved ones and change, but ninety-five percent of them fail. Here's my advice. If you commit to changing to become a decent guy, don't do it for Summer or to appease the harpies. Do it for yourself. That's the only way it'll stick."

* * *

Mollie entered Alex's small isolation room and found him sitting on the padded floor, eating grapes. "Good morning, Alex," she said, and sat down beside him.

"You are late and your coffee is cold." He handed her the cup.

"Sorry. I was on the web with a job interview. It took longer than I planned."

Alex frowned. "You have a job. It's here with me."

Putting her hand against his chiseled face, she smiled. "No, Alex. Our time together is almost over. You're nearly grown, and I've taught you all I can. Soon you'll be with your harpy family, flying like a freed bird through Dora's jungle. You don't need me anymore."

Alex stood, shaking his head. "I will always need you." He fell to his knees and took her hand. "Mollie, you're all I know, all I love."

She sighed. "We'll stay in touch, but you must move on and be with your kind. Learn to be a real harpy."

He coiled up next to her and placed his head on her lap. "I am uncertain, even a little afraid of my future. As you said, I am not a real harpy and different from them. They might detest me, like the humans."

Mollie stroked his long back between the wings. Alex was normally confident, and his bravery and defiance bordered on dangerous, but every so often he revealed childlike insecurities to her. "Alex, you shouldn't worry. You are different, special, but that's why the harpies will love you. If you need me, just call. I'll come to Dora. You are, after all, my boy."

At noon the mirror in Alex's small room turned into a screen, and Dr. Collins appeared. "Hello, Alexander and Miss Harris."

Mollie noticed Alex's innocent, wide-eyed expression shifted to an angry glare. He hated Collins.

Alex stood. "I don't feel like dealing with you and your stupid tests today."

"Come now, Alexander," said Collins. "For weeks you've cooperated and done very well."

Looking upward at the screen, Mollie said, "Maybe we should cancel the session today. Alex is little upset."

"That's the perfect time to test his limits. What's bothering you, Alexander?"

"You," Alex growled.

"Let's get this over so I can leave you alone." Collins placed a blank card against the screen. "Concentrate and tell me what you see on the other side of the card."

Alex looked at the white card. "It is a dog, a poorly drawn black Lab used to retrieve waterfowl for game hunters. It is also a sickening reminder that harpies were once hunted and killed like ducks." Alex's eyes turned to slits. "Furthermore, you drew the picture. Proof you're not only an incompetent psychiatrist but also a lousy artist."

Mollie covered her grin. When he wanted, Alex could devastate an ego, and the administrator's bewildered expression proved he had succeeded.

Collins gazed at his drawing. "Umm, yes, I did draw the dog. How did you know?"

"You don't want me to go there."

"But I do," Collins said. "Tell me how you knew that I drew the picture?"

"Don't say I didn't warn you," Alex said, "Call the nurse to the screen."

The nurse who monitored the panels in the isolation ward appeared next to Collins. Alex crossed his arms and gazed up at her. "Miss, you're uncomfortable with Dr. Collins and for good reason. I've seen his thoughts. He longs to shove you against the monitors, rip off your clothes, and rape you. It's his fantasy to overpower you and hear your screams."

"Alexander, that's a lie! It's an absolute lie," Collins barked, and addressed the flushed nurse. "I've never thought such a thing. He's saying this to make me look bad. Don't believe him."

"But she does believe me." Alex smiled. "The woman has good instincts and you, basically, give her the creeps. That's why she avoids you. Ironically, you're the pervert, but I'm the one caged. It doesn't seem right."

"Shut up, shut up, you monster," Collins hollered. "You winged freak."

"That's no way for a psychiatric to talk to his patient." Alex smirked. "But you realize I would have to respect you for your insults to offend me. This isn't the case."

"Turn off the screen," Collins ordered the nurse. "Turn it off."

The screen became a mirror. "The sicko runs a mental hospital, but should be a patient," Alex said, "It's ridiculous, Mollie."

Concerned, Mollie stood. "The things you said about Collins, are they true?"

"Of course, exposing a horrid truth is far more upsetting than a lie. And as you have often said harpies are truthful."

Mollie held her forehead and paced. "Oh, Jesus, this isn't good. You shouldn't have let him know that your telepathy penetrated the electronics and probed his mind."

"It's no big deal. I can't force my will on anyone."

"It is a big deal. Collins knows that you'll soon be able to coerce someone to open the door and let you out. God knows what he'll do. Alex, we only had a week to go."

"I'm tired of his crap and want him to leave me alone,"

"I'm not so sure he will. He'll tell your mother what happened and might suggest drugging you again. They might even reschedule your brain surgery and wing amputation."

He leaned against the wall, and his fist struck the padding. "I don't care anymore. Let them take everything, even my life. I'm sorry, Mollie. I know you wanted to save me, not fail me like you believe you failed my father, but I can't take anymore."

Mollie stepped to him and stroked his head. "I understand. You're becoming an adult and your nature is growing stronger. This confinement is causing you to lose hope, but it's almost over."

He lifted his head, and his eyes met hers. "You can't understand unless you're a harpy in a cage. When you're here, I'm okay. But alone, it's painful. My whole body aches and is weak. I feel like vomiting rather than eating. And the worst is the helplessness." He shuddered. "It gets so bad that the only way out is to curl up, shut down my heart, and end it. I now know why the captive harpies died."

Mollie grabbed his shoulders and shook him. "Alex, get a grip," she growled. "If you don't, I'll drug you myself. Is that what you want?"

"No," he whispered. "Are you certain they're coming for me?"

"Your grandmother assured me, and as you know harpies don't lie."

He glanced up at the mirror. "What about Collins?"

She held her forehead. "I'll talk to him, reassure him that you're still harmless and can't control people. Maybe he'll do nothing." She stood on her toes and kissed his forehead. "Just remember— one more week and you're free."

* * *

At her mansion, Monica closed her eyes and relaxed face down on her bed while the robot massaged her back. Nearly asleep, she heard a door knock, and grumbled, "What is it?"

Lilly, her private secretary, stepped into the room. "Dr. Collins is on the com."

"Tell him I'm busy and will call him back."

"He sounded upset and says it's urgent."

"For Christ's sake, the man is always upset, but I half-expected his call. Alexander can't behave for long." Monica waved the robot away, sat up, and put on a silk robe. She faced the small com on the nightstand and touched the keys. Seeing the doctor on the small screen, she said, "What has he done now?"

"I just finished a session with Alexander, and I'm afraid I have to discontinue treating him. He's become dangerous."

"Isn't that why he's there?"

Collins pulled at his pencil-thin mustache. "Yes, well, he's learned to project his telepathy through the viewing screen and enter a person's mind. He did it to me this morning."

"Can he manipulate you?"

"Not yet, but it's only a matter of time. Miss Harris swears he's still harmless, but I've taken precautions. All personnel were removed from the monitoring room, and robots, instead of nurses, are bringing him food."

"None of this surprises me. Your little institution was never equipped to handle him. I've already made other arrangements. At the end of the month, he'll be immobilized, put in a comatose state that's used to transport animals, and be shipped to an Earth sanitarium. Can you manage him for ten more days?"

"I think so. If he shows signs of influencing the staff, he'll be gassed. We can hook him up to a feeding tube and keep him unconscious until he goes." He weakly smiled. "It's regrettable, Miss Carlton, but we were in over our heads with Alexander. He's very problematic."

"Tell me something I don't know." She disconnected without a goodbye and said to Lilly, "I hate that long, boring trip to Earth, but I am his mother and have to make sure he gets proper care at the sanitarium. Inform Agatha about my trip. She can help me pack, and after I'm gone, she'll only be needed once a week to keep up the house."

"What about my duties?" Lilly asked.

"Don't worry, dear. You'll be here full-time to pay bills and handle correspondence with the mining companies."

"Earth, that's so exciting. I've heard their stores are fabulous."

Monica sighed. "I wouldn't know. The last time I was there, I discovered I was pregnant with Alexander, so it was a short stay. On this trip I can do some serious shopping."

CHAPTER NINE

In the main ship cabin, Bloom lay curled up in feathers on the couch with his eye closed, but unlike the others asleep in their berths, he was awake. He felt the vessel's slight vibration and heard the rhythmic hum of the engine along with Jim's steady snore in a back compartment. From the start of the voyage, Bloom had staked out these cushions for a nest and lookout so he could oversee everything, while Ribot guarded Summer and was on the floor beside her bed.

The creak of a bunk and the quiet footsteps in the aisle told Bloom it was Matt who had a troubled nature and didn't rest long. When the pilot tiptoed into the cabin and tried to sneak past the couch, Bloom said, "Again you do not sleep."

Startled, Matt flinched and cursed. "Damn it, Bloom. You scared the shit out of me. Thought for sure you were asleep. You're like a friggin' guard dog."

Bloom lifted his head. "You compare me to those human pets? Dogs are not equal to harpies."

"Yeah, yeah, I know." Matt collapsed in a nearby chair. "Don't get your feathers up. It's just a saying."

"You have many strange sayings, even for a man. Why do you rise now?"

"I need to check our course." Matt patted the hull. "Sometimes this old girl's computers go on the blink, and we're getting close to the planet."

Bloom stretched out and rested his head on a hand. "You speak of this star vehicle—." He paused and corrected himself, "this spaceship as though alive."

"I like to think she has a heart. *Dream Weaver* has gotten me out of a few scrapes."

"To feel for a metal thing says you are a lonely man."

"Wait just a minute. A lot of guys love their ships. It doesn't mean …" Matt gazed at the floor and chuckled. "I've never felt lonely, but I'm afraid when this mission is over, I might. Are you married, Bloom?"

"I bonded with three mates and have many fledglings."

"Was it worth it? I mean, do they make you happy?"

Bloom knitted his brow. "It is instinctive for a harpy to seek a family. They fulfill his life and give him a reason to live, but harpies are not like men. We bond for life, and if the male is lost, another takes his place. When humans are unpleased with their mate, they abandon them and offspring. In these broken bonds, how do the young grow up strong and sure without male guidance?"

"They don't. My parents split up, and I'm the screwed up result."

"When we met, you were a flawed and selfish man, but I sense a change, a longing to care and love. There is hope for you, Matt."

"Really?" Matt grinned.

A beeping sound came from the front of the ship, and Matt stood. "That means we're coming into range of the planet." He and Bloom walked into the cockpit, and Matt pointed at the small orange ball hovering in the distance. "There's Oden. We'll soon be setting down. Are you getting nervous?"

"Yes, but not nervous of capture or death," Bloom said. "I fear failure. I must save Shail's son."

* * *

Mollie tapped her nails on the desktop and stared at the communicator, willing it to buzz. The ship from Dora should be here by now, but anticipating its call made her anxious.

She reflected on her morning visit with Alex. He too was restless with the expectation of his freedom. Rather than lounge around, he had paced, puffed up his feathers, and flexed his wings. But Mollie was glad he showed no sign of depression, like last week.

She was concerned about Dr. Collins. She had convinced him that the harpy couldn't coerce a person to act, and for further proof, she consented to a lie detector test. The doctor was still obviously angry and worried about Alex's claims that if known could destroy his career. When seeing her, he scowled and snubbed her. Today she bumped into Collins in the hallway. He smiled and asked pleasantly about Alex. His congenial behavior aroused Mollie's suspicions. The man was acting too nice, and Alex had to escape before learning why.

"Come on, you stupid contraption," she grumbled to the com. "Buzz, damn it."

Hearing her voice, Frankie woke and left her feet. The little furball stretched, looked up at her, and chirped softly, conveying his hunger.

"All right, Frankie." She petted him and walked into the kitchen. She placed Frankie's bowl on the counter and filled it with pet kibble. The buzzing of the com caused her to drop the food bag. "Thank God," she said, and hurried to the desk.

She hit the connect key and her excitement fizzled when she saw Agatha on the screen.

"Oh, Mollie, I'm so glad I caught you at home," said the sweet old housekeeper. "Have you heard about Miss Carlton's newest plans for Alexander?"

Mollie slunk into the chair. "What plans?"

"She's sending him away, putting the poor boy in a sanitarium on Earth." Agatha dabbed her moist nose with a tissue. "I'll probably never see him again."

"When is he going, Agatha?"

"The ship arrives in a few days," said Agatha. "Lilly told me about it this morning. Alexander will be knocked out and placed in a narrow animal crate for the long voyage. Lilly's a horrible person. She was so happy about it. I'm busy packing Miss Carlton's bags and closing up the house, but I took a minute to call you."

"I knew something was up. Today Alex's doctor was way too happy, knowing Alex will soon be out of his hair."

"I worried sick, Mollie, but what we can do?"

Mollie gazed at the distressed old woman who loved Alex and had risked her job to call, hoping to help him. "It's already done, so stop worrying. Alex will be fine."

Agatha blinked away her tears. "What's been done?"

"You can't tell anyone, but I contacted Alex's harpy grandmother. She's the ruler on Dora. She arranged to rescue Alex, and the ship with harpies should arrive before he's sent to Earth." Mollie breathed deeply. "But we're cutting it close."

Agatha grinned. "That's wonderful, Mollie."

"We probably won't see him again, but it's nice knowing he'll be free to fly with his own kind."

"He often told me his dreams of flying until his wings gave out."

"With any luck, his dream will become reality."

In the study, Lilly noticed the blinking light on her desk com, indicating a kitchen transmission. Without turning on the screen, she listened in on the conversation between Agatha and Mollie. After their call, she rose with a smirk and went to find Miss Carlton.

* * *

Oden loomed outside the cockpit window as Matt maneuvered the ship to orbit the planet. "In a few hours we'll be over Mirage and I'll make the descent," he said to Jim and the harpies.

"That's one big planet," said Jim. "It's huge compared to Earth and Dora."

The harpies stared somberly at the bleak surface of brownish-black mountain ranges and rusty-orange deserts. No oceans or forests. For harpies, Oden probably seemed like hell. "Humans live there?" Bloom asked quietly.

Matt chuckled. "Yeah, Bloom. We'll live in any godforsaken place if we can make money. Oden has some valuable rocks." He turned to Jim. "So once we set down in Mirage port and get the paperwork squared away, Summer and I will see the exhaust guy, set up a night for the rescue, and give him a deposit while you guys visit the Harris woman and get the hospital layout."

"Not quite, Matt," Jim said with a headshaking grin. "You and Bloom will see your exhaust guy. Summer is with me and Ribot."

"Still don't trust me."

"As far as I can see you," said Jim.

"Thanks a lot, but speaking of seeing," Matt said, and glanced at the harpies. "What about their wings? They'll stick out like sore thumbs, and we don't want to draw attention on this planet."

"Already ahead of you. I brought three cloaks to hide the wings. Summer can use Alex's for now. They're packed in cargo along with the weapons and portable coms."

Matt slapped Jim's back. "That's what I like about you; always prepared."

In a few hours, Mirage was below, and the ship broke orbit and started the descent. Matt flipped on the com to contact the port. "This is *Dream Weaver.* We're on a ten-nine heading and asking for permission to land."

"We have you on radar, *Dream Weaver,*" said the dispatcher. "Maintain your course. After entry, switch to a ten-twenty heading. Gate sixty-three at Mirage port is available."

"Roger that, dispatch," said Matt, and turned off the com. He throttled back as the little ship entered the atmosphere and rumbled and shook.

As the harpies stared out the cockpit window, Summer said happily, "We made it, Bloom. Isn't it exciting? When you get home, you can tell your family and flock how you flew through the stars to another world."

"I am a creature of flight, but I prefer to have my feet on dirt than in these stars," Bloom said. "Only a golden finds this journey exciting."

"And it's about to get more hairy," Matt said. "Everybody go back and buckle up. Hitting the atmosphere, she's as rough on entry as takeoff."

"Great," Jim grumbled and addressed the harpies. "Let's go. I'll help you strap down those wings." He and the harpies left for the cabin. A few minutes later, he returned and took the co-pilot seat. "Those males are trembling. It's safe to say that harpies will never become space travelers."

"Not so sure," Matt said. "Summer likes it."

"Yeah, but like Bloom said she's a golden, and they're slightly nuts, get off facing death."

"But you're married to one."

Jim smiled. "Yes, I am and life is never dull."

The ship approached the desert surface with the engine roaring to slow down. The violent shuddering subsided as the ship leveled off and flew a mile above ground. Matt pointed toward the massive, see-through dome in the distance. "There's Mirage."

"I believe that's bigger than any dome city on Earth."

"That's because it's centrally located to black holes and trade routes. Earth and Dora are off the beaten path." They flew past the city, and Matt swung the ship around and sailed down to a hub of huge warehouse-type buildings that spread out across the desert. He found gate sixty-three, but the hangar door was closed, and Matt's ship had to hover before it.

"Incompetent shitheads," Matt said, and hit the com switch "Mirage port, wake up in there. This is *Dream Weaver*. We're outside sixty-three. Open the damn door."

"Sorry, *Dream Weaver*," said dispatch. "You arrived before schedule."

The hangar door opened, and Matt steered the ship inside. With a thud and a dust cloud, it settled on the floor. The door quickly closed to keep out the searing heat. "We got a few minutes to kill. The temperature has to drop before the port clerk shows up. Once he checks our papers and drones run a ship scan, we can catch the underground shuttle into the city."

In long black cloaks Bloom, Ribot, and Summer stood quietly in the cabin and watched a small drone fly through the ship, searching for contraband. The port clerk checked the papers and questioned Matt and Jim about their purpose in Mirage. After the clerk and drone left, Jim said, "That went smoothly."

"Yeah, arrival is always easier than departure," Matt said. "You smuggle things out, not in, and the drones and scent robots take forever, inspecting every inch of your ship before takeoff."

After boarding the underground monorail that made the round-trip excursion from the port to the city, the five got off at the first stop to contact the exhaust system employee and Mollie Harris.

Jim talked to Mollie on his portable com. "We're in front of a big jewelry shop on the corner of Diamond and First. Okay, see you in a bit."

Meanwhile, Matt made arrangements with the exhaust system guy. He closed the com with a huff. "First hiccup," he said to Jim. "After tomorrow, the guy has a shift change and won't be back on nights for weeks. That means this has to go down tomorrow evening. On top of that, the son-of-a-bitch wants double for the payoff."

"Tomorrow?" Jim exclaimed. "That's not enough time to examine the hospital layout and deal with security."

"We do this in daylight and the harpies fry in that desert. Besides, the longer we stick around, the more people get suspicious and we're busted." Noticing Jim's frown, he added, "Lighten up, buddy. You have to play this game fast and loose. Overthink a plan and it turns to shit."

"I'm too old for this game," said Jim.

"I got to hook up with this guy," Matt said, and hailed down a driverless cab. "I'll call you in a few hours. Come on, Bloom." He and the harpy ducked into the vehicle and were on their way.

Mollie pulled up to the curb and recognized the big man from the com call. Jim stood near two slender figures in cloaks, but a glance at their large haunting eyes, high cheekbones, small noses, and full lips, giving them an elfish look, told her they were the harpies.

"Jim?" she called.

Jim walked to her vehicle. "Hello, Mollie. This is Summer and Ribot. They're . . . ."

"Harpies," Mollie said. "I never get over how beautiful they are. Get in."

Ribot nodded to her and climbed into the backseat. Summer followed him as Jim took the front passenger seat next to Mollie.

Summer pushed back her hood. "Thank you, Miss Harris, for helping the harpy."

Mollie turned and saw Summer's long blond hair. "My God, you're one of Shail's."

"Did you know my father?" Summer asked.

Mollie pulled away from the curb. "I knew him back when harpies were hunted. Shail was so gorgeous that I called him prince. But wait until you meet Alex. He's just as handsome as his dad."

"All my brothers and sisters resemble Father."

Mollie smiled. "Are there just three of you?"

"There're another harpy and the pilot," said Jim. "They're checking on an escape through the city exhaust system."

Mollie turned down a street, heading for her apartment. "I'm glad you weren't delayed. I recently learned that Alex's mother is shipping him to Earth in five days."

"We're also working under a time frame," Jim said. "We're freeing Alex tomorrow."

* * *

Jim, Ribot, and Summer arrived at Mollie's apartment, where she offered them juice. At a table Jim and Mollie milled over the city map and discussed the clinic location and layout. Ribot stood at a window and stared at the modern city. Summer reclined on the couch with Mollie's pet.

Mollie pointed at the map. "Here's Mirage Mental Institution, and there's the exhaust port for their escape. The distance between is clear across the city."

"The distance isn't a problem for a harpy. Does this eight-story clinic have rooftop landing?"

"Yes, when visiting Alex, I've seen emergency hovers land on the roof."

Jim leaned back in the chair and rubbed his jaw. "I imagine the roof has guards, but the harpies should be able to handle them."

Ribot moved from the window and stepped to the table. "Bloom and I can land silently behind these guards and do away with them."

"Ribot, I don't want them killed," Jim said, "just rendered unconscious."

"As you wish," Ribot said.

"Okay, so we'll take Alex out from the roof," Jim said. "He can fly to the exhaust port with Ribot and Bloom."

"That might be a problem," said Mollie. "Alex's doctor had his long flight feathers clipped two months ago. They've grown back some, but I'm not sure he can fly."

"They cut his wings?" said Summer. "His doctor must be very cruel."

"How many lights are in these months?" Ribot asked.

Summer held up her fingers six times to show him the days.

Ribot nodded. "He can flutter and soar a short distance, but he lacks fast flight."

"You can't carry him," said Jim. "He'll slow you down, and you'll never make the desert crossing before sunrise."

"If the golden opens his wings and glides, Bloom and I can pull him and go faster."

"That could work." Jim turned to Mollie, who was refilling their juice glasses. "That leaves you and me. Any thoughts on breaking into the building and busting Alex out of his room?"

Mollie sat down at the table. "I can get Alex out of his room. I've watched Dr. Collins punch in the code at Alex's room door and memorized it. It's just getting to that room. There is always a receptionist and guard at the front desk and surveillance cameras. Motion sensor robots are in the hallways on every floor."

"You're forgetting the alarms," said Jim. "I can disable cameras, take out a robot, and even handle a guard, but the trick is doing it quietly. The alarms trigger and we're screwed."

"There might be a way around all this security." Mollie stepped to a closet and produced a blue doctor's gown. "I stole it thinking it might be useful. You go in disguised as a doctor. We let Alex out and leave discretely the same way."

"It's worth a shot." Jim pulled on the scrubs. "What do you think? Can I pass for a doctor?"

Mollie grinned. "With a shave, you'll look very distinguished."

Summer rose from the couch. "If you won't let me help Ribot and Bloom on the roof, I might as well return to the ship with Matt and wait in the cave."

"It's already been decided, Summer," Jim said. "You're not going with Matt or facing danger on the roof. It's bad enough that you're crossing the desert with the harpies."

"Who is Matt?" asked Mollie.

"Matt guides the ship," said Ribot.

"He's lovesick for Summer," Jim said, "and I don't trust him alone with her."

"Jim, how will you get back to the ship?" Mollie asked.

"Once I'm out of the clinic, I'll book a flight to Oden spaceport and meet Matt's ship. If that doesn't work out, I'll catch a shuttle to Dora. And Mollie, you'd better come with me. They'll blame you for the missing harpy."

Mollie looked around at her small apartment. "I can't go tomorrow. What about my things, my vehicle, my poor old Frankie?"

"Leave everything behind except the pet. My wife will give you a fresh start on Dora."

Mollie smiled. "Alex wanted me to come with him. He'll be so happy."

Matt called Jim, who directed him and Bloom to Mollie's apartment. Matt swung his leg over a kitchen chair and sat backward with his elbows on its back. "We're all set for tomorrow. Bloom knows the location and layout of the exhaust systems. As soon as it's dark, the guy will meet the harpies at a side door. And remember, Bloom, don't give him the money until after you're through the vent systems and outside in the desert. The guy's a snake, and…." Matt chuckled. "It takes one to know one."

Jim filled Matt and Bloom in on the hospital plan.

Matt said, "Bloom and I also went to a lookout tower of the eastern desert, and I pointed out the mountain where I'll be. See, Jim, just like I said, fast and loose. We got a plan."

Jim ran his fingers through his hair. "Yeah, it sounds perfect if nothing goes wrong."

CHAPTER TEN

In her apartment Mollie drew the drapes to block the bright light from the two suns and simulated night. The small band of rescuers settled down for sleep. Summer shared Mollie's bed. Jim crashed on the couch, and Matt stretched out in a large, stuffed chair. The two male harpies were content on a soft rug.

Hours later Mollie woke and found Summer gone. She walked into the living room, and all her visitors were there and awake.

"I took the liberty of making breakfast," Jim said, standing in the kitchen over the stove.

The male harpies were on the floor and nibbled on jam-covered toast. Summer sat at the kitchen table with Matt who lowered his coffee mug and said, "Morning, ma'am, sorry we took over your place."

"No, it's fine," Mollie said, sitting down next to Summer. "I feel bad I'm not a better hostess. I should have made breakfast."

Jim handed her a cup of coffee. "Don't feel bad. I've done all the cooking on a cramped ship and know what this crew likes to eat. It's now a routine."

"Since yesterday I've been puzzled about your crew," Mollie said and looked at Summer. "I know a lot about harpies, which is why I was hired to care for Alex, but I've never heard of a winged female harpy." She turned to Bloom, "Or a male with black hair and feathers."

Summer smiled. "Black-winged males have always existed, but it takes a special cross to create one so Bloom is very rare. I, however, am new to the harpies. My mother is human, and male harpies had never mated with women. But my father did. I and my three sisters are the results. We have wings like the boys."

"Shail has four daughters?" Mollie said.

"Counting Alex, he has eight sons with his three mates," Summer said.

Jim grumbled, "Yeah, and they not only look like Shail but have his temperament, obstinate, blue-eyed blonds with an in-your-face attitude. They know nothing about congeniality."

Summer smirked. "You can't hide your feelings, Jim. You love us."

"I love your grandmother and father," said Jim. "The rest of your clan I can do without." His comment seemed aimed at Summer who shook her feathers and raised her head.

"Jim, I'm afraid Alex isn't any better," Mollie said. "He can be difficult. Speaking of him, I better get dressed and go to the clinic. I can't wait to tell him he'll be freed tonight." She rose and placed a hand on Summer's shoulder. "Twenty years ago your dad was the last golden male, and his bloodline was one heartbeat away from extinction. I'm glad to learn of his many offspring."

Matt also stood and placed his cup in the sink. "I also need to get going. I want to recharge the ship before leaving the port for the mountain. If there's trouble, I might have to skip the spaceport and make a straight run for the wormhole."

"I'll go with you," said Jim. "I have to pack my gear and bring the laser guns." He looked at the harpies. "You all lay low here. I should be back in a few hours."

Summer left the table and stepped to Matt. "I will see you tonight." She embraced him and nuzzled his neck.

"Yep, sure will." Matt clutched her face and kissed her lips. "I know you're tough but please be careful, doll."

"Matt, you're pressing your luck with those males," Jim said and went to the door. "Let's go before you really piss them off." With a sigh, Matt followed Jim out of the apartment.

"Matt is very cute and charming, Summer," Mollie said.

Summer's eyes lit up with a smile.

An hour later Mollie pulled up to Mirage Mental Institution and parked. Sitting in her vehicle, she thought that the next time here, she'd free Alex. The escape attempt had her keyed up with joyful relief and worry. Something could go wrong.

She entered the clinic and, behaving as usual, she said hello to the staff on her way to the elevator and fifth floor. In the hallway, a robot was stationed in front of Alex's room, and its electronic voice acknowledged her. "Good morning, Miss Harris."

"How's Alex?"

"Alexander Carlton woke at 6:13 am," said the robot, "urinated at 6:20; received a breakfast of grapes, melon, and orange juice at 6:40—all melon not consumed; napped at . . . ."

"That's enough," Mollie said, and inserted her visitor pass into the monitor.

The robot followed up and pressed a sequence of numbers that Dr. Collins or a nurse had previously done on the keyboard. When the door opened, the robot said, "Please push the red key when your visit is over and you wish to leave."

Mollie stepped into the room and saw Alex, sitting in a corner with wings wrapped around him and his head resting on his knees. He looked up and she smiled. "Tonight, Alex."

* * *

Jim sat in the passenger seat of Mollie's vehicle, tapped his knee, and his other hand clutched the small bag, holding his laser gun and equipment for the break-in. "You nervous?" he asked Mollie.

"God, yes," she said, and drove into the clinic parking lot.

Jim climbed out of the vehicle and gazed up at the eight-story building. "You know, Mollie, I've been a cop all my life, but for the second time I'm breaking the law to save a harpy. The first time was Shail and now his son."

"And they're both worth it." Mollie left the vehicle and looked to the west through the dome. One of Oden suns had slipped below the horizon and the other hung low in the yellow sky. "Judging from that sun, it'll be dark in fifteen minutes."

Jim wore the doctor gown and carried the bag, following Mollie into the building. A nurse sat at the reception desk and a security guard stood nearby. Mollie grinned and said, "This is Dr. Jones and we're here to see Alexander Carlton."

"At this hour?" the nurse said with a scowl and turned to her computer. "There's no scheduled visit from a Dr. Jones or anyone else."

"So much for the doctor disguise," Jim said, and pulled the blaster out and stunned both the nurse and guard. Glancing at the unconscious bodies, he said, "We'd better hustle before they're discovered." He retrieved a small device from the bag, and as they raced down the corridor, he zapped the surveillance cameras. In the elevator, he said, "I took this zapper off a thief, thinking it might come in handy some day."

"Let's hope the darn thing works," Mollie said, and hectically pressed the elevator button to the fifth floor. The door opened and Mollie peeked out. "All clear," she said as Jim braced the door open with his bag for their return escape.

They stepped out into the hallway and between them and Alex's room was the ward robot. Its motion sensor lights came on, and it moved towards them. "No staff or visitors are scheduled at this time. Please leave the fifth floor. No staff or visitors are scheduled...." The robot's message was silenced when Jim ripped out its circuits.

"Get the kid," he said, "while I'll take out the cameras on this floor."

Mollie raced to Alex's room and punched in the numbered keys on the monitor, but nothing happened. "The door won't open," she called. "They must've changed the code."

Jim rushed to her and drew his laser weapon. "So much for doing this quietly," he said. "Stand back." He blasted the controls and as the door opened, a siren went off.

Alex stepped into the noisy hallway. "Is this your idea of a subtle break in?"

"No, but shit happens," said Jim.

Mollie grabbed Alex's hand and yelled over the screaming siren. "We have to hurry and get you on the roof." The three ran to the open elevator and leaped inside. Jim pressed the button to the top floor.

"Alex, this is Jim," Mollie said, out of breath. "He's married to your grandmother."

"I would say I'm glad to meet you, but I'll reserve judgment," Alex said smugly.

"He's definitely one of Shail's brats," Jim said, and looked at his watch. "I hope the harpies took care of things upstairs."

* * *

On the roof of an adjacent building to Mirage Mental Institution, Bloom, Ribot, and Summer stared across at the two security guards milling around the hover landing pad.

Bloom looked down at the parking lot and saw Mollie's vehicle arrive. Jim and Mollie soon disappeared inside the building. "It is time," Bloom said, spreading his wings to fly. "Wait."

A hovercraft flew close into range and landed on the clinic roof. Several people climbed out and briefly talked to the guards. The hover occupants disappeared through the rooftop door.

Quietly now, Bloom relayed to Ribot and turned to the female. *As agreed, Summer, you shall wait here until we have the golden and fly from the roof.*

I know the plan. Summer huffed.

Bloom and Ribot soared downward and rose up to the rooftop. Hovering in unison, they dropped on the unsuspecting guards and applied a sleeper-hold to their necks. They quickly rendered the men unconscious.

When lowering the man's body to the ground, Bloom glimpsed the flutter of gold wings. He wheeled around to Summer and so annoyed he spoke aloud, "You were told to wait until we had your brother and left. You promised Jim."

"I thought about it and decided three harpies are better than two." She reached down and removed the weapons from the guards. She kept one blaster and tossed the other to Bloom. "They might wake up and use them on us."

Quiet your voices. Ribot conveyed and tilted his head. *I heard a weapon inside. There is trouble.*

A siren suddenly blared from the building. The three harpies cringed with the piercing noise.

"Summer, go now," Bloom ordered. "We stay for the golden."

Summer planted her feet. "I am not leaving."

The rooftop door flung open, and Jim rushed out, followed by Mollie and the golden male. Seeing Summer, Jim shouted at Bloom. "What the hell is she doing here?"

"Disobeying him and you," Summer said and stepped to Alex. "Brother, can you fly?"

Alex spread his shortened wings. "I don't know."

Jim saw the parked hovercraft. "Mollie, there's our way out of here. You all take off." He and Mollie hurried across the roof as the harpies stepped to the ledge and prepared to fly. Bloom called to Jim. "I hear hovers, too many to flee."

In seconds, fifteen fast-moving hovers appeared and sealed off the airspace surrounding the building. A voice blared from a loudspeaker system. "This is the police. You're completely surrounded. Drop your weapons and kneel on the deck."

Over the roar of hover engines and loud siren, Jim yelled to Mollie. "They had to know we were coming."

The stationary hovers vibrated the rooftop, and their strong wind stirred up the sand and dirt. Like being in a sandstorm, everyone on the roof crouched against the building wall and shielded their eyes, except one. Alex glared at the police hovers and strode across the landing site to the roof edge. He hopped up on the parapet and brazenly faced them.

"Everybody down or we'll shoot," shouted the loudspeaker.

"No, Alex!" Summer called. Placing her arm over her eyes, she rose to get him.

Jim grabbed Summer and wrestled her down. "Stay down, damn it."

"Alex, don't confront them," Mollie screamed.

Alex glanced over his wing at her. "Mollie, I will never go back to that room." He arched his wings, preparing to fly or fight.

Mollie scrambled across the pavement toward him, but a weapon blast rang out from a hover. In mid-stride, she dropped to the hard surface.

"Cease firing," yelled the loudspeaker.

"Mollie? Mollie!" Alex sprang to her. Cradling her lifeless body, he screamed, "Noooo!" He buried his face into her side and gasped, "Please don't be dead, please don't leave me, Mollie."

For an agonizing long minute, all eyes focused on the grief-stricken young male. Alex gently released Mollie's body. With his face wet with tears, he stood and shouted at the hovercrafts. "You killed her. You killed my Mollie. You'll pay, pay for what you've done."

Bloom conveyed to Ribot. *He has lost reason and shall die.* Wrapping a wing to his face to protect his eyes from the blowing debris, he stepped toward Alex, intending to save him.

The loudspeaker rang out. "Don't move. We don't want any more bloodshed."

Alex fluttered to the building ledge and lit on the low barrier. "You might not want bloodshed, but you're getting it," he growled, and focused on the hover that had fired the fatal shot.

The pilot in the hover seemed possessed. He pushed the throttle forward, and the aircraft took a nosedive and disappeared. The frantic screams of those aboard was followed with the loud boom from the metal craft colliding with pavement. A billowing smoke plume rose to the rooftop.

Alex turned his attention to another hover. It followed the first, hurtling downward to crash and burn on the street.

"Shoot them. Shoot them," the loudspeaker ordered. A hail of laser blasts hit the roof.

Bloom and Ribot ducked behind the door and returned fire. Jim rolled on Summer to shield her, but groaned when a blast hit his leg.

Alex appeared invincible. Not one weapon discharge came near him. "Stop," he growled, and the weapons ceased. "Now you all die." Two hovers flew into each other, and in midair, burst into flames.

Bloom was mesmerized, unable to think or move. He could only watch. The young male stood brazenly against a backdrop of black sky that highlighted his arched yellow wings and wind-whipped blond hair. Below him was the bright glow that resembled a sunrise, but the golden male, not a sun, had created the radiance that came from the hellish inferno of flames and carnage.

"Stun him, Bloom," Jim shouted. "He's not right."

Bloom switched the weapon to "stun" and pointed it at Alex.

Alex turned to Bloom. "You can't stop me. No one can."

Bloom tried to pull the trigger but couldn't. He looked helplessly at Jim.

Jim moved off of Summer and gasped, "Go to him. You're his sister, and he'll listen to you. He can't keep killing these poor officers."

Summer walked to Alex. "Brother, you must end this massacre."

"But they murdered Mollie." Alex sobbed and used a wing to wipe the tears off his cheeks. He sucked up his resolve and growled, "It ends when they are dead." Underestimating the little female, he looked away from her and refocused on the hovers.

When he turned his back, Summer flew at him and kicked him off the ledge. As he fell, his head hit the slight wall. She bent down and shook him. "Alex?" she cried, but he was unresponsive. "Alex, wake up."

The hovers, no longer under Alex's spell, fled the scene, and Bloom rushed to the golden harpies. The side of Alex's face trickled with blood. Summer looked up with panic, afraid she had seriously injured or killed him. "Oh, Bloom, what have I done?"

Bloom knelt and felt Alex's forehead. "Do not fear, Summer. His thoughts remain good and clear. He shall recover." He looked to Ribot, who bent over Jim. "Ribot, can he rise?"

"I'm done," Jim said, and nodded toward the smoldering hovercraft on the roof. "And my escape is done, too."

Bloom hurried to Jim, knelt, and examined his wound. "You are not done. This shall heal." From Jim's doctor's grown, he ripped off a strip of blue material and bound the man's leg to stop the bleeding. "Ribot and I shall carry you."

Jim clasped Bloom's arm. "No, just go. I'll slow you down, and you'll never reach the mountain in time. Besides, one of you has to carry Alex."

"I do not feel right leaving you."

"You've got no choice, Bloom. You're in charge now. Take the harpies and get to the exhaust systems. Those cops won't be scared off for long."

With a nod, Bloom straightened and stuffed his weapon into his sash. He walked to Alex and lifted the comatose golden male into his arms. "We fly," he said to Ribot and Summer.

Summer's startled eyes glared at him. "We're not going without Jim." She rushed to the man, hugged him, and cried. "You must come with us."

Jim brushed away her tears. "Oh, sweetheart, it's okay. You promised to obey me, so do as Bloom says. Just tell Windy I love her."

Holding Alex, Bloom stepped to the ledge and stared down at the burning rubble of hovers. Countless vehicles with flashing red lights and screaming sirens were merging on the scene. On the city skyline, the police hovers were regrouping and heading toward them. "Ribot, take her. We have no time."

"Come, princess," Ribot said, and pulled her off the fallen man. Placing a brown wing around the distressed female, he guided her to Bloom and the building ledge.

"The exhaust building is near the tunnel to the port, but many hovers lie between it and us," said Bloom. "We shall fly low through the buildings so we are harder to find and follow." Spreading his wings to fly, he felt a blast from the opposite structure hit his wing tip and smelled his singed flight feathers. "Fold your wings. We dive." He gripped Alex and leaped headfirst off the ledge. Summer and Ribot followed suit.

More blasts erupted and zipped past the three harpies, but with wings folded tightly against their bodies, they moved downward like bullets, traveling too fast to be targeted. Nearing the street, they opened their wings, leveled off, and flew rapidly through the canyons of buildings. To avoid colliding with the bustling air-traffic, they stayed twenty feet above the sidewalks. Their presence caused a commotion among the pedestrians, many screaming and yelling in alarm. Bloom looked back and seeing no stalking hovers, he breathed a sigh of relief.

After several anxious minutes, they arrived at the exhaust system building, between the dome wall and desert. Returning to the silent harpy talk, Bloom relayed to Ribot, *Take him while I speak to the man.* He placed Alex in Ribot's arms and tapped at the side door.

The thin man in grimy clothing, who Bloom had met with Matt on the previous day, opened the door. "You're late." The man looked past the harpies at the searching floodlights on the police hovers in the city. "What's going on?"

"It is not your concern."

"No, no, I don't want any part of this," the man said. "The deal's off." He attempted to shut the door, but Bloom shoved him back and entered the building full of noisy machines.

"You shall honor our agreement, or face my wrath," Bloom said, looming over the man.

"Okay, okay," the man said, and led them through the dimly lit building, past giant, rotating fans and tall, grinding machines. Toward the back, they reached a narrow access door. The man inserted his pass card and unlocked it.

The door opened, and Bloom gazed out at the shadowy desert and inhaled its fresh air. From a hanging pouch on his hips, he pulled out the credits to pay the man, but when their hands touched, Bloom sensed treachery. He whipped the weapon from his sash. "You chose to betray me?"

The man backed away. "No, I haven't."

"Lies," Bloom said, and fired the weapon. The man collapsed, and Summer looked at Bloom with shock. "He is stunned but should be dead. He told the police of our desert crossing. It shall be more dangerous." They stepped outside into the desert, and Bloom pointed to a mountain. "Matt's ship is at the base of that mountain. You should know in case I fall."

* * *

At Mirage port Matt fired up *Dream Weaver* and left hangar sixty-three. Guiding the ship toward space, he muttered, "Hope Jim and those harpies don't screw up." Out of reach of Oden satellites, he descended toward the mountain range miles west of Mirage. He approached the largest peak and slowed, looking for the large cave that could hold and hide his ship.

For hundreds of years, men had mined the mountains for rare black diamonds and created numerous cavities. With the stones depleted, the range near Mirage was abandoned. All that remained in the rocky cave were discarded drilling equipment and small pools of water that attracted the giant sand tortoises and small creatures, like Mollie's pet.

At the base of the mountain, Matt maneuvered his ship inside the cave. He decelerated, and the ship settled on the grayish and purple stone. He killed the engine but didn't open the door. The Devil's breath bore down hard on Oden during daylight, and even the dark, quiet cave was hot. To kill time, he flipped on a city police scanner and propped his boots up on the dash. Night and the harpies' arrival was hours away.

He massaged his chin, thinking about Summer. Although they were different species, they shared similar passions. Under her delicate frame and feathers lurked a witty daredevil. Like Matt, she sought adventure, and whenever he gazed at the slender beauty, he melted. She had to be the one.

Matt reflected he was also fond of Jim. The man treated him like a long-lost son in need of advice. Matt hated to admit that he'd even grown to like and admire two male harpies. They were so darn brave and noble, prepared to die for this cause. He realized he was the only wild card in the bunch, willing to sell his soul for the right price. Being among them, he felt inadequate. He shut his eyes and dozed to the murmurs of police reports.

Matt woke to alarmed voices on the scanner. Through the cockpit window, he viewed the cave entrance dimmed with the approach of night. He slowly turned the dials, trying to make out the garbled communication and grasped a few words.

"They're called harpies," said a man's voice.

"All units, Mirage Mental Institution," said another.

Matt held his head. “Holy shit, they’re busted!” He jumped up and paced, trying to decide whether to stay or go. Then he heard the relay that made up his mind.

“Officers down!” said the frantic speaker, “Multiple officers down. They took out four hovers and killed a dozen of our men. It’s a shoot to kill, a shoot to kill order, take out those flying bastards.”

Matt could barely swallow. Smuggling a harpy kid out was one thing, but shooting down cop hovers was far more serious. “I love her, but I’m not going to prison for her.” He slid into the pilot seat and fired up the ship.

CHAPTER ELEVEN

Under cover of darkness, Bloom and Summer flew over the vast desert. Ribot trailed, carrying Alex. Even at night the heat was oppressive, and their wings labored against a blistering wind. Accustomed to a moist climate, their lungs ached in the bone-dry air as they panted through parched mouths. The elements along with Alex's weight slowed them down, and Bloom worried if they would reach the mountain cave before sunrise.

After several miles, Bloom assumed they had eluded the police, but his notion vanished when he heard hovercrafts over the howling wind. Glancing back, he saw their lights leave the port and fan out in search mode. No doubt the exhaust system man had recovered from the laser stunning and told the police they were in the desert.

Summer also heard the hovers and thought the same thing. *You were right about that man, Bloom. You should have killed him.*

Enough have died this night. Bloom noticed that Ribot had fallen behind and was struggling with the golden's weight. *Land, Ribot. I shall carry him.*

Ribot set down and gasped for breath. His brown wings drooped in the sand, too played out to fold. *I am sorry, Bloom.*

Bloom stepped to him. *This thirsty orange land sucks out the blood and strength of the living. You need not apologize.* He took Alex from Ribot's arms while estimating their distance to the mountain. They had reached the halfway point in their journey, but the hovers were closing in fast. He faced Ribot. *You and Summer fly ahead to the ship. If we stay together, we risk losing both goldens.*

No, Bloom, said Summer. *I'm not flying off without you and my brother.*

"Do as told, Summer," Bloom growled. "There is no time to argue. The hovers shall soon be here, and neither I nor Ribot can carry Alex and out fly them."

Ribot placed his hand on Alex's forehead. *I swore to obey you, but to save him I must break my vow.* He shifted his eyes to Bloom. *This is the only way.* He spread his wings and flew toward the army of hovers.

"Ribot, don't go," Summer screamed.

"Come, Summer. Let us not waste his sacrifice." Holding Alex, Bloom lifted off the ground, but Summer remained. With teary eyes, she watched Ribot disappear into the darkness. "Now, Summer!" Bloom yelled. She reluctantly extended her wings and flew alongside him.

After several miles, Bloom heard the heartbreaking laser blasts that echoed across the desolate land. The heat sensors on the hovercrafts had located Ribot. In hot pursuit of the harpy, the police and their spotlights had moved toward the western desert and away from them and the mountain. In the distance, more weapons fired, and then there was only the whistling of the haunting wind. Bloom felt the gripping anguish and recalled telling Aron that Ribot was the bravest of the brown-winged males.

Summer sniffled. *Those were blasts, not stunners, Bloom. They killed him.*

Yes, I fear my loyal friend is gone, but Ribot knew the risks and accepted them.

I didn't. I didn't consider the risks. Now Ribot and Mollie are dead. Jim has been captured or killed because he tried to protect me. I should have listened to my grandmother and not come.

We needed you, Summer. You stopped your brother from killing more men.. Bloom glanced down at the slender male in his arms. *I am still in awe of this young male. Never have I known or heard of a more powerful harpy.*

Powerful and twisted, she relayed. *When I kicked him, I sensed his mind. I am unsure we should have freed him. He is not like us.*

You sensed his anger and sorrow, but it is true. Humans raised him and he is different, but I believe when Alex lives among us, he shall change and learn to protect life. With his influencing gifts, he might become the greatest of all harpies.

Or the worst, Summer added.

Guided by starlight, they flew across the harsh landscape, increasing their distance from the police hovers, and the threat faded. They had traveled forty miles with another twenty to go. But then something more deadly than police weapons arose. The pale gray light of dawn crept over the horizon and invaded the black sky. At their current pace, they'd never make the mountain in time. *The first of the two suns rise,* Bloom relayed. *Without Alex's weight, you fly faster, Summer. Go ahead and seek the mountain.*

Matt's ship can reach us before dawn. Land, Bloom, and I'll call him. She tilted her wings, fluttered, and set down.

Exhausted from the heat and the suffocating dry atmosphere, Bloom welcomed the short break and landed beside her. Lugging Alex, his arms throbbed, and his wings were worn out from fighting the strong air current. He placed Alex on the sand, reached into his pouch for the small portable com, and handed it to her. *Matt might not come,* he relayed, puffing. *To travel into the desert exposes his ship to the enemy.*

He'll come for me. Summer punched in the numbers to Matt's ship and spoke into the com. "Matt, it's Summer. We're more than halfway to the mountain, but the suns are rising. We'll never get to you in time. Please come for us."

Instead of Matt answering, a com computer voice responded. “The party you wish to reach is not on the planet. An intergalactic call is required.” It repeated the message before clicking off. Summer’s lips parted and in shock, she looked to Bloom.

Bloom sighed. “He has fled, Summer.” He took the com from her, returned it to his pouch, and picked up Alex. “We must move on or die here,” he said, opening his wings.

“But maybe Matt heard me.”

“Summer, the man betrayed us. He is not coming for you. We are on our own.”

Summer and Bloom winged their way toward the mountain, racing against heat, light, and time. The night temperature was already over a hundred degrees, but when the first sun broke the horizon, the heat became brutal. Bloom could hardly breathe, and his eyes burned in the abrasive wind. His sweaty skin felt scalded, and his fatigued body neared collapse. Summer had fallen behind him, and he saw that she too was suffering and tired. “Keep up,” he yelled. When the second sun crested, they would roast alive.

“I can’t, Bloom. I cannot keep going. I’m …” Delirious with heat exhaustion, her wings sagged, and she spiraled downward, hitting the scorched sand, and she tumbled to a stop.

Bloom circled back and landed beside her. He stood over her fanned-out wings and drained little body. “Summer, you must rise,” he pleaded.

“Forgive me, Bloom,” she muttered. “I’m too weak to move.”

Bloom stared at her, and then at the golden male in his arms. Whom to save? He set Alex down and spread his wings over his frame. The feather cover might protect him. He then picked up Summer.

She opened her eyes, “What are you doing?”

“I can only carry one, and you are the more worthy. Once you are safe in the cave, I shall return for him,” he said, but knew to go back for Alex would be suicide.

Carrying the lighter female, Bloom traveled faster. He soon reached the mountain, and the cave was easy to spot in the morning light. He sailed inside and placed Summer on the stony floor near a puddle. She was barely conscious when he knelt and splashed water on her face. She swallowed and blinked her eyes. "Better?" he asked.

She nodded.

"Good," he said, rising. "I must go for the young male."

Summer lifted her head. "No, Bloom. We both know you will die, and Alex is probably already dead. Stay here."

"Princess, I promised to save him. If I fail, tell Aron I tried." He stepped to the cave opening and saw the second sun cresting on the horizon. Standing before the rusty landscape was like facing down a forest fire. Undeterred, he spread his ebony wings and flew.

* * *

After Bloom left, Summer moaned, "Oh, Bloom." His courageous attempt to rescue Alex was futile. Her tears blended with sweat as she thought about the noble black-winged harpy, then Ribot, the kind woman, Mollie, and Alex. They were all gone now. Jim might also be dead. He had protected her and warned her about Matt. Reflecting on the deserter, she curled up and sobbed.

She was alone and had never known such despair. She then heard a telepathic male voice in her subconscious. *Get up, Summer. You are a golden harpy. Behave like one.* She suddenly recognized it was her father's. Whether the message was a hallucination or a telepathic connection, she sat up.

Okay, Dad. To cool off, she lifted her wings and splattered puddle water on her sunburned face and body. The cave was sweltering but survivable. She staggered to her feet and tossed back her long, drenched locks.

She considered her options. She could fly out of the cave and burn up like a phoenix, or stay here and slowly starve to death, or she could return to the dome on the following night, but she would surely go to prison, a death sentence for a harpy. "I do have another choice." She knew about the lethal trait in harpies. A chromosome became active when a harpy was severely depressed. Her generation had never been hunted and caged, so none had suffered the fatal heart attack, but now she considered it as a dignified alternative.

Time passed, and any hope of Bloom's and Alex's survival had vanished. She paced the cave and tried to venture outside, but the heat was unbearable. She walked deeper into the cavern that was darker and cooler, skirting mining apparatus that told of man's mark on the land.

In frustration, she kicked a small bucket and lay down on the purplish dust. What would her dad do? Shutting her eyes, she wondered if her family would ever learn of her fate. Thoughts of her loved ones led to Matt. "Why did you leave me to die? I loved you."

* * *

In the back seat of the idling limo, Monica fidgeted with impatience and concern. She stared ahead at the flashing lights on numerous police vehicles that had created the traffic jam. Sirens blared and hover searchlights flooded the dark domed city. "Can't we move?" she asked Lilly, next to her.

Lilly lowered the window between the front and back seats and asked the driver, "Is there any way around this mess? Miss Carlton is in a hurry."

"Sorry," said the driver. "Every street is backed up for blocks. According to traffic reports, there are a lot of casualties and hover crashes at the clinic."

Lilly clasped Monica's arm. "The police wouldn't harm Alexander. I'm sure he's all right."

With a venomous glare, Monica jerked her arm away. "I shouldn't have listened to you. Now people are dead, and one might be my son." She addressed the driver. "How far is the clinic?"

"About three blocks, Miss Carlton."

Monica flung open the limo door before the driver could hop out and do it. She stepped onto the sidewalk and stomped toward the clinic.

Lilly climbed out. “Wait, Miss Carlton, I’ll go with you,” she called, chasing after her.

Monica marched on, ignoring her. In the next block, she encountered a police barricade and stopped at the yellow tape. She covered her mouth at the sight of billowing smoke and flames of burning hovercrafts on the street. There was no question that Alexander had caused the catastrophe when the police tried to stop his escape. In her attempts to control him, she had pushed him too far. “My God, did they kill him for this?” she mumbled to Lilly.

“I’ll find out.” Lilly pushed through the spectators to a young police officer. “We have to get through. One of the dead might be her son,” she said as Monica came alongside.

“Sorry, ladies,” said the officer. “The area is off-limits. It’s a crime-and-disaster scene.”

Lilly launched into a curt retort. “This is Miss Carlton. Before you lose your job, I suggest you let her pass.”

“Just one minute, please,” the officer said, and spoke into his radio. “Sir, Miss Carlton is at the southern barricade and wishes to enter.”

“Let her in,” was the response, “and accompany her to our temporary command post here.”

“Yes, sir,” the officer said and lifted the tape. “Come with me, Miss Carlton. I’ll take you to Chief Richards. He’s in the mental institution lobby.”

Monica and Lilly followed him down the sidewalk. Near the clinic, the scene became more chaotic. Firemen were hosing down the flames on the rubble of downed hovers. Armed policemen shouted and raced toward landing hovers, which sped off into the city. In the parking lot, ambulances and their medics sat idly, suggesting that few were injured. Only the coroner vans were in use, being loaded with covered gurneys.

Monica stopped and sniffled. "I can't believe he did this. I just can't."

"Maybe Alexander is not to blame," Lilly said. "The Dora harpies probably caused this tragedy."

Monica glared at her. "You don't believe that."

The officer escorted them around the bedlam to a clinic side entrance. Inside the building, they hustled down the hallway and entered the hectic lobby. Officers rushed around and shouted to each other. Nurses and orderlies appeared dazed, and several huddled around Dr. Collins. Collins spotted Monica and darted down the opposite corridor. At the center of the commotion was the portly, silver-haired Chief Richards. He was hollering into his com as Monica approached.

"Goddamn it, get every hover out into the desert," Richards yelled. "The harpies aren't in the dome anymore. Start the search at the southern exhaust systems. What? You tell that little prick in port authority to open the gates or I'll have his goddamn job." He slammed down the com lid as an office raced to him.

"Sir," the officer said, "the director of air quality isn't complying with your order. He says he needs a directive from the mayor."

"You tell that son-of-a-bitch to crank up those exhaust fans before this dome fills with smoke and chokes everyone to death. This is an emergency. He doesn't need the mayor's okay. If those fans aren't working at full capacity in one minute, I'll come down there and throttle the bastard." The startled officer stared at Richard. "Goddamn it, tell him." The office hurried toward a table serving as a desk.

Richards glanced at Monica and sighed. "As you can see, Miss Carlton, I'm extremely busy."

"I don't give a damn about your problems," said Monica. "Where's my son?"

"Honestly, we don't know," Richards said. "After the police hovers crashed, the harpies flew from here to the exhaust system. They forced a worker to unlock a side door and then stunned him. The man has recovered and confirmed that one harpy was holding an unconscious, yellow-winged male that fits your son's description. Details are sketchy, but we assume he's in the desert with this band of murderous harpies."

"He'll die from the heat at sunrise." Monica, upset and angry, shook. "Chief Richards, you were warned days ago about this kidnapping. You knew that Mollie Harris arranged for a ship of harpies to come here and take Alexander, and you still botched it."

"We followed procedure. We couldn't arrest Harris and the harpies until they committed a crime. After they broke into the clinic and had your son, we intended to take them into custody, but all hell broke out on the roof. Miss Carlton, I lost thirteen good men when the hovers crashed, and we still don't know how the harpies accomplished that, but believe me, I want those bastards caught."

"What about Mollie Harris?" Monica snapped. "I'd hope you've finally arrested her."

"She's dead, killed in the crossfire. A man with harpies was wounded and has been arrested, but he's in pretty bad shape. We haven't gotten his statement yet."

Learning of Mollie's death, Monica lowered herself into a chair. She now understood why Alexander went berserk and forced the police to kill themselves. He loved her more than anything.

"Excuse me, Miss Carlton. I have to handle this situation," Richards said and stepped away.

Monica waited in the lobby and watched the commotion. She nervously clutched her medallion, hoping to learn more on Alexander's whereabouts and wellbeing. Forty minutes later, Richard answered a com call from an officer in the field.

"He's dead?" said Richards.

Monica jumped up. "Who is dead?"

Richards continued to talk on the com. “Damn it. That shoot-to-kill order was canceled. I want them alive. Use stunners and reroute every hover to the western desert, and fast. Morning comes in a half-hour.” He closed the com and turned to her. “It wasn’t your son. They shot down a brown-winged harpy. Don’t worry. We’ll find him.”

Monica’s ruthless tenacity was gone with the realization that Alexander might die, and it was her fault. When she tried to control him, make him human, she’d had him confined where he was subjected to drugs, and cruel doctors, until he fled with strangers. Losing Mollie was the final blow. He turned deadly. “Why didn’t I leave him alone and let him have his stupid tree and nanny? He really was a good boy,” she cried. Distraught, she trembled and wept, “Alexander, I’m so sorry.”

Richards turned to Lilly. “She shouldn’t be here. I’ll have an officer take both of you home.”

Lilly nodded. “Come, Miss Carlton. Let’s go back to the house.”

CHAPTER TWELVE

Summer woke when someone lifted her off the hard cave floor, and she opened her eyes to Matt's worried face. Instead of his usual jacket and jeans, he wore a metallic protective suit. "You'll be okay, Summer," he said, carrying her through the cave.

Her eyes narrowed. "Traitor," she screamed and slapped his face "Put me down. I don't want to be near you."

Ignoring his busted lip and her demand, Matt kept walking toward his ship near the cave opening.

She writhed in his arms and yelled, "Let go of me. You weren't here, and now Bloom and Alex are dead. How could you betray us: betray me?" When he carried her into the ship, she sobbed. "Jim was right about you. You're a selfish, horrible man who never loved me."

"Jim was wrong about him," a soft voice said from the aisle that led to the back berths.

As Matt released her, Summer saw Bloom. "You're alive!" She sprang across the cabin into the harpy's arms. "But how…how did Matt find you?"

"It wasn't easy," Matt said. "Summer, I got your com call but couldn't respond without giving away my location to the cops. Then it was hit-and-miss, trying to track the com signal on a fast-moving harpy. First, Bloom was in the desert, then the cave, then back in the desert. I followed his coordinates and found Alex. Then I just waited.

I knew Bloom would show up. He wasn't about to abandon the golden kid and let him bake."

"Is Alex all right?" asked Summer.

"I scanned his noggin and body," Matt said. "He's got a bad case of heatstroke and will probably wake up with a hell of a headache. Aside from that, he's okay. But we've screwed around long enough and need to get out of here." He slipped out of the heat suit and headed for the cockpit.

Summer walked to Alex's bunk in a back cabin and saw the icepacks on his forehead and chest.

Bloom followed and answered the question in her mind. "He suffers more from heat than we do because he was not raised in a hot jungle."

Summer nodded and embraced Bloom again. "You did great, Bloom. You saved us both."

"I hope to hear those words when home." When the engine fired up and the whole ship rumbled, Bloom shuddered. "The danger is not over."

The ship's vibration and roaring engine woke Alex. With squinted eyes, he pulled the icepack off his head and asked, "Where am I?"

"You're on the ship," said Summer. "We're leaving Oden."

Alex struggled to sit up, but then plopped back down. "I have the worst headache and feel dizzy."

Summer sat down on his bunk. "When I knocked you down, you hit your head on the rooftop."

"I don't remember that, but…." Alex hesitated. "Mollie is dead, isn't she?"

Summer nodded.

Bloom put a water bottle to Alex's dried lips. "Drink, it shall help you heal."

Alex swatted the bottle away and growled, "Leave me alone." He curled up and covered himself with his wings. Under the feathers, he sniffled and whimpered.

Hearing him cry, Summer caressed his head and sensed his despair and loneliness. Despite what he had done, she felt sorry for him. "Alex, Mollie is gone, but I am here for you."

The ship left the cave, and they prepared for blast off. Soon *Dream Weaver* cleared the planet's atmosphere and travelled in space.

* * *

In the cockpit, Matt stared at the com buzzing nonstop, but he didn't answer it. Bloom came up beside him and stared inquisitively at the flashing, noisy instrument.

"It's Oden dispatch trying to hail me," Matt explained. "That little trip in the desert for you guys will cost us. The satellites picked up my ship in the mountains and monitored our illegal takeoff."

"They seek us now?" asked Bloom.

"Yep," Matt said, and hit a few switches.

"Can your ship out fly them?"

"Nope."

"What shall you do?"

Matt sighed. "The cops will soon be on our ass, but I've got a few tricks up my sleeve. We're taking a detour and hightail it to that nearby asteroid field. It saved my ass before. It's our only chance."

"Asteroids?"

"They're big floating rocks, Bloom. But my ship is quick and turns on a coin. We'll outmaneuver them. Plus, I doubt the feds will follow us into a field."

"These floating rocks are dangerous?"

"Very," Matt said. "A pilot has to be mad as a hatter to fly through asteroids."

Bloom patted Matt's shoulder. "You are that pilot."

"Gee, thanks."

"How long before we seek the shelter of floating rocks?"

"I have her wide open. Just hope she holds together. If we're not cut off, we should reach the field in half a day."

Bloom stroked a door bracket. "Stay well, old girl, and fly swiftly."

Matt smiled, seeing that Bloom had become a believer. Then his grin faded, and he looked up at the lanky harpy. "I want you to know I feel really bad about losing Jim and Ribot. Without them, it isn't the same."

"Matt, no words are needed. I am a harpy and sense your feels."

* * *

Bloom left the cockpit and entered the back berths to check on Alex's recovery. Summer knelt beside his bunk and placed a water bottle to his mouth.

"I told you I don't want it," Alex snapped. He turned away and buried his face in a pillow.

Summer looked up helplessly. "He won't drink or eat."

"Move away from him, Summer." Bloom reached over and grabbed Alex's shoulders. He jerked him up, and shook him harshly. "You shall do as told and survive."

Alex's eyes widened with alarm. "Get your hands off me," he stammered. "I'm a golden harpy."

"Yellow feathers do not make a golden." Bloom glanced at Summer. "Your sister is a golden harpy, strong, brave, and honorable. You behave like a feeble human who cares only for himself. You dishonor those who died for your freedom, including Mollie. Come, Summer. He is not worth saving."

Summer raised an eyebrow and dropped the bottle on the bunk. They stepped out of the cabin.

Alex yelled. "You can't treat me like this. I could kill you, kill you with a glance. I am a golden harpy."

Bloom slammed the compartment door, drowning out Alex's ranting.

In the main cabin, Summer said to Bloom, "You were hard on him. Mollie was like his mother, and he cannot get over her death."

"To baby him makes him more pathetic and hopeless. His anger toward me shall replace the sadness. It is the best way to help him."

Summer reclined on the couch. "I am not that strong. In the cave when I thought everyone was gone, I considered ending my life."

"But you did not. I too have wished for death when Alex's age and hunters took my father. He was a powerful flock leader, and I worshipped him. But then Aron took me under his wing like a mighty tree, steadfast and true, but with rough bark." Bloom smiled slightly. "If not for Aron, I would have died." He noticed Alex standing in the aisle.

Alex lowered his head and stepped into the cabin. "I'm sorry for being ungrateful and an egotistical jerk. I want to be a real harpy. Will you teach me, Bloom?"

Bloom wrapped Alex in his dark wings. "I shall. You are under my feathers as I was under Aron's."

Alex hugged him. "Thank you."

In the cockpit Matt sat at the controls when Summer strolled in. "How's the kid?" he asked.

"Better," she said. "Bloom has accepted him into his flock and will treat him like his younger brother. Though, I don't think Alex realizes this."

Matt chuckled. "Brothers tend to beat the crap out of each other."

"Harpy brothers do the same, challenging each other to fights. Alex has some tough lessons ahead." She took the co-pilot seat, tucked her legs under her, and let her wings hang off the backside of the seat. "We haven't spoken since we left Oden. I owe you an apology."

"No, you don't. I should've come sooner."

"But you did come."

Matt noticed three green dots on the radar screen that were moving toward the red dot, his ship. "Shit, here they come, and the fuckers are closing in fast."

"The police?" she asked.

He frowned, "Yeah, but these ships look too big for Oden security." He fidgeted with the radar knobs. "Damn, those are federation ships. The kid's mother must have pull."

"Can we escape them?" Summer asked.

"Don't know." He pushed the throttle to maximum speed. "At the rate their gaining, they could get into range and fire a few blasts. Our only hope is the asteroids." His knuckles tapped the wooden handle of the knife on his belt. "Knock on wood. It's going to be close."

Bloom entered the cockpit. "We move much faster. Do the police come for us?"

"On our tail," Matt said, and pushed the throttle to wide open. "Okay, sweetheart, give me all you got." *Dream Weaver*'s hull rattled as the ship surpassed a safe velocity.

Bloom put a hand on the shaking rivets. "She breaks her heart to save us."

"Come on, *Weaver*. Hold together, baby," said Matt, staring at the radar. "Damn, there's another one, and he's trying to intercept us. They want us bad."

They reached the outskirts of the asteroid field. An alarm sounded and flashed red on the instrument panel. "Hang on, here come the blasts." Matt banked the ship sharply, and two laser blasts zipped past the ship's right window. "That was close, too close."

He steered the ship straight into the field. "It's time to separate the men from the boys." Another blast hit an asteroid to the left of the ship, and it exploded into a million flying pieces. "Son-of-a-bitch, they aren't screwing around. You must have really pissed them off. What happened on Oden?"

Bloom and Summer didn't answer.

Throttling back, Matt maneuvered behind a giant asteroid and glanced at the radar. The federation ships had changed direction and were skirting the field. "Figured they'd back off and won't follow. Now it's us against the asteroids, and this ride isn't for wimps."

"I'll go back and stay with Alex," Summer said and left the cockpit.

Matt mumbled to Bloom while intently guiding the ship around boulders. "Summer says you've kind of adopted the kid."

"Alex has never known a father and needs male guidance." Bloom squatted alongside Matt's cockpit chair. "Thank you for saving him, but if you had stayed in the cave, you would not face this danger now."

"Honestly, Bloom, I nearly skipped out on you guys. Then realized I couldn't live with myself if I left her." He banked the ship to avoid an asteroid. "Besides, you're thanking me too soon. We're not out of the weeds."

"Harpies live day to day, not thinking about what might be. So today you have my thanks."

"Okay, then," Matt said, and looked at the radar. "Damn feds are deploying around the field, planning to lie and wait. They figure we'll either crash or come out, eventually."

"What shall you do?"

"We stay here and we'll definitely bite the bullet. I can't keep dodging these rocks. I'm heading for that big asteroid and then we'll pull the wool over their eyes. Go in the back storage and load the garbage chutes with everything we don't need: some of my clothes, the extra ship parts, a few weapons, and some of your feathers."

"My feathers?" Bloom asked.

"Yeah and make sure you get some yellow ones off Alex and Summer. We got one shot to make this look good. After you're done, bring me the red box that's in a cabinet over my bunk."

"What is in it?"

Matt grinned. "A second chance."

He left and returned several minutes later. "All you have said is done," Bloom said, handing Matt the red box.

Summer came in. "Why did you want our feathers in the garbage?"

"They're a decoy, so the feds will back off." Matt popped open the red box and smiled. "I've been saving this sucker for a rainy day."

Bloom looked out the window. "I see no rain."

"Just a cliché, Bloom," Matt muttered while eyeing the looming gigantic asteroid that resembled a small moon. He checked his watch and adjusted a timer inside the box.

Summer peered into the box. "What are those orange tubes?"

"Uranium blasting caps." Matt closed the box lid. "When triggered, they create one hell of an explosion. I set the timer for twenty minutes, about when we'll crash-land on the asteroid."

"Crash-land?" said Summer.

"Yeah, it's gonna be a bumpy ride. Everyone needs to strap in tight." Matt handed the box back to Bloom. "Add this to the garbage. I'll jettison the chutes near the asteroid. When the bomb goes off, I'll kill the engine. On radar, the feds will think the ship hit the asteroid and blew up. And without electronics, the blast should give us enough momentum to set down on the rock without thrusters. I just have to hope our hull won't break up."

"I understand your decoy," said Bloom. "When hunters shot at harpies, we faked injuries and death to draw the men away from our fledglings."

Matt nodded. "Let's hope these feds are as stupid as hunters and fall for it. That's why the feathers. Drones will analyze the debris. If they find harpy feathers, they'll believe we're goners and leave."

"Have you done this before?" Bloom asked.

"Hell, no," Matt said with an uneasy chuckle. "I'm not even sure it'll work, but there's a first for everything."

Bloom and Summer stared at him with disbelief.

"Look, I can't keep ducking these rocks," Matt said. "Sooner or later we'll hit one. It's either this or turning ourselves in."

"No, we would rather crash and die," Summer said.

Alex walked into the cockpit. "What's happening?"

"You don't want to know," Summer said. "We are apparently in for a bumpy ride and must buckle up." She and Alex left for the cabin.

Bloom picked the red box. "I trust you, Matt." He walked out, heading for the garbage chutes.

Matt huffed and uttered, "Glad he trusts me. This is the craziest damn thing I've ever done, and it could be my last." He steered for the asteroid while the minutes ticked by. He fastened his rarely-used seatbelt and called back, "You all ready?"

"Yes," Bloom answered.

Matt hit a switch and the garbage chutes opened, releasing the miscellaneous gear, feathers, and bomb into space. He looked at the ship clock. "Five minutes," he yelled. With the countdown, he clenched teeth, and his sweaty hand clutched the throttle. "Here it comes!" He pulled back on the throttle, killed the engine, and slammed down the electronic switches. A huge flare burst behind the ship. Seconds later, the shock wave hit. *Dream Weaver* flipped end over end. He hectically pushed the manual flaps to right the vessel before it hit the asteroid surface. "Come on, baby, straighten out."

He stared anxiously at the starter switch. Thirty more seconds and he'd have to fire up the engines to prevent a fatal crash. They'd be saved, but their hoax would be exposed. "Bitch, level out!" he screamed and frantically pumped the flaps.

With a few seconds to go, *Dream Weaver* finally stabilized and glided silently toward the grayish, rocky terrain. He pushed down the flaps and released the grappling hooks, normally used to tether the ship when stationed on windy planets. The hooks slowed the ship's speed, but didn't stop it from sliding over the gravel and stony surface. The loud banging, bumping, and scraping from the hull rattled his nerves.

"Holy fuck!" Matt said with terror, seeing a huge canyon ahead as the ship neared its sheer drop off. He released a left hook so the ship would slide sideways. It slammed against a large boulder and stopped.

The creak and groan from sheared, dented, and bent metal echoed through the dark ship.

Matt leaned back with his pounding heart like it might leap out of his chest. "Remind me never to do this shit again." In the creaking, shadowy cockpit, he closed his eyes. A minute later, he felt a kiss on his lips and looked up to Summer's silhouette against the glow of stars.

"You did good, Matt."

He unbuckled his seatbelt. "Is everyone okay?"

"Alex and I are fine, but Bloom says he will never travel in space again."

"I don't blame him." Matt switched on the ribbon of tiny running lights along the floorboard. Powered by batteries, the lights were undetectable on radar. He and Summer walked into the cabin.

Alex stood and grinned. "Man, what an unbelievable rush. It was great."

Bloom still strapped into his seat and said solemnly, "Yes, unbelievable."

Matt clasped his shoulder. "You all right, buddy?"

"I shall be in time," Bloom said, with a shake of his locks.

"Well, don't relax. We're not out of the woods yet." Matt opened an overhead hatch, pulled out several blankets, and tossed them on the couch. "I can't run the generator without giving us away. That means the filter system can't create oxygen, and the heat is off. We need to lie low to conserve air and bundle up in the main cabin. It's going to get real cold real quick." He walked back and closed the doors to the berths to preserve heat and went down in storage for a flashlight. When he returned, Summer was on the couch.

"You and I will rest here," she said to Matt.

On the floor, Bloom lay on a blanket, and the kid stood over him, scowling.

"I'm not curling up with you," Alex said crossly. "I don't care how cold it gets." He grabbed a blanket and plopped down in the large, stuffed chair.

Matt lifted an eyebrow, wanting no part of the harpy feud, and reclined on the couch with Summer, and she wrapped him in her warm feathers.

"Male harpies do not sleep alone like humans," Bloom explained. "We live in flocks, and when single, we share a nest to shield each other from rain and cold."

"I don't care," Alex said. "I'm not bedding down and have a guy hug me."

Summer lifted her head. "Alex, you have the wrong idea. Male harpy closeness is a bonding that demonstrates devotion and friendship."

"I've survived fine without harpy friendship," said Alex.

"You really believe you are fine?" Summer asked.

"Let him be, Summer," Bloom said. "He shall learn from his misery." He curled up and covered himself with a blanket and wing.

Matt snuggled against Summer and waited for the federation ships to leave. If they didn't go soon, everyone on Matt's ship would die from cold or lack of oxygen. For the harpies, surrender was not an option.

CHAPTER THIRTEEN

In the dark cabin, Alex clutched the blanket and shivered under his tightly folded wings Even though the lights were out, his cat-like vision revealed in the starlight the three strangers who had rescued him. He heard the slight ruffle of Bloom's feathers, Matt's whisper, and Summer's soft giggle. He sniffed toward them. Having grown up with humans, he was familiar with the pilot's scent, but the two harpies had a sweet, animal-like fragrance. Mollie had often told him that he smelled like a flower. He now understood why.

All his life he had longed to be with his own kind, but finally here, he was having reservations. His instincts and telepathy made him superior to humans, but Summer and Bloom had the same attributes and were his equal. And at times they even snubbed him, saying he was like a weak, flawed human. The worst insult was sensing their disdain and horror when he killed the cops on Oden and showed no remorse.

Mollie had claimed he was special, a golden prince of the harpies with extraordinary gifts. But on the ship, he had a rude awakening. No one treated him like a prince, and his mind-controlling powers made them uneasy and distrustful. He buried his face in feathers. Like humans, the harpies thought him a dangerous freak.

"I miss you, Mollie," he whispered. She had loved him unconditionally.

Sighing deeply, he saw his breath. The cabin temperature had dropped rapidly. Bitter cold invaded his limbs, making his joints ache, and a prickly burn stung his skin. He trembled uncontrollably and could barely move his numb fingers and toes. He knew harpies were tropical beings with thin blood, and designed for flight, they had light-weight bones, and no fat. With these characteristics, they couldn't endure frigid weather like humans. He was in pain and with growing fright, he thought he might die and no one would care. His only option seemed to give in and warm up with Bloom.

He crept to the large, black-winged harpy on the floor. "I'm freezing."

"Come," Bloom said, lifting his wing.

Alex crawled next to him. Bloom embraced him and covered him with his thick and heavy adult feathers, much warmer than Alex's shortened, teenage wings. Snuggling against Bloom's chest, Alex stopped shaking, and the ache subsided.

Alex, do not worry, Bloom relayed to Alex's mind. *We care about you and do not think you are a dangerous freak. In time you shall fit in and be happy with us.*

Alex had never heard a harpy's silent talk. Rather than being comforted, it alarmed him. Their physical contact had revealed Alex's private thoughts to Bloom. In the future Alex vowed not to touch other harpies.

Several hours later, Matt sat up and said to Summer, "I've got to check the radar and see if the feds are still around." Crawling out from under her wing, he left the couch, clutched his jacket, and turned on his flashlight to see in the dark cabin. "Damn, it's frigging cold," he said with a burr.

Alex raised his head. "Isn't that risky? If you turn on the radar, they'll also see us."

"I know, but if I switch it on and off fast, they might see a blip, but probably think it's only a false echo. I got to take the chance. Our oxygen is low, and we'll soon freeze to death." He left for the cockpit.

Alex followed him, pressing his wings tight against his body. Summer and Bloom joined them. Matt slipped into the pilot seat. Looking up at the harpies, he said, "Okay, kids, let's keep our fingers crossed." He flipped a switch, and the screen came on. The red line swept the asteroid field.

"They're gone," Alex said.

Matt smiled. "They sure as shit are, and my scanner is a souped-up model, equal to the feds. It's time to fire up *Weaver* and blast off this rock."

"So we journey home?" Bloom asked.

"In a roundabout way," Matt said, turning on the ship's lights, heat, and oxygen. "No way am I stopping at Oden spaceport and entering the James wormhole. It's too dicey, with the feds looking for us." He turned on the computer and studied a star map. He pointed to a dot beyond the asteroid field. "We'll head for this little star called Bella. Its second planet has a substandard mining colony and is near a wormhole that comes out at Dora. It's a longer trip, and the wormhole is unstable, barely a thread but at least the Federation ships can't use it. The bad part, there's no law enforcement in the area, so the smugglers are ruthless. They don't just highjack ships; they murder the crew. I've heard some outrageous stories."

"No worries, Matt," Alex said, standing in the threshold. "They won't touch us if I'm aboard." Everyone turned and stared at him.

Bloom breathed deeply. "Matt, how much longer is our journey?"

"This many days," Matt said and held up his fingers repeatedly, so Bloom understood.

"Fourteen," Alex said.

"A harpy who knows numbers," Matt commented.

Alex folded his arms. "I have several college degrees and probably know more about this ship than its ignorant pilot."

"Alex," Summer scolded.

Matt chuckled. "Hey, I'd rather be ignorant than an irritating, ungrateful asshole like you."

"Careful, human," said Alex. "One more insult and it might be your last."

Summer wheeled around and shoved Alex hard against the cockpit door. "You better be careful," she growled. "You harm this human, and I will tear you apart."

"Jeez, I'm sorry, sis," Alex said, and rubbed the back of his smarting head. "I was just kidding. I'd never hurt your future mate." Tousling his feathers, he took a step to leave but glanced back. "I know you love him, but you could do better."

Summer noticed Matt's startled expression and bit her lip. Exposing her feelings and hopes to Matt was Alex's payback for the shove. She had wanted to entice Matt into bonding with her, but he'd been blindsided with a commitment.

Bloom said to them, "I am sorry about Alex. Few have loved him, and he has learned cruelty from others and become defensive and spiteful. I shall talk to him."

"That's your opinion," Matt said. "I think the arrogant brat needs a good kick in the butt."

After Bloom left, Summer took the co-pilot seat. "Matt, be careful with Alex and do not harass him; he is more dangerous than you know. The police hovers on Oden did not crash because of a mishap or from being shot down. Alex's telepathy forced the pilots to drive their hovers into the street and commit suicide. Bloom and I are worried about his powerful mind control. He grieves for Mollie and is unsure where to aim his anger."

"You mean we've risked everything for a psychopath who should have stayed in the nut ward?" Matt shook his head. "And here I thought the feds where after us because his mother is a big shot. Turns out, they're going all out to bring down a cop killer." He turned to her. "Summer, what are you going to do with this kid? You can't turn him loose on Dora. If someone pisses him off, he might waste them."

"Bloom believes he can change him."

"Bloom has his work cut out." Matt took her hand and smiled. "But speaking of the little brat, he says you want to marry me. Is that true?"

"Yes," said Summer.

Matt grinned and said jokingly, "Where I'm from, the guy usually does the asking."

"With harpies, there is no asking. It is a meeting of the minds. Do you love me enough to bond?"

"I do." He leaned over and passionately kissed her.

Bloom stuck his head in the cockpit. "Are we leaving now?"

Still kissing Summer, Matt pushed the door shut in Bloom's face.

* * *

After blasting off the asteroid, Matt steered his ship through the floating boulders. Some were the size of houses while others could support a city. Having cleared the field, he set a course for Bella and placed the ship on autopilot. He left the cockpit to unwind and found the harpies lounging around the cabin and nibbling on nuts and dry fruit.

Matt walked to Alex resting on the couch. "I think we got off on the wrong foot, Alex. It's a long journey and we need to be friends." He offered his hand.

Alex stood and took Matt's hand. "Bloom told me you risked your life to take me from the desert. I was ungrateful." He shrugged. "Men locked me up for a long time and then killed a person I loved, but it's no excuse for insulting you. I'm sorry."

"Hey, kid, no harm done," said Matt.

* * *

Over the following days, *Dream Weaver* left the shipping channels and traveled farther and farther from civilization toward Bella. Bloom noticed that a temporary peace had settled among them, but underneath was an unspoken tension.

On this return voyage, Bloom no longer harassed Matt about Summer. The man loved her and proved it in returning to Oden to save them. Besides, Bloom had bigger issues than keeping the man away from the harpy princess. He had to deal with Alex.

He spoke at length to the teenage male about harpy beliefs, culture, and loyalty. Alex seemed a willing student, asking questions about the part he should play among his kind. But Alex's mindset was a mystery, becoming a master of concealing his feelings and thoughts from Bloom's telepathy. His nasty attitude disappeared, but instead of interacting with his shipmates, he became distant. No one trusted him, and he knew it. For hours he stared out the window into space or used the computer to read, but his aloofness raised concerns. Would he behave or pounce?

Matt sat at the galley table with a deck of cards, facing Summer. "I know a great place for a honeymoon, doll. We could hit the casinos on Earth's moon. The way you can read minds and cards, we'll make a killing and get rich."

"That would be dishonest, Matt," she said. "When we live on Dora, we will not need wealth."

Matt sighed and dropped the cards. "There are drawbacks to marrying a harpy. You all are too darn honest." He leaned back. "Let's talk about this bonding. You're underage, so do you need permission from your father to marry?"

"The doctor on Dora says my father suffers from post-traumatic stress disorder. Some days his mind is clear and other times, he does not know me. He cannot make such decisions. My grandmother rules Dora, but my older brother, Will, soon replaces her. One of them will give us permission to bond."

Curled up on pillows, Alex lifted his head from his feathers. "I wish I had known our father when he was well." Everyone looked surprised because he was normally quiet.

"Me too," Summer said subtly.

Alex flung his hair from his narrowed eyes. "I know what you insinuate, Summer. If Shail had raised me, I wouldn't be trouble now. Just remember, Father killed many men too."

Summer sprang up, glaring, "Father killed men who hunted and murdered harpies. They deserved to die, unlike those poor policemen who accidently shot Mollie. Father was as bold and warm as a sunrise and defended us. And he regretted the killing so much that his despair took him from me. Never compare yourself to our father. Alongside him, you are a heartless shadow."

Matt reached up and took her hand. "Summer, just leave it alone."

Summer jerked her hand away, and her feathers quivered with anger. She looked at Bloom. "You think he'll become a great harpy? He's not even good enough to be one of us." She stomped off to the back berths.

Matt rose. "Sorry, kid. Your sister is pretty defensive when it comes to her dad. I'd better go back there." He strolled toward the berths.

Alex stood and stared at the floor. "Am I evil, Bloom, a heartless shadow? Didn't I only inherit yellow wings from Shail and nothing else?"

Bloom sighed. "In some ways you are like him. You have his intelligence and raw courage. I shall never forget seeing you on the rooftop. While we hid, you faced the police and their flying machines. I thought there is Shail's spirit reborn in his son. But Shail was also honorable and generous. He loved his harpies and was willing to die for them."

"And I'm a selfish son of a nasty bitch."

"Along with our instincts, harpies are compassionate and take pride in protecting life," said Bloom. "When I was your age, the harpies fought a great mercenary army. We won the war, but did not celebrate. Every male gazed at his bloodstained hands and hung his head, many falling to their knees and cried in shame. Killing the men, we had disgraced our gentle race. You must learn to care about others."

"That might be impossible. Any compassion I had died with Mollie. The only thing I have left is my mother's callous nature." He sighed. "You want to help me but it's doubtful I can be fixed."

CHAPTER FOURTEEN

In a mossy treetop nest, Will stirred from the tiny footsteps on his face and shooed away a little spotted lizard. The reptiles had a symbiotic relationship with sleeping harpies, eating the stinging insects. He lifted his head and gazed at the sunrise that was transforming the shadowy jungle into a feast of color. "Wake up," he said to Freely, who slept nearby. "I want to be in Terrance by midday."

Freely stretched and yawned. "Do you think your grandmother knows if the rescue was successful?"

"She might. The ship left over a month ago, and the mission should be done. I am concerned if they freed this half-brother and got away safely."

Freely rose. "Will, you do not care about this human-raised brother who is likely troubled. You are worried about Summer."

"I will not judge Alex until we meet. But true, I am mainly concerned for my sister."

Before departing, they picked several plum-like fruits, peeled off the rubbery purple skin, and ate the sweet white flesh and nut for energy. They took flight, and at noon landed on Windy's porch.

Will stepped inside and called to his grandmother. There was no response, so he used his telepathy and focused on her. "She is here, but something is wrong." Rather than mount the stairs, he flew to the second level, leaving Freely near the front door. He walked down the hallway to Windy's bedroom.

"Grandma, it is Will," he said, stepping in the room. She lay on the bed, wrapped in the sheets and hugging a pillow. Harpies rarely slept during the day, and his anxiety grew. Kneeling beside her bed, he asked, "Grandma, what is wrong?"

She rolled over and gazed at him with bloodshot eyes. "Oh, Will, I had a terrible vision during sleep. Jim was hurt and dying."

Will stroked her head. "Your worry for him caused a nightmare. I am sure he is fine."

Windy sat up. "It was not a nightmare or dream, but stronger, clearer. He said he loved me, and I believe we connected telepathically. Another thing that troubles me. He promised to call when they had Alex, and he has not."

"There are many reasons why he did not call. The mission was delayed or there was space interference with the connection. It also might not be safe yet. A com call can pinpoint his whereabouts for the police."

"Yes, all could be true, but I am mostly disturbed with the vision. With all his heart, mind, and soul, he reached out to me."

Will sighed. "All right, show me these images." He wrapped his arms around her and closed his eyes. Focusing on her, he saw the mental picture. Flames and smoke invaded a black skyline. On a rooftop Jim lay in his own blood as an explosion erupted, shaking him and the building. Summer knelt beside him and gripped his hand. He said weakly, "Just tell Windy that I love her."

The image ended, and Will released his grandmother. He too was now troubled. Despite the vast distance in space, he could not ignore a possible telepathic connection. "I shall send for my mother. She can comfort you until we know if your vision is true."

"No, Kari and others must not know of this mission. Ted, Aron, and I are guilty of breaking the law. We cannot involve others."

"But you told me."

She cupped his cheek. “When you discovered Jim was gone, I told you because you will soon rule and must learn about hard decisions. Should I place my mate and granddaughter in danger to rescue this unknown grandson, or should I have not interfered and left Alex to his fate? Soon I will know if my choice was wise.”

“I do not know Alex, but he is my father’s son. Given the choice, I would accept the risks and save him. No harpy should perish in a cage.”

* * *

Over the next few days, Will and Freely stayed at Windy’s home, all hoping that Jim would call. Will normally slept in the trees at night but took up dozing at the bottom of his grandmother’s bed. She tossed and turned with nightmares, but when he crawled alongside her and covered her with his wing, she slumbered quietly. They made attempts to contact Mollie and find out if the ship had arrived, and they rescued Alex, but no one answered her com. This added to Windy’s anxiety. Something had gone wrong.

This morning, Will and Freely sat on the porch railing and enjoyed pastries. Windy joined them with a cup of herb tea.

Freely slipped off the railing and bowed. “Did you sleep well, my queen?”

“Yes, thanks to my grandson. His wing keeps the demons away, but I fear his worry has aged him.” She sat down at the table. “Before, he was carefree and only interested in females and adventure. He has now matured into a responsible adult. I am sorry, Will. I would have preferred you kept your innocence longer.”

“It was time I grew up.”

“Very true,” Freely said with a smirk.

Will glared at him but was not about to chastise him on his grandmother’s porch. He massaged his jaw and changed the subject. “This waiting and not knowing is killing me. It is risky, but maybe we should call the Oden authorities. We could claim to be friends of

Mollie Harris and are concerned that we cannot reach her. We might learn she is in jail for freeing Alex."

"That is a good idea, Will," said Freely.

"We might also learn she is dead," said Windy, "And it is risky. The authorities could guess we are part of the kidnapping. But I am willing to try anything."

"So we will call Oden." Will heard a vehicle pull off the road and hopped from the railing. "Are you expecting anyone?"

"No," Windy said. The vehicle came into sight and stopped at the house. "It's only Ted."

Ted climbed out and said, "Good morning, Miss Windy. Will, I didn't expect to see you and Freely, but I'm glad you're here."

Will noticed the man's slump as he trudged toward the porch. Ted was born with a grin on his lips, but he wasn't smiling now. "You are sad, not glad. Tell us the bad news."

Ted glanced at him. "Jesus, you're just like your dad when he crawled in my head. I'm here to talk to your grandmother, but alone."

Windy rose from the table. "If it's about the rescue mission on Oden, Will and Freely know about it. You can speak to all of us."

Ted, staring at the floor, avoided their eyes. "It is about the rescue. I came here in person because you shouldn't hear it on a com. I just got a call at the Terrance airport from a Federation officer wanting information on some Dora harpies that boarded a ship bound for Oden. I told him I didn't know anything. When I asked what it was about, he said these harpies planned to break into a mental hospital and free another harpy, but the police were tipped off and waiting for them. They surrounded the hospital roof." He paused to swallow.

Impatient, Will snapped, "What happened?"

"It's bad, Will," Ted said, cringing. "There was a shootout. Thirteen officers died when their hovers crashed. A woman was killed, and a man was severely wounded. The police shot one of the harpies but the rest made it to their ship and took off. The Federation ships pursued them into an asteroid field." Ted covered his mouth and trembling chin. "It was reported that ship hit an asteroid and exploded. Miss Windy, they're all dead."

Windy collapsed into a chair and moaned, "Oh, Jim and my beautiful Summer." She dropped her head and cried.

Will stepped off the deck and strolled to the edge of the jungle. For a half-hour, he gazed at trees but saw nothing. Harshly wiping the tears off his cheeks, he sniffled up his resolve. He'd grieve later for his brave little sister. Returning to the porch, he asked Ted, "Who was the wounded man?"

"I don't know. The officer didn't say. He might have been a hospital worker, a security guard, or just a bystander."

"Or he might be Jim," said Will. "Find out the man's name and if he survived."

"I'll get online for Oden news. They might have it." Ted hurried toward his vehicle and stopped short. "If it is Jim, things will get sticky around here. He was the chief of police and the harpy ruler's husband. With all those dead officers, the feds will be looking to arrest co-conspirators. That means me, your grandmother, and maybe even you."

"Let them come," Will said, and ruffled his feathers. "They will arrest no one."

"Well, if they have Jim, he'd never rat anyone out, but to be on the safe side, discuss nothing about the mission on a com. I guarantee the feds have started surveillance and are recording every call on Dora. That evidence could come back and bite us."

After Ted left, Will took his advice. Shunning com use, harpies directly would convey information. He hailed Freely. "Fly home to your father and tell him that Bloom and Ribot are dead. Aron can tell the tragic news to their families."

"My father shall take this very hard. He and Bloom were very close."

"I share the burden of delivering this news," Will said. "I fly to Westend to see my mother. As Rachel's best friend, she should be the one to inform Rachel of her daughter's death. The golden family will long mourn Summer's loss."

Freely placed his hand on Will's shoulder and nodded. There was no more to say. He flew off the porch and disappeared into the jungle.

Will stepped to his grandmother, who sat sobbing. "Grandma, I must go to the west coast. Before I leave, let me help you to your bed."

"You go to see Kari?"

"Yes, but I will be back here tonight."

"Poor Rachel," she said, faltering when she rose. He caught her and swept her up in his arms.

She buried her face in his chest and mumbled, "Forgive me. I have not felt this crushed since your grandfather died. Now I have lost Jim."

"But he is not dead."

She looked up with questioning eyes.

"Your telepathic vision is proof. The wounded man is Jim."

* * *

Kari woke before dawn in the Turner house. After dressing, she tiptoed down the dark stairs to the kitchen and quietly placed several slices of nut bread and a jar of honey in a small basket, then slipped outside. To the east, golden sunlight broke through the massive trees, pursuing a gray sky. Morning was coming. She gazed westward at the pasture of rolling hills. A small herd of wild zel grazed in knee-deep silver grass that sparkled from the light of the twin moons, still low on the horizon. She hurried through the vegetable garden off the kitchen and crossed the backyard. At the edge of the jungle, she stepped onto the shadowy path. Birds chirped and other creatures hooted, greeting the day. Miles away a red dragon roared. Kari had often traveled the lush trail, and each time it was magical.

Fifty yards down the path, she came to a small clearing and sat down on a wooden bench with the basket in her lap. She waited, and after several minutes, he appeared among the trees.

Hello, Shail, she relayed.

He flung his shoulder-length blond locks from his face and sniffed the air as his wide blue eyes cautiously searched.

It's all right. No one is here but me. Please come out.

Coaxing him from the trees, he stepped warily into the clearing and shuddered.

She held up the basket. *Look, I brought your favorite, nut bread and honey.* She rose and approached him.

Shail backed away, half raising his yellow wings, and his darting eyes suggested that he might flee.

It's me, your mate, Kari. Don't be frightened.

Shail sniffed and caught her scent. *Kari?*

Yes, my love. She smiled. Although over forty-years-old, Shail could have passed as an older brother of his sons. A full-blooded harpy, he was spared from wrinkles and age and had kept his little-boy face and slender, muscled frame.

He tiptoed within arm's reach and inhaled her scent. *It is you.* Embracing her, he lowered his face into her long hair and nuzzled her neck. *For many lights I have searched for you and feared your father had sent you back to the stars.*

Kari pulled away. *Shail, I saw you yesterday. Don't you remember? And Father can't send me to Earth again. He died long ago.*

He looked puzzled. *Turner is dead?*

Dad died before our first son was born, and Will is grown now.

I am sad to learn of his death. Turner hated me, but I admired his honor and courage. He blinked hard. *I remember. He stepped in front of a laser blast to protect me.*

She smiled. *That's right. He died saving your life so he didn't hate you. Now let's have breakfast.* Going over the past to refresh Shail's memory had become a ritual. They sat down on the grass, and she handed him a slice of bread.

He gazed at the bread but didn't eat it. *I do not know what is happening to me, Kari. Things I should know are gone. I am always afraid but do not know why.*

She stroked his head. *You have nothing to fear. You destroyed your enemies and saved your flock. The jungle is at peace. You only need to remember that you have many beautiful sons and daughters and everyone on the planet loves you.*

You spoke of my son Will. Tell me of him.

He is beautiful, wise, and brave, just like you. Soon he rules the flocks. You should be very proud.

He dropped the bread and hung his head. *I am not proud, but ashamed. I have not been a good father. I do not know my offspring or their names.*

Shail, you are the best of fathers. You sacrificed everything for your family. If not for you, all living creatures on this planet would be gone.

If you say so, he relayed and looked up into her eyes. *I only know one thing, and it is more feeling than a memory. I love you, Kari. If I forget that, I am truly lost.*

After visiting Shail, she strolled down the trail toward the house, feeling uplifted. It had been one of his good days. He was calm and coherent and before parting, they had made love. On a bad day, he reverted to his feral ancestry. Unable to communicate, he hissed and was unapproachable. Unfortunately, the bad days were outnumbering the good. She hoped, as always, that this wasn't their last time together.

Lost in her thoughts, she pushed aside a blue fern and rounded a large tree along the path. She stopped abruptly, seeing Will ahead.

"I thought you would be here," he said. "How is Father?"

"He was good. We even spoke about you and your coming reign." Coming closer, she noticed his drooping wings and weary face, but it wasn't from a long flight. "Will, what has happened?"

He wiped the sweat from his forehead and stepped to a log. "Please, sit, Mom. I must tell you terrible news."

She gulped, sat down, and took his hand. Never had she sensed such gloom and anxiety in her son.

He proceeded to tell her the whole story, starting with the ship voyage to Oden to save a golden harpy, one of Shail's sons. When he concluded, they were both in tears. "I must return to Terrance and be with Grandma," he said. "She has been given hope that Jim still lives, but she might start blaming herself for Summer's death. She chose to rescue Alex, and it was the right decision. No harpy would abandon a son of Shail."

Kari stood and hugged him. "You have changed and now have the worries of an adult. You are so much like your father when he was young."

"I wish to be like him but never shall. He has no equal."

After Will left, Kari returned to the house, dragging her feet with the terrible news. In the kitchen, Rachel sat at the table, drinking coffee. Lea, Shail's third mate, stood behind her youngest son. "Hold still," Lea growled and jerked on his yellow feathers.

"Ouch. That hurts, Mom," whined the fidgeting ten-year-old.

"Kari, look at this mess," Lea said, focused on the wing. "Whirly got into a fight with a harpy and was thrown into sticky vines. Do you know how to get the burrs out?"

Whirly said defensively, "The brown was bigger and older than me, but I won the challenge."

"You won burrs that are ruining your feathers," Lea grumbled.

"Oil down his wings and the burrs will fall out," Kari said to Lea. "For a few days, his feathers will be greasy so he can't fly far, but at least they won't be damaged."

Rachel looked up. "Kari, your eyes are red and puffy. Have you been crying" She stood and took Kari's hand. "Is it Shail? Is he all right?"

Kari embraced the tall woman and broke into tears. “Oh, Rachel, it’s not Shail. It’s your daughter, Summer.”

CHAPTER FIFTEEN

In *Dream Weaver*'s cockpit, Matt chewed a fingernail and stared at a flashing red light on the control panel as Bloom, Alex, and Summer stood behind him. "Shit, just what we need."

"What does it mean?" asked Bloom.

"It means trouble," Alex responded. "A propulsion component under the ship is failing. It was probably damaged during that rough asteroid landing."

Surprised, Matt looked up at Alex. "How'd you know?"

Alex rolled his eyes. "I said I know all about your little ship. Any idiot can read a manual. The question is, can you fix it?"

"Sure, Alex, I could hop into a spacesuit, go outside, and slap in a new component, but I don't have one." Matt looked back at the controls. "And it's gotta be replaced before we enter that little wormhole. Break down in there and it might be years before another ship comes along and find us."

"What can we do?" Summer asked.

"Change course," Matt said, and veered the ship to the left. "We got no choice but to head for Bella's second planet. The component is standard, and the mining colony should have one."

"But what of the outrageous stories about the planet?" asked Summer.

"Yeah, that's a concern," Matt said. "Ships venturing there have either disappeared or been found stripped and abandoned. Even freakier, the crew is gone; no sign of a struggle; no blood or bodies. Some say the area is haunted."

Alex chuckled. "The human imagination always amazes me. The miners probably double as pirates, but if you're worried about ghosts, I'll protect you, Matt."

Matt glared at the cocky young harpy. "Alex, I don't need your damn protection, but I am concerned about you. When we land on this planet, we don't need you going off on another killing spree because someone ruffled your feathers. The feds will hear about it, even out here, and know you harpies survived the asteroid field. We'll exit the wormhole at Dora, and the law will be waiting. I'm not going to jail because a snot-nosed harpy lost his cool."

Alex raised his head and his gaze shifted from Matt to Bloom to Summer. "You obviously believe I'm a mindless killer and don't trust me. Fine, you're on your own. I'll stay on the ship, and you can deal with whatever's there." He flung back his hair and swaggered out of the cockpit.

* * *

The small gray planet loomed in the distance. Matt flipped on the com to contact the domed mining camp. Summer sat in the copilot seat and watched.

"This is the ship *Dream Weaver*," Matt said into the com. "We've got an emergency and seek permission to land."

A grey, humanoid robot appeared on the screen. "What is the emergency, *Dream Weaver*?"

"A damaged propulsion component and we need a new one for an X-class."

"One moment while I check inventory," said the robot. The screen went blank, but a minute later it returned. "According to our stock records, the component is available. What is your passenger count?"

"Two aboard," said Matt.

"Approach from the west end of the compound and initiate landing. The last hangar is available and will be open. I have notified our head mechanic, and he will assist you with the repair."

"Roger that and thanks," Matt said, and flipped off the transmission.

"You lied about our numbers." Summer said.

"It's called poker, doll. You don't reveal your cards, until the game is over and we're outta here." Matt turned back to the controls. "So far so good; they got the part. It won't take long for Bloom and me to get it and fix the ship."

"I should go with you," said Summer.

"I'd like that, but it's better if you stay aboard and control your brother."

"No one controls Alex."

"Yeah, but he'll listen to you. He doesn't respect me and Bloom as much."

Matt maneuvered the ship closer to the planet. Alex and Bloom came into the cockpit to watch. The ship pierced the atmosphere of grey haze and smoke as it neared the black surface. The barren, mountainous landscape contained active volcanoes that spewed molten rock and yellow rivers of boiling lava.

"This land looks angry," said Bloom.

"It's a newly forming planet," Alex said. "I checked it out. There's no water or oxygen, and except for the human colony, no life."

Matt glanced at the panel that analyzed the planet. "It's also plenty hot. Hell of a place to live."

They left the volcanoes and cruised over a flat, scorched wasteland broken periodically with deep canyons created by earthquakes. At the domed encampment, Matt guided the ship into the open hangar.

"Bloom, dig out two laser guns," said Matt, "and a cloak for your wings. Even here, they might have heard about the harpies and what happened on Oden. No sense in tempting fate."

The ship set down, and the hangar door closed behind them. Fans came on to lower the temperature and distribute oxygen. Matt left the cockpit and walked into the cabin. "It'll be a little while before Bloom and I can leave the ship," he said to Alex and Summer. "After we go, hide in the berths and stay away from the windows," he said to Alex and Summer.

A flashing light on the hangar wall conveyed the air quality was safe, and passengers could disembark. Matt double-checked a monitor. "It's still hot out there, but the oxygen is okay."

"Be careful," Summer said, and kissed him.

In the cabin Bloom flung the robe over his wings and stuffed a laser gun in his sash. He handed the other weapon to Matt, who tucked it into his jeans waistband under his jacket. "Ready?"

Bloom nodded.

Matt hit the latch and the ship door opened. They walked down the ramp into the empty hangar. Dirt covered the floor and tired equipment rested along the walls. "It doesn't look like they've used this hangar in a while."

Bloom sniffed the air. "It has been long. I smell no human scent except yours."

Matt called out, "Is anyone here?" His voice echoed through the large, eerie building, followed by silence. "I'm getting a bad feeling."

"I too."

Hearing a sliding metal door, they turned and saw the robot enter. "Welcome, welcome," it said. "Follow me, follow me."

"Where is everyone? Where are the people?" Matt asked the robot as they approached it.

"Follow me. Your ship component is this way."

"I hate robots," Matt grumbled. "If you want a straight answer, don't ask a robot." They trailed the robot through the door leading down a long hallway. Once they had passed the threshold, the door slammed shut, cutting them off from the ship.

Matt wheeled around and saw there wasn't a control panel to reopen it. Even more alarming were white scar marks on the metal door. "Those are laser blasts. Someone wanted to get back to their ship."

The robot had rolled farther down the hallway.

"Hey, come back here and open this door," Matt called to it.

A second door crashed down ahead, separating them from the robot and passage. Matt and Bloom found themselves trapped within a small room. Matt pulled out his lazer gun as Bloom threw off the robe, arched his wings, and withdrew the weapon from his sash.

Matt called to whoever might be listening, "Hey, guys, we seemed to have been cut off. Care to open these doors?"

Bloom sniffed the air and looked up at the vent in the ceiling. "A foul odor enters." He pointed upward.

"I don't smell a thing."

"You are not a harpy."

Matt staggered and leaned against a wall. "Bloom, I'm feeling dizzy. It must be gas." He fired his weapon at the door, scoring the metal with a fresh mark. He reeled and collapsed in Bloom's arms.

Bloom gently rested him on the floor and stood. "You shall regret taking us." He wobbled and fell beside Matt.

"Damn, I fucked up, Bloom," Matt muttered before passing out.

* * *

Alex curled up on a bunk, buried his face in feathers, and closed his eyes.

Summer anxiously paced back and forth between the bunks. "How can you sleep?" she snapped. "They have been gone too long and might be in trouble."

"I offered my protection, but apparently I'm not trustworthy," Alex muttered. "If they're in trouble, it's their fault."

Summer huffed. "There you go again, thinking only about yourself. When you needed help, Matt and Bloom came for you."

Alex sat up. "What do you want from me, Summer? I'm wrong when I offer to help and wrong if I don't."

"You could show some concern."

Alex left the bunk and stood before her. "All right, I'm up and concerned. Are you happy?"

Summer raised her hand to hush him. *Quiet, I hear voices outside,* she relayed into Alex's consciousness. *We speak like silent harpies now.* She tilted her head. *It is not Matt or Bloom.* She tiptoed into the cabin and peeked out a window for a view of the hangar.

Alex followed her. *Can you see them?*

No, I believe they are under the ship. Both knelt and placed their ears to the floor and heard a drill.

"Here's the damaged component, Father Rimes," said a deep voice. "No surprise, looking at the dents and scrapes on the fuselage. They must have had a rough landing. I can slap in the new part and don't need the pilot's help."

"Very good, my son," said a higher-pitched voice. "He can be taken to the sisters and be prepared for the sacrifice tonight."

"I better hustle then," said the deep voice. "I don't want to be late. It's been a while since the camp had fresh meat."

"Our prayers have been answered," said Rimes. "Others can remove the ship valuables while you work."

"On this piece of junk, I doubt they'll find anything worthwhile."

"You're wrong. The ship brought us the exotic winged beauty. I already contacted several sex traffickers on the red-light planets and have an interested buyer."

The deep voice chuckled. "I imagine they'll work his feathers off, but it is better than roasting, like his buddy." The voices faded.

Summer watched the robed men leave the hangar and frowned. *What kind of humans are these?*

Cannibals, Summer. They eat their own kind.

* * *

Matt woke with a severe headache, and his body ached from its awkward position. Trying to move, he found that his tethered wrists and legs had been pulled to his backside and bound together. Even more discomforting, he was nude and laying on a stone floor within a tiny cage. "What the hell," he said, and wiggled in his bonds. "Who took my damn clothes?"

"Matt, are you all right?" asked Bloom's soft voice.

Matt twisted his head. In the dim light, he saw Bloom in a nearby cage, also stripped of his sash and tied.

"I'm not hurt, but I'd hardly call this all right." He tussled, trying to free his hands.

"It is no use to struggle. I have used all my strength to break my bonds and failed."

"What do you think they'll do with us?" Matt asked.

"I woke like you and know nothing, but I do not believe their intentions are good."

"No shit," said Matt. "We should've brought the kid."

"Alex can control a mind," said Bloom, "but he cannot open doors or stop gas, proved when he could not escape the hospital. If he had come, he would be like us now."

"Maybe, but—" Matt hadn't finished his thought when a door opened and an overhead light came on. Three men in long robes entered. The older man wore red and Matt's leather boots. The others were in black. Matt's eyes widened when he saw they each had four arms. Accustomed to adapting to the strange in his travels, he forced a grin and asked, "Hey, fellas, since you have extras, could you give me a hand and untie these ropes?" None cracked a smile.

The older man bent over Matt's cage. "How old are you, boy?"

Matt hesitated. "I'm a…twenty-four."

"He is a perfect age, mature, but still lean and tender. Take him to the sisters."

"What about his tongue, Father Rimes?" asked a dark-robed man. "If they don't remove it, he'll be yelling profanities on the altar."

"Wait just a damn minute," said Matt. "What do you plan to do with me?"

Rimes paid no attention to Matt's question. "He can keep his tongue. When gutted, his screams will stimulate the hood and make the sacrifice more enticing."

"Sacrifice?" Matt shouted. "You can't be serious? You can't do that shit to me."

"Shut up," growled the dark-robed man, kicking Matt's back through the cage bars.

Matt groaned. "I hope you sick freaks burn in hell."

Rimes chuckled. "My darling boy, you are the freak who will burn."

"But why?" asked Matt. "I've done nothing to you."

"You are a man. That is enough reason, but you deserve an explanation. Scientists created us, believing a worker with four arms would be more efficient, but our mental makeup was also altered. Some of us became murderers. As a result, they scrapped the program, and we were rounded up and discarded on this hellish planet to mine for the two-arms. We revolted and for revenge, we sacrifice the two-armed humans and their flesh sustains us."

"And what of me?" asked Bloom.

"You are not a man and won't be slain, my feathered friend. The council and I have decided that because you also have six limbs, we hope your genetics matches ours for breeding. Once your sperm has been extracted, you'll be sold for sex. Many will pay a fortune to ravage your body."

"You and they shall die before I am touched," said Bloom.

Rimes grinned. "Gorgeous and aggressive, you'll be very popular." He nodded to his henchmen. "Take the man away."

The men wheeled the cage out of the room while Matt yelled, "Wait a minute, Rimes. Can't we talk about this?"

The men took Matt down a sloping hallway that branched into caves. Deep in the bowels of the planet, they entered a large cavern. They removed Matt from the cage and placed him face down on an iron table. Raising his head, he saw two robed women, one young, one old.

"Girls, do you really plan to eat me?" He chuckled nervously, hoping his boyish charm would save him.

"Gag the beast," the older woman said.

A man shoved a rag into Matt's mouth and fixed it in place. A chain that hung from the ceiling was strung through his bonds, and the two men hoisted him about a foot off the table. With his bowed spine and backward-stretched arms and legs, he experienced excruciating pain. He moaned, and his eyes stung from sweat and tears.

The four robed people sat down on a bench and watched him squirm. After about twenty minutes that seemed like an eternity, he quit moving, exhausted, and in agony with his arm joints on the verge of dislocation.

The old woman stepped to him, grabbed his hair, and jerked his head up. Staring into his drained eyes, she said, "Brothers, you can leave. He's finished and will be easy to handle."

After the men left, the two women went to work. The older woman turned to a cart alongside the table that held a battery with two wires attached to the posts. She taped one wire to Matt's sweaty ribs. Meanwhile, the young woman placed a bucket beneath Matt's penis.

"I like him," the young woman said. "He's very handsome."

"Sarah, don't get attached. He's food. And you're here to learn. Several steps must be taken when preparing a creature for slaughter." Using a glove, the old woman picked up the loose wire and touched the bare end to Matt's side. With the jolt of electricity, Matt jumped, twisted and shook.

"Come on, boy," the old woman said. "I don't have all night." This time she held the wire to his stomach, allowing the current to course through his entire body. For several long and excruciating minutes, he screamed into the gag. His stunned body constricted and became as stiff as a statue. Losing control of his bodily functions, he urinated in the bucket.

"That's a good boy, get it all out," the old woman said. When the flow ceased, she stopped shocking him.

Matt had never known such pain or been so scared in his life. His heart pounded, and he trembled and hyperventilated through his nose.

The old woman turned to the girl. "You understand why this was necessary?"

"So he doesn't piss on the altar."

"That's partly true, but a creature should never be gutted with a full bladder. When cut open, he'll wiggle and the sacrificial blade might pierce his bladder. The urine will saturate the flesh and ruin it."

"I see," the girl said, and removed the bucket.

The old woman pushed the battery cart aside. Running her hand down Matt's arm, she shook her head. "The trouble with these young males is they're strong and recover quickly. Right now, he's too tense. Feel his muscles."

The girl ran her hand down Matt's arm. "He's rock solid."

"Yes, and tight muscles and adrenalin before death will cause his meat to be tough. He should be relaxed and weak. I'll have to drain him to make him docile as a lamb."

Distracted and in pain, Matt paid no attention to the women, but when the woman injected a large needle in his arm, his eyes flashed open. Through the syringe, his blood flowed down a tube and into a large jar. Panicked, he tossed on the chain and huffed with terror. He pleaded to the girl with his watery eyes but was ignored.

Before long he felt light-headed and was too tired to move. Cracking open his eyes, he saw the jar was full of his blood. The woman pushed the battery alongside the table and hit him with a round of shocks. Matt whimpered and could barely flinch.

"All his fight and resistance is gone," said the old woman. She removed the syringe and applied a bandage to stop the bleeding. "We can bathe and oil him down now."

"He looks dead."

"He's anemic and has just enough blood to keep his heart and brain functioning. When they're young and handsome like this one, Father Rimes will probably prolong the sacrifice and castrate him. Father enjoys seeing their reaction, watching their sex organs cook."

The girl petted Matt's damp hair. "That sounds so cruel."

"Life is cruel. Look where we live."

The women bathed Matt with warm soapy water and then rubbed him down with herb smelling oil. "Go tell the brothers he's ready."

The henchmen returned, unhooked the chain, and lowered Matt onto the table. Grabbing his arms and legs, they carried him through the many tunnels. They eventually arrived at an expansive auditorium containing hundreds of people. Cheers and laughter filled the air when they paraded him among the crowd. Bound, nude, and frail, he was spanked, slapped, and groped. By the time he reached the raised platform and altar, he was emasculated to tears and ready to die.

He was placed on a stone altar with a view of the mob. To his left was a spit turning slowly over a pit of smoldering lava rocks. To his right, ten men stood in red robes.

Father Rimes approached the altar and raised his four arms. The room grew silent. "Let us give thanks to the gods for this fine young specimen that shall nourish our bodies and deserving souls."

A low, monkish chant rose from the crowd and echoed throughout the auditorium. The henchmen removed Matt's gag, bonds, and rolled him onto his back. Though too anemic to resist, his arms and legs were tied down to expose his chest, stomach, and sex. The chant became louder and bloodcurdling intense. He shuddered and breathed deeply, knowing his death would soon satisfy a deranged, evil cult. He closed his eyes, resigned to his fate and thought about Summer and the life they might have had.

CHAPTER SIXTEEN

"Release him," shouted a voice from the back of the auditorium. The eerie chanting diminished to whispers, and the crowd switched its attention from the altar to the speaker. "Release him, I said."

Matt opened his eyes and saw the audience part, allowing a blond head to advance through them.

Father Rimes, holding the sacrificial knife over Matt, yelled, "How dare you interrupt the ceremony. Who are you?"

"Alexander."

Matt smiled.

When Alex came into full view, Rimes hollered to his henchmen. "He has wings like the other one and must have come off the ship. Seize him before he flies out of reach."

The men pulled their blasters from under their robes, leaped off the stage, and raced to the harpy. Alex stood calmly with folded wings. With his subtle glance, he halted the advancing men who dropped their weapons and froze. Alex strolled towards the altar through the crowd as the people lowered their heads in reverence and moved aside, giving him a wide berth.

Matt watched in astonishment. Summer had told him about Alex's incredible powers, but he now witnessed them firsthand. It was hard to believe that the slight, blond male could command such authority.

Rimes whirled around to his red-robed councilmen in red robes and asked anxiously, "What…what is going on? What is wrong with everyone?"

Matt said weakly, "You're so screwed."

With a flutter of flashing wings, Alex was on the raised platform. The men, who had restrained Matt, stumbled away from him, and Rimes huddled among his council.

Alex stepped to the altar and Matt. "Are you okay?"

"I am now. Seeing you, I've never been more relieved."

Alex shook his head. "I should've insisted on going with you and Bloom, but my stubborn pride got in the way. I'm sorry."

"I wanted you on the ship," Matt breathed. "That was the worst decision of my life." Managing to lift his head, he watched Summer and Bloom fly over the crowd and land beside him. "Oh, doll, I thought I'd never see you again," he said with tears flowing.

Summer hugged him and sniffled. "My sweet Matt, they hurt you, hurt you badly."

Bloom snatched a banner off the platform and draped it over Matt's naked body. "We could not find you. We searched, but there were too many tunnels. Then we learned they would bring you here."

"Can you walk, Matt?" Summer asked.

"I don't think so. The suckers electrocuted me and drained my blood."

"I shall carry you," Bloom said.

Alex had heard enough and stepped away. He flung the hair from his eyes and arched his wings, confronting Rimes and his council. "You tortured my friend and should die."

"No, Alex," Bloom said, stepping beside him. "That is not the harpy way. Their deaths shall only haunt you."

"Bullshit," Matt growled. "Kill 'em, Alex. Make the twisted fuckers walk outside and commit suicide like the cops on Oden. The bastards planned to castrate me. Do it, Alex."

Alex thumbed his chin and looked to Summer. "What should I do? What would our father do?"

"I don't know," Summer said. "Father killed evil men but forgave others. But surely not everyone here deserves to die."

"Yes, they do, Summer," said Matt. "They're all guilty."

"You must now choose to be a harpy or man," said Bloom. "Do you have a vengeance of a human or the compassion of a harpy? These people are bad, but it is not your place to judge and punish."

"If I don't judge, who will?" Alex asked.

"No one," said Matt. "There is no law out here. These bastards have hijacked ships and slaughtered the crews for decades. You can end it."

Alex looked at Matt, then Bloom. "Go back to the ship. I'll come later."

Matt pointed at Rimes as Bloom lifted him off the altar. "That fucker is wearing my boots. I want them."

Rimes quickly removed the boots, and Summer picked them up. She followed Bloom as he carried Matt down the steps, through the humbled crowd, and out of the auditorium.

In the long corridors leading to the hangar, Matt said, "I hope Alex kills all those pricks."

"I sense the terror and suffering you endured," said Bloom. "Great fear turns into anger. I understand how you feel, Matt. But Alex should spare those people—not for their sake, but for his own. His decision this night determines who he is."

* * *

Alex stepped to the edge of the platform and gazed out at the silent crowd. "Do you feel me?" he asked. "I am deep within your minds and sense the poison that has grown. Many of you are followers, too ignorant to question the horrors. Others knew better but went along out of fear." He turned toward Rimes and the red-robed men. "And then there are these, pure evil and lusting for blood and power. They brainwashed you and turned you into a murdering cult."

Alex spread his wings, tilted his head back, and closed his eyes. Using hypnosis and his telepathic powers, he penetrated the psyche of every soul. “Embrace me. I remove the vile, the delusions, and give you back your humanity.” He opened his eyes. “Now see clearly and judge yourselves.”

With gaping mouths and shocked, wide eyes, the stunned crowd realized their ghastly transgressions. A woman cried out, “Father Rimes and the council turned us into monsters!” Many rumbled in agreement, and their voices grew louder.

“Be calm, my children,” Rimes cried frantically. “The sacrifices were necessary. The four-armed hood had to be protected and kept secret from trespassers.”

“That’s a lie,” yelled a man. “The crews on those ships were not a threat.”

Alex descended the stairs and walked toward the hallway. The people now became a livid mob. Men shouted and shoved their way to the stage. Rimes pleaded, trying to calm them.

Alex reached the hallway and looked back. Several men threw the council men from the stage and into the hordes. Their hysterical screams rang out as they were beaten to death. Rimes backed away and, still holding the sacrificial knife, cut his throat and collapsed. The sound of laser blasts and wild shrieks and wails filled the auditorium as the enraged mob attacked the henchmen and anyone deemed guilty.

Alex turned away and continued down the hall, not troubled or pleased. His form of justice could only be described as tolerable.

“Wait,” cried a woman as she and two others ran to him. Dropping on the floor, they huddled at his feet. “Please stay with us,” she said, looking back at the chaotic auditorium. “Our leaders are dead. We need you.”

“I have opened your eyes and given you choice and reason. It is now up to you. You can become decent human beings and live in peace or continue your sick, murderous way. Either way, it no longer concerns me."

"But you have the power to help us. We'll do anything for you."

Alex stepped out of their grasping hands. "There is nothing you can do that I want." He proceeded down the corridor. He strolled into the hangar and approached the three unconscious men lying beneath Matt's ship. When he and Summer left the hangar to find Matt and Bloom, he had followed Summer's wishes and placed the men in a cataleptic state rather than harm or kill them.

"Wake," he said to the men. The men opened their eyes, coming out of the trance. "You will go to the controls and open the hangar door, allowing our ship to leave. Is that understood?"

The terrified men nodded and scurried from the hangar. For a moment, he stood on the ship ramp and considered that these humans feared, respected, and even worshiped him like a god, but his harpy shipmates disapproved of him. He took a deep breath and went aboard.

In the cabin he found Matt resting on the couch with his head in Summer's lap as Bloom gave him a sip of water. Every eye focused on him and questioned what he had done to the planet inhabitants.

"We can go now," Alex said.

Summer said. "We heard laser blasts and screams on our way to the ship. You killed everyone, didn't you?"

Alex crossed his arms, offended that she thought the worst of him. But he was too proud to justify himself and explain his actions. "Believe what you want, Summer. Just keep in mind that you asked me to save your boyfriend, and I did."

Matt leaned forward. "Alex, I've got to know. What happened to that bastard Rimes?"

"He's dead," said Alex.

"Good," Matt said with a grin.

Bloom hung his head, and his fleeting glance conveyed disappointment. Summer's harsh stare made Alex flinch and look away. As when he had killed the Oden cops, he felt the harpies' distain. He ruffled his feathers and changed the subject. "The propulsion component is fixed, and those bozos will open the hangar door for the ship. The question is, can Matt pilot it?"

Matt managed to sit up. "Unsure, I'm still dizzy. I'd hate to pass out on liftoff."

"I'll do it, then," Alex said. "I wasn't bragging about my knowledge of the ship."

Matt chuckled lightly. "Alexander, I'm starting to believe you can do anything. Put me in the co-pilot seat and I'll help you if I can."

"Maybe we should wait until Matt recovers," Summer said.

"No way," Matt said, struggling to rise. "I'll recover when we're off this shithole. The kid says he can handle the ship, and I believe him. Let's do it, Alex." With Bloom's help, Matt entered the cockpit and took the co-pilot seat.

Alex secured the latch on the ship door for takeoff. He lifted his wings when sitting down in the pilot seat. Gazing at the controls, he recalled everything in the manual he had read when bored. He flipped a series of switches, and the engines fired up. He glanced at Matt.

"Yep, you got it," Matt said, smiling. "You really are a smart son-of-a-bitch."

"I've been called many things but never stupid." Alex hit a lever, and the ship lifted from the ground and rotated to face the open hangar door. He then guided *Dream Weaver* outside.

"Good, you're doing great, Alex," Matt said, and looked up at Bloom and Summer. "You'd better go back and strap in. We're about to blast off."

Alex steered the ship a short distance across the scorched black surface. Nosing the ship skyward, he said, "Here we go." He punched in the throttle that pushed the thrusters to full power. With a deafening roar and violent shaking, the ship fought gravity and lifted off. A few minutes later, they left the atmosphere. He shut down the thrusters and leveled the flight. Turning on the space scanner to set a course for the wormhole, he tapped the screen. "I assume this where we're going."

"Yeah, put her on a two-nine heading," Matt said, pointing at a gauge. He unfastened his seatbelt and turned to Alex. "There's something I got to say. Throughout this voyage, I've treated you like an arrogant, spoiled brat, but I've been totally wrong. When you walked through that mob, took control, and saved me from those lunatics, it was nothing short of miraculous. And now with no training, you handled this ship like an expert. Alex, you blow me away."

Alex produced a little smile. "Well, you weren't wrong. I am a brat, but working on it."

Matt chuckled. "I guess I'm trying to say you've impressed me. You're brilliant, gifted, and I'm lucky to call you a friend."

"Thanks, Matt." He glanced back into the cabin. "I wish others felt the same."

Matt patted his shoulder. "Don't worry about it, kid. Those harpies will come around."

"But I do worry."

* * *

Summer sat on the edge of Matt's bunk as he slept. She gazed at the rope burns on his wrists and ankles—injuries similar to her father's scars when long ago he too was captured and tortured. She was glad Alex had killed the cruel miners who had done this to Matt, but her brother had condemned everyone. Surely, some were innocent, like the dead policemen on Oden. Alex's lack of empathy was disturbing.

Matt opened his eyes and whispered, "How long have I been out?"

"Several days. You were so pale and ill that you needed sleep to heal and regain your strength."

"Several days…" Matt lifted his head. "That means we should be near the wormhole. I gotta get up. To navigate that hole's twists isn't easy. One mistake and we'll hit the outer debris."

"Alex can handle it. He is good at some things."

Matt climbed off the bunk and grabbed his jeans. "Summer, you need to give that kid a break. He can't help that humans raised him, but he's trying hard to fit in with you guys."

"He rescued you, so it's understandable why you admire him, but Bloom and I criticize him for good reason. Soon he will be on Dora, and the entire flock will condemn his selfish nature. He will suffer less if he changes now."

"I suppose you got a point," Matt said, putting on a shirt. "I just feel sorry for him. I better make sure he has the right coordinates."

She followed Matt into the cabin where Bloom rested on the couch, eating nuts. Alex was curled up in the stuffed chair and was reading a pamphlet.

Alex looked up and smiled. "Glad to see you, Matt."

Out a port window, Matt saw the white and yellow clouds flying past. "Jesus Christ!" he exclaimed. "We're already in the damn wormhole."

"Wasn't that the plan?" said Alex.

"Shit, Alex, you should have woke me up so I could check your coordinates before we entered," Matt growled, hurrying through the cabin. "Charting a course in this narrow bastard takes precision and knowhow." He disappeared in the cockpit.

"He's feeling better," Alex commented and resumed his reading.

"But he is not the same man," Summer said dismally. "Those men broke his spirit."

"Yes," said Bloom, "but his suffering and near death taught him what truly matters. Matt shall never roam and leave you, Summer. He shall love you all his life."

Alex looked up with a sneer. "How could you know that?"

"You can peer into minds," Bloom said, "but you cannot know hearts until you open your own."

"Whatever."

Matt returned to the cabin, scratching his head. “Umm, yeah, we’re right on course. The autopilot is perfectly charted through the wormhole. You can’t learn that in a manual, so how’d you do it, Alex?”

“I studied the procedure and star map on the computer.”

“You studied it?” Matt questioned. “That’s a hell of a lot of grasping to comprehend.”

“For a normal person, it would be,” Alex said. “But my fanatical mother had me tested. Turns out I have a photographic memory and never make mistakes with machines. I only screw up with people and harpies.”

CHAPTER SEVENTEEN

In his customary spot on the couch, Bloom dozed with his black wings covering his coiled body as the ship sped through the narrow wormhole toward Dora. Nearby, Alex preened a wing in the large stuffed chair that Jim had once occupied. Bloom missed the man and wondered if he had survived his wound on Oden. He opened his eyes, hearing Summer snip at her brother.

"Alex, you're doing it wrong," she said, standing over him. "Lick your fingers and then force the oil from the quill down the shaft. Your feathers will be cleaner and healthier."

Alex elevated his head. "Unlike you, I didn't have a harpy to teach me these things and had to rely on instinct, but my feathers are fine. They have nearly grown back to full length."

"I'm trying to teach you now, but you are too stubborn to learn."

"Little sister, it would take a millennium for you to learn what I know."

Bloom sighed. Throughout the voyage, Alex and Summer were at odds, every discussion turned into bickering. Perhaps, they argued because they were siblings, the same immature age, and were born with combative golden natures. The confinement in the small space for a long time added to their stress. But the murdered Oden policemen and now the miners were the main contention. Summer was angry and frustrated with Alex's refusal to discuss what he'd done to the miners. Blocking his mind from her, he prevented her from using her telepathy to learn the outcome. Despite their quarreling, Bloom believed they cared about one another.

"You might be smart about the human world," she said, "but know nothing about harpies."

Matt, who had become the referee, closed his computer with a sigh and rose from the booth. "Will you two knock it off? Jesus, you're arguing over feather maintenance and giving me and Bloom a headache. When we're back on Dora, Alex will learn this stuff from his family."

"With his attitude, my family will have nothing to do with him," said Summer.

"That's nothing new to me, Summer," Alex said. "My mother didn't want to be around me. Actually, I'm glad she thinks I'm dead. I hope she's suffering."

Summer launched back. "My family cares about me and doesn't deserve to mourn my death. My poor grandmother let me stay on this ship and is probably sick with regret. Please, Matt, we must contact Dora and let them know we survived."

"Doll, we already talked about this," Matt said. "A com call can be traced. If we give ourselves away, we'll be screwed."

"Matt is right," said Alex. "An intergalactic call is foolish."

"Of course, you two agree," Summer griped. "You're buddies, and neither has a concerned, loving family. It's different for me and Bloom. Our families are in anguish, and terrible grief can turn to despair with harpies." She sat down beside Bloom and sniffled.

"Hush now," Bloom said and cloaked her with his wing. "I too worry that my mates and fledglings suffer my loss, but we have traveled far, risked much, and lost friends. We must remain cautious until the journey ends, or consider we had done all for nothing." He lifted her chin. "Summer, you must imagine their great joy when seeing us alive."

With a nod, Summer wiped her moist eyes. "Matt, it was cruel to say that you and Alex never had a loving family. I'm sorry."

Matt shrugged. "Hey, we play the hand we're dealt, but I like to look on the bright side. We'll soon be part of your family. You and I will be married, and Alex will blend right in with his brothers and sisters."

Alex lifted a skeptical eyebrow. "I have my doubts about blending in. But tell me about our harpy family, Summer. You mentioned our grandmother, and Mollie told me she's the harpy ruler. I'm wondering why a helpless, old female governs the flocks when a male is more capable."

Summer jumped up with arched wings and stood over Alex slouched in the chair. "How dare you say my grandmother is old and helpless? Stand up, you sorry-excuse of a harpy, and I'll show you the capabilities of a female."

"Boy, you've pushed her buttons now," said Matt.

As Alex started to rise, Bloom hastily left the couch and stepped between the golden harpies before their clash of words turned physical. "That is enough! You are royal golden harpies. Show some dignity. Summer, this is not the time or place to challenge him to a fight." He turned to the young male. "And, Alex, our queen is beautiful, strong, and wise. All harpies respect and cherish her. You need to rethink your words."

"Okay, okay," Alex said, raising his palms in surrender. "I apologize, didn't mean to insult Grandma."

Reluctantly, Summer lowered her wings and stepped away, but continued to glare at Alex.

Bloom breathed with relief that Summer's attack was postponed for now. Although Alex was far bigger, she would've taken down the city-raised male with no combat experience. If Alex had lifted a wing in opposition, she might have seriously hurt him.

"Kid, you're lucky," Matt said. "I saw your sister locked horns with four big guys in a bar, and she knocked their lights out. Bloom just saved your hide."

"Of course she'd have whipped me," Alex said. "I'd never strike a female." He turned to Bloom, who had returned to the couch. "I'm still curious as to how my grandmother came to rule when I've read that a golden male has always led the flocks."

"That is true," said Bloom. "Windy is our first female monarch. Her only son, your father, Shail, was the last of the golden males and reigned before her. Those were terrible years. Hunters had invaded our jungle and were slaying our males. They captured and tortured Shail. When peace finally came, he had lost the will to lead and asked his mother to take his place until one of his sons came of age and could rule. That time soon comes. Shail's offspring approach maturity."

Alex stroked his jaw. "My father has eight sons, so one of us will reign."

Summer laughed. "Alex, you're not even a consideration. You're more human than harpy and fall way short of a ruler. Besides, my older brother, Will, is the next monarch."

"Who chose him?" Alex asked.

"Everyone," said Summer. "He is the best male harpy on Dora and has no rivals."

"But I'm not on Dora yet," said Alex. "Maybe this brother needs some competition."

"You? Competition?" Summer giggled. "You are not in his class."

Alex frowned and turned to Bloom. "What happens if two golden males want to rule?"

"As I said, Shail was only golden male and had no opposition. The last flock gathering to choose a monarch was during your grandfather's time when many golden males filled the trees. They took part in challenges that proved their speed, strength, bravery, wisdom but mostly their honor. The flock elders chose the winner of each challenge. At the end of three lights, the two remaining males fought for dominance, the animal way. I have heard some males died in these battles. Brown-wing harpies lack the aggression to dominate others, but golden harpies are a breed apart. That is why they have always ruled."

"What would I have to do in these challenges?"

"I do not know. Only the elders are aware of such things. But you could not use your powerful telepathy against Will or any harpy. The flocks would disapprove, and without it, you have no chance of winning."

Alex stood and flexed his wings. "We'll see."

"Alex, to ponder this challenge is unwise," Bloom said. "I do not wish to see you crippled or killed. You are a stranger to the harpies and their ways. Grow, learn, and become a real harpy. This should be your goal."

"My goals are higher," said Alex.

"You are confident and smart, but that is not enough to beat Will," said Bloom. "I saw him fight at a harpy gathering. He was only half-grown, but challenged many big teenagers twice his size. He struck like a yellow flash of lightning and overwhelmed them. One teen had a broken arm and another, a fractured wing. Will is fully mature now and undefeatable."

"Stop discouraging him, Bloom," said Summer. "If he challenges Will, Alex will learn humility."

"I will learn nothing from him," Alex growled. "Will is an ignorant barbarian who lives in the trees and hardly my equal. I look forward to meeting him."

* * *

Over the coming weeks of the voyage, Alex was consumed with the challenge for rule and questioned Bloom about it daily. At first the black-winged harpy tried to dissuade him from competing but finally settled for explaining how males fought one another.

Summer found it amusing that he even considered opposing Will. A huge fan of her oldest brother, she asserted that Will would be the perfect, noble ruler. He loved the jungle, its creatures, and the harpies and would sacrifice his life to save them. Unlike Alex, Will was compassionate, honorable, and wise, as well as the fiercest male on the planet. While praising Will, she ridiculed Alex for being uncaring, self-centered, and deceitful. His human upbringing had left him damaged and a heartless killer.

The more Summer talked, the more Alex despised Will and became committed to his goal. Oddly, he didn't crave power or fame. He wanted what Will had always had, something that had eluded him his entire life. He longed for love, respect, and happiness. When he reigned, all this would be his.

* * *

In Terrance, Will stood on the airport landing strip and braced his wing-wrapped body against the gale winds and heavy rain. It was the height of the Dora wet season. Flinging his long, drenched hair out of his eyes, he gazed at the black sky as thunder rumbled across the distant tree canopy. Over the howling gusts, he heard the hum of an approaching hovercraft and felt relieved. They had made it through the storm.

Ted's red hovercraft appeared out of the dark clouds and descended on the strip, not far from the airport building. Rather than fly against the wind, Will walked to the craft. The doors opened, and Ted and Will's mother stepped out.

"What nasty weather," Ted shouted. "I hate flying at this time of year."

"Thank you for bringing my mother," said Will as he embraced and covered her with a wing.

"Heck, I'd do anything for Kari," Ted responded. "You harpies don't mind rain, but I'm heading in. I'll see you inside." The man raced across the puddle lot and disappeared in the building.

Kari clutched her hooded cloak and asked, "How is she?"

"Not good, her depression grows worse, and she stays mostly in bed. Grandma is afraid she will never see Jim again."

Discussing these matters in private, they strolled slowly to the building. "On the trip here Ted updated me that Jim survived the gunshot wound and is recovering in a prison hospital. He's been arraigned for the murder of the policemen, but a trial date hasn't been set."

"Yes, that is all we know. Grandmother fears he will die in prison. Mother, I must seek news, but am afraid to leave her alone with Freely." He smiled slightly. "He is the toughest of brown males, but acts like a pet that never leaves her side. I never realized how much he loved her."

"Everyone loves Windy, but you were right to send Ted to fetch me. I know too well how it feels to wonder and worry if I'd ever see my mate again. I'll take care of her."

They stepped inside, and the little airport was empty of passengers and employees. Due to the severe weather, all flights were canceled.

"Do you want some coffee, Kari?" Ted asked.

"Thank you, Ted, but I better go straight to my mother-in-law's house."

"And I must leave for Hampton immediately," said Will. "I only waited for you to arrive."

Ted put down the coffeepot. "You can't be serious about flying across country in this storm? The East is getting slammed with hurricane winds and small tornados, and this front is heading our way. You'll be fighting a dangerous headwind. Wait till it blows over."

"I cannot wait. Sam Waters expects my arrival. He can tell me how to help Jim."

Kari stepped to a rain-pelted window. Outside, a thrashing tree battered the roof and was on the verge of being uprooted. She turned to Will. "Even the bravest harpy wouldn't fly now. Can't you call Waters?"

"A com call holds more risk than a flight."

"Not sure about that, but a call is dangerous," Ted said. "Federal agents have been snooping around Terrance, asking about Jim and his trip with harpies to Oden. They're monitoring incoming and outgoing calls. Jim's mission shouldn't be discussed over the airways."

Will kissed her forehead. "I'll be all right, mother. Ted can drive you to Grandmother's home."

Ted smiled. "I'll be glad to. I just need to let my wife know I'm back. I'm sure she's worried."

Kari hugged Will. "Please be careful and I'm not only concerned about the weather. Most people in the East have never seen a harpy, and you'll be treated like an oddity. But the criminals there will see you as beautiful, valuable creature to be captured and sold off-planet. Keep your guard up and don't trust anyone."

"You're afraid I might end up like Father."

"Will, you were never told the worst of his captivity. It would terrify a youngster, but you are now grown and should know. Shail was not only abused, but men brutally raped him. He never recovered, and that is why his mind is damaged."

Will was filled with outrage. "What happened to those who did this?"

"Shail killed them." She hesitated. "Should I have told you?"

"Yes. I understand Father better and his suffering. Most harpies would curl up and die from such cruelty. He truly is the strongest of us."

"He was," Kari said sadly. "His memory loss is upsetting, but it probably has kept him alive." With a forced smile, she changed the subject. "When you get to Hampton, tell Sam I said hello. When he was the Dora governor and your father ruled the flocks, they worked together and were the best of friends."

"I have heard this from Grandma," said Will. "Waters has never met me, but I hope with his knowledge of laws, he can help Jim."

"Actually, Sam has seen you. He visited the Outback when you were a few days old. Then we were captured and shipped to Earth. Do you remember any of it?"

Will stared at the floor, hesitant to disclose an inner torment. "I sometimes dream of it, Mom. It's night and I'm in a tiny cage and cold. A man takes me out and holds me by my wing. It hurts and I call out into a dry, barren land for Father. He comes and tells me he loves me. The cold and pain end, but Dad is gone. I wake with pangs of guilt. My pleas caused his downfall. I should have been braver."

Kari slowly shook her head. "I hoped you had forgotten that incident in the desert. But, Will, you were not even two years old, and all baby harpies call for their fathers when hurt and frightened. It was Shail's duty to protect his son. The blame lies with those heartless men."

"Perhaps, but bad memories that come in dreams cannot be stopped. Maybe I am a little like Dad. We share emotional scars." Will kissed her forehead. "I must go, Mother." He walked outside and spread his wings. With a leap, he flew into the ominous sky.

Through the afternoon, Will fought the thunderstorm, hammered with the torrential rain and intense gusts. Unable to glide, he constantly beat his wings to avoid being tossed around like a leaf. He lowered his head so his locks protected his eyes from the stinging droplets. The sun disappeared, but pressed for time, he flew on in darkness. Lightning brightened the landscape and kept him on course.

Halfway through the night, he gave up. He was making little progress battling the powerful eastern wind, and his taxed wing muscles burned with shooting pain. Drenched, shivering, and exhausted, he decided to wait out the storm. He soared down and landed in the closest tree. Curled up on a small limb, he covered himself with his warm, waterproof feathers. The rumbling thunder and swaying tree rocked him quickly to sleep.

In the morning he woke to the sound of a man's voice. He jerked his head up from the feathers and looked below. A man standing under the tree grumbled, "What a mess. We'll be cleaning up limbs for months." Gazing upward, he spied Will and muttered, "Son of a gun, a harpy." He yelled to his partner, "Roy, get over here. There's a little male harpy in this tree."

A second man soon joined him. "I'll be damned," Roy said. "I've seen pictures, but never a live one because they don't leave the Outback. I bet this one was blown off course in last night's storm."

Will looked at the overcast sky and was satisfied the rain and wind had let up. He could resume his journey. but where was he? The surrounding landscape surprised him. The jungle was gone, and for miles, the rolling hills held rows of fruit trees. So dark he didn't realize he had bedded down on a huge human farm.

"What's the matter, little guy?" asked one. "Are you lost?"

Will was annoyed with the *little* references as he was taller than either men, but he was slender, half the mass of a large man, and that probably accounted for the comments. He stood and ruffled his feathers to dry them.

"Jesus, Larry, he's got yellow wings. He's a golden harpy," said Roy. "They're rare but dangerous. I read they've killed people."

Will fluttered down to the ground, and the two men backed away. Roy grabbed a fruit-picking pole and held it defensively.

Will tilted his head. "I am dangerous to those who would harm me."

"He…he talks," said Larry. "I heard they couldn't talk."

"We can but avoid speaking to humans," Will said. "You asked if I was lost. How far is Hampton?"

Roy lowered the pole. "That city is a long way off." He pointed to the rising sun. "Best to travel south and pick up the highway. It takes you right into Hampton."

"Thank you," Will said. He picked up a fallen fruit off the ground. "If you don't mind, I will take this for breakfast."

"Take all you want. It's just going to rot," said Roy. "Mr. Harpy, it's been a real pleasure meeting you."

"Yeah, same here," said Larry. "My wife will never believe me. Wish I had a camera."

Will gave them a nod, and with a bound, was in the air and winging south. By mid-morning, the grey clouds had given way to a clear greenish-blue sky. He increased his speed to make up for lost time and only glided when totally spent. Reaching the highway he felt distressed with the lack of forest. There was no place to hide. He soared over the patchwork of cattle pastures, vegetable farms, and orchards, all dotted with dwellings. Sad and angry, he thought about the beautiful jungle trees and wildlife that had once dwelled here. Man's selfishness to destroy nature for his needs was perplexing.

That afternoon Will searched for a quiet place to land and drink. The populated road offered little opportunity to slip in and out undetected. He wasn't afraid of humans, but they were aggravating. His brief encounter with the two fruit pickers proved his mother had been right. The Easterners perceived him as a wild jungle creature, more animal than human. Only when he spoke did they realize he was an intelligent mortal.

Even in Terrance, humans clamored around the winged-male harpies. To avoid harassment, he stayed out of cities. "Soon I shall rule and must walk among them," he thought. His father had ended his reign because of the human cruelty but also because he was done facing them. Will related.

Up ahead in a small off-road park, he saw clusters of trees and a stream. People milled around their campsites and parked vehicles. Licking his parched lips, he decided to stop and chance it. He zeroed in on the stream, fluttered, and landed in the knee-deep water. Bending over, he sucked up the cool water and tried to ignore the excited voices that soon surrounded him.

"It's a harpy! A harpy landed in the stream," the people yelled, racing to him.

Rather than engage them, Will played the part of a mute, dumb animal that was so thirsty it risked going among humans for a drink. He kept his wings slightly arched for fast flight or fight, but quickly sensed that these people were harmless. They giggled, gawked, and talked about his appearance. After drinking his fill, he straightened, and with the back of his wrist, he wiped the dripping water from his mouth. He shook back his hair, still panted slightly from the flight and gazed at the crowd.

A little girl approached the edge of the stream, holding out a round red fruit. “Here, boy, come get the apple. Come on, boy.” A heavyset woman stood behind her.

“Jane, get our kid away from that thing,” barked a skinny man. “You don’t know what it might do.”

“He’s okay,” said the woman. “He’s only thirsty and won’t harm her. I can’t get over his incredible blue eyes and gorgeous long body.”

The little girl gave up coaxing Will to her and tossed him the apple.

Curious about the strange fruit that bobbed before him, Will picked it up and sniffed it. But he suddenly got goose bumps, sensing a threat. His ears twitched under his locks, and he focused on the whispers of two men who stood under trees, out of earshot from the others.

“That is one handsome buck, and brazen, typical of a golden,” said a low, coarse voice. “He should fetch three million on the black market. Nabbing him will save us the trip to the Outback.”

“Yeah, but how are we going to get him?” asked the other man. “We can’t stun him in front of these campers.”

“I’ll go back to the truck for the rifle and bring him down when he flies out of the park.”

“I hate shooting one in flight. The fall might injure or kill him.”

“Don’t matter. His wings are worth a fortune.”

Will smiled inwardly, thinking about his mother's warning about the criminals. Besides stunning and intelligence, she had good judgment. No wonder his father had pursued her for his mate.

He had heard enough from the men. Forging the stream, he strolled toward the two scruffy hunters under the trees. The campers followed him. Standing before the hunters, he said, "Go ahead and fetch the rifle from your truck, but know that when you aim it at me, I will kill you. I believe humans call it self-defense."

Baffled, the hunters said nothing at first. Finally, one spoke, "You—you couldn't have heard us."

"Aww, you underestimate your prey," Will said. "Harpies can hear a slight bird chirp from miles away, and we sense danger. That is why we survived centuries of man's hunting."

The woman with the little girl stomped forward and raged at the men, "You planned to shoot him?"

"No, no, no," said the coarse-voiced hunter. "We don't have a rifle."

She nudged the skinny man. "James, go check their truck for a weapon. Firearms are illegal in a campground, and harming a harpy is a felony."

"Let's get out of here," said the other hunter.

Several men closed in and surrounded them. "You better stay put," one said. "The rangers will come and sort this out."

At the hunters' campsite, James held up a rifle and yelled, "They got a gun."

"You bastards," the woman growled at the two hunters. "You're going to prison."

The campers seemed to have the situation under control, so Will stepped to the little girl. To be eye level with her, he went down on one knee and held out the apple. "I have never eaten one of these, but thank you for it."

"It's really good. My grandfather brought the tree from Earth." Unable to contain her excitement, she grabbed his neck and kissed his cheek. “You’re the prettiest boy I’ve ever seen and have super wings.”

Her mother smiled. “She’s only seven, but I think she’s in love with you.”

He bit into the apple. “It is good.” He stood and patted the girl’s head. He turned toward the two hunters, longing to attack them, but this land fell under human law, not harpy. Compared to Will’s punishment, the hunters got off easy. He said goodbye to the woman and her child and resumed his trek.

Winging his way high above the road, he rehashed the incident in the campground and realized that a year ago he would not have been diplomatic or restrained his impulses and anger. He would have flown at the hunters and maimed or killed them. His mother and grandmother had noticed the change in him, saying he had mentally matured. Perhaps it was true. He was nearly ready to rule the flocks.

CHAPTER EIGHTEEN

Will flew a mile above the highway to avoid being seen and shot, learning from campground experience that East, unlike the Outback, held some corrupt humans. As an added precaution, he took up the old ways when harpies were hunted and only descended at night to drink, eat, and rest. Darkness was the ally of game animals. The trip that should have taken two days was going on three. The storm had blown him far north of the direct route.

The farther east he traveled, the more he saw human dwelling and activity. The two-lane highway had become four with an increase in traffic. He had heard about the human expansion from his stepmother, Rachel, who visited Hampton once a year to shop for things, unavailable in Terrance. She said that outposts and small villages had become towns, and town had grown into cities, and Hampton, the capital, was now a metropolis. Will wondered when enough was enough. Would the human invasion ever end?

Toward evening the dark horizon glowed with an eerie white dawn, but it was not from the sun. The cause was the gleaming lights from massive high-rises and giant spaceport. Another thirty miles and he would arrive in Hampton. He had learned that Sam Waters lived north of the city in a large pink house beside the ocean, but finding it in the dark among so many homes could prove difficult, and he hesitated to disturb the man at this late hour. He also needed to recoup and bath after the long, grueling trip. Wanting to make a good impression, he would meet Waters in the morning.

He reached the city and soared above the tall buildings swarming with hovercrafts. The streets were crowded with vehicles and people. He shuddered and flew on but found the ocean equally congested, its harbors containing all manner of boats, barges, and ships. He headed north along the coast to the quieter outskirts of the city. He glided down and followed a narrow strip of beach sandwiched between high cliffs and water. After a few miles, he spotted a place that could suit his needs. The small white cottage overlooked the ocean and was surrounded by fruit trees. Its front yard had a large vegetable garden, a pond, and a huge, moss-covered tree. The place was ideal for a tired harpy. Even in a land of concrete, plastic, and steel, this homeowner still appreciated nature.

He fluttered over the pond and looked, listened, and sniffed the air. Detecting no danger, he landed in the pond and collapsed in the soothing water, too tired to douse and preen his wings. He reflected on what he'd seen today. Humans were spreading like wildfire across the land, and more and more of them wanted to settle in the Outback, his homeland. His father and grandmother had permitted many to enter, but Will considered ending the practice when he ruled. For the good of the jungle, wildlife, and harpies, the human wave had to stop.

He ate a little fruit and settled in the big tree near the garden. In the last few days, he had only caught brief naps and was exhausted. Instead of coiling up under his feathers, he stretched out on the soft moss, letting his worn-out wings hang loose off the tree limb, and fell asleep.

* * *

Will normally woke at dawn but continued to doze after the strenuous flight. A few hours later he heard the cottage front door close. Folding his wings, he looked down at a middle-aged woman. She strolled into the garden and started raking around the tomatoes. A large white cat sat beside her, but when it spotted Will, it meowed and flicked its tail.

The woman glanced at the cat. "Max, if you kill one more bird, you're going." The woman posed no threat, so Will thought he would ask her for directions to Waters home. He stood and stretched his wings, unintentionally spooking the cat. It hissed and fled under the front porch.

The woman frowned at her hiding pet. "What is wrong with you today?"

Will sailed down from the tree and landed behind her. "I'm afraid I frightened him."

Glancing over her shoulder, the woman jumped and dropped the rake. "My Lord," she shrieked. "You scared me half to death."

"I'm sorry," Will said. "I will be careful not to scare you twice."

She shook her head and chuckled. "Sweetie, if you startle me again, I won't die. I'm aware that harpies take things literally," she said, picking up her rake. "So what is a handsome golden male doing here?"

He glanced back. "I slept in your tree last night. There was no place else."

"I meant what are you doing on the East Coast? With all this civilization and little vegetation, it has to be distressing for a jungle dweller."

"It is troubling, and I will be glad to leave, but first I must find Sam Waters. I was told his home is near here."

"If you mean the old governor, everyone knows where he lives. His big pink house is just a few miles north before the next curve in the road. You can't miss it."

"Yes, that is who I seek. Thank you." He spread his wings to fly.

"Hold on, young man. It's too early to drop in on him. Come up on my porch, and I'll feed you some coffee cake that I baked yesterday."

Will accepted the invitation and folded his wings. He was famished, and the cake would be a nice break from fruit and nuts. He followed her to the porch that held a small table, a few chairs, and a multitude of hanging and potted plants.

"No wonder the cat was having a fit." She laughed, leaning her rake against a post. "Max finally met his match, a bird big enough to eat him."

"We don't eat cats."

She smiled. "You are so darn cute. Now you wait here, and I'll be right back. I want to tell my daughter you're here. She'll be thrilled to meet a harpy."

The woman went inside, and Will heard her speaking about him. While waiting, he crouched near the porch steps and sniffled softly to the cat hiding below the deck. The cat meowed, came out, and purred when he stroked it.

The woman returned with the cake and a bowl of fruit. "I'll be. Max never takes to strangers."

"Harpies are not strangers to animals. They sense we will not harm them."

"My daughter also has a way with animals. She's studying to become a veterinarian." She placed the food on the table. "Well, hop up here and eat."

He stepped on the deck, and she handed him a slice a cake oozing with berry jam, which made his mouth water. He took a large bite when the door opened behind him.

"I thought he might also want some juice," said a girl's voice.

Looking over his wings, he saw her. She was his age with a petite frame, large blue eyes and her long blond hair was pulled back into a ponytail. Stunned with her beauty, he couldn't swallow the cake and began to choke and cough.

"Sherry, quick, hand him a drink," said the mother. "The poor dear is gagging."

With a sip of juice, he managed to get the food down but lost interest in eating. The sight of the girl had taken his breath away, and Will never lost his breath over anything. Further, his legs felt as flimsy as grass, and his feathers quivered with nervousness.

"Are you okay?" Sherry asked.

He nodded, too flustered to speak. He sucked up his wits and set the juice glass on the table, careful not to drop it.

Sherry grinned. "Mom said there was a harpy in our yard, but I didn't believe her."

"I am…I am a real harpy."

"Of course you are," Sherry said with a chuckle. "You're right, Mom. He is very cute."

The mother said, "Well, I'm Frances, and this is my daughter, Sherry."

"I am called Will."

Sherry extended her hand in the human greeting. "It's great to meet you, Will."

He clasped Sherry's hand and became even more rattled, sensing her. Hastily withdrawing from her touch, his elbow knocked a potted plant off the windowsill. The crash of pottery made him jump and whirl around, causing his wing to knock several plants off the railing. He leaped back, overturning the little table that sent juice, cake, and fruit flying. Bounding backward, he tripped on the woman's rake and fell with his flopping wings taking out more plants. Lying sprawled on his back with extended wings, amid broken pots, plants, soil, and smashed cake, he looked up, mortified.

"I am sorry. I'm so sorry." He scrambled to his feet and leaped off the porch before his jitters destroyed everything.

"It's all right, Will," said Frances. "Accidents happen."

"I must go." He glanced at Sherry, who covered her mouth and giggled. Losing face with his clown act, he extended his wings to flee.

"Will," Sherry said. "Please, come back and see me."

"I must meet a man but will return tonight."

* * *

Will flew up the coast above the beach road, searching for the large pink house. "Idiot," he cursed with each flap of his wings. So taken with Sherry, he had lost all grace and self-control. He recalled that his father once told him about his first meeting with his mother. "Kari called it 'love at first sight,' Shail had said. "It changes your life. Nothing matters except her. Someday you shall find the right female and understand." Will now understood.

Reaching the pink house, he landed in the front yard and ruffled his feathers, trying to regain composure and block Sherry from his mind. The door opened and a tall, silver-haired man appeared.

He grinned. "You have to be Will, Shail's son. You're the spitting image of your dad."

"I have been told this, Governor Waters."

"Call me Sam. We met when you were only a fledgling. Come in."

Will folded his wings and stepped to the door. Peering over the threshold, he noticed that the large home held many valuable and breakable things. "Thank you for seeing me, but could we speak outside?"

"Sure, I know harpies are claustrophobic. We'll go to the back veranda."

Will wasn't concerned with confinement like older harpies, terrified of being trapped under a roof, but he didn't want to repeat the cottage mishap. Embarrassed, he didn't explain his outdoor request.

They walked around to an expansive deck with a view of the ocean. A maid in a uniform brought out a large tray of arranged fruits, breads, and drinks and set it on a table. "Thanks, Diane," Waters said, sitting down in a large wicker chair. "Help yourself, Will."

Feeling at ease in the open space, Will picked a slice of bread. "I appreciate anything you can do to help Jim. My grandmother is very worried."

"I'm deep in debt to the harpies. Your father and his flock killed the beetle swarms and saved everyone on Dora, including my family. I'll do anything to help Windy, but wish she had contacted me when learning about this grandson locked in an Oden mental hospital. Rather than send Jim, I could have gotten him out legally. Though, it might have taken some time."

"You mentioned that harpies are claustrophobic. The grandson did not have much time. Before you had the courts free him, he would have died from despair. The rescue had to be done quickly. But rather than discuss what should have or could have been done, we should focus on the present."

"You're right, no sense crying over spilled milk," Waters said, and picked up one of the drinks. "Okay, I contacted Jim's lawyer on Oden, informing him I'd be co-counsel in the case. He sent me copies of the file and police reports. They've charged Jim with a long list of felonies, starting with breaking and entering, assault, kidnapping, but the worst is the second-degree murder charge for officers killed in the commission of a crime. The good news, the prosecutor will have difficulty making the murder charges stick. He has to prove *los ipsa laquatory*."

"Los ispa la..."

"It's Latin and means 'without any doubt and for no other reason' Alex's telepathy caused the officers to crash their hovercrafts. His doctor testified that Alex was capable of this, but he's dead, so there's no way to prove it. Without him, the murder case is weak." Waters sipped of his drink. "But they have a strong kidnapping case against Jim."

"How is it kidnapping when my brother wished to go? Jim only helped him?"

"It's irrelevant what Alex wanted. He was underage. His mother was his legal guardian and had the right to commit him. Two doctors agreed with her. If Alex had been eighteen, he could have requested a competency hearing. The doctors would have had to establish he was a danger to himself or others."

"I question the fairness of your laws with a harpy," said Will. "Lock up a harpy for even a minor misdeed and confinement kills them. How is this justice?"

"It's not. The problem is that the situation has never been addressed. Since harpies became citizens eighteen years ago, they haven't been charged with a crime."

Will walked to the porch railing and gazed at the ocean. "All this talk means nothing when I sense the bleakness in your mind. Jim cannot be saved."

Waters rose and stepped next to Will. "You not only look like Shail, but are intuitive, brutally honest and get straight to the point." He sighed. "Jim will most likely be convicted, and at his age, he'll die in prison."

"Without her mate, my grandmother will also die of depression."

Waters was visibly shaken. "Can't a doctor or drugs help her?"

"Harpies do not take drugs." Will shut his eyes and breathed in the ocean scent for a long moment. He turned to Waters. "Perhaps there is a way to save her and maybe Jim. She could travel to Oden with you and explain that the harpy depression is deadly for us. Jim had to free Alex to save his life."

"That's a great idea, Will. She's the harpy ruler, and a jury is apt to believe her. But we'd have to be careful she doesn't incriminate herself in the kidnapping."

"My grandmother does not care about that. If all fails, she can at least say goodbye to her husband and be at peace."

"I'll do everything in my power to win Jim's case. As soon as the courts set a trial date, I'll make arrangements for Windy and I to travel to Oden. We'll pray for the best."

"This is then the course we take."

"Yes," Waters said. "I used to have these same talks with Shail. We'd have a problem, figure it out, and resolve it. Most people don't know he was brilliant. I miss him."

"You loved him."

Waters chuckled. "No one has put it to me that way, but yes. I loved him. He's the noblest being I ever met. I understand you'll soon replace Windy and be the next harpy ruler. If you need a friend or help with laws, I'll be there for you. You're going to be a fine ruler."

"I'm not so sure. I have a temper and struggle to control it."

"So did your dad." Waters smiled. "When angry, that slender harpy put the fear of God into some big men. Still, Shail was fair and accomplished great things."

* * *

Will spent the rest of the day talking to Waters, at first about Jim's trial and Windy's trip to Oden. Then they discussed Will's forthcoming reign. He told Waters about his journey to Hampton and his disgust with the human sprawl. He didn't want it to happen in the Outback and planned to close the border to new humans. Waters advised him to go slowly, and for his first few years in power, to set limits on the number of people who could enter. An immediate border shutting down would harm the human economy and might be met with resistance.

At dusk Will bid Waters farewell, understanding why his father trusted this man. He was honest, caring, sensible, and encouraging. Will's thoughts shifted to Sherry and his promise to return tonight. His confidence had been restored, and he was ready to prove his worthiness to her. He sailed down into the dark yard.

A few lights burned inside the cottage. His approach, though, triggered the outside motion sensor lights on the porch. He flung the hair from his face, and with a wing shake smoothed his feathers while waiting for her on the lawn.

A minute later Sherry strolled out onto the deck, wearing a bathrobe. "I've been thinking about you all day."

"I know."

His earlier buffoon performance seemed to be forgotten. He stood before her, a poised young male seeking a mate and had earlier sensed her desires for him.

She left the porch and stepped to him. Caressing the feathers on top of his wings, she said, "They're so soft." She ran her hand over his bare shoulder and down his chest.

He didn't move, letting her inspect his body, but breathed hard when her hand reached his hip sash. She gazed into his eyes, lifted the cloth, and fondled him sexually. Immediately aroused, he was blinded with the urge to breed. He took her into his arms and passionately kissed her moist lips, then lowered her onto the grass while covering them under his quivering feathers.

"I want you," she gasped and bit his neck, further stimulating his sex drive.

He opened her robe, exposed her nude body, and suckled her breasts. Rubbing his erection against her, he hoped to make her receptive to his seed and create his baby. She parted her legs, her yearning matching his. So excited, he nearly exploded. But then, sensing that something was amiss, he withdrew and knelt before her. "Sherry, we must be clear about this. I am not a man who takes breeding lightly. I am a harpy. Once we bond you are mine and I am yours until our deaths."

She lifted her head, confused. "Will, I…"

The front door flew open, and Frances yelled from the deck. "What are you two doing?"

"I don't know." Sherry sat up, closing her robe. "I don't know what came over me," she said, standing. "I couldn't resist him."

"You nasty creature," Frances growled. "Are you seducing my daughter?"

"Yes," Will said, rising. "I wish her to be my mate."

"Mate?" Frances snarled. "Go back to your jungle and prey on your own kind."

"But she is my kind," Will said. "She is a harpy."

Both females stared at him in disbelief. "I'm not a harpy, Will," said Sherry. "I wasn't even born on Dora."

"A harpy knows another. I sensed and smelled you. You are like me." He turned to Frances. "You have kept the truth from her."

"Mom?" Sherry asked.

Frances wearily rubbed her forehead. "I should never have brought you back to this damn planet, but you were so adamant about going to school here and seeing the wildlife."

"Back?" Sherry questioned. "Was I here before?"

"You were born on Dora."

"Whether or not you wished it, Sherry would have returned to the jungle," Will said, stepping before the porch. "When mature, harpies, like some animals, are driven by strong instincts to seek their birthplace and raise their young."

"You think she's a harpy, and maybe she is," Frances said, "but I swear I didn't know."

"You did not know because you are not her birth mother," he said.

"Oh, Mom," said Sherry. "Is that true?"

France sank into a chair and nodded. "I always meant to tell you, but was afraid you'd stop loving me and leave."

Sherry hurried onto the porch and hugged her. "How could you think that? I will always love you, but if Will is right and I am a female harpy, I have to know about my parents."

Frances wiped her moist eyes. "Your parents…no, I need to go back to the beginning. In nursing school I learned I couldn't have children. Since having a family was out of the question, I sought a livelihood in space. I was on the first ship to reach Dora after the beetle swarms destroyed Hampton. The steel-domed port was the only building left, and it was transformed into a temporary hospital."

France turned to Will. "That's where I saw my first harpy. These magnificent beings had not only killed the swarms but brought jungle food to the people so they wouldn't starve. The place was in utter chaos. Every day they pulled injured survivors from the rubble, and as a nurse I treated them. Nearly a week after the disaster, two men dropped off a newborn baby girl—you, Sherry. They had found you fifty miles outside of Hampton in the ruins of a farmhouse. You were wrapped in a blanket and had been placed inside a filing cabinet to protect you from the swarms. The skeletal remains of your parents were nearby."

"You never found out who they were?" Sherry asked.

"Birth records, land deeds, all information was gone. I located one of the men who brought you in. Turned out he was a neighbor of your parents, and he said your father came from Earth five years earlier. After buying his farm, he married a local girl, a pretty blonde who was very shy."

"She was not a girl, but a harpy," Will said. "Back then, male harpies were hunted and scarce, so many females disguised themselves as women and bonded with men to save our species."

"It must have been a terrible time." Sherry looked at her mother. "How did you end up with me?"

"Weeks went by and no one claimed you. I took care of you. You were so beautiful and good, but I should have realized you were different when you never cried. My supervisor informed me of plans to send you to an orphanage on Earth." She cupped Sherry's cheek. "I couldn't let that happen. I wrapped you in your blanket, boarded the next ship off Dora, and claimed you were my daughter. Hampton was still in turmoil, and no one questioned me. I thought God had answered my prayers. I had a child."

"Can I see her baby blanket?" Will asked, figuring something so precious wouldn't have been discarded.

"It's in a chest in my bedroom. I'll get it." Frances rose and walked inside.

Disheartened, he said, "You have learned who you are, but now have doubts about us."

"My feelings for you haven't changed, but I'm a little overwhelmed. I need time to sort out my life before I make a commitment."

Frances returned with a small cream cloth. "It's a very strange material. The loose stitching is like nothing I've ever seen."

Will held out the trailing tie of his hip sash and placed it alongside the blanket. The material was identical. "Now you have seen another like it. Insects weave the cloth inside caves, and only harpies used it. It is the final proof that Sherry's mother was a golden harpy."

Will left Hampton and Sherry, disappointed they'd come so close to bonding, but it was not to be. He flew home, determined to win her love and make her his mate. Sherry, having learned she was a harpy, planned to visit the Outback and meet her people. Once assured of her nature, she could be ready to bond.

Will had suggested that Sherry speak to his mother on her visit, as Kari had a similar experience. Her harpy mother had died giving birth to her, and her human father hid that she was a harpy, even sending her to Earth schools to keep her from the truth. Grown, she returned to Dora and bonded with Shail, when discovering her true nature. Both Will and his father shared similar situations, attracted to golden females, who believed they were women. Will hoped the result would be the same. Sherry would be his.

He would have stayed and courted her, but the importance of governing the Outback overshadowed his love life. His grandmother had shut down, and he was forced to take charge. Officially, he was not yet the harpy ruler, but no harpy or human questioned his authority. On the day of Will's birth, his father had chosen him to reign, and his younger brothers accepted the decision, leaving Will unchallenged.

With good weather and a heated pace, he crossed the eastern half of the continent in two days, but this time he avoided the highway and its troublesome humans. At sundown, he saw the mighty river that separated the landmass. Terrance was only a few miles downstream. Longing to bathe and to cool off before going to his grandmother's home, he sailed down and dove into the swift current. In swimming toward the bank, he detected a manmade smell. On the shore, he sniffed the breeze. The faint odor of overheated metal, charred brush, and fuel drifted out of the jungle.

Angry, he ruffled his wet feathers and leaped skyward to follow the scent. It wasn't uncommon for a ship to avoid Terrance airport, sneak into the Outback, and land among the trees to poach the rare wildlife. Sometime, these men stunned and took brown-winged harpies. Beautiful and docile, they made perfect sex slaves and were in demand on the black market.

Within a few minutes, Will located the oblong spaceship that was wedged between trees and concealed under layers of fan branches. He pushed aside a branch and touched the ship's warm metal side. It hadn't been here long. Sensing a harpy, he turned to confront two brown-winged males exiting the heavy brush. "What is this doing here?" he vocally snapped.

They quickly bowed and one relayed, *It is good news, master. Your sister lives. Summer has returned from the stars with Bloom and your new golden brother. Bloom summoned us to hide and guard the star vehicle.*

Learning about Summer, Will tilted his head back and felt the torment of loss lift from his heart. It was good news.

CHAPTER NINETEEN

Dream Weaver had left the small, unstable wormhole and approached Dora from the outer reaches of space, avoiding the shipping channels to and from the Hampton spaceport. The ship entered the atmosphere at Dora's northern pole to elude satellite detection and traveled over the mountain range toward the West Coast. Turning left, it flew over jungle unoccupied by humans toward Terrance.

In the cabin Alex sat on the couch with his head pressed against the window, fixated on the vast ocean and colorful towering trees. In the cockpit Bloom directed Matt, who was piloting the ship. Alex's shipmates were familiar with the planet and didn't share his wonderment of the landscape, so beautiful his eyes watered.

Summer stepped into the cabin smiling. "We are almost home, Alex. What do you think?"

Hiding his excitement, he stayed focused on the scenery. "It's different from Oden."

Summer chuckled. "You can't fool me. You're elated with Dora." She called to Matt, "How much longer before we land?"

"We're close, should see the river soon."

Alex wandered into the cockpit. "I hope you're not planning to land at an airport. We'd definitely be busted."

"I've already considered that." Matt glanced up at Bloom. "Got any ideas on where to put down where we're not spotted?"

"North of the city is jungle, no homes or farms," Bloom said. "I know of a clearing where two red dragons fought for a female and knocked down the trees. It was a few seasons ago, but you should still be able to land there."

"Red dragons?" Matt questioned with a frown.

"They're largest animals on Dora," Summer said. "A full-grown male could crush your ship."

"Great," Matt said sarcastically.

"I'd like to see one," Alex said.

"And a dragon would love to see you," Summer said. "A city-raised harpy is an easy meal."

The ship reached the river, and they headed south. "There." Bloom pointed. "There is the spot."

Matt maneuvered the ship over the clearing. "You call that a landing site? The trees are over thirty feet tall."

Bloom shrugged. "Trees grow fast, but these are still small compared with others."

Matt huffed and scrutinized the area. "I can wedge her down between trees, but liftoff will be a bitch."

Summer slung her arm around Matt's shoulder. "Do you plan to leave?"

"Probably not," Matt said as the ship descended into the forest. They heard shearing and snapping limbs along with the scraping of metal. "I'm so sorry, sweetheart," he said to his ship. It settled on the ground, and he powered down the thrusters.

Alex went back into the cabin to unlock the hatch door. As it opened, Bloom rushed past him and, not waiting for the ramp, flew to the ground. Dropping on his hands and knees, he to kiss the forest floor.

Alex smiled. "I believe Bloom is happy to get off your ship, Matt."

Matt looked out the door and laughed, but his mood turned grim. "Summer, how am I going to walk through this shit and get to town?"

"It's not far," said Summer. "But if you wish, Bloom can carry you over the trees."

"He carried me when I was an invalid, but I got no excuse now." Matt grabbed a knapsack of personal gear. "I'll be a sweaty and dirty mess after this hike." He turned to Alex. "Let's go, buddy. I believe we're home." Matt and Summer walked down the ramp to join Bloom.

Alex hesitated in the doorway, breathing the warm humid air with its sweet, strange fragrances. The howls, hoots, and songs from the creatures rang out through the exploding colors of vines, enormous ferns, and massive trees. He then looked back into the cabin—his world of human comforts: machines, trouble-free food, and cool filtered air. He felt like a zoo animal released from its cage after a lifetime of security and forced to face a hazardous wilderness. He had longed for freedom and this place, but was now uncertain. Could he adapt?

Bloom must have sensed his apprehension. "Come, Alex. All shall be fine."

Alex fluttered down to them. "No worries, Bloom. I always land on my feet."

Matt pulled a small remote from his pocket and tapped a key. The ship ramp went up and the door shut. "She's locked up, but a hovercraft might spot her. The word will get out we're here."

"You and Summer go ahead," Bloom said. "Alex and I shall hide the ship with brush and meet you at our queen's home."

"Sounds good," Matt said. "Okay, doll, lead the way." They penetrated the foliage.

Alex crossed his arms and eyed Matt's long ship. "Thanks a lot, Bloom. My sister and the pilot take off, and we're stuck with this job. It'll take forever to cover this."

"A harpy is not above hard work."

"Physical labor is for inferiors, not me."

"You have so much to learn." With a head shake, Bloom flew off.

Alone, Alex grumbled, “He’s got a lot to learn about me.” He heard the crunch of branches, and a dozen reptilian-type beasts with green bodies and red heads appeared. They stood head-high on their thick back legs and seethed at him. Frightened, Alex flew to the top of the ship and peered down as the animals sniffed and nosed the ship. “Bloom,” he called.

Bloom soared out of trees and landed before the creatures. He extended his wings and hissed at the animals. Intimidated by the harpy, they fled back into the underbrush. He looked up at Alex crouched on the ship. “The jungle is beautiful, but dangerous for those lacking knowledge.”

Alex dropped on the ground. “All right, what were those creatures?”

“They are called zels, plant eaters, and are harmless unless attacked.”

“They had damn big teeth.”

Six brown-winged harpies sailed out of the forest. Landing before Alex, they went down on one knee and bowed their heads. “What’s this?” Alex asked Bloom.

“They know you are Shail’s son and believe golden harpies deserve reverence.”

“You’ve never bowed to me.”

“That is because you have failed to earn my respect.”

Provoked, Alex arched his wings. “You’ve been ragging my ass throughout the voyage, and I’m sick of it.”

“Do not raise your wings unless you are challenging me to fight. Fold your wings. I have no wish to harm you.”

Humiliated in front of the other males, Alex was angry and not giving up. He lowered his wings and waited for Bloom to turn his back. Alex lunged at him and swung his fists, but Bloom, anticipating the attack, ducked. He grabbed Alex’s arm and flung him to the ground. Alex, dazed and hurt, sat up shaking his head.

"Stand up," Bloom growled, seizing his arm and jerking him to his feet. "A golden should not lie in dirt. Do you wish to continue this fight, or are we done?"

Alex couldn't defeat the older, bigger, and more experienced male in combat and considered using his telepathic powers to hurt Bloom, but he liked the black-winged harpy. In frustration, he resorted to yelling. "I should have left you with the miners. Right now men would be raping you, and your self-righteous attitude would be gone."

"I owe you my life, but vowed to make you a true harpy. Your lessons have begun. Shall you help us cover the ship?"

"No, I'm not helping."

Bloom gazed skyward and mumbled, "Some vows are hard to keep." He whirled a finger in the air, and he and the harpies soared into the foliage.

Alex shook his wings to remove the dirt and leaves and brushed off his knees and arms. Several minutes later a harpy carrying a bundle of fan branches set down on the ship. After scattering the branches, he left, and a second male arrived with a bundle. The work didn't seem hard.

Alex was growing bored and needed to strengthen his wing muscles. "Fine, I'll play along." He winged upward nearly a half-mile to the treetops. He saw a red tree with thick purple vines. Fluttering before a fan limb, he reached out to grab it.

A harpy flew into him knocking him away from the tree. *No, master,* he said into Alex's subconscious. *Do not touch that one.*

Alex turned to the young brown-winged male, fluttering nearby and growled, "What the devil is wrong with you?"

"You speak aloud and so shall I." The teen lowered his head. "I am sorry I pushed you, but you faced danger. These purple vines snare and eat harpies." He pointed at the vine.

Alex saw the outstretched vine tentacles reaching for him. Alarmed, he fluttered backward further out of reach. "Damn, that's creepy."

The teen grinned. “Yes, these vines creep up on unknowing creatures. If you wish to collect fans, you also chose the wrong tree. This one is bright red, so it is young and strong. It shall not easily yield its branches. Come, master. I shall take you to the right trees. I am Westly.”

Alex trailed Westly. He had only been on Dora an hour and, during that time, he fled huge reptiles, fought Bloom, and escaped a vine that had nearly turned him into lunch. He was apprehensive about the coming days. They approached a yellow tree, and Westly grabbed the bark and clung with hands and feet like a squirrel.

“These are good,” Westly said, and dropped a loose fan leaf on the ground.

Alex copied him, having trouble at first with his foot grip. When a pile of fans lay below, they flew down, gathered them in bundles, and took them to the ship. The chore soon became fun.

Alex wiped the sweat from his brow, feeling exhilarated with his accomplishment. He realized Bloom’s reasons for having him help with the job. Alex was being educated about his new home. More importantly, he was learning how to fit in with a flock rather than be a loner. He collected branches off the ground for another trip to the ship. “Westly, I didn’t thank you for saving me from the vines.”

Under Westly’s dark locks, the olive-green eyes twinkled. “It is a great honor to protect a golden. My father shall be proud.”

Alex became suspicious. “Do you know Bloom?”

“All harpies know Bloom. He is a powerful flock leader.”

Alex dropped his bundle, his misgivings confirmed. When Westly came to his rescue, it was not a chance meeting. “Bloom sent you to watch over me.”

“Yes,” Westly answered, and tilted his head. “You do not know the dangers and must have a guardian. Our golden harpies are too few.”

Alex quietly re-collected the fans. He had underestimated Bloom, judging him as flunky, but in fact, he was a high-ranking and respected member of the harpies. And he was clever, manipulating Alex. It was time for a new strategy.

Alex and Westly returned to the ship and added their palms. Bloom landed beside them with his arms full of fans and said, "I am glad to see you are helping, Alex."

"It's actually kind of fun." Alex stepped to him. "Look, Bloom, I'm sorry I took a swing at you. It was uncalled for, but I don't take criticism well."

Bloom tossed the fans over the ship. "All golden harpies are temperamental and arrogant, but they are also noble and have earned their behavior. You have not."

Alex didn't argue. To accomplish his goal, he needed Bloom and had to suck up and behave.

They concealed the ship under branches and were done. "Come," Bloom said to Alex. "I shall take to your grandmother. She shall be happy to see you."

Before leaving, Alex said to Westly, "I appreciate your help and hope I see you again."

Westly smiled. "It was an honor to serve you, master."

Alex and Bloom soared over the endless, multicolored canopy. Trying to be sociable, Alex said. "You were right to ask me to work. I learned a lot. When will you teach me to fight?"

"First you must cast out your human flaws and gain honor. Then you learn combat."

Alex breathed deeply. "Casting out my flaws is easier said than done."

"You are smart and can change, but I question that you wish it. In your challenge, you underhandedly struck when my head was turned. Even now you are insincere, acting friendly because you seek the training. Harpies are loyal and never dishonest."

Alex couldn't deny the allegations, and deceiving Bloom wasn't working. "That's true. I'm trying to warm up to you so I can learn to fight in a challenge. It's the only way to prove myself and gain respect."

"You are being honest, but your aim is wrong. Winning fights causes fear in others, not admiration. Once you become whole and care about others, respect shall follow."

"So you say. And Bloom, I do like you, just not the crap you dish out."

"I know."

They came upon a wide river, and in the distance to the south was Terrance with its buildings strung along the banks. "I do appreciate your advice, and I'll try."

Bloom tilted his wing downward toward the city. "Since you are interested in fighting, I shall give you guidance. Your mistake was fighting like a human. A slight harpy can defeat a large, heavy man. With six limbs and flight, we do not stand and swing our fists, but flutter and deliver powerful blows with, mostly, our feet. A challenge between harpy males is a sparring dance of speed, balance, and nerve. It is graceful like birds."

"Good to know," Alex said as they soared over city streets and then the homes in the rural area of town. He started to feel nervous about meeting his family. "Bloom, if I step out of line, you can throw me in the dirt again."

Bloom smiled, rare for him. "I do not have to. Your brother, Will, shall do it. Besides, once I deliver you to your family, I leave to be with mine. When you are ready to become a harpy, seek me. I shall be there for you."

On the edge of the jungle, they landed in the front yard of a grand Victorian-type house with its windows and doorway adorned with wood-carved flowers. A wide veranda holding wicker furniture faced a hedge with enormous flowers. It was a place befitting a queen. Alex anxiously ruffled his feathers and followed Bloom onto the porch.

Bloom knocked on the door, and Alex stood behind him. A petite woman with waist-length blond hair opened the door. One whiff of her told Alex she was a golden harpy.

"Bloom, you're alive!" she cried.

"Yes, Mistress Kari," Bloom said, bowing. "Summer also survived the journey and comes with the pilot." He turned to Alex. "Here is Shail's lost son, Alex."

"So you're Alexander." She stepped to him and kissed his cheek. "You're as handsome as your brothers. This is so wonderful. Your grandmother will be ecstatic. We thought you had all died." She stepped back and wiped her watery eyes. "Come in, come in. I'll go upstairs and get Windy."

They walked inside as she raced up the staircase. Alex asked, "Who is she?"

"She is Kari, your father's first mate," Bloom said.

"Will's mother," Alex grumbled. Kari was another reminder of his brother's charmed life. She was gorgeous, affectionate, and kind, unlike Alex's unsightly, callous mother, who hadn't kissed him in years. How different his life might have been if Kari had raised him.

Kari stood on the upper stairs with a bright smile. "Come on, Windy. It's a huge surprise."

Alex's grandmother appeared, wearing a long white gown on her slender body, and at her side was a young brown-winged harpy. She stared down at Alex and Bloom and covered her mouth. Sweeping back her waist-length blond hair from her blue eyes to make sure her sight didn't deceive her, she said, "Bloom, you have returned."

"Yes, my queen, I am here with your grandson, Alex."

Windy descended the stairs with her head high, showing strength, but a tear on her cheek displayed her heart. On the ship Summer had been right, Alex thought. Windy was majestic, hardly fitting a weak, elderly grandmother.

Bloom knelt, his wings spread on the floor, his head lowered. "Summer should also be here soon."

At the bottom of the stairs, Wind stroked Bloom's locks. "My beautiful black-winged guardian, you have never failed us. Thank you, Bloom, for bringing them back safely." She turned to Alex and, without a word, embraced him. He tried to gently break free, but she gripped him tightly.

"My precious grandson, you are home," she whispered in his ear. "You can let go of your anger, fear, and hurt. No matter what you have done or might do, you will never lose my love. Trust me, Alexander. All shall be well."

Alex sniffled, fighting his emotions. He had sworn never to allow another harpy to touch him and peer into his mind, but caught off guard, he couldn't resist her embrace. She sensed his flaws and didn't judge him. The last time he felt such affection was with Mollie. Regaining composure, he murmured, "Thank you, grandmother."

The door opened and Summer bounded into the house. "Grandma," she screeched, and clasped Windy into her arms. "I've missed you so badly, and I was worried that you thought I had died." Tearfully, she pulled back. "I'm sorry about Jim."

"He is alive and recovering in a hospital," Windy said.

"That is good to hear," said Bloom. "We feared his death."

"Summer, you must call your mother," said Kari. "She's been inconsolable, believing she'd lost you."

Matt ambled inside and heard Kari. "Doll, be careful with that call. The feds are probably listening in."

Summer grabbed Matt's hand and dragged him to Kari and Windy. "Grandma, you remember Matt, the pilot? He's so brilliant. He rigged a bomb to explode in space so it looked like our ship hit an asteroid and blew up. It was the only way to escape the Federal ships."

Windy looked at the couple holding hands. "It seems you are fond of him. Is this young man joining our family?"

Summer grinned. "Yes."

"Ma'am, with your permission, I'd like to marry Summer. I love her."

Windy's questioning eyes focused on Bloom.

Bloom sighed. "The man has many flaws and struggles with honor, but has tried to improve and be worthy of Summer, He does love her, and I fear their attachment has grown too strong for separation."

Matt frowned. "Gee, thanks for the referral, Bloom."

"My queen," said Bloom, "if you have no further need of me, I am eager to see my mates and fledglings." With Windy's nod, he headed for the door, but in passing Alex, he said, "I shall see you again."

The brown-winged harpy went to Windy "My queen, with so many here, I shall gather more fruit for your table."

Summer asked, "Freely, you're always with my brother. Where is he?"

Kari answered. "Will flew to Hampton to talk to a lawyer about Jim's criminal case, but he should be back soon. Now come, Summer, let's call Rachel. The whole family will be relieved."

"Like I said, doll," Matt put in. "Don't mention our little trip to Oden." He moved next to Alex. "Let's go on the deck, buddy." On the veranda, he dropped into a large chair and asked, "So, how'd it go, meeting the grandmother?"

Alex grasped the railing and gazed at the pink and golden sunset. "She's not what I expected."

"Yeah, she's hot. Best looking grandma I've ever seen"

"How was your walk through the jungle?"

"Miserable. That hike damn near killed me." Matt rubbed the back of his neck. "I'm wondering if us city boys will be content here."

Alex glanced at him. "Using one of your clichés, are you getting cold feet?"

"Maybe lukewarm," Matt said with a chuckle. "It's not the place or doubts about being with Summer. It's giving up star travel."

"I'd give up anything to have a mate like Summer."

Matt nodded. "You're a smart kid."

Out of the shadowy jungle, a yellow-winged male flew onto the porch and with a smile, he approached Alex. "You must be my brother Alex. I came from the ship and was so glad to learn you and Summer survived. I am Will." When he reached out to embrace him, Alex stepped back.

"I know who you are," Alex said stiffly.

"It's all right," Will said. "You don't know harpy customs. A hug is a gesture of friendship, and I do want us to be best friends. We will have great adventures and tear up the trees with fast flight."

"So you're Will?" Matt said before Alex could respond. "Summer's been bragging about you, and Bloom claims you're the toughest harpy on the planet."

Will smiled. "I can hold my own. You are the pilot." He stepped to Matt and shook his hand. "I am thankful you brought my sister and brother home safely. Where is Summer?"

Matt pointed a thumb toward the door. "Inside, she's on the com with her mom."

"We'll talk later. Right now, I'm anxious to see her. Alex, if you need anything, you only need to ask me." He went into the house.

Matt slouched back into the chair. "You're taller than him, but no question that you two are brothers. Kinda strange, though. For being a badass, Will seems like a nice guy."

"He's a fool. We will never be friends."

CHAPTER TWENTY

In his grandmother's home, Will stood back and watched Summer chat on the com. She noticed him and grinned.

"Mom, I got to go. Will is here," Summer said. "I'll be home tomorrow and you'll meet Matt. I love you." She disconnected and rushed into Will's arms. "I am so happy to see you."

He lifted and twirled his little sister around and then set her down and kissed her forehead. "I never thought I would hold you again. We were told your ship hit an asteroid and exploded."

"Matt faked the explosion so we could escape the feds. Did you meet him?"

"I did, briefly."

Windy said, "Your sister cares about this man, and they talk of bonding."

"That human outside?" Will frowned. "I shook his hand and sensed him. Summer, he is not good enough for you."

"Please don't get your feathers up," Summer pleaded. "Matt isn't perfect, but I love him."

With a raised head and a huff, he shot back, "And I love you, Summer. I want you to have the best." Seeing her concerned teary eyes, he took a deep breath. "Maybe he can prove his worthiness to me. For now I promise to do nothing."

Summer nodded sadly. “Bloom also disliked him at first, but Matt won him over.”

“I have great respect for Bloom’s judgment, so we shall see. Right now I wish to know why this rescue on Oden went bad? So many died; the police, Alex’s nanny, one of our harpies. And Jim was wounded and captured.”

“It was a trap,” Summer said. “Somehow the police knew we were coming and surrounded us.” She glanced toward the porch. “Alex’s nanny was killed, and he went crazy, using his telepathy on the police so they committed suicide. I knocked him down, and he hit his head. If he had remained conscious, more would have died.”

Will glanced out the window at Alex in the yard. “In Hampton I saw the police reports and his doctor’s claim that Alex’s telepathy killed the police. But how is that possible? Harpies can sense a human but they cannot control their mind.”

“Alex is not like us. He has a gift, or maybe a curse. His telepathy can force humans to do anything, even suicide. I’ve seen him do it twice, on Oden, and again at a mining colony.”

“It’s time I have a serious talk with this brother. Killing humans will not be tolerated.” He took a step toward the door.

Windy had listened to their conversation and now stepped in. “Stop, Will,” she said sternly. “You are to leave Alex alone. Come with me.”

Irritated, Will ruffled his feathers but obeyed his grandmother. They went upstairs to her bedroom, which usually meant a lecture. “Grandma, Alex must be straightened out now before anyone is hurt.”

Windy sat down on the bed. “He knows he has done wrong, and confronting him about past mistakes will not help. He’ll only grow more resentful. I sensed him. Although he tries to hide it, he is very defensive, hostile, and confused. A heartless mother raised him and then had him locked up for a long time. What he endured would kill most harpies. He was then freed, only to see the one person who loved him — his nanny — killed before his eyes. Imagine your life if it had been his. Heartbroken and enraged, you also might have struck down those policemen. Alex needs love, not badgering. I want you to be his friend."

"I already offered my friendship, but if he proves difficult..." He shook his head. "I shall try to support him." Changing the subject, he asked, "Do you wish to hear what Waters said about Jim?"

"Not now," said Windy. "This is a time for joy, and everyone waits for us to celebrate downstairs. We shall speak in the morning."

Will and his grandmother left the bedroom and found the household on the porch. His flight partner, Freely, placed fresh fruit on the table, alongside a platter of baked goods. Summer poured juice into the glasses as Kari came out with a steaming bowl of cooked tomatoes and squash. Windy took a seat and Matt and Kari joined her.

Summer stood behind Matt with a hand on his shoulder. She picked up a yellow fruit ball and said, "I've been dying for a trisom. You can't get them in space."

Matt looked at the food. "Wow, totally vegetarian. This will take some getting used to."

Windy smiled at him. "You sound like Jim. He could give up drinking but not his meat. Summer, there is a bag of jerky in the kitchen cabinet. Bring it for Matt. The restaurants in town serve a variety of animal dishes."

Will sat on the rail next to Freely. To take a chair, he would risk his long wings being stepped on and damaged.

The sun slipped below the horizon as they feasted and talked about the trip to Oden. Only Alex was absent from the gathering. He stood alone at the other end of the veranda and gazed at the jungle.

Summer said, "Will, your mom said you went to Hampton. How was the trip?"

"Yes," said Kari. "What did you think of Sam?"

"I was very impressed with him," Will said. "I understand why Father trusted him and liked Sam." He cleared his throat. "Also, on the visit, I met a golden female harpy who is my age."

Summer grinned. “Is she a possible mate, Will? Was she pretty?”

Will scowled at his prying sister. “Obviously, she was pretty, but I’m not about to discuss her or my love life. She and her mother are coming to the Outback, so you’ll meet her and judge for yourself.”

“Another golden,” Windy said, amazed. “All this time, I thought we were the last of them, but now there are two more—this Eastern female and Alex. When I was young, many yellow wings soared through the sky. It gives me hope for our future.”

Evening approached and Will glanced down the long, dark veranda. In the shadows, Alex’s tall, silhouette leaned against a post. “Come join us, Alex.”

“I am fine here.”

Will gazed at his estranged brother. Earlier he had failed to sense Alex’s emotions, assuming his new half-brother was uncomfortable or shy. After speaking with Summer, he reconsidered Alex’s aloofness. Possibly he was hiding his sinister nature and deeds. Was it possible for a golden harpy to be evil?

At dawn Will woke in a tree nest beyond his grandmother’s home. Freely slept nearby, no longer needing to comfort Windy. He saw Summer sitting on the porch steps with wet hair and wings, and he flew to her.

“Good morning, sister,” he said, landing before her as she preened a feather.

She smiled. “I could not wait for daylight to find a stream. With space travel, water is limited and a bath is short.”

“Do all still sleep?”

“I think so, but I don’t know about Alex. Grandma offered him a bedroom, but he never came in the house last night. But that’s normal. He’s moody and likes being alone.”

“Grandma told me to give him time and don’t confront him, but he concerns me.”

"He should. Alex has it in his head to become the next harpy ruler, and you're the only one standing in his way. You need to watch your back."

"Him, rule?" Will smirked. "He just got here and knows nothing about us or Dora."

"Alex is more like a spoiled, selfish human than a harpy, but don't underestimate him. He's not only dangerous but extremely smart. Before he blocked his thoughts from me, I sensed him after he killed the police. He was full of hate and felt no remorse. His telepathy is scary, but I'm unsure if he can use it against a harpy." She shook her wet locks. "My guess we'll soon find out."

Will lifted his eyebrows and said cynically, "That is reassuring."

"Bloom believes he can change Alex. But I doubt it."

"I will speak to Bloom about him." To lighten the mood, he smiled and said, "so you and the pilot. Are sure you want this man? Matt is a wanderer, not satisfied in one place for long."

"We plan to stay on Dora, but if we end up in the stars, I will still be happy. After last night's dinner, have you changed your mind about him?"

"He's a strange character, tries to hide his shortcomings with a joke and a grin. But he suits you. Summer. You have always sought adventure and would never be content with a quiet male harpy. Matt shares your passion, and I understand why you choose him."

She stood and hugged him. "Thank you. I value your opinion above all."

The veranda flooded with the early morning light, and Matt wandered out to them. "Morning, doll," he said, leaning over to kiss her. Barefoot with an open shirt, he scratched his chin stubble. "Do you think there's any coffee in this house?" he asked, easing into a chair.

"Grandma kept some for Jim. I will make you a cup." She went inside.

After Summer left, Will stepped on the porch and approached Matt. With arched wings, he growled, "What makes you think you are good enough for my sister?"

Matt's drowsy eyes popped open. He jumped up and stumbled backwards. "Oh, Christ, it's too early for this macho bullshit. You got your wings up and want to fight? Okay, I've had my fill on the ship with this harpy intimidation." He leaped off the deck and held up his fists. "Let's go. I know you can kick my ass or maybe even kill me, but fuck it. I'm not giving up Summer."

"You're willing to die for her?"

"Yeah, without her, I'm nothing," Matt said with watery eyes. "I got nothing to lose, Will, so hammer away."

Will studied the flustered man and folded his wings. "You have proven your love for her. There is no need to harm you."

Matt lowered his fists and looked baffled. "Really, you're okay with us?" When Will didn't answer, he stepped back on the porch. "You harpies sure like to test a guy."

"The tests are necessary," said Will. "We are part animal, and in nature only a worthy male earns a mate. A cowardly, selfish male does not protect or care for his family and some even desert them. His female and fledglings suffer, but also the male's undesirable flaws can be passed to his sons. Our flock is small but honorable. We wish to keep it that way."

"Makes sense," Matt said, "weed out the scum. Mankind could take a lesson from you harpies. Will, I promise to be good to Summer. If I fail, you won't need to kill me. I'll do it myself."

Summer returned with a cup of steaming coffee. "Are you two getting along?"

"We're just having a meeting of the minds," Matt said, taking the cup.

A few minutes later, Windy and Kari came out and served breakfast. Freely soared out of the jungle and landed among the group.

Windy looked around. "Where is Alex?"

At that moment, Alex emerged from the woods and flew across the lawn to the steps.

"Are you hungry, Alex?" Windy asked.

"No."

Leaving the porch, Will walked to him. "I would like to spend some time with you."

"Why?" asked Alex.

"You are my brother. I want to know you and show you your new home."

"That's crap. Summer told you what I did, and you already have an opinion of me."

All chatter on the porch ceased, and everyone watched Will and Alex.

Will took a breath. "I have no opinion, yet, and what you have done, right or wrong, is of no interest to me. We share the same father and blood. I wish to understand you and be your friend."

"Maybe I don't want your friendship." Alex sneered. "Do I puzzle you, brother? I should. You wish to understand me but you're not capable. My IQ is light years ahead of yours while you have the brains of Neanderthal. Stick to your trees and leave me alone."

Will had never heard of a Neanderthal, but knew it was an insult. He glanced at his grandmother, fighting the urge to knock Alex senseless. He forced down his anger and said calmly, "I am sorry you feel this way. Because you have endured much, I will excuse your rude behavior, but don't try my patience, Alex. The next time I will not forgive you." His dead-serious gaze conveyed that one more slight, despite his grandmother's wishes, would be met with an attack.

Alex's feathers quaked, and he clenched his fists. Glaring at Will, he opened his mouth to respond, but must have reassessed his situation. He sprang into the air and jetted into the brush.

Will shook his locks, amazed that he had mustered his restraint and not popped Alex in the mouth. He returned to the porch. "Grandma, he needs a good thrashing."

Summer spoke up. "I agree."

"Beating a frightened, bewildered creature does not make it sound or gentle," Windy said. "Alex has been taunted enough. Only kindness will heal him."

* * *

Alex flew furiously through the trees, not caring if his wings tore through branches and dangling vines. "I should have made him crawl like a worm," he growled. Rattled with Will's threat, he had nearly used his telepathy to hurt him, but fear had stopped him. He wasn't afraid of his brother but was terrified of the consequences. Bloom had warned him that if he harmed a harpy with his telepathy, the flocks would object. Deemed dangerous, he could face banishment, prison, or another mental ward.

After several miles, his rage diminished, and he felt pain. He slowed to a glide and saw the blood seeping through his feathers. His wings had paid for the reckless flight. He landed on a wide tree limb. Parting the feathers, he examined his cuts and broken quills. His arms and legs were also bruised and scratched. Even his cheek suffered a minor slash. He sat down and felt ridiculous. Rather than harm Will, he had beaten himself up. "At least it is done. He knows I am not a brother or a friend, but his enemy."

Throughout the space voyage, Alex had planned the altercation with Will that would lead to a challenge for harpy rule. Summer had fueled the conflict, speaking highly of her older brother while peering at Alex with disdain. Bloom had added to Alex's contempt, saying he could never defeat Will in a fight. Alex had arrived on Dora and stepped off the ship, hating this brother who possessed everything that Alex lacked.

He'd even lost Mollie, his soft place to feel love and reassurance. If she had lived, what would she think of his plan to fight a brother and rule the harpies? "I miss you," he whispered. "You would tell me what to do." Though committed to his goal, doubts had crept in after meeting Will. His brother was hard to hate. Under different circumstances, Alex would have treasured his friendship. When Matt had said Will seemed like a nice guy, Alex had to shake off the sentiment and replace it with determination. Something he had practiced all his life.

Alex leaped off the branch and flew toward the river. Spotting Matt's ship, he sailed down and spoke silently into the trees. *Come out.* Two harpies appeared and bowed to him. *I seek the young male named Westly.*

One of the harpies answered. *Westly is my brother's son. I shall bring him to you.*

Within a half-hour, the harpy returned with the teenager. Westly asked, "You have need of me, master?"

"I want you as a guide."

Westly stared at the ground. "I am greatly honored, but unworthy. I am not old enough to protect a golden on my own."

"I didn't ask for protection," Alex said, irritated. "I just need someone to show me around."

"I must get my father's permission."

"Fine, do it," Alex said. "I'll wait." Westly took flight and was gone over an hour. Alex wondered if the young fool had a change of heart.

Westly came back. "My father says I can go with you, master."

"Stop calling me master. It's Alex." They spread their wings and bounded into the sky.

"Mas..., Alex, where do you wish to go?" Westly asked when they reached the clear air above the tree canopy.

"Somewhere far from people and harpies," Alex said. "I don't trust them, and I also don't want them to see I can't fight, but you're going to teach me. I must learn how take down a harpy in a challenge."

"Me? I cannot train you. A golden attack is very different than a brown's. My father says a golden harpy charges his opponent and does not stop until he wins, is severely injured, or dead. Brown-winged harpies are not as violent."

"I'm an amateur, so coach me on what you know. It'll be a start."

"I thought you wished to learn about the jungle and animals."

"That can wait. Once you've taught me enough, we'll go to Bloom. Do you know how to find him?"

"I have never been to his nest, but it is said to be a full day and night of fast travel west in a valley of red trees near the ocean. If you wish to avoid other harpies, we must fly northwest to the cold mountains."

After several hours of grueling flight, they reached the northern foothills. Alex dripped with sweat, and each beat of his wing brought pain. "I used to dream of flying until my wings gave out." He panted. "That was a stupid dream. I must stop and rest."

They descended into the trees and landed on the forest floor. Alex sat down on a log, puffing. Too exhausted to fold his wings, he let them extend across the ground. Westly stood before him and showed no sign of fatigue.

"It's my wings," Alex said, huffing. "My feathers were cut in half and only recently grew back. Then I got reckless and damaged them flying too fast through the trees."

Westly examined Alex's wings. "You have a few minor wounds, but the feathers are solid, plush, and full length. I am afraid it is your heart, lungs, and muscles that fail you. You have not flown far in some time."

"Westly, I've never flown this far," Alex said, ashamed. "I was raised in a glass cage, couldn't fly much at all, and for the last several months, I was confined in a small hospital room and then shut up on a cramped spaceship."

Westly bowed his head. "Master and I call you *master* because you are one, your body might be weak, but you had the strength of spirit to survive such a life. I could not."

Alex smiled. "Thanks, Westly."

"Before learning the challenge, you must get in shape or the fight shall be short with your defeat."

Alex dropped his guard and allowed the teenager to massage his shoulders. Through the contact, Westly transmitted his devotion for Alex. He realized why male harpies, unlike men, were such feely, touchy mortals. He thought about Will. Perhaps his brother wanted to hug him, not to probe his mind, but to reassure Alex and show him affection. Too late now; an unbreakable divide rested between them.

Rather than move on, they stayed put so Alex could recover. Westly retrieved fresh fruit for dinner, and after a soothing bath in a clear pond, Alex curled up for the night in soft tree moss with the teenager. Alex relaxed and enjoy the companionship. For the first time, he had a real pal.

At dawn Westly shook Alex awake. "If we travel today, the cool morning is better."

Alex yawned and scratched his head. "Let's stay here a few days. I want to try a challenge."

After a breakfast of strange fruit, Alex felt good. The soreness in his wing muscles was gone, and he was ready to take on Westly.

Westly explained, "First, there is the circling." He backed away ten feet and walked around Alex with arched wings and tossing his hair. Alex watched him.

"No, you must lift your wings and also circle me."

"Why?"

"It builds your nerve and intimidates your rival."

"I'm not prancing around, flashing my wings like some damn bird," Alex said. "Just get on with it." Westly flew at him, kicked his shoulder, and knocked him down. Alex looked up from the dirt. "I wasn't ready."

Westly pulled Alex up. “You shall never be ready if you do not circle. With the pacing, your mind becomes alert, your muscles tense, and you sense the other’s weaknesses. You are prepared to attack or be attacked. Do you wish to try again?”

Alex shook the leaves from his hair. “How old are you?”

Westly spread his fingers and held out his hand three times.

“Pathetic, been knocked down by a fifteen-year-old.”

“I understand you long to learn a challenge, but first we should build up the muscles in your wings, legs, and arms. If feeble, you cannot flutter long while kicking and punching another harpy.”

“I suppose you’re right. I’ve heard Will is tough.”

Westly’s eyes grew big, and he gasped. “Will, Shail’s eldest son, you…you wish to fight him?”

“I do. I can accomplish anything if I put my mind to it.”

“Alex, you cannot accomplish this. My father said that Will is true to his name. He has great willpower and is undefeatable. He shall only hurt you, Alex.”

“Let me worry about that.”

CHAPTER TWENTY-ONE

After Matt had watched the dispute between the harpy brothers, he kicked back on the porch and finished his coffee. He wasn't surprised that Will and Alex had clashed. Both were prima donnas with big egos and short fuses, who had gotten into Matt's face. If the yellow-winged suckers did square off, he was unsure who would win. He had seen Alex in action at the mining colony and had heard Will was as deadly as they come. The match would be a coin toss.

Will and his flight buddy, Freely, stood in the yard and nuzzled one another's necks before Freely took off. "Strange bastards," Matt mumbled. He had also noticed that except for Alex who was city raised, harpies rarely smiled and frowned. Like animals, they express their emotions with their eyes.

He questioned his decision to remain among them. He walked into the kitchen with his empty cup. Kari was washing the breakfast dishes, Summer was drying and putting them away, and the grandmother sat at a table.

"I'm heading to the airport, ladies," Matt said, putting his cup on the counter. "It shouldn't take long to pick up a hover and get back."

"We'll be ready," said Kari. "I'm anxious to check on Shail."

He kissed Summer's cheek and said to Windy, "Ma'am, I appreciate the use of Jim's vehicle until I get one."

He strolled out to the veranda and waved to Will. "Catch you later, man."

Will, standing like a statue, didn't acknowledge him.

"Harpies, pompous pricks," Matt groused and walked to the parked vehicle at the side of the house. Sliding into the driver seat, he thought about its poor owner. Jim had treated him like a wayward son, giving him advice. He liked the man and hoped he'd beat the rap. He drove through the small town of Terrance to the airport. Inside the building, he strolled past people at the ticket counter and baggage claim and went straight to Ted's office. Ted sat at his desk, speaking to a man on the com screen. Matt leaned against the door jamb and waited.

"I ordered that part weeks ago," Ted griped. "It should be here." Swiveling his chair, he saw Matt. "I got to go." Disconnecting, he shot out of his seat. "I'll be damned. We heard you were dead."

"Nope, still kicking," Matt said.

"But the report....your ship blew up in an asteroid field."

"I made the Feds think that. I said I was a damn good smuggler."

"So Bloom, Summer, and Shail's son...?"

"Fit as fiddles; they're at the grandma's house. Summer and Kari want to go home to Westend. I'm here for a hover."

"I am so relieved," Ted said. "And I'm sure Windy is too."

"Yeah, yesterday was one big, happy family reunion, though it didn't last. Will and Alex had words this morning that nearly came to blows, so much for brotherly love."

"Will is back from Hampton?" Ted said. "I expected him tomorrow at the earliest. He took off in one heck of a storm, and it's a long trip, but I should've known, considering that harpy." He sat down in his chair and motioned to another. "So, Will and his new brother got into a scrap. They just met each other."

"After spending a couple of months with harpies, I've learned to handle them like nitro. One little spark sets them off."

"That hasn't been my experience. Maybe you rub them wrong."

"Oh, hell," Matt said with a chuckle. "I rub everyone wrong, but wait until you meet Alex. That kid is something else. He killed a bunch of Oden cops, which is why the feds were after us. He did save my butt, so I've tried to warm up to him. Just when I think we're buddies, he turns those cynical blue eyes on you. Then you remember this boy can kill with a blink. He's spooky. He plans to duke it out with Will and become the next harpy ruler."

Ted massaged his chin. "A golden harpy challenge for rule. That hasn't happened in nearly sixty years. I once saw their father Shail level a huge guy in Hampton port. I can't imagine two goldens fighting it out. Alex might be dangerous, but Will is no slouch."

"Neither is their sister. I'd never tangle with Summer." Matt rose. "Speaking of her, she and Kari are waiting for me."

Ted stood. "I'll show you the rentals. By the way, where's your ship?"

"North of here," Matt said. "She's jammed between trees. It's going to take a shitload of chainsaws and some fancy maneuvering to free her."

"It's good you didn't land here. The Federal agents could still be hanging around."

They walked outside, crossed the tarmac to the parked aircraft, and stopped in front of four small hovercrafts. "Here are the rentals. The blue one came in last week. It's brand new."

"You want to sell it?"

Ted blinked at a space pilot's interest in purchasing local transportation. "Matt, are you planning to stick around?"

"Afraid so," Matt said with a grin. "Summer clipped my wings and I'm grounded."

Ted laughed.

* * *

Will stood on the dewy lawn as a cool morning breeze blew the long locks off his shoulders. His flight companion, Freely, had taken wing on a joyous mission. He would convey the good news to Aron that Bloom and others had survived the journey and returned to Dora. The rest of the household was inside, leaving Will to reflect on his earlier altercation with Alex. Antagonistic and unstable, his younger brother created a dilemma. How to deal with him? His grandmother proposed patience and compassion, but Will disagreed, believing firmness would work better.

Matt came out of the house, but Will, absorbed in his thoughts, ignored him when he left for the airport. The pilot was another problem, but Summer was stubbornly committed to him. Nothing would change her mind. Maybe the relationship would work out, and Will wouldn't have to intervene.

He had to talk to his grandmother about her trip to Oden with Sam Waters. Saving Jim and preventing her from despair was another concern. He closed his eyes, feeling the burden of family troubles. His worries would be amplified when he ruled the Outback, unless Alex killed him.

He sensed the approach of harpies and wondered what now? Two brown-winged harpies, a teenager and adult, landed in the yard.

After kneeling, the adult relayed, *I seek your wisdom, master.*

Normally, they would ask his grandmother, but word had spread that she was sick with the loss of her mate; Will was the temporary monarch. Only eighteen years old, he felt inadequate in his role.

How can I help you?

Your brother who came from the stars has requests that my son be his companion in the jungle, the adult relayed, placing his hand on the teenager's shoulder. *Westly is smart and brave, but not full grown. To watch over a golden is a great responsibility and much to expect from one so young.*

Perplexed, Will tilted his head and asked Westly. *Why has Alex chosen you?*

When covering the star vehicle, Bloom said I should watch over him and be his friend.

He does need a friend, Will said. *Alex is new to our way and could use help adjusting. This has been his only request and should not be denied. Go to him, but do not tell him you sought my permission. He would resent it.*

Yes, master, Westly said, and flew away.

Thank you, master. The father conveyed and opened his wings to leave. Will motioned him to stay.

I sense your concerns. My brother is willful and ignorant to dangers, and your son appears to idolize him because he is a golden. Westly might be unable to dissuade him from foolishness and risk. Pick two of the most trusted males in your flock and have them guard Alex and your son. These guards are to stay out of sight and not interfere unless there is a great threat. Alex must be kept safe.

I agree, said the father. *I shall rest easier tonight*. Flying skyward, he passed a shiny blue hovercraft.

The hover landed in the yard, and Matt stepped out. "What do you think, Will? I just bought it."

Will walked to the craft. "No scratches and dents, it must be new."

"Yep, straight from the factory and it's the fastest hover in its class. Bet it'll give your wings a run for the money."

"I have no wish to rob you."

Matt, Summer, and Kari loaded up in the hover and left for the Turner estate near the West Coast. Windy waved goodbye to them from the porch. After the hover disappeared over the treetops, she turned to Will. "I am not eager to discuss what you learned from Sam, but it must be done." She stepped to a chair and sat down.

"Yes, it is bad news. The charges against Jim are strong, and more likely than not, he faces prison." He knelt before her and placed a hand on her knee. "But, Grandma, a small light glows in the darkness. Waters plans to postpone Jim's trial until he can travel to Oden and defend him. Waters and I have agreed that you should go with him. You can be a witness and explain the harpy depression, the reason Jim had to rescue Alex from the hospital. Also, seeing Jim again shall be good for you."

"I feared our talk, feared you would say that Jim and I would be forever parted. But your bright light encourages me. I look forward to going." Her eyes twinkled.

"I am glad and no longer have to worry about you."

She took his hand. "I am sorry you had to agonize over my survival while ruling the Outback in my absence. But you have done so well. You handled the human disputes with fairness and wisdom. Everyone in the Outback respects and trusts you. Before I leave, we shall have a little ceremony with the flock leaders and human officials, and I shall renounce my reign and name you as my successor."

"It can wait until you return to Dora."

She eyed him. "You are clever, Will. You fear that things might go badly on Oden, and I will never return, but the responsibility of leadership will save me."

He dropped his head and nodded.

She lifted his chin. "My sweet Will, to ease your mind, the ceremony shall take place with my homecoming. But whether I live or die, everyone accepts you as the next ruler."

"Not everyone," he mumbled, thinking of Alex.

* * *

In her luxurious mansion on Oden, Monica Carlton sat on a bench inside the glass solarium. A row of little pink flowers grew at her feet, and she recalled that Alexander had been more fascinated with plants than toys. He even preferred sleeping on the hard tree limb than in his spacious bedroom and soft bed. Daily she came to the warm, uncomfortable greenhouse in search of answers. Her son had grown up a stranger, and she had lost him before word of his death.

The tragedy was burnt in her mind. Chief Richards had come to her home and said that Alexander and his kidnappers perished when their ship hit an asteroid. First, there was numbness and disbelief.

Then she felt the rage that slowly turned to agonizing sorrow. Despite their strained relationship, she missed him.

The outside door opened, and Jerry, the elderly black gardener, stepped inside. "Oh, Miss Carlton, I didn't know you was here. Lilly called and asked me to come back to work and tend the plants, but I'll do it another time."

"No, take care of them now." Monica rose and dabbed her bloodshot eyes. "I changed my mind about tearing down the solarium, so you have your job back."

"Thank you, ma'am." He bent over and put a finger in the soil. "They're in bad need of a drink." After turning on a sprinkler, he removed a rake from the storage locker and went to work on the fallen leaves.

Monica watched him for a few minutes. My son never liked people much, but he loved Mollie and cared about you and Agatha. Mollie is dead and I fired Agatha, so I'm asking you. Why did he get along with you?"

Jerry stopped raking and leaned on the rake handle. "I believe people misunderstood Mr. Alex, expected him to act like a human. He wasn't. One look into his eyes, I saw his wildness. I treated him like a bird, gave him space, and kindness. Even a wild bird warms up, given time." He looked up into the tree. "T' ain't the same place without that rascal."

"Apparently you understood him better than I did." She stood. "I'll leave you to your work."

Jerry reached down and picked up a small yellow feather that his rake had unearthed in the leaves. "Ma'am, I'm thinking you might want this." He held it out to her.

She brought the feather to her lips and kissed it. "Thank you, Jerry." The precious plume was all she had left of her son.

Monica walked through the house to her secretary's office for a morning report on the hospitalized kidnapper. At her desk Lilly leaped to attention.

“Well?” Monica asked.

“He’s recovered enough from surgery to be moved to the prison hospital tomorrow, but he’s still not allowed to have visitors. I’m not sure it would do much good to see him anyway. He refuses to talk to police and has only spoken to his attorney.”

Monica’s earlier grief became irritation. “Ridiculous,” she fumed. “I don’t give a damn about the hospital or police policies. Inform Chief Richards I’ll be at the hospital in half an hour and expect to meet this kidnapper.”

The limo pulled up to the hospital, and Monica strolled to the reception desk. “I’m Miss Carlton,” she announced to the two nurses in attendance.

One rose and said, “We’ve been expecting you, Miss Carlton. Chief Richards said to escort you to the prisoner’s room. Please follow me.”

Trailing the nurse down the hallway, Monica wondered if she should scream at the man who had taken her son from the hospital or calmly question him.

They came to the prisoner’s room where a guard sat outside the door. He rose and unlocked the door, “Miss Carlton, for your protection, the chief insisted I remain with you when you speak to the prisoner.”

Monica huffed a consent, but the prisoner was less apt to talk with the guard present. Inside the room, she stepped past the guard and gazed at the large, sleeping man. His light hair was streaked with silver, and his features were ruggedly handsome. “Excuse me,” she said. “I wish to talk with you.”

The man slowly opened his eyes and grumbled in a low, tired voice, “Who the devil are you?”

“I’m Monica Carlton, Alexander’s mother.”

His eyes focused. “Oh, Jesus, what do you want?”

“Why did you kidnap my son?”

"Lady, you and I both know it wasn't a kidnapping. He was dying in that mental hospital and wanted out. Now go away."

"But he was killed, and it's your fault," Monica thundered.

He glared at her. "You want to point fingers? Start with yourself. You locked him up, and despite his suicide attempts and Mollie's warning that harpies die in cages, you kept him there. At least the poor kid's suffering is over."

"Alexander was dangerous and had to be committed."

"Typical parent of a kid gone bad, blame everyone but herself."

Monica fought back tears. "You don't know anything about my son."

"No, but I damn well know harpies. I'm married to one, and your boy's father was my best friend. Unless threatened, they're reasonable and gentle. If you hadn't been so hell-bent on breaking his spirit, neither of us would be here, and Alexander would be alive." He yelled to the guard, "Get her out of here!" He rolled on his side with his back to her.

"You haven't seen the last of me. You're going to pay for what you've done," she shouted, but the man didn't respond.

"Miss Carlton," said the guard. "Perhaps it would be better if you left now."

Monica sniffled up her resolve and swept past him with her head held high. She strode through the hospital and out to the waiting limo. Realizing everything the man had said rang true, she recalled Alexander's short life. When a small fledgling, he had curled up at her feet and nuzzled her legs, begging for affection. She pushed him away and scolded him for behaving like a dog. As he grew older, she forced the human culture and education down his throat. He had tried hard to please her, but as a teenager he rebelled, using his telepathy to play embarrassing pranks to be noticed and loved. He became dangerous with the attempt to amputate his wings. When the police shot Mollie, it was the final blow.

"It is my fault, all of it," she said, sobbing.

The limo pulled up to her mansion. She wiped away the tears and went inside.

Lilly met her in the foyer. “Did you speak to the kidnapper?”

Monica stared at her skinny, red-headed secretary, who for six years had been her partner and co-conspirator in the war against her son. Lilly had spied and tattled on his every move, had encouraged her to fire Mollie, and to take more drastic measures to control Alexander. It would be easy to blame Lilly for the end result. But she knew better.

“He told me who was responsible for Alexander’s death, and it’s me.”

“Miss Carlton, that isn’t true.”

“My son was very perceptive and saw right through people, including you. I recall his favorite word for you was ‘snake.’ But Alexander’s death is my doing. I should have taken Mollie’s advice and not listened to you and those doctors. I should have been a better mother.”

“Miss Carlton, you were a good mother. You gave Alexander everything.”

“Everything but love,” Monica said. “Lilly, you’re fired.”

CHAPTER TWENTY-TWO

Alex fluttered several feet off the ground and kicked at bowling ball-size fruits that hung on vines. He landed and gazed at the smashed and dripping target, making sure he hadn't missed any. Bending over, he rested his hands on his knees. Panting, he was totally spent from the all-day exercise.

"Alex, you must get faster," Westly said. "Watch my hand." He swiftly waved his hand past Alex's face. "Did you see it?"

"Not really," Alex gasped.

"If you wish to beat Will, you must strike with such speed."

"That's impossible."

"You have chosen the impossible. I have heard that Will is a blur of yellow when he fights. His challengers never see the blows that dropped them."

Alex straightened. "My brother might be better prepared, but he's only flesh and blood. He can be beaten."

For several weeks from sunup to sundown, Alex had worked in heat and rain to strengthen his muscles and develop his fighting skills. Tired of sleeping on soggy tree moss, he took to a mountain cave for the rainy nights. Westly had taught the basics for a challenge, but Alex needed Bloom to complete his training.

On the ship Bloom had been modest, never revealing he was one of the toughest harpies in the flocks. Alex now regretted his cavalier behavior toward the black-winged harpy. He'd have to swallow his pride to gain Bloom's help.

The sun was low on the horizon when Westly began to hang more fruit. Alex pulled his sore, drooping wings off the ground. Tossing back his sweat-drenched hair, he said, "I'm done and going to the stream." He started down the jungle path with Westly following. "You don't need to be with me every second. Go find us dinner."

Westly lowered his head submissively. "Sure, Alex."

Alex sighed. "Don't take it personally. Sometimes I want to be alone. I'll meet you back at the cave."

Westly took off, and Alex continued through the head-high blue ferns. "God, he's worse than a shadow," he grumbled. At the familiar stream, he untied his new hip sash woven by cave insects. After washing it and hanging it on a rock to dry, he lay nude in the cool water and noticed that his once pale body bore a dark tan, and hard muscles had replaced soft flesh. Even his flaxen hair had brightened to bleached blond. Amusingly, his body now resembled Will's.

He leaned back against grass on the bank, closed his eyes, and let the rushing water soothe his weary body. When hearing a snap of twiges behind him, he assumed the harmless zels had come for their afternoon drink. He suddenly became aware of a warm, foul breath on his face, opened his eyes to huge teeth, and froze with terror. A massive reptile with a snakelike, yellow-and-black striped body seethed over him, ready to chomp down on its cornered meal. But a knocking sound of wood against wood came from the trees. The animal swished its enormous tail and lifted its head to investigate. With its attention diverted, Alex scrambled out from beneath the creature's head and took flight. Behind him he heard the angry, shrill bellows.

He flew rapidly to the cave, still shaking with fright.

In the cave Westly, snug in the nest of moss, popped a berry in his mouth. He tilted his head. "Where is your sash?"

Alex walked to the nest and collapsed. "On a rock near the stream," he gasped. "Some big, yellow and black bastard nearly ate me. Damn thing looked like a snake."

"A snakon, they are bad but slow. They mostly eat the rotting flesh of dead animals. Harpies are too fast for them."

"Well, this one snuck up and got right over me. I should've been paying more attention."

"So the scare taught you a valuable lesson, stay alert on the jungle floor. We are the most intelligent of creatures, but that does not make us less vulnerable. If you continue to reject the knowledge of the wild animals, they shall kill you before your brother does."

"Yeah, yeah, yeah," Alex said, and sat up. "What kind of animal knocks against wood? The noise distracted the creature and allowed me to get away."

He scratched his head. "I know of no animal that makes such a sound." He rose. "I shall retrieve your sash."

* * *

In Terrance the sheets of rain pounded the windows and metal roof of the large community building. Will slipped inside the rear door and stood behind the noisy crowd of humans that filled the seats and lined the walls. All focused on the stage. Will clasped his hands to hide nervousness. His grandmother stood at the podium, and behind her sat the mayor, city council members, and Larry, Jim's replacement for chief of police.

When his grandmother smiled at him, many turned their heads, mumbled, and gawked at him. They knew he was Shail's eldest son, destined to rule the Outback. Windy lifted her hands, calling for silence. "Thank you for coming out in this nasty weather. You have heard that my husband, Jim, will stand trial for crimes on Oden. Those that know him know he is innocent. I will leaving Dora to be with him during this ordeal. In my absence, my grandson Will shall take over. He has full authority to make all decisions, and upon my return, he will officially replace me as the harpy ruler. Will, please come forward."

Will walked up the center aisle and sensed the uncertainty of people. Many thought he was too young, too wild, too aggressive, the well-known traits of golden male harpies, and that he had no experience for leadership. Most hoped that Windy would remain in power.

Reaching the podium, he faced the crowd and said softly, "I feel your concern and see the doubt in your eyes. I understand you do not know or trust me as the harpies do. I promise I to be fair and wise with my decisions, but I must warn you that change is coming."

A rumble of voices filled the room. An older, heavyset man stood and approached him. "Will, I'm Ed Jackson, the mayor of Terrance. I worked alongside your dad when we rebuilt city after the swarm strike. So, what kind of changes do you have in mind, son?"

"Mayor, I recently flew the length of the land." Will looked back at the crowd. "The eastern jungle is nearly gone, replaced with human sprawl. The same is slowly happening to the Outback. Every season more homes, farms, and businesses appear. Man is the only creature that destroys nature rather than blends with it. This human spread must end."

Jackson chuckled. "Son, you can't stop progress."

"But I can, Mayor, and we are not related, so do not call me son. No more humans will be allowed to move here. Those who already live here can remain. But if you long for more land, more money, more things, I suggest you go elsewhere." In response to the grumbling, he unconsciously arched his wings slightly.

Jackson stepped toward his grandmother. "Miss Windy, you can't agree with your grandson's radical policies of shutting our borders. We have a lot of residents who work in construction. Half our economy will be wiped out, and I have a long list of people who have applied for residency plus a stack of building permits waiting for your approval."

Windy moved next to Will. "Toss your list and permits away, Mayor Jackson. I agree with Will. For many years, I have been too lenient and sympathetic to human demand and have let more and more people cross the river and stay here. Terrance is growing into a large city. Remember, Mayor, this is harpy land. When my son, Shail ruled, he invited you and the humans into his home as his guests. A good guest does not take advantage of his host."

In the crowd a middle-aged woman stood. "I'm very happy here and want the jungle preserved, but I have a small restaurant that relies mainly on tourists. Are you also putting a stop to visitors?"

Will said, "I realize the human need for money. The tourists can come and enjoy the city and a small portion of our jungle, but they can no longer wander the forest roads, littering, and killing animals with their vehicles."

Jackson huffed. "With such restraints, tourists won't come. Business will suffer—."

"They will come," Will said, cutting in. "The Outback is one of the few remaining places where ancient trees and mighty dragons reign. Our precious jungle must be protected. Can you not see this as a harpy does?"

The audience broke out in chatter. A bearded man stood, "I agree with the young harpy," he shouted. "I was born here and have seen how people are destroying the jungle. Those people who want a comfortable city life, wide highways, and tall buildings should get their asses back to where they came from. I'm with you, Will. It's a good idea."

Will stared at the people, amazed that so many supported his cause. Windy took his hand and relayed, *Some disagree with you, but you have earned the respect of all, just like your father did.*

* * *

After the town meeting, Will flew through the downpour to his grandmother's home. Windy remained to talk to the mayor and officials. Landing in the yard, he saw Bloom on the porch.

“Bloom, I am glad to see you,” Will said, ruffling his wet feathers under the veranda roof. “We have not talked since your return.”

Bloom bowed and then they clasped each other’s shoulders. “Yes, there is much unspoken, but the jungle says you do well as a ruler.”

Will sat down on the railing. “I am not so sure. The harpies accept me, but I just left some unhappy humans who disapprove of me. So what brings you here?”

“I came to see Alex, concerned if he is adjusting.”

“He is not here. After one night, he left with the young male named Westly. I have been told they are in the a cave in northwestern mountains.”

Bloom nodded. “I know Westly’s father. The young male is a good companion, but hardly fit to protect a golden.”

“I have sent two adults to secretly watch over the pair, and it was lucky I did. My brother recently had a scare. A snakon nearly attacked him, but the males intervened. I am told Alex works hard, learning to fight like a harpy.”

“The fight is for you.”

Will lifted his eyebrows. “For some reason Alex dislikes me.”

“It is not dislike but envy. He wants what you have. He believes if he defeats you and rules the flocks, he shall be admired and loved.”

“He has the mindset of a human and a negative outlook. Even if he won, the harpies would not love him.”

“On the ship I have encouraged him to change, learn our values and ways, but he is very stubborn and has had a troubled upbringing.”

Will ran his finger through his wet hair. “I do not have time for this brother. My grandmother leaves soon for Oden to save Jim, and I must deal with the humans who object to my decisions. When Alex is ready, let him come, and fight me. He shall learn about defeat and humility.”

“I fear that even if beaten and shamed, Alex shall grow worse, not better. Do not take him lightly. His telepathy is powerful and deadly. Your mind must be strong — stronger than his.”

"Summer has already warned me, but I am not concerned." Will sighed. "I feel sorry for Alex. Great sacrifices were made for his freedom, yet he remains a prisoner of his own making."

"Yes, even here among his own kind, he is unhappy. He asked me to teach him to fight, but I refused until he becomes a true harpy. This is why he sought Westly for combat training."

"If Alex thinks as I do, he knows that only a dominant male can prepare him to face me. He shall seek you again, Bloom. I want you to embrace him and give him the skills for a challenge. My father would expect me to be fair to his wayward son."

* * *

At the Turner estate, lightning struck a distant tree in the sprawling pasture. Under the covered porch, Summer lay curled up on the settee with her head on Matt's shoulder. They gazed out at blowing rain that had flattened the long grass and listened to the thunder.

"This is the life," Matt said, rubbing together his bare feet that were propped on the small coffee table. For a week his beloved boots had lain on the bedroom floor.

"I am glad you are happy here," Summer said. Initially, she had been nervous when introducing Matt as her boyfriend and future mate to the family. Her mother, three sisters, six half-brothers, and her stepmother, Lea, were at first surprised, but Matt's charm and down-to-earth nature won them over. She was also was concerned about Matt's fitting into the rowdy bunch of young golden males who often postured and clashed. But he had said the household reminded him of a redneck bar and he felt right at home.

Today the house was quiet. Summer's rambunctious siblings, ranging in ages from ten to seventeen, were in the jungle playing in the rain and seeking adventure. At dusk they would return for dinner on the back porch. Summer smelled the baking bread that Kari and Lea prepared in the kitchen, the aroma comforting after the turbulent space journey. Hearing the front door open, she turned.

Her mother, Rachel, stepped out on the porch. "You two look cozy despite the horrid weather."

Matt straightened and put his feet on the slippery wooden floor. "I like the rain, ma'am, as long as I don't have to work in it. Summer says the wet season is nearly over."

"Yes, it's like a faucet, abruptly starts and stops." She wandered to a chair and sat down beside them. "I'd like to talk to you about your marriage."

"Mom, I already said we are in no hurry," Summer said. "We sleep together but do not mate."

"That's true," Matt said with a sigh. "I mind my p's and q's with Summer. She's worth the wait."

"I appreciate that, Matt," Rachel said. "A scoundrel would grab my daughter, hop on his ship, and disappear. I'm glad you're a decent guy."

Matt chuckled. "Not that decent because it's crossed my mind to take off with her."

Summer swatted his arm. "As if you could force me onto your ship."

Rachel smiled. "You probably know Summer's reason for remaining a virgin. If you took advantage of an unattached female, the male harpies would sense it and likely harm you."

Matt turned to Summer. "Is that right? You're holding back to protect me?"

Summer chewed a lip. "Yes, but I prefer your reasons, waiting because it's honorable."

"Let's talk about his pairing of a man and harpy," Rachel said. "What custom will you follow, bond in private like harpies, or have a wedding?"

Matt grinned. "A great party usually follows a wedding, and I'm overdue for some serious drinking."

"We'll have a wedding," Summer said. "Beside Matt's party, I want my family to hear our vows."

"This makes me very happy," Rachel said. "I always expected my daughters to take harpy mates, and I'd never celebrate their union. If it's a wedding, we need to start planning it. You must decide where and when it will take place for the invitations and the guest list. Then there's your dress, the food, flowers, and so on."

"Mom, slow down. We have plenty of time."

"You have the time but others don't. Every day your father grows worse. I fear he won't be with us long. Your grandmother leaves for Oden. If she loses Jim to prison, she might never return. A wedding brings so much joy and our family needs some. You should wed while Shail and Windy are still with us."

Summer rose and stepped to the railing. "I'm ashamed I haven't visited Dad since I came back, but I get so depressed when he doesn't recognize me." She turned to Matt. "Tomorrow we will see him."

The next day the rain had stopped and the sky was clear and bright. Matt held Summer's hand and followed Kari down the jungle path behind the house. On the ship he had heard stories about Summer's celebrated father. Shail's intelligence and fierceness had saved all life on the planet. But his reputation as a man-killer and the fact that he was losing his mind made Matt apprehensive. Shail might go berserk and murder a lowlife who was marrying his daughter.

Summer whispered, "Don't worry, Matt. Dad won't hurt you."

"Shail will be more afraid of you than you are of him," Kari said. "A man's voice can rattle him, so this visit will go better if you don't speak, Matt."

The path ended at a small clearing, and Kari told them to sit on the bench while she urged Shail from the jungle. After several minutes he stepped from the trees. Matt was astonished by his youthful looks. Shail had to be in his mid-forties, but he could pass for Summer's brother. His pretty face lacked wrinkles, and he had lush long hair and a streamlined frame. His genes were obviously stronger than his mates because his kids had inherited his blond hair, yellow wings, and striking features. However, that's where similarities ended. His offspring were fearless, but Shail was timid, creeping from the brush like a terrified animal.

Kari took Shail's hand and coaxed him closer yet with one glance at Matt, he planted his feet and trembled with his eyes filled with panic. He jerked free from Kari's hand and fled into the air, vanishing over the treetops.

Kari turned to them and sighed. "Men abused him, and Matt frightened him. More and more he relies on his animal instincts to function and is losing human reasoning. Some days I can't get near him."

"Mom is right," Summer said. "He has gotten worse since I left."

"I'm sorry, Summer," Kari said, "I'm afraid the father you knew is gone."

* * *

At the Terrance airport, Will stood beside Ted on the tarmac, waiting for the noon commercial flight from Hampton.

Ted rocked back and forth on his heels. "So-o-o, are you going to tell me about this girl?"

"She is not a girl, Ted. She's a harpy."

"Whatever she is, you must have made an impression for her to fly all this way to see you."

"She is coming to see the home of the harpies."

"Yeah, sure," Ted said, grinning. "Summer is getting married, and you're next."

Will shook his feathers and didn't respond to the meddling man. Across the river, the large, circular hover came into view, slowed, and landed on the airfield. The door opened and passengers walked down the ramp. Some stopped and gaped at Will's wings. When several started to approach him, Ted interceded.

"Don't pester the harpy," he said. "They don't like it." He motioned the people toward the port building. "You can collect your baggage inside."

An older woman ignored Ted. “Can I touch you?” she asked Will.

Irritated, Ted growled, “Lady, keep your hands off him. He’s not a pet and far from friendly.”

Will quickly forgot the annoying passengers when he spotted Sherry. She and her adoptive mother, Frances, were the last to leave the hover.

Sherry saw him and called out, “Hi, Will.” Coming closer, “It’s so great to see you again.”

Tongue tied, he managed to say, “Hello.”

Ted elbowed him. “Wow, she’s a knockout!”

“Shut up, Ted,” Will grumbled as Sherry and her mother strolled to him. “It’s…um…great to see you too. This is Ted, the manager of Terrance airport. He will drive you to my grandmother’s home.”

Frances shook Ted’s hand and said, “Pleased to meet you. I’m Frances and this is my daughter, Sherry.” She turned to Will. “Are you sure we won’t be a bother? We could stay in town at a hotel.”

“My grandmother has a large home and wishes your company.”

Ted placed their bags in his vehicle, and he, Sherry, and Frances drove off. Will flew ahead and landed on Windy’s porch. He paced, waiting for their arrival. Freely and Windy came out of the house and joined him.

Freely said, “Will, I have never seen you so nervous.”

“He is,” Windy said with a smile, “but it is a good nervous. He is attracted to her, and his heart flutters like his wings.”

Will stopped pacing. “I am not nervous,” he lied. The moment he saw Sherry again, he became flustered. He took a breath to gain control.

The vehicle pulled into the drive, and Ted, Sherry, and Frances climbed out. Windy walked out to them and introduced herself while Ted brought their bags to the house. Will remained on the porch and watched them chat, walking to the house.

Freely nudged him. “She is lovely, a good choice for your mate.”

"We are not committed to a bond. She could choose another, Freely."

They gathered in the living room, and Windy served refreshments. Ted, trying to be supportive, said, "Did you know that Will is the next Outback ruler? He's just like his dad, Shail."

Frances spun around to Will. "My goodness, your father is Shail?" She explained to Sherry. "When I first came here, everyone talked about the beautiful harpy leader who destroyed the swarms and saved everyone. Shail is a great hero. Why didn't you tell us, Will?"

With all eyes focused on him, he fidgeted. "Harpies do not boast about such things, and I am only one of my father's many sons. Ted, are you not needed at the airport?"

Ted laughed. "Yeah, he's modest, but we all know Will is the best of the harpies and a shoo-in to rule. But I believe he just gave me my cue to shut up and go. Ladies, it was nice meeting you," he said and left.

Sherry smiled at Will, and then sat on the couch next to his grandmother. "Miss Windy, do you know anything about my harpy mother?"

"Many years ago, my father took me to the last harpy gathering where a new ruler would be chosen from many competing golden males. I was there to find a mate. I remember three males who had flown in from the East for the challenges. We later learned the three Eastern goldens were killed defending their flocks from hunters. It was assumed that their mates and fledglings also perished."

"My mother must have descended from one of those males," Sherry said.

Windy took Sherry's hand. "Yes, one was your grandfather, and if your mother had lived, she'd be the same age now as my son, Shail, just as you are Will's age. It is the only explanation."

"But my mother married a man," Sherry said.

Windy grinned. "As have I. Back then, males were hunted and few in number. Many females took the identity of a woman and wed men to conceal their nature and survive. The offspring of these females kept the harpies from extinction, especially the golden bloodline. Your mother chose wisely. Had she bonded with a harpy, your parents would probably have perished, and you wouldn't be here."

Will stepped forward and said softly, "My mother is half-human, and the mother of my four sisters is a woman. My father was the last golden male and took three mates to increase our numbers but we still are few. You are very important, Sherry."

Sherry clasped his hand. "And apparently so are you."

CHAPTER TWENTY-THREE

Alex staggered to his feet and, using his arm, wiped the blood and dirt from his mouth. He straightened and glared at Bloom. He had gone from kicking fruit and playing footsy with Westly to serious competition.

"Again," Bloom said.

Alex took a breath, arched his wings, and walked in a circle with his eyes fixed on Bloom who outweighed him and had overshadowing black wings. Bloom, poised and confident, began to stroll around him.

Alex's only fan, Westly, stood on the sidelines with other males from Bloom's flock. "Come on, Alex," he called. "You can take him."

Alex glanced at the group of brown-winged males, who obviously enjoyed seeing their leader beat the crap out of a pompous young golden.

"Lose the resentment, Alex," Bloom barked. "You cannot focus on the task, and therefore, second guess your next move."

Yellow and black feathers fluttered off the ground, and they engaged in combat. Alex kicked Bloom's ribs, and Bloom countered with a wing whack that sent Alex downward and tumbled end over end into ferns.

Alex lifted his head and hissed, conveying harpy rage. He stood, flung the ferns aside, and marched back to Bloom in the clearing. Fed up with the ridiculous circling, he crouched and flew at his opponent. Bloom jumped aside, kicking Alex's stomach. The blow put Alex on his knees doubled over and coughing.

Bloom grabbed Alex's arm and jerked him to a stand. "We are done today. You are frustrated and angry. In a fight you must think clearly, ignore embarrassment no matter how many times you are knocked down."

Alex swept the hair from his sweaty brow. "That's easy for you to say. You're not eating dirt."

"I met the ground often when I was your age but learned that mind control is more important than speed, strength, and skill." Bloom patted Alex's back. "As with all things, you grasp knowledge quickly and come far in a short time."

With the clash over, the other males took flight into the jungle. Alex and Bloom walked down a narrow animal trail to a stream. "I have trained many young males," said Bloom, "but never a golden. Your temperament is different. You accept punishment and come back for more. Brown-winged males lack this resolve." Reaching the stream, Bloom knelt for a sip while Alex collapsed into the cold water. Bloom gazed at Alex's bruised body. "Tomorrow you rest and heal."

Alex splashed the blood off his face. "No way. I'll take a break when I'm good enough to beat you and Will."

"You could already win a challenge against most males, and someday soon, you shall beat me. But Will is your brother, and you are wrong to make him an enemy. He has a good heart and would give you the love you seek."

Alex touched his sore chin and rose from the water. "I don't want his damn love, Bloom. When I rule the harpies, I'll have everyone's love."

Bloom sighed. "For one so smart, you are a blind fool. The power you seek shall not make you happy."

"Let me worry about that."

"You should be worried. The challenge for rule is more than a fight for dominance. You shall also face tests that prove one's wisdom and honor."

"You know I'm smarter than Will."

"In human school knowledge, yes, but Will has jungle insight and good judgment—qualities not taught in books, but experienced. For you, the toughest shall be your character. You must prove you are trustworthy, decent, and caring. Above all things, harpies prize honor."

Alex considered his dilemma. Could he fake his way through it?

An unfamiliar harpy fluttered down and bowed to Alex. "Our queen sent me to summon you and Bloom to the Turner estate."

"That's where my lame relatives live," Alex said. "I don't want to see them."

Bloom asked the harpy, "What is the purpose of the summons?"

"It is a human bonding. In three lights, Shail's eldest daughter marries a man. Our queen wishes you to be at the ceremony."

Alex sat down on a smooth boulder to preen his feathers. "Summer hates me. She doesn't want me at her wedding. Tell my grandmother I'm not coming.

Bloom said to the harpy, "Forget his words. Relay to our queen that her grandson and I shall be there." With a nod, the harpy flew away.

"Bloom, I'm not going. They think I'm a monster."

"Their thoughts intimidate you? How can a coward rule?"

Alex leaped up from the rock. "I'm not intimidated. I grew up with criticism and overcame it. When I face Will, I just want to be ready. This time I'm not flying away from him."

"Your family gathers to rejoice the bond of Matt and Summer. Will shall not challenge you unless you provoke him. You should meet your other brothers and sisters."

"I don't care about them."

"And what of your father?" asked Bloom. "He should also be there."

Bloom had ended the argument. Alex wanted to meet his illustrious dad.

* * *

In an upstairs bedroom at the Turner estate, Summer gazed out the window at the arriving vehicles with wedding guests. "I'm getting nervous, Mom. I'd rather stare down a pride of grogins than face these people. We should have bonded in private and forgot Matt's party."

"You'll be fine," Rachel said, standing behind her and weaving tiny white flowers into Summer's long blond hair.

Summer shook her head. "Those flowers pull and are annoying. Are they really necessary?"

"Yes, now hold still. Don't you want to look pretty for Matt?"

"He thinks I am fine without foliage in my hair and in this long, heavy dress."

"This pearl-beaded gown with the custom-made back for your wings cost a small fortune. I want my daughter to be beautiful on her wedding day."

"I am going through with this wedding to make you and Matt happy. Harpies don't care about ceremonies." Alex and Bloom landed in the yard, and Summer huffed. "Unbelievable, my long-lost brother showed up. I hope he doesn't ruin everything."

Rachel stepped to the window. "So that is Alex. He's very handsome, doesn't looks anything like his mother. But he did inherit her size. He's taller than your father and brothers."

"How well did you know his mother?"

"I met Monica on the voyage to Earth when we both slept with Shail. I was never her friend. She's the cruelest woman I've ever met, enjoyed abusing and molesting your father. Someone that heartless should never have had a child. I feel sorry for Alex, having that terrible woman for a mother."

"Mom, if you had been on the spaceship with that jerk, you wouldn't pity him. Alex takes after his mother. Every time he opened his mouth, I felt like hitting him."

Rachel clasped Summer's shoulders and glared at her. "I raised you to be charitable and understanding. That poor young male has probably never known a mother's love. You should overlook his shortcomings."

Summer lowered her head. "He rarely mentioned his mother, except after the asteroid explosion, he said he was glad that she would believe he was dead. I'll try to be kinder to him."

Rachel smiled. "Now you truly resemble an angel."

"I better go down and face the music, as Matt would say." Summer picked up the bouquet of wildflowers, hoisted the gown so as not to trip, and walked to the staircase. Will and her three sisters awaited her in the foyer.

Will looked up at her. "You look lovely, Summer." When her sisters giggled at her outfit, he hissed at them.

Descending the stairs, Summer said to Will, "Alex is here. He and Bloom landed beside the house."

He lifted an eyebrow. "I heard Grandmother invited him, but I am surprised he came. Do not worry. Bloom will make him behave."

"I doubt it."

Rachel joined them and kissed Summer's cheek. "Thank you, sweetheart, for letting me have the wedding." She turned to her other daughters. "Let's go, girls." They left the house to join the guests.

Arm in arm, Summer and Will strolled down the jungle path to the clearing where the ceremony would take place. A small group of harpies and people faced an arch trellis bearing pale yellow flowers. Windy stood under the trellis, and Matt was off to the side, cleanly shaven, boots polished, and wearing a new black jacket. He winked at Summer, and she blushed. As she and Will approached, she scanned the guests. Alex and Bloom stood beyond the gathering under the trees, but Summer was searching for another. "He didn't come."

"I am sorry, Summer," said Will, knowing she spoke of their father.

They stopped before their grandmother, and Will gave Summer's hand to Matt. "I give you my sister. Treat her well."

"I will. I give you my word."

Windy smiled at her and Matt. "We are gathered here..." She stopped when the harpies looked to the jungle and fell on their knees. Shail with Kari holding his hand stepped from the jungle. Behind them was Aron, Shail's lifelong friend. The humans went down on their knees with lowered heads. Only Windy stood and gazed approvingly at her son. Shail hesitated and glanced at Aron.

"I am here, brother," Aron said quietly. "I shall always be here for you. Now be with your family on this important day."

Shail released Kari's hand, and his posture straightened. He walked directly past the guests to Will. "You are my oldest, yes?"

Will rose. "I am, Father. I am Will."

Shail clasped his shoulders. "I feel the honor and strength in you. You make me proud, son."

Will's eyes watered. "Thank you, Father."

Shail stepped to Summer and kissed her cheek. "So beautiful," he said, and then glanced at Matt. "You chose a man?"

"Yes, Father. I love him." Summer bit her lip hard, trying to prevent tears. "Daddy," she sniffled. "I am so glad you came."

Shail brushed away the tear. "I am too." He turned to Matt, his soft voice becoming stern. "My daughter is a precious flower. If you take her into your nest, you must love, nurture, and guard her with your life."

"Yes, sir, I promise, sir," Matt said.

"Break that promise, and I shall find and end you."

"Yes, sir," Matt said. "I believe you would."

For a brief moment in time, Shail was the father Summer had known — confident, powerful, majestic. But sadly, it wouldn't last.

Shail stepped to his family, patting his sons and kissing his daughters and mates. Alex, the only one absent, had stayed under the trees and watched the father he had never known.

Shail hugged Windy. "Thank you, Mother, for all you do and have done." He glanced anxiously at the gathering. "I must go."

Windy sobbed openly. "I know this was hard for you. Remember, I love you, son."

Shail swallowed. "I shall try to remember." He turned to Aron.

With Aron's nod, the two legendary harpies took to the sky and faded into the trees.

Windy wiped her eyes and regained her composure. She took Summer's and Matt's hands, placing them together. "Your father accepts this man as your mate, Summer, and so do I. You now belong to Matt, and Matt, you are hers. Cherish this day and never forget your vow to love each other." Summer leaned over and kissed Matt's lips.

Matt embraced her, making the kiss long and passionate. They pulled apart. "We're married now?"

"Not until tonight," said Summer. "A harpy bond takes place when we unite."

* * *

After the wedding, the guests left for the reception at the house. Will remained and gazed across the clearing at Bloom and Alex. With a wing shrug, he stepped toward them, deciding to give his estranged brother a second chance. Perhaps their initial rocky encounter could be mended. "Alex, I would like to talk to you."

Leaning against a tree trunk with crossed arms, Alex straightened, tossed back his locks, and lifted his wings. "We are beyond talk."

"Give me patience," Will thought, and took a few steps toward Alex. "I do not wish to fight you."

Bloom tried to mediate. "Alex, his wings are folded. Speak with him. He offers a truce."

"Bloom I don't give a shit what the moron is offering. I don't want to hear it."

Will had warned that he would not ignore one more insult from Alex. He raised his wings, intending to pummel the brashness out of him.

Alex stepped from the tree with his wings open, and ready to engage him.

As Will approached him, he heard Sherry calling for his name from the path.

"Another time, Alex," Will said, deciding not to bloody his brother in front of Sherry. He turned toward the path and called, "I'm here." Stepping to her, he said, "Sorry; I had hoped to resolve a problem, but it can wait." He took her hand, and they walked up the trail to the house. "What did you think of the wedding?"

"It was beautiful but so emotional. I cried, listening to your father. He was so elegant yet commanding."

"I'm glad you saw him as he once was."

* * *

Alex lowered his wings and watched Will leave with the striking female. "Who is she?" he asked Bloom.

"I know not her name, but the word among the flocks is she is a golden harpy Will discovered in the East. You fulfilled your grandmother's wishes, but it is unwise to stay, after antagonizing your brother."

"I'm not worried about him," Alex said. "Besides I want to meet this female from the east."

"Will is clearly interested in her. If you try to come between them, you shall further enrage him."

Alex just chuckled and kept walking toward the path. At the large house, he stepped onto the long porch and heard the chatter inside. Opening the front door, he entered the foyer. Those gathered in the living room saw him and talk ceased. All knew about him: the dysfunctional brother, the freak more human than harpy, the dangerous cop killer. "What was I thinking?" he murmured.

Alex was used to ogling and snubs on Oden, but this group included harpies, his own kind. The stares crushed him, and he sought a graceful way out. Lowering his eyes, he stepped back to the door and fumbled for the handle.

To his surprise, Summer stepped forth and rescued him. "Alex, I'm happy you came to my wedding." On tiptoes, she kissed his cheek. Given their bickering on the ship, her affection was unexpected and left him speechless.

Matt walked to them, holding a beer bottle. "Hey, kid, are you ready to party?"

"If that's okay with you and Summer," Alex said quietly. With Summer's acceptance, the judging stares ceased, and the cheerful prattle resumed.

"Sure, it's okay," said Summer. "If not for you, there'd be no wedding or Matt."

Alex was baffled. Why was she being nice to him? He squelched the skepticism and tried to be gracious. "Congratulations on your marriage. I'm glad you found love. It makes me envious."

"Alex." His grandmother strolled to him. "Come and meet your other brothers and sisters." Pulling him away from Summer and Matt, Windy introduced him to his siblings, and the guests. Alex relaxed, sensing no animosity. He spotted Bloom at the door, standing like a sentry with Alex in his sights. Was he concerned for Alex or the safety of others?

Alex smiled, mingled, and spoke politely, hoping to dispel the nasty rumors about him. All the while, he searched for the gorgeous female and watched out for Will.

Through a window he saw Will outside with Aron, the harpy who had left the clearing with his father. Bloom had whispered that Aron was Shail's nest brother and lifelong companion. At the wedding, Alex had longed to meet his father, but feared rejection. After all, he and Shail were strangers, only connected by genes. When Shail fled, Alex realized he too had insecurities.

With Will outside, Alex wandered through the house, searching for the pretty female. After checking the study, library, and family room, he entered the dining room with a long table laden with dishes of food. Small groups talked and nibbled on the cuisine, but she wasn't among them. With sagging shoulders, he ate a slice of melon.

"Kari, this is the last platter in the refrigerator," said a female voice in the kitchen.

Alex perked up. Like a breath of fresh air, Sherry breezed into the dining room and placed a dish on the table. Restraining his enthusiasm, he ambled to her side. "Hello, I don't believe we've been introduced. I'm Alex."

She smiled warmly. "No, and I thought I met all of Will's brothers. I'm Sherry."

"I'm considered the black sheep of the family." Alex grinned. He'd been taught etiquette but rarely practiced it. With Sherry, however, he poured on the charm. When she offered her hand, he brought it to his lips and softly kissed it. "You're a beautiful addition to the Outback."

Her eyes sparkled. "Aren't you the gentleman?"

"I'm different from my brothers, who were raised in trees. I was born on Oden with humans, so I'm a bit more civilized and educated. I received my first college degree when I was thirteen."

"Wow, thirteen, you must be brilliant. I was also raised with humans and went to college. Right now I'm studying to be a veterinarian at Hampton University."

"That's a noble occupation, helping those who can't speak for themselves, but the science is hard. A vet must learn twice as much as a physician."

With upraised eyebrows, she said, "Yes, the biology of different species is a lot to comprehend."

"If you ever need a study partner, I'm at your service. I grasp books rather quickly."

"What did you study, Alex?"

"I have degrees in engineering, computer science, art history, sociology, psychology. If you want your head examined, I'm your man, or harpy." He smiled.

"I can see why psychology would interest a harpy. We do have scary intuition. I never understood how I could sense people's thoughts until Will told me I was a harpy. That freaked me out."

"But the fog you lived in has finally lifted. You clearly see who you are. Knowing your nature, you are more confident and comfortable."

For a moment her mouth parted in thought. "Yes," she said slowly, a little astonished. "I do understand myself better and am more positive." She lifted her eyes to his. "Alex, you explained it so perfectly."

Will came into the dining room. Seeing Alex with Sherry, he hot-footed it to her side. "Are you having a good time?" he asked, with a smoldering glare on Alex.

"I'm having a wonderful time with your brother," said Sherry. "Alex is so intriguing."

"Is he?" said Will. "Would you like to see the estate now?"

Alex straightened to his full stature. "She's busy talking to me."

"Your talk is over," Will said in a low, threatening tone.

"I'll decide that," Alex snapped. "Why don't you buzz off to some bush?"

Out of nowhere Bloom appeared and edged between them. "Alex, this is not the time or place."

Alex lifted his wings and growled, "This is none of your business, Bloom!"

"Bloom is right about the place," Will said. "We need to take this outside."

"Agreed," said Alex.

Everyone in the house heard the friction in the dining room. Windy rushed to them. “Will, you promised not to hurt him.”

“Hurt me?” Alex seethed. “I’ll have this idiot begging for mercy.”

“Grandma, he has slighted me for the last time,” said Will. “Shall we go, Alex?”

As Alex and Will started toward the door, Sherry grabbed Will’s arm. “Please, Will, not a fight, not because of me. Show me your home.” She turned to Alex. “And, Alex, we’ll talk another time. Okay?” Bloom and Windy could not stop the clash, but Sherry had their full attention.

Will nodded. “I will not mar my sister’s wedding with bloodshed.” He focused on Alex. “Next time we meet, we settle this.”

“That’s fine with me.” Alex sneered. “But, Will, this won’t be a fight between feuding brothers or over a female. It will be a challenge for Outback rule.”

“I look forward to it.”

* * *

Thanks to the gossip of the wedding guests, the confrontation between Will and Alex spread quickly across the Outback. The following day the Terrance newspaper carried the headline: Who Will Reign? The article explained that the last time the harpies had gathered to pick a ruler was nearly six decades ago. and the winner was Shail’s father. Two generations later, the grandsons would make their bid for leadership and fight it out.

The press was familiar with Will, Shail’s eldest son; they had photographed and written about him since birth. In his later years, though, he had become elusive. When he showed up in public at the Terrance City Council meeting, it was a surprise. His announcement to close the Outback proved unpopular with officials and some of the residents, but their opinions didn’t matter. Humans were guests in the harpy land, with no vote as to who ruled and how.

The story said little about Alex, except that he was ten months younger than Will and had a college education. No information on where he had been all these years or how he came to Dora.

The harpy chatter in the trees was more telling. The flocks trusted Will and his judgment and wanted him to be their next leader. And with his incredible fighting skills, he was the favorite to win. Yet many harpies were curious about this younger, audacious brother from another world. Some flew great distances to watch him train in Bloom's valley. Alex was open to challengers. A brown-winged harpy, who subdued a golden, gained great stature in the flocks.

* * *

Exhaling through clenched teeth, Alex gave a low, unnerving hiss to his opponent, a flock leader from the South. The brawny, older male with an enormous wingspan appeared massive compared with Alex's wiry frame and smaller, yellow wings. But what Alex lacked in size and weight, he made up for in speed and an uncompromising determination. Bloom and harpy spectators watched the challenge from the sidelines.

Alex flexed his wings and strutted around, opposite his rival. Then he saw the telltale signs: the pupil dilation in the male's green eyes, the raised hair on his arms, the hesitation of step, and the slight shudder of dark feathers. The male's body language conveyed that he was anxious and having reservations about exchanging blows with a golden. Alex knew the fight was over before it began.

He flew at the big male, catching him off guard with a shoulder blow to the gut. The male frantically flapped his wings to keep from falling backward and stay airborne. Alex launched into a full assault of swift kicks, punches, and wing whacks. Overwhelmed, the male never even struck back. A hard foot blow to the groin brought him crashing down. He curled up, coughed, and held his crotch. But Alex wasn't done. Fluttering above, he kicked his opponent's face until bloody. The harpy huddled under his wings for cover, so Alex targeted them, stomping the brown feathers to break the quills and ripped out the down, making it rain as brown fluff. To show dominance, Alex lifted his sash and urinated on the loser.

"That is enough, Alex!" Bloom marched into the circle and shoved Alex away from his victim.

Alex tousled his feathers in anger. "Watch it, Bloom, or you're next."

"Shut up." Bloom knelt over the injured male and relayed, *It is all right now. He shall not harm you again.* He glared at Alex. "What is wrong with you? When he hit the ground, the fight was over."

"I've been waiting for a big, bad male to show up so I could make a point." Alex gazed at the harpies on the sidelines. They lowered their heads to avoid eye contact. "You see? They respect me now."

"That is not respect but fear. They think you are vicious and unbalanced. You not only defeated this male but practiced the old animal ways of marking him as a slave."

"At least I didn't drink his blood."

"Do you realize what you have done? The humiliation has destroyed his life. He shall lose his flock and maybe even his mate. You should be ashamed."

Alex retreated into the dense forest and reflected on the challenge and his apparent shameful behavior. He regretted disgracing the large male, not out of compassion, but because his excessive actions might harm his standing with the harpies.

With the daily fights, he had rapidly gone from an amateur to a skilled terror. The battles also made him feel good, beating out his sorrow and rage. Whenever he faced an opponent, images of his future reign danced in his head: Will, bloody and broken, cowering at his feet: Sherry at his side; the adoration of his harpy family; and the respect of the flocks and humans. But mostly he envisioned his mother, to whom he was no longer an embarrassment or problem, but a worthy son.

* * *

Will had kissed Sherry goodbye at the Terrance airport. She and her mother then boarded the commercial hover to Hampton. They had discussed a relationship, but Sherry wanted to finish school before committing. He sensed her fondness for him, but an inquisitive seed had been planted when she met Alex. She questioned Will about his brother, but he refused to speak about him. To disclose Alex's faults to gain her favor would be dishonorable. Sherry could discover for herself that despite Alex's intriguing behavior, he had a dark side.

Days later Will rested on his grandmother's bed and watched her pack for the trip to Oden. "Do you want me to go to the airport?" he asked.

"No, we shall say our goodbyes here." Windy closed the bag. "I do not like leaving you with all these problems, especially Alex."

Will rose and held her. "I can handle things, Grandma. And concerning Alex, our challenge for rule shall wait until your return. Your troubles lie ahead on Oden. Stay strong. We need and love you."

"This challenge..." She looked up. "Do you think Alex could win?"

"No, not even if he trained a lifetime. I have the advantage. Father taught me to fight. It is sad, though. Alex longs to rule more than I, and I would gladly yield to him, but he is unfit to govern others."

"I still believe that someday he will change and be an impressive harpy." A vehicle pulled up to the house. "There is my ride."

Will picked up her bag, and they strolled outside to the porch. Larry, who had taken over for Jim as police chief, sat in the driver seat, but jumped out. After opening the passenger door for Windy and stowing her bag, he waited.

"Thank you, Larry," Windy said. "We will go shortly."

Larry smiled. "No hurry, Miss Windy. The hover will wait for you."

She hugged Will and said, "I will call you when Sam and I reach Oden."

Freely flew out of the jungle, and stumbled to a kneeling position before her feet. His green eyes watered, saying, “Please, my queen. Promise you shall return to me.”

She stroked his brown locks. “My devoted companion, you never left my side when I was ill and depressed.”

Will sighed. “I would also ask for your promise to return, but know you will not make that vow. If things go badly for Jim...”

Windy put her finger over his lips. “I shall try to stay well.” She kissed his cheek and climbed into the vehicle.

As the vehicle drove off, Will wondered if he would ever see her again.

CHAPTER TWENTY-FOUR

Windy took the commercial flight to Hampton. Sam Waters greeted her at the terminal and drove her to his lovely oceanfront home. The years had been kind to the retired governor. Although he had a few wrinkles and his once-black hair had turned silver, he was still a tall, lean, and handsome man.

She had met Sam two and a half decades ago when her second mate, a wealthy man, ran for governor, and Sam was his running mate for lieutenant governor. Sam was unaware Windy was a harpy or of her and her husband's plans to end harpy hunting, but Sam was a good, honest man who frowned on killing creatures that looked so human.

When he and her husband won the election, Windy thought the nightmare was over. The harpies would finally dwell in peace. But it was not to be. Windy's husband died of a heart attack, making Sam governor. In the end Shail saved his harpies, and Sam worked with him to implement the ban on harpy hunting. She now needed the man's help again.

They spent the evening rehashing old memories. Like Jim, Sam was deeply devoted to Shail. The following day she and Sam boarded a private spaceship for the long voyage to Oden. Throughout the trip, he catered to her every need and tried to be upbeat when discussing

Jim's trial. Windy smiled, not wishing to contradict him. She had read his mind and knew Jim's circumstances were bleak.

After a month the ship reached Oden and landed at Mirage port, Windy and Sam stepped off the vessel, not expecting a greeting, but were swiftly surrounded with an anxious press of a dozen journalists.

"Miss Windy," called a reporter. "You're the harpy ruler. Why did your husband and the harpies kidnap the Carlton boy?"

Another reporter pushed closer. "Do you have anything to say about the thirteen officers who were killed during the hospital raid?"

"No comment," Sam interceded, and put an arm around her, leading her to a waiting vehicle.

"Your husband goes to trial soon," said a woman journalist. "Are you here to support him?"

"She has no comment," said Sam as they reached the vehicle.

The reporters kept firing questions. "You're Shail's mother," yelled another man. "During your son's reign, he caused the death of over a thousand men. Is that harpy policy—kill people when it suits you?"

After Windy was in the vehicle, Sam wheeled around and yelled, "My God, man, get your facts straight. It was a war. Those men were hired mercenaries who invaded the Outback to exterminate harpies." He climbed into the back seat of the vehicle and slammed the door, ending the interrogation.

"Get us out of here," Sam said to the driver and took Windy's hand. "I'm sorry, I had no idea they'd be here."

"Harpies have always fascinated humans. I wasn't surprised to see them."

The vehicle took a tunnel from the Mirage port and entered the domed city's bustling streets. "When we get to the hotel," said Sam, "you can relax and freshen up."

"I would rather see Jim first."

Sam instructed the driver to go straight to the prison.

There Windy and Sam were screened and led into a stark, windowless room with a table and two chairs. Because of attorney-client privilege, the visit wouldn't be monitored. Sam took a seat while Windy walked back and forth. After months, she would finally see her mate. The door opened, and two guards escorted Jim in room.

Windy's eyes welled up, and she rushed into his arms.

Jim hugged her. "Oh, babe, I'm so glad to see you, but you shouldn't have made this long trip."

"I had to. You breathe life back into my soul."

Sam stood and extended his hand. "Jim."

They shook hands. "Governor, I don't know what you can do," Jim said with dejection. "My lawyers say if I go to trial, I'm facing a life sentence. The prosecution has offered a plea, twenty years. At my age and given cell mates don't care for ex cops, I'm still might to die in prison. Being honest, it's not looking good."

"I'm meeting with your attorneys tomorrow," said Sam. "Maybe I can do better, negotiate protective custody and a reduced sentence for only the kidnapping charge."

"But Alex died because I sprung him. That's not going to play well." Jim looked at Windy. "Babe, I so sorry about Summer."

Windy whispered into his ear. "They survived, Jim. They're on Dora, and Summer has married the pilot."

Jim looked upward and breathed out, "Thank God. I've been sick about those youngsters." He eased into a chair and chuckled. "So Matt and Summer…I couldn't keep that sucker away from her, but the boy was in love. I'm glad they're together."

The one-hour visit flew by. After discussing Jim's case, Windy and Sam left the prison. In the vehicle Windy stared in a daze. "You and Jim believe there is not much hope for his release."

"It doesn't look good."

They pulled up to the hotel and were relieved that the media wasn't in the lobby. After escorting Windy to her room, Sam said, "Would you like to meet later for dinner?"

"I am very tired and not hungry."

"Get some rest. I'll have room service bring you a fruit plate in case you change your mind."

"Thank you, Sam," she said, and closed the door. She crawled onto the big, soft bed and felt the familiar gloominess. Seeing Jim made her realize how much she'd miss him.

An hour later she heard a door knock and rose, expecting room service. She opened the door to a large, middle-aged woman with curly dark hair, dressed in expensive clothing and jewelry. "Can I help you?" Windy asked.

"You're the harpy ruler, correct?"

"I have no comment," Windy said, assuming she was a reporter. She started to shut the door, but the woman put her foot in the doorway.

"I'm not with the press." The woman lowered her gaze. "I'm…I'm Monica Carlton, Alexander's mother. I need to talk to you."

Windy was taken aback, not expecting her. The homely woman bore no resemblance to her beautiful son, but knew that Monica spoke the truth. "Come in."

"I saw you on the news," Monica said, stepping into the room. "You look like Alexander."

"He was my grandson."

Monica wheeled around and snarled, "That didn't give you the right to take him. I know you sent the ship with harpies and the man in prison."

Windy's instincts were on high alert, sensing more anger than sorrow. On the trip, Sam had repeatedly warned her not to discuss the kidnapping lest she be implicated. And for Alex's sake to prevent his arrest, don't tell anyone except Jim that he was alive. "Does it matter who sent them, Miss Carlton?"

"It matters! My boy is dead. He'd still be alive if you hadn't interfered."

Windy strolled to the window and stared out at the city. "Your son was a harpy, and they die in cages. If he had remained in the mental hospital, it would have killed him anyway."

"Maybe, maybe not," Monica said, slumping into a chair. "We'll never know. I regret locking him up. I'm sorry about many decisions I made with Alexander." Her eyes became angry slits "That still doesn't excuse that man in prison. He took my son and caused his death. I'll make sure he spends the rest of his life in prison."

Windy turned from the window. "That man is my husband."

"I know."

Windy nodded. "If I lose Jim, we will share the anguish of loss. Besides having that in common, we are also powerful females who influence many lives. I rule a country, and with your wealth and authority, you can manipulate the government on Oden."

Monica looked up. "What's your point?"

"I believe we can do business. You could sway the prosecutor to drop the charges and free Jim."

Monica chuckled sarcastically. "I probably could, but why would I?"

"Because I can end your sorrow, just as you can prevent mine."

"Ridiculous! There's nothing you could do that would make me feel better."

"You are wrong, Miss Carlton."

* * *

Outside of Terrance, in the jungle, Will stood with Matt and Summer alongside a massive blue tree with a trunk the size of a house. "Is this what you seek, Matt?" Will asked.

"Wow, this sucker is huge," Matt said, looking up at the mile-high branches. "Never knew trees could grow this big."

"The old forests in the west have many such trees," Will said. "But in my father's youth, humans cut down most of the ancient trees near Terrance. This one was spared and is rare."

"Do you like it?" Summer asked Matt.

"It's perfect, close to town and your grandma's," Matt said. "Before long we'll be living like the Swiss Family Robinson in a tree-house. It's a great compromise. Thanks, Will."

"Summer would be unhappy in a house, and you would duck raindrops in a nest. The local river flock will help you build it."

Matt chuckled. "It's going to be so damn cool. Well, I gotta get going. I need to see Ted and find out when the next cargo hover leaves Hampton. I want to get my tour bus on board."

"You do not seem to miss star travel," Will said.

"Hell, smuggling is a hairy business, and long stretches between ports can be boring and lonely. Rather kick back and haul tourists around, showing them the jungle and critters." He kissed Summer's cheek and strolled towards his new hovercraft. He stopped at its door. "Speaking of lonely, Summer and I have been ambling around in your grandma's big house. Why don't you and Freely come for dinner? We could use the company."

Summer smiled. "Yes, please come, Will. I have learned how to bake your mom's bread."

"I have missed that bread. I will see you at sunset."

At dusk Will stood on the veranda at Windy's home, leaned against a post, and watched the sun slip behind the horizon of dark trees. Freely perched on the railing and munched on a slice of bread. Matt sat in a chair and sipped a beer. Among the empty plates was Matt's rough sketch of his tree house.

Matt shook his head in frustration. "Will, you won't let me use nails and saws on the tree. How am I supposed to build this place?"

"I gave you permission to live in the tree, but it is not yours to harm," Will said. "Vines can replace nails, and bind the branches and fans for walls, a floor, and roof. Show your picture to the flock leader. His harpies will give you what you want."

Matt lifted a skeptical eyebrow. "If you say so."

Summer came out on the porch and set a pitcher of fruit juice on the table as the com buzzed inside the house. "Will, it's probably the mayor looking for you about a meeting. When you turn off your portable com, they call here and bother us." She left to answer it.

Will had removed the small com from his hip sash, shut it off, and placed on the table. He had carried it for emergency, but quickly learned he couldn't escape the pestering humans with their insignificant problems. He glared at the com. "I hate that thing. Everyone can track me down."

Matt laughed. "You're in charge. It comes with the territory."

"And like a fool, I will fight Alex to remain in charge. I should let him win."

Matt glanced toward the door. "The call is taking a while. It must be Summer's mom."

Summer finally returned, looking astonished. "Will, it was grandma. She and the governor are boarding a ship for home."

"What?" Matt said. "They just got to Oden."

Will studied her. "It was a good call."

She grinned. "Jim is coming with them."

* * *

In a high fan tree, Alex looked around to make sure he was alone. Sitting down, he tapped the keys on his portable com. "Hi, Sherry," he said to the lovely female on the small screen.

She didn't smile. "Alex. I told you this morning that I'm busy studying for tests."

"I know, but I had to tell you I finally beat Bloom in a challenge, I'm ready to face Will."

"I don't understand this fight. Will cares about you and could help you adjust to your new home."

"He thinks I need help? He told you about the cops on Oden to turn you against me."

"Will hasn't said anything about you, but I can tell you're cynical and unhappy."

"That'll change when I defeat Will and become the harpy ruler. Sherry, I can be what you want. Just give me a chance. We have so much in common" He lowered his gaze "I admit I'm cynical. That happens when you've been stepped on all your life."

"Alex, you have so much going for you. You're gorgeous, charming, and brilliant, but I have to be honest…"

"You prefer Will."

"I'm sorry. I fell in love with him the first time we met."

Alex jumped up. "But he's an animal, a moron who can't even read."

"Actually, his mother taught him to read, but you're missing the point. Will is my soul-mate."

He glared at her image. "That's a lie. You think he'll be the next harpy ruler and want the prestige. You'll reconsider when I knock that loser off his pedestal." He slammed down the com lid, fluttered to the ground, and angrily paced. He had poured his heart out to the bitch, and for what? She was no different than the rest. He threw the communicator against a tree trunk.

Bloom strolled out of the forest. "Upset?" he asked, eyeing the broken com pieces.

"What do *you* want?" Alex barked.

"Your grandmother comes home soon."

"Good, then I can tear Will apart. If he survives, he'll be so disfigured that no female will have him."

* * *

After recovering in an Oden hospital and spending several months in jail, Jim had boarded the ship with Windy and Sam for the flight to Dora. A month later they arrived in Hampton, said farewell to Sam, and boarded the commercial hover to the Outback. Jim sat at a window and looked below at the Terrence airport and an awaiting crowd. He clutched Windy's hand and smiled. His horrendous journey was over, and he was finally home.

The large hover descended on the airstrip, and he and Windy walked down the ramp to cheers from hundreds of people. Several harpies near the crowd silently bowed. Will was the first to greet them. He hugged his grandmother and shook Jim's hand. Jim had met Shail's son when a small rambunctious fledgling, but Will was now a regal adult. Jim suddenly felt old.

Summer leaped into Jim's arms. "I'm so happy to see you." Clinging to his neck, she sobbed. "I'm so sorry, Jim. If I had listened to you, you wouldn't have been hurt protecting me and then caught and put in jail. It's my fault."

"Summer, things don't always go as planned, and you're not to blame. And you were needed to stop Alex from killing more officers."

Matt wandered up to them. "Hey, old man, it's great having you back."

Jim grinned. "So the smuggler married the princess; sounds like a fairy tale."

"Well I'm pretty irresistible. Even got harpies to like me."

Jim clutched Matt's shoulders. "I'm proud of you, son. Windy filled me in. You got everyone home in one piece."

"Heck, all your damn preaching rubbed off on me, opened my eyes to what's important. Otherwise, I might have left everyone's sorry ass behind on Oden."

"Without the preaching, you never would have done that. Summer nailed it. You're a good guy."

Windy embraced her family and then addressed the crowd. She expressed her happiness to be back with Jim and thanked everyone for coming. After bidding them farewell, she and Jim climbed in his familiar old vehicle.

Jim placed his hand on her knee. "A few more miles, and we'll finally be home. It was great, seeing everyone."

Windy solemnly gazed out the window. "Everyone, but Alex."

"Throughout the voyage, you've dwelled on that kid and worried about this fight with Will. Most brothers, even harpies, test each other."

"Jim, it is more than a fight between brothers. The future of harpies rests on the winner's wings."

Jim massaged her shoulder. "Will is going to beat him."

On the ride to the house, Jim had reassured Windy, but he also had concerns. He had seen Alex in action, using his telepathy to kill on Oden. Would he use his power against Will?

They pulled up to the house, and the veranda was lined with the yellow wings of Windy's grandchildren, who had flown from the airport for a welcome-home party. Soon the house bustled with activity and gleeful voices. Jim stepped into the kitchen to assist with the food, but the girls had it under control, preparing a traditional harpy meal.

Matt walked to him, holding a white package. "Screw that vegan crap, I picked up steak for you and me. Let's fire up the barbeque."

In the yard Jim watched Matt light a fire in the stone pit. Will, Freely, and the six golden brothers joined them. It was a gathering of males. The young harpies played around, taunting one another, but when Will spoke they became quiet. Jim saw that Will had gone from the oldest brother to an admired hero. With his cocky and joking nature, Matt fit in with the brash bunch.

Jim wandered from the group to gaze at a brilliant gold and pink sunset. Will stepped to him and said, "You have missed this."

Jim nodded. "I never thought I'd see Dora again."

"I too had my doubts," said Will. "Waters said your chances of freedom were bleak, yet you are here. My grandmother has not told me how this happened."

"It was Windy's doing." Jim smiled. "The best lawyers can't compete with harpy shrewdness. I should have known. I watched your dad argue before the Supreme Court on Earth. With his brains and telepathy, he had the lawyers ducking for cover and impressed the judges. It was a major ruling. Harpies went from being animals, property, and slaves to mortals with human rights." He turned to Will. "That was Shail."

"I miss him." After a moment, he asked, "But how did Grandma save you? You never had a trial."

"Windy talked to Alex's mother, who told the prosecutor that I had her permission to take her son. That ended their kidnapping case. And there was no proof that Alex's telepathy caused the deaths of the officers, so that charge was never pursued. On the assault and damages, Miss Carlton coughed up the money and settled those cases. Besides, no one on Oden dared question her, so I got off."

"What did my grandmother say to make this woman help you?"

"Windy told her the truth—that Alex was alive and living on Dora. In exchange for my release, she'd arrange for Miss Carlton to see him. She's on her way here."

"Summer has said that Alex dislikes his mother. He might be unwilling to meet her."

"He has no choice. Windy is still the ruler, and what she says goes."

CHAPTER TWENTY-FIVE

Alex tied his creamy hip sash around his bronze frame, ripping with newfound muscles. Gazing at the sky through towering trees, he savored the jungle aroma on the moist breeze and listened to the distance roar of a reptile. All this will soon be mine, he thought. He tossed back his locks and fluttered his wings. A small yellow feather dislodged and danced in the air. Like his past uncertainties, it would never again be part of him. He knew who he was and what he wanted.

He had arrived on Dora as a pale, gangly youth, but the fresh air, sunshine, and humid climate were conducive to harpies. With daily rigorous exercise and a healthy diet, he had transformed into a sleek-muscled male on his eighteenth birthday. His blood ran hot with testosterone and the eagerness to fight an opponent. All males, even Bloom, avoided him. Only one contender stood in his way.

Bloom sailed down to him. "It is time, Alex."

They flew up to the treetops and headed northwest. "Why must we go to this sacred mountain?" Alex asked.

"It is our birthplace, the origin of harpies," Bloom said. "We have always gathered at the mountain base to pick a new ruler," Bloom said. "Long ago a spacecraft with several men crashed into the mountain, and the survivors bonded with the jungle loca eagles. Their offspring were—."

"Bloom, I know our history, probably better than you. So all the harpies will be at this mountain for the challenge?"

"All the males," said Bloom, "Females without newborns shall also be there. And our queen has invited a few humans, like Jim and Matt."

"Good, they'll see me beat Will."

"Alex, you are focused on the fight, but your honor and wisdom shall also be tested."

"What kind of tests?"

"I still do not know the council elders' choices for the three challenges." Bloom tilted his wings to the north.

Alex wasn't worried about the physical fight or proving his wisdom, but his honor might be a problem.

Several hours later, they reached the towering black mountain and soared into the heavily treed valley at its base. Like thousands of bees at a hive, harpies covered the forest floor. Landing, Alex noticed that individual flocks had their encampment. Followed by Bloom, he proudly raised his head and walked through them, displaying authority. The brown harpies soberly dropped their heads and backed away. They obviously wondered if Alex was their next monarch.

"Alex," Westly called happily, rushing to him. "I hope you win."

Alex smiled at the brown-winged teenager. "I believe you're my only fan." He looked around. "Is Will here?"

"You are the first golden harpy to arrive. Even our queen has not yet come."

An hour later Will and his companion Freely flew in and landed in the gathering. Will spotted Alex and gave him a nod, but Alex returned an icy stare. Will turned his attention on the flocks. Their interaction was different from Alex's; they encircled Will, showing no fear and treating him like a brother. Will patted the shoulders of the males, stroked female heads, and ruffled the locks of fledglings. The flock leaders embraced Will and nuzzled his neck. No doubt, the harpies were fond of him. Troubled, Alex kicked a fern and growled, "Bloom, when does the challenge begin?"

"In the morning, but you must relax, Alex," said Bloom, "Your envy shows, and it shall defeat you."

Alex sighed. "Do you want me to win?"

"I want you to be happy and whole, but winning this fight shall not do that for you."

"Please, no more lectures." Alex glanced at his brother. "Why do they love him?"

"The love is mutual, and they trust him. They know Will would die defending them. Would you do the same?"

Alex brushed off the question, unsure of his answer. "It doesn't matter how they feel. This isn't a popularity contest. Come, Westly. Let's go to a stream so I can bathe."

* * *

At dawn Alex woke in the moss nest with Bloom shaking his wing. "Get up, Alex. Your family is here." Alex saw a small, yellow-winged flock of his brothers and sisters flying above the black mountain peaks with the backdrop of a pink sky. Trailing them were two hovers, obviously Matt's and Jim's.

The golden harpies landed among the browns, and the hovers set down on a grassy ridge overlooking the valley. Alex watched Matt and Summer climb out. Kari, Rachel, and Lea, whom Alex had met at Summer's wedding, left the back seat. Will flew to his mother and they hugged.

Seeing the mother and son affection, Alex unconsciously mumbled, "I wish." He stopped, withholding his pathetic feelings from Bloom.

"I know, Alex," Bloom said. "I have long sensed your wish for a mother's love."

Alex straightened. "I don't care to discuss it."

Jim, Windy, Sherry and her mother left the second craft. Alex's confidence was jolted when he saw the large woman crawl out of the back seat.

"I know not the dark-haired woman," Bloom commented.

Shocked and incensed, Alex exhaled. "My grandmother has betrayed me. That woman is my mother." He leaped skyward and rapidly flew west, despite Bloom's calls to return.

After several miles, Alex reached the coast and landed on a cliff overlooking the green ocean. He fell to his knees and hung his head as his mind churned with sick frustration. She didn't love him, so why was she here?

Bloom arrived and stood over him. "Alex, get up. If you do not come back to the gathering, you forfeit the challenge."

Alex looked up at him. "You don't get it. She's here to take her pet back to the Oden mental hospital. My grandmother arranged it, probably because I caused trouble with Will and disrupted your perfect little world. The harpies hate me anyway."

"Alex, for one so smart, you lack common sense," Bloom said, shaking his head. "Our queen risked the life of her mate and granddaughter to save you. She would never send you back to a cage. And you confuse hate with fright. Every harpy would defend you."

"So why is my mother here?"

Bloom reached down and pulled Alex to a stand. "Use your instincts. Her hands fidgeted with nervousness. Her sinking shoulders and lowered head with eyes focused on the ground display a lack of dignity and strength. She is a sad, defeated creature with no power left to control you."

"Don't be fooled, Bloom. She's a lying, cruel bitch putting on an act. After eighteen years of practice, she knows how to trick a harpy."

"If you lack the courage to face her, perhaps you should end this challenge. The golden monarch fears nothing, even his scheming mother."

Alex stared into Bloom's steady green eyes and slowly nodded. "Once I rule, I'll charge her with child cruelty and see how she likes a cage. Thank you, Bloom. You've given me another reason to defeat Will."

They flew back to the harpy gathering. On a mountain ledge, Windy, Aron, and several elder males overlooked a small clearing where Will stood alone. In the surrounding trees and forest floor, thousands of harpies waited for the challenge.

"They await you," Bloom said, and veered off to join the flocks.

Alex fluttered momentarily, took a breath, and landed beside Will. Grinning, he said, "Sorry to disappoint you, brother, but I didn't change my mind."

"For your sake, I wish you had, Alex."

On the higher meadow, a woman's voice cried out, "Alexander, Alexander, I'm here. It's your mother."

Alex turned his back, refusing to acknowledge his mother.

Windy walked to the edge of the rocky cliff and smiled at Will and Alex. "I love you both and hope neither of you are harmed." She then lifted her gaze to the flocks. "This gathering and the challenges between my grandsons mark the end of my reign and the beginning of a new one. When a winner stands here alone, I ask you to honor him as you have with me." She stepped aside, and Aron came forward.

"My best friend is not here today," Aron said, "but if Shail were, he would be proud. He gave us our lives, freedom, a lasting peace, and these two noble sons. They are here, willing to prove their worthiness as the next flock guardian. May the winner possess the same fine qualities as his father."

Then Aron addressed Will and Alex. "Will, may you fulfill your destiny. And Alex, I do not know you, but if fate chooses you to lead, you have my loyalty, as did your father."

"Thank you, Aron," said Will.

Alex nodded.

Aron continued, "There shall be three contests, one each light, and all testing these goldens' bravery, nobility, and intelligence. The first challenge confirms honor. These two males must risk their lives and prove their devotion to the flock. It begins in the narrow canyon to the south."

Before Alex knew it, Will shook his hand and said, "Good luck, brother."

At a loss for a snappy comeback, Alex whispered, "You, too."

Abruptly the surrounding harpies rose above the trees. Their brown wings created a huge shadow, eclipsing the sun above Alex. He marveled at the sight until he realized he was alone. Will, Aron, and the elders had left the ledge. Jim's hover swept down and picked up Windy.

Alex leaped into the air and flapped hard to catch up with the massive cloud of wings. Although they were all brown-winged harpies, their wing color ranged in a variety from light tan, chocolate, dark sable to a reddish mahogany. Like migrating birds in tight formation, their instincts avoided air collisions. He looked for Bloom, but finally glimpsed black and jetted through the congested sky. Coming alongside Bloom, he panted slightly. "I'm here. When the harpies took flight, I was a little overwhelmed."

"Yes, a harpy swarm is an amazing and rare sight. In my lifetime, I have only seen it twice, once in my youth during the war and now. I hope not to see another. A gathering would mean the loss of our ruler or another threat." He pointed ahead. "There is the valley that leads to the canyon."

With tilted wings, they descended into a lush valley of trees that narrowed into a rocky, barren gorge with a dried-up riverbed. Sheer cliffs left only one way out for flightless creatures. Two large pens made of timbers stood on the canyon floor and held elephant-sized red reptiles.

Alex's eyes widened. "What are they?"

"Red dragons," Bloom said. "You would know had you learned about the jungle instead fighting."

They set down on a cliff and Alex said, "I'm guessing these creatures aren't gentle plant eaters."

"No, dragons are deadly and swift. They have their strong back legs and can leap twice their height, so do not fly too low. And remember that Aron said this is a test of honor. There is no time for more advice. Be careful, my young friend," Bloom said and left Alex to join the large flock had settled on nearby boulders and surrounding trees overlooking the canyon. The two hovercrafts landed on a ridge above the gorge. Seeing Will near the animal pens, Alex sailed down to him.

He tiptoed closer for a better look at the penned reptiles. He had studied Earth's history, and the dragons resembled a T-Rex, over twenty-feet tall and including their tail, nearly forty-feet long. As Alex approached, a dragon crashed its coned head against the cage, rattling the wooden bars. Its huge, snapping mouth could have swallowed a harpy whole. Startled, Alex fluttered backward.

"Alex, it's not wise to tempt a dragon in a weak cage," said Will. "For him, you are a meal."

Alex felt queasy with the setback. His education was worthless and hadn't prepared him to deal with these animals. Will, on the other hand, was a master in this realm and confidently gazed at the monsters. Alex swallowed and stepped beside him.

Aron flew down and explained the challenge. "Hidden among those trees are thirty cloth bags filled with stones," he said, pointing toward the valley. "Each bag represents a helpless harpy that you must save. The bags have been soaked with female dragon urine to draw these two males. Each of you shall take your turn and retrieve the bags before the dragon is upon it. If a dragon touches a bag, it cannot be taken. When your dragon leaves the valley or all bags have been rescued or lost, the contest is over. The harpy who saved the most bags is the winner of the challenge, proving his honor. Will he risk his life to save others? The first challenger has the choice of a dragon."

"The decision is yours," Will said to Alex.

Alex faced a dilemma. If he let Will go first, Alex could copy him, but he had noticed that one dragon was larger than the other. The smaller dragon should be slower and less aggressive. "I'll go first."

"Stay safe, brother," Will said, and flew to a cliff.

"Stand before your dragon, Alex," Aron said. "When he leaves the cage, your challenge begins."

Alex stepped next to the smaller one, and Aron joined Windy and the elders. Alex peered up the canyon and spotted a bag in the trees. Two harpies flew down, fluttered over the cage, and tugged on the vines that secured the door. The wooden door dropped open, and the smaller dragon stepped out. Alex leaped into the air and raced to the forest for his first bag of stones. Lifting the stinking meshed bait, he found it matched his weight. He heard a tremendous roar and turned. Through the trees, he saw his dragon cower before the bigger caged male and then it rapidly fled.

Alex flapped hard to a cliff out of a dragon's reach and set his bag down. His dragon scampered across the open canyon as if it had wings. Alex realized his mistake; he had chosen the wrong dragon. Terrified of the larger male and having an agile, lighter body, the younger dragon had swiftly arrived in the trees. Alex sighed and flew into the valley, searching for another bag.

Rather than eyesight, the dragon used its massive nose and sniffed the air to locate the elusive "female." It stopped and bellowed, hoping she would respond. Catching the strong scent, it stomped toward a bag. Alex dove down, snatched up the bag, and beat his wings hard with the heavy load. The dragon lunged, barely missing its prey's legs. Alex placed the second bag on the cliff, but the dragon had already located another bag and was licking and rubbing against it.

With the reptile preoccupied, Alex retrieved six others without interference. For the next hour, the contest continued up the valley.

Racing against time and the eager young reptile, he was barely one step ahead of the creature. Altogether, he collected twenty-six bags. The dragon claimed four.

Alex dropped the last bag on the cliff and bent over, puffing with exhaustion. His body ran with sweat and his wings sagged on the ground. He watched as the dragon lumbered out of the valley. The two harpies soon retrieved the bags from the cliff to reset the challenge. To make the next contest fair, Will had left the canyon so he would not know the bag locations.

Bloom landed next to Alex. "You did well."

Alex tossed back his drenched hair, still panting. "The dragon was too fast and the bags too many and heavy. Not even Will can collect them all."

"We shall soon find out." He and Alex stepped to the ledge to watch.

Will flew over a ridge and descended into the canyon, landing near his large dragon. As before, the two harpies opened the cage door. When the dragon stepped out, Will sped to the trees. Instead of seeking a bag, he returned to his dragon, holding two round purple fruits.

"What's he doing?" Alex asked Bloom.

"Watch and learn, Alex."

Will set the fruit on the ground and flew directly at the dragon. Swooping down, he kicked the reptile's cone head repeatedly. With the harassment, the dragon became angry, and its thunderous roar could be heard for five miles. The reptile, forgetting about the female scent, thrust its massive frame into the air to kill the annoying harpy. Will shot out of range, but continued to toy with the monster's six-inch, chomping fangs. Like a pesky insect, he buzzed and prodded the dragon until it shook with rage, wildly flailing its tail. Its once dull-red scales beamed a bright scarlet.

Alex stared in awe as his brother fearlessly played a dangerous game, tormenting the enormous beast. "Will's insane."

"He is a golden harpy."

The dragon grew noticeably tired with its attempt to catch the swift little harpy. Its hurling jumps became shorter and less frequent as its large nostrils flared with the effort.

Will landed and with hands on his hips, he gazed at the creature. He casually picked up the fruit and fluttered over the dragon. When the reptile made another sluggish leap, Will dropped the fruit inside its nostrils. The dragon crashed to the ground sneezing and shaking its head to dislodge the thick syrup.

Will landed dangerously close to the animal and lowered one of his wings. He paced in front of the dragon, dragging the wing and shaking its feathers. The agitated animal lunged for him, but Will fluttered back and landed a few feet away. Once again he pulled his wing across the dirt and hissed at the flustered creature. With his extended wing on the ground, he turned and walked toward the trees with the dragon in slow pursuit.

"It's following him," Alex said in amazement.

"Yes," said Bloom. "Will behaves like a wounded bird, easy prey for a tired meat eater, and with the strong fruit odor in its nose, the dragon cannot smell the female urine and ignores the bags."

With a parted mouth, Alex witnessed his brother guide the dragon up the canyon and past the trees. The beast occasionally rushed him, but Will remained out of reach. Eventually, the two disappeared from sight.

Alex reflected on the contest rules: the challenge ended when the bags were saved or the harpy's dragon left the valley. Rather than retrieve the heavy bags, Will had removed the threat and saved all thirty of the mock harpies. "He won, didn't he?"

Bloom nodded.

* * *

On a rocky, dark ledge, Alex stood alone, braced against the cold, blustery winds with his wings wrapped around him. The sacred black mountain was a hellish place for a harpy. Through his long whipping hair, he peered below at the harpy gathering. The treetops swayed in a crisp breeze, but the valley was considerably warmer. Harpies normally slept at sundown, but tonight they celebrated Will's win. At each encampment, a small pit fire burned, creating hundreds of flickering lights in the black forest. Like fairies, small fledglings flew through the soft glow and streams of smoke. The adults ate and renewed old friendships.

He sniffled and harshly wiped his nose. At times on Oden, he'd been lonely, but until now, he'd never felt like an outcast and, even worse, a failure. He could hardly join his family; they all backed Will. Alex had even sent Westly back to his river flock, in no mood for companionship. Bloom had invited him to be with his family, but Alex had declined. Better to sulk over his loss in private.

All those days of hard training and he had been unprepared for the dragon challenge. It was especially distressing that he'd underestimated his brother. With shrewdness, courage, and skill, Will had manipulated his dragon and won without hoisting one lousy bag. Will was serious competition, and Alex's anger and humiliation shifted to worry. What other surprises did the council of elders have for him? Would he be ready for the next challenge? The mountain gusts tugged at his wings like the questions tugging at his mind.

He had expected a straight-out fight with Will and maybe some tricky questions concerning honor and wisdom. Giant reptiles never crossed his mind. With rattled confidence, he sat and hugged his legs. The eerie wind seemed to wail that he didn't belong here, didn't belong anywhere. Resting his head on his knees, he felt sick inside.

A harpy voice entered his mind. *Master, I have been searching for you.*

Alex lifted his head and saw a brown-winged harpy bowing before him. "What is it?"

Our queen sent me. She wishes your presence.

"Tell her I'm busy."

The harpy cocked his head, bewildered. *You refuse to come? You refuse our ruler's command?*

Alex considered the consequences. His grandmother could rally dozens of harpies and physically force him to come. If he used his telepathy to stop them, he'd be in deeper trouble. They might drug and ship him back to Oden and his mother.

Rising, he grumbled, "All right, damn it."

Trailing the messenger, he soared downward over the dark mountainside to the valley dotted with campfires, and to the small meadow where the hovercrafts rested. Beyond the parked hovercrafts, several white canvas tents encircled a large bonfire that crackled and flicked sparks to the stars. A small crowd of shadowy figures, probably relatives, stood around the fire, enjoying the warmth. Alex ignored them and followed his harpy guide to a large tent.

At the entrance, the harpy relayed. *Our queen waits within.* With another bow, he took flight.

For a moment Alex stood outside, trying to calm his anxiety. He heard a familiar chuckle at the fire and saw Matt. With glowing faces, the pilot stood next to Summer. Alex now recognized the others: two of his younger brothers faced off with their pale arched wings appeared deep gold in the firelight. Jim's bigger frame and deep voice stood out in the group.

Alex then spotted Will and stepped back into the shadows. He felt like retching at the sight of his brother's arm over Sherry's shoulder, her head rested against his chest and her arm around his waist. That should be me, Alex realized. Will might have sensed him, gazing directly into Alex's eyes.

Alex felt awkward like an exposed spy. He shoved the canvas flap aside and stepped inside the tent that was dimly lit with old fashion candles. His grandmother stepped to him and kissed his cheek.

"Alex, I am pleased you are here," Windy said, and took his hand to draw him further inside. "I am very proud of you."

"But I lost today."

"A loser is one who does not try. You faced a red dragon, not knowing the creature or danger. That is to be admired." She turned toward a dark tent corner. "There is someone here who wishes to speak to you."

The large silhouette rose from a chair, and Alex detected her scent. "Grandmother, you said you loved me. Why did you betray me and tell her I was here?" He pulled back to leave. "I have nothing to say to that woman."

"Stay, Alex," said Windy. "Your resentment towards your mother may be justified, but the anger is destroying your peace. I believe this meeting shall do you some good." She nodded to Monica and left.

Monica came forth. "Oh, Alexander, I thought you were dead, and I've been crying my eyes out for months. I can't even eat." She reached for his arm, but he jerked away.

"Don't touch me," he snapped.

"Please, Alexander," said Monica. "I traveled all this way from Oden, and I'm staying in a tent in this horrid jungle just so I could talk to you. I want you back. I could—."

"I, I, I," Alex sneered. "It's always about you. How I continue to ruin your life. God, I'm sick of it. I'm eighteen now, and you have no legal authority over me. Go back to Oden and leave me alone. I don't want to see you again." He swept out of the tent and flew rapidly away into the night, till he could no longer hear her cries.

Alex left the valley and winged upward along the mountainside. Soon the jungle warmth, trees, and animal sounds disappeared, yielding to a howling cold wind that lashed the bleak black stone. The higher he flew, the temperature dropped and turbulent updrafts increased. He relentlessly beat his wings to prevent colliding into the jagged rocks. Most harpies would not risk these hazards, especially in the dark, but he aimed to reach the crest of the sacred mountain, where he'd surely find solitude. He finally reached the top and landed on the toothy stones.

Drawing his wings close to stop shivering, his eyes watered when he gazed across the dark wilderness. "I will always be alone," he whispered.

All goldens stand alone, relayed a male voice. *They do not need the security of others.*

Startled, Alex jumped and then located the speaker. The shape of a harpy stood several yards away on a boulder. His tall, lean frame was unwavering in the blustery weather, and the yellow hair and wings looked white in the starlight. Only one harpy could create this image.

Figuring his grandmother had sent Will after him, Alex arched his wings. "Go away, Will."

I am not Will.

Alex realized the harpy's resonant voice was deeper and softer than Will's. When the harpy hopped off the boulder and approached, Alex recognized him. "Father?"

Shail sniffed Alex's feathers. *Yes, you are one of mine, although I do not know you or your name.*

"I'm Alexander, but we have never met."

Alexander is a long, strange name, Shail relayed, *and you speak like a human. Your mother is a woman.*

Alex dropped his head and nodded.

Son, you are cold. Shail wrapped his arms and wings around Alex, shielding him from the freezing gusts. Nuzzling Alex's cheek, he relayed, *my poor son, I feel your heartbreak, confusion, and rage. I am sorry I failed you.*

Alex would normally resist the closeness that allowed his father to read his mind, but he had longed all his life for this precious moment. He clung to his father and wept. "I'm the failure, Dad. I'm competing against Will for harpy rule, but am losing. I want the respect that the harpies had for you. But it will never happen."

Destiny brought you to this mountaintop and me so I can help you. Your mind, though troubled, has more strength, power, and determination than I have ever sensed in a harpy. You shall succeed and rule many.

Alex looked up. “You truly believe I’ll win?”

You shall win all you desire. Of this, I have no doubt.

Alex brushed away his tears and smiled. *Thank you, Father.*

Shail gazed down at the valley and this time spoke. “The flocks gather and two of my sons challenge each other for rule. My vow is nearly complete. The demons shall soon leave me.”

Alex frowned. “What vow? What demons?” He trembled, sensing his father’s thoughts. “Once a son rules, you plan to kill yourself.”

“I am a burden, Alexander. After the birth of my first fledgling, I promised to give the flocks a worthy ruler. Now it comes to pass. My work is done, my vow fulfilled.”

“But you can’t die. I need you.”

Shail placed his hand against Alex’s cheek. “You need no one, son.” He gazed out at the dark landscape, crowned with silver peaks. “Look out there. What do you see?”

“Mountains, valleys, stars,” Alex said hastily.

“You do not truly see, but someday you shall. This night is a dark cave that leads to tomorrow’s light. When you find the opening, all shall be clear.”

Alex wondered if his father was brilliant or insane. Shail stepped to the ledge. “I often come to this mountain. The icy air drives off my fears and awakens cherished memories. Long ago I bonded with Kari within these stone walls. I loved her so much it hurt.” He extended his wings. “When you feel lost, come here, Alexander. It shall renew your spirit.”

“No, wait,” Alex called, but Shail leaped off the cliff and glided down into the dark jungle.

CHAPTER TWENTY-SIX

Alex woke at daybreak in a tree nest, eager for the next challenge. Last night's meeting on the mountain had restored his confidence. He placed his faith in his father's prediction that he would be the next ruler. He flew to the stream for a quick bath, and feather preening. After snatching a few yellow fruits from a tree, he headed for the gathering.

Will was already there below the ledge where Windy and the elders would come, and Aron would explain today's contest. Alex landed near Will, smiled, and tossed him a fruit. "Good morning, brother. Breakfast is on me."

Will caught the fruit, looking puzzled. "Good morning, Alex," he said slowly. "Thank you."

Alex nodded smugly, bubbling inside. He longed to gloat about their father's visit, which forecast his win. Will would be crushed, but Alex refrained. Bragging and then losing (if Shail was wrong) would be mortifying. After the challenge, he would tell Will.

Aron arrived and landed next to Alex and Will. "Our queen and the council wait for you near the ocean. This is where the next challenge shall take place. It is a test of courage, speed, and wisdom. Follow me." He took to the air, and Alex and Will followed. The massive flock and two hovers trailed them.

Once again, Bloom's wing tips nearly touched Alex's soaring nearby. Alex nodded toward Aron. "You told me he was my father's friend, but this Aron seems to carry a lot of weight with the flocks."

"He is the greatest brown-winged harpy, but I have no time to talk of him. Alex, the next challenge is about wisdom, but it is not the wisdom found in your books. I believe you must use reason and common sense."

"Sure, coach." Alex smiled. "But no matter what it's about, I'm going to win."

Bloom rolled his eyes and peeled off. Alex landed next to Aron and Will on a sheer cliff overlooking the Western ocean. The elders and other harpies took positions along the bluffs and beach rocks. The hovers set down on the wide stretch of shoreline, and the passengers unloaded.

Alex gazed at his grandmother, mother, and Sherry. Besides Mollie, they were the three most influential females in his life: his grandmother, who had saved him and believed in him: his heartless, disgruntled mother, who gave him the anger and determination to prove himself; and now there was Sherry, the first to pull at his heartstrings. After defeating Will, he hoped Sherry would choose him as her mate. A lot rested on today's challenge.

The two harpies that had released the caged dragons arrived, each holding a bag, and took positions beside Alex and Will.

"This is the second challenge," Aron said. "Inside each bag are hand-sized red stones. Your harpy shall fly out over the ocean, drop a stone, traveling further out and drop another until the stones are gone. You must locate your stone, dive to the bottom, and retrieve it. Then proceed out to finding the next one. When they grow too heavy, you can place them in a pile here." With Aron's nod, the harpies took off, heading out to sea with their bags.

Alex wondered how this challenge concerned wisdom, but figured the one who collected the most stones would win. His focus was on his harpy, watching where he dropped the stones in the rough surf. He swallowed, again ill-prepared for the daunting task. Raised on a desert planet, he had just recently learned to swim in a calm lake. Will was probably like a fish in water.

The two finished dispatching the stones in the ocean and returned. Aron lifted his hand. “Stay safe, young goldens,” he said, and drop of his hand, signaled the start of the challenge. Alex and Will leaped off the cliff and flew out over the surf. Reaching the area where the harpies had dropped the first stones, Alex and Will hovered above the clear water and scanned the bottom.

Alex spotted his bright red stone on the sandy ocean floor. Will also seeing his stone, they dove simultaneously into choppy surf. Ten feet down, Alex grabbed the rock and swam for the surface. Coming up for air, he considered swimming for the shore to get out of the water but saw that Will used his kicking legs and flapping wings to thrust his upper body above the surface, allowing him to fly out like a seabird.

Alex copied him and was soon airborne. Will wrapped his rock in his sash and soared out to get his second. Alex followed his lead.

The second rocks were deeper, twenty feet down. Alex folded in his wings, took a full breath, and pierced the water. He kicked his feet and beat his wings as in flight to swiftly propel him downward through the water. He grabbed his second rock and quickly surfaced. But Will had already left water and was moving out to claim his third rock. Alex panicked, realizing his brother was getting ahead, and he might never catch up.

Seeing the third rock below, Alex tightly clutched the two in his sash and plunged into the water as Will surfaced. Swimming to the bottom, Alex grabbed the rock, but found that three rocks weighed him down. He struggled to reach the surface and then had more difficulty leaving the water.

Will must have faced the same problem and was winging toward land to deposit his rocks on the beach. Alex thrust himself from the water and pursued the same course. To carry three and go for the fourth, he risked losing all his stones and precious time if unable to leave the water.

Alex dropped the rocks in the sand and headed out for his fourth. Will was way ahead of him, surfacing with his fourth rock, and he was flying to claim his fifth. Alex plummeted into the ever-deeper water and came up with his rock. Further out, Will also broke the surface. They left the water in unison, Will heading toward shore as Alex flew out. In passing each other, Will called out, "Stop, Alex," he said, fluttering in place. "I could not get the fifth rock. It is too deep. Come with me to shore. We both have four rocks, and the challenge shall be a tie."

Alex hovered near him. "Maybe it's too deep for you."

"It is too deep for any harpy. If you try to retrieve it, you shall die."

Alex huffed. "You'd say anything to win." He jetted farther out into the ocean, but glancing back, saw Will hadn't moved. He still fluttered stationary above the surf watching him. Lingering over the translucent water, Alex saw the red object, his winning stone. He tied the fourth stone in his sash so his arms would be free for faster swimming.

"Please, Alex," Will yelled. "Do not go for it. You can have this win."

"I don't need charity to beat you," Alex called. He gulped down a deep breath and nose-dived. Kicking, flapping his wings, and swimming a breaststroke with his arms, he descended deeper. Halfway down, he realized the crystal-clear water was deceptive, and he still had a long way to go.

Undeterred, he pressed on. He reached the bottom and snatched up his rock, but his inner ears and sinuses throbbed with pain, and his lungs were about to burst. To relieve the pressure, he exhaled and slid the stone into his sash.

He swam upward, following his own air bubbles. Now his starved lungs screamed for oxygen, and the chest pain was unbearable. The surface seemed miles away. Gripped with terror, he realized he'd never make it. With his brain deprived of oxygen, his thoughts became hazy. He couldn't tell if he was swimming up or down, and he struggled to stay conscious. His eyes closed and his instincts took over. To relieve the stabbing lung pain, his mouth opened, and he inhaled the deadly water.

* * *

On the sandy beach, Alex grew aware of lips pressing against his mouth and breaths of air being forced into his lungs. "Come on, Alex." Will puffed, using mouth-to-mouth to resuscitate him. "Don't be stubborn now."

Alex heard Bloom's frantic voice. "Breathe, Alex, breathe!"

Alex lifted his head slightly and choked and coughed to remove the foamy white water out of his lungs. Through squinting teary eyes, he saw Will kneeling over him and, beyond, glimpsed Bloom's black feathers.

"That's it. Get it out," Will said, and rolled him on his side.

"Is he all right?" Bloom asked anxiously.

"I believe so," said Will, "but it was close."

"He is lucky you were there," Bloom said. "I could not have reached him in time." He dropped on his knees in the sand and stroked Alex's head. "I am sorry, Will. You asked me to train him, and he knows how to fight but has learned little else."

Will stood. "You are not at fault, Bloom. From what I've seen, Alex does not take advice well."

Aron landed beside them and gazed at Alex. "He is fortunate to live. Goldens have died in these challenges." He turned to Will. "You are the winner."

Still hacking, Alex struggled to sit up and pushed Bloom away. "He's not the winner." He fumbled with his sash and produced two stones. "I have more stones than Will."

"The challenge was not about stones," Aron said. "It was about wisdom. The fifth stone could not be safely retrieved, but you lacked reason and sought it. Our ruler must make sound choices and not place his flock at risk. Furthermore, Will chose to save you, putting your life ahead of his and his victory. That shows consideration, another important quality in a ruler. You are here holding those stones only because of your brother. He has won two of the three challenges and is our next ruler."

Alex scrambled to his feet. "But there's one more challenge. It's my right to compete."

Aron said. "The gathering is over.

"If Alex wishes," Will said, "I will compete in a third challenge. There should be no question of who is best."

Aron sighed. "It is your choice, Will, but I have seen enough. Your brother's misguided actions prove he is unfit to lead." He spread his wings, and said, "The challenge shall take place at the mountain."

Will playfully ruffled Alex's wet hair. "If nothing else, you are tenacious. Even a near-drowning doesn't stop you. I respect that." He took off, flying toward the hovercrafts.

Alex bent over, coughed up more water, and shook his body and wings to remove the clinging sand. "These contests are rigged," he grumbled to Bloom. "They knew I didn't know anything about dragons and swimming."

"But a harpy ruler *should* know such things," Bloom said.

Alex straightened and his eyes narrowed. "And what's this shit about apologizing to Will for not training me? Did he order you to do that?"

Bloom gazed out at the ocean. "I refused to teach you to fight until you learned honor, but Will said to train you, anyway."

Speechless with hurt feelings, he stepped back and ran his hand through his hair. "All these months together..." He rubbed his forehead. "I thought we were friends, Bloom—that you cared about me—and now, now I learn it was a lie. You had to be with me."

"Long before Will's request, I took you under my wings on the ship and vowed to help you. I am your friend, Alex, and wish to see you happy, but you are blind to the truth. Winning these challenges shall not fulfill you."

"Fuck you, Bloom, We're done. I don't need you or your training. And fuck Will too. He wanted me to learn to fight so he'd have competition and look good. He pulled me out of the water for the same damn reason. Tomorrow, he's in for a surprise." Before Bloom could respond, he fled the beach and rode the ocean thermals offshore.

At dusk Alex flew to the sacred mountaintop, hoping to see his father. Again the trek was deadly, taking great effort of thrashing his wings to avoid smashing into the slope. He reached the peak and landed, but Shail wasn't there.

It was probably a good thing. Angry, he would likely have trashed out his father for lying about winning the challenge. "He's like everyone else in my life," he said, reflecting on Bloom, Sherry, and his grandmother. "I place my trust in them, and they stab me in the back." He picked up a stone, threw it, and heard it strike the cliffs below. "Dear old Dad had one thing right. I don't need anyone."

He gazed out at the wilderness, strung with ribbons of color from the sinking sun. The land, without a trace of man, was beautiful and worth fighting for. His father had said to come to this mountain and it would renew his spirit. Indeed, it had. His resentment vanished like the tossed stone, and he felt at peace. His father also said he'd win all that he desired. Could it still happen?

* * *

After the ocean challenge, Will flew to the tents on the meadow and received a hero's welcome from family and friends. Flock leaders arrived at the encampment, congratulating him. With their warm embraces, Will sensed their joy but mostly relief that Alex was unlikely to rule. The merriment lasted throughout the afternoon. He and Sherry hung out mostly with Summer and Matt. The two golden females had become fast friends. His grandmother and Jim reunited, never looked happier. His two preteen brothers got into a scrap, and nearly overturned a food table. Will yelled at them and put them to work collecting firewood for the night's bonfire.

His only solemn moment was when Miss Carlton pulled him aside and profusely thanked him for saving her son's life. The woman babbled on about her regrets with Alex. He responded, "Miss Carlton, you dwell on past mistakes. Prove you love him now. That is what he longs for."

In the evening, Will and Sherry rested on a blanket near the campfire. The blaze had diminished to embers and flickers of flame. She clasped his hand and said, "You've been awfully quiet, like you're in another world."

"Sorry, I have a lot on my mind."

"I can imagine thinking about tomorrow, but you were so brave, saving Alex today."

He looked into her eyes. "Sherry, I was terrified, seeing his lifeless body floating below. When I dove down and pulled him to the surface, he wasn't breathing. I thought I was too late. And in those waves, I could never have lifted off with his added weight, if not for sheer fright. It gave me the strength to do it."

She hugged him and whispered, "Humans called it adrenaline. It gave you the grit to perform the impossible and save Alex."

Will raised an eyebrow. "Yes, I saved a brother who wants me dead. Forgive me, but I need a little time alone." He kissed her and rose, and she left for her tent.

Will strolled through the meadow, knee-deep with fragrant wildflowers, and gazed at the stars. His thoughts were on Alex and the fight. By all reports, Bloom had taught his brother well for the challenge, but Will had years of experience and could defeat Alex in physical combat.

The concern was whether Alex would use his deadly telepathy in the challenge, and whether Will had the stronger mindset and concentration to resist the hypnotic suggestions. Alex's power was like all weapons. The danger lay in the user. As Aron had said, Alex was unfit to rule. In a fit of rage, he might annihilate humans or start a war devastating to the flocks. With leadership in the wrong hands, bad things could happen.

Will also considered Sherry. Alex might force her to be his mate. She and Will had decided to bond after her schooling. He wondered now if that was a mistake.

"You too cannot sleep?" said a voice.

He turned to his grandmother. "My mind is so occupied that I did not hear you approach."

"I imagine it concerns tomorrow. I will be glad when it is over."

Will smiled. "For a temporary reign, yours lasted twelve years while you wait for me to grow up."

"I kept hoping your father would recover and take over again, but it was not to be. I am glad you allowed the third challenge. It gives Alex another chance to prove himself. At times he reminds me of Shail. Both were abused, angry, reckless, and willing to lash out and kill. Shail was a trailblazer, the first harpy to attack men. Alex is also unique. I believe someday he will be a remarkable harpy."

"If he is so much like Father, perhaps he should reign?"

Windy smiled. "No, back then Dora was a different place. We were in a war to survive. The harpies needed an edgy, tenacious ruler who could throw his flock into battle. I believe most harpies feared Shail more than men. But today we are at peace. Our ruler should be honorable, patient, and wise, the qualities that you also inherited from Shail. Alex has a good soul, but his mind is muddled. He must learn to control himself before he rules others. Now is not his time."

"I hope you are right about him. I allowed the third challenge because he lacked experience in the first two trials so we were not equals. And I admire his determination and courage. He tried so hard to win that it nearly killed him. Tomorrow I face him and must consider his other motives, besides proving himself."

"Even if you lose tomorrow, you have won two out of three challenges and would rule."

"That is not necessarily true, Grandma. You care about Alex but he has a sinister side and powerful telepathy. If he kills me, he will be the next harpy ruler."

CHAPTER TWENTY-SEVEN

At the base of the sacred mountain, thousands of harpies gathered on the valley floor. Many formed a large circle while others surrounded them on tree limbs. Looking down at the fighting arena from the stone ledge were the council of elders, Windy, a few humans, and the golden family. At the center Will and Aron waited. Only Alex was absent.

At midmorning Aron turned to Bloom standing on the sidelines.

Bloom shrugged, conveying that he didn't know where Alex was.

Aron said to Will, "Maybe your brother had enough with dragons and drowning and has changed his mind about this last challenge."

"He will come," Will said. "Only death would stop that one."

Alex finally sailed down and landed beside Will and Aron.

Will, nose to nose with Alex, said. "To make us wait shows a lack of respect for others."

Alex chuckled. "Perhaps none of you deserve my respect. But patience, brother, you'll soon have a chance to beat the flaws out of me."

With slow deliberation, Will raised his eyes. "Nothing shall please me more."

Alex arched his wings and glared. "Me, too, I have dreamed of this moment."

Before the confrontation became physical, Aron moved between them. “Step back from each other,” he ordered.

Will and Alex separated, strolling to the perimeter of the imagined circle for a fighting challenge. Will stood motionless with his hands on his hips and studied his opponent. Alex tossed his hair and strutted back and forth with a pace so light that he barely left a footprint. He ruffled his long, luxurious wings in anticipation, his sparkling eyes burning with confidence. To Will, Alex’s plucky behavior could mean only one thing; he would use his powerful telepathy to win.

Aron stepped into the center of the arena and looked at the harpies. “Few here have witnessed a battle for dominance between mature golden males. It is majestic as well as ruthless, often resulting in maiming and death.” He glanced at Will and then Alex. “I pray you both stay well. There are no rules. When one of you can no longer rise and fight back, the challenge is over, and the last standing is the winner.” He raised his arm. “It starts.” Dropping his arm, he flew from the arena to the ledge with the elders.

Alex grinned and called to Will, “Brother, are you ready to meet your match?”

Will didn’t answer.

They circled with poised heads and half-opened wings, their feathers still the pale yellow of youth. Their intense stare was blue against blue. They treaded into striking distance, and Alex made the first move.

Fluttering, he rose six feet and kicked at Will’s head. Will dodged the blow and shot upward in a full-out attack. He hammered Alex’s face with hard punches. A knee to Alex’s stomach knocked out his wind, and he flailed his wings backward to escape the assault, but Will kept up the pounding with lightning fast strikes from his fists and feet. Alex covered up in defense, unable to return the thrashing. A powerful kick to Alex’s gut sent him to the ground.

Will landed near him. “Have you had enough?”

Alex lifted his head and huffed for air through a split lip. “No,” he growled but his watery, distressed eyes expressed the reality; he was outclassed and incapable of defeating Will in a physical match. He slowly rose and spit out the blood. “Let’s try this again.” He lifted off and fluttered at sparring height.

Will extended his wings to engage him but heard Alex’s voice in his mind. *You cannot fly, Will. You cannot fight.* Will tried to flap his wings, but they wouldn’t respond. Alex hovered above and kicked at him. Will ducked but was struck in his chest. He rolled and sprang to his feet.

“What’s wrong, brother?” Alex asked with a menacing smile.

Will took a breath to still his fast beating heart. He closed his eyes, focused on his father’s training, and became calm. *No one controls me,* he relayed to Alex (but more to himself.) He glared upward at Alex and, in a flash, flew at him.

Believing Will was under his spell and couldn’t fly, Alex never expected Will’s attack. In a flash he flew at Alex and hit him with a shoulder blow to the stomach. Alex doubled up and received a hail of wallops to his face and torso. Will spun in midair, and his wing whacked the side of Alex’s head. Knocked silly, Alex hit the dirt. Holding his thumping head, he scrambled into the sidelines of brown harpies.

Will landed to continue the battle on foot. His rage tittered on uncontrollable. “Come on,” he shouted. “This is a fight of flesh, blood, and feathers, not of mind tricks.”

Crouching, Alex tried again to enter Will’s mind, but Will concentrated on his father’s belief that he was destined to rule. Alex swallowed hard, aware that his hypnotism and strategy had failed. Will was too headstrong, and the contest had switched to his advantage.

Alex glanced up at his mother and Sherry, and that bolstered his resolve. He sniffled up his courage, entered the ring, and cautiously approached his brother. Again, they circled each other with edgy steps and extended wings, each waiting for the other to move. Like streamlined wading birds, they did the dance of intimidation. A flinch, nod, or glance sent both fluttering into the air and exchanging blows.

Alex managed a few hits, but Will brushed off the pain and kept up the assault. At one point, they collided with their bodies pressed together, gripping, striking, as their wings furiously flapped. A bash to Alex's nose separated them. They landed and paced, taunting.

The grueling challenge continued for another half hour. With each encounter, Will's brutal hits were swifter and more accurate, and Alex suffered the worst of the fight, being knocked down several times. Most males would have given up, but Alex persisted, returning for more punishment.

Will had seen enough to size up his brother's skills. Like all browns, Alex fought defensively, taught to hold his ground. His weakness lay in not being trained by an aggressive golden harpy who thrust himself into battle and risked injury and death. It was time to end this. He hissed at Alex, a final warning to yield.

Alex raised his head that was smeared with the blood and sweat. He answered Will with a low, hostile seething. They lifted from the ground, but Will didn't flutter in place. Like a rocket, he crashed into Alex and, with a severe punch to the cheek sent Alex tumbling backward. Again he crumbled to the ground. Slowly he lifted his head and rolled over to rise.

Will landed near him. "It is over, Alex. Stay down!"

"Never!" Coughing and holding his side, he staggered to his feet and limped toward Will. "It's never over. I will never quit." With a wrist, he wiped his bloody nose and raised his wings.

Will sighed. "I believe you, brother." Alex's bruised body was smudged with dirt, and his tattered wings had broken quills and patches of missing feathers. Blood ran down his face and dripped from his chin. One eye squinted from a swelling cheek. He was no longer the handsome, flashy golden male from an hour ago. Will barely had the heart to continue.

Once again, they lifted off the ground. Will battered his brother into a dazed state and then flipped in mid-air flip, coming up behind him. He quickly wrapped one arm around Alex's neck as his other arm braced the back of Alex's neck. He clasped his wrist, keeping the chokehold firmly in place.

Alarmed, Alex wildly thrashed his wings and kicked in the air as he pulled at Will's arm and elbowed his ribs. But Will held on and applied more pressure, cutting off his oxygen. Alex continued to struggle, but it was hopeless. Too obstinate to give in, he wanted to die in a glorious bloodbath, but Will foiled his plan. Not wanting to inflict a devastating injury, he slowly rendered Alex unconscious.

"Do not fight me, my brave brother," Will whispered into Alex's ear, clutching him in the sleeper hold. "You fought well and are a true golden."

Will? Please, Will, don't do this to me, Alex relayed, gasping and unable to speak. His terrified eyes closed with lost awareness as their feet touched the ground.

Alex was out cold. Will gently laid him down, knelt, and kissed his brother's lips. He had never faced a tougher competitor. Brushing the sweat off his brow, he rose and lifted his gaze to the flocks.

The harpies fell to their knees with profound bows. Will turned toward the ledge and all, even his grandmother, lowered their heads. Aron stepped forward. "Behold our golden prince, your monarch."

* * *

Alex regained consciousness with a familiar, heavy smell of perfume and a clammy, nervous hand on his forehead. Before opening his eyes, he knew his mother bent over him. He looked up into her worried face and noticed he was on a cot inside a white tent.

Monica stroked his head. "Oh, Alexander, you're finally awake, thank God. I sent for a doctor."

More orientated, he raised his head and felt the widespread pain: the scrapes and bruises, his stressed wing muscles and torn-out feathers, the throbbing fractured ribs, and a pounded stomach. His face ached and was swollen so he could barely see out of one eye. His throat was tender from the throttling, but he managed to say, “I don’t need a damn doctor. I want outta here.”

“Please, Alexander, please give me a minute.” She lowered her head with a sob, “I’m sorry, I’m so sorry for everything. I pushed you away and did horrible things to change you when you were already perfect. It’s my fault you ran away and entered in those barbaric challenges. A monstrous lizard nearly ate you, and you almost drowned. And you’re lying here half beaten to death.”

Alex cringed, rising on his elbows. “The challenges were my doing, not yours.”

“You wouldn’t be on this miserable planet if I had been a good mother and shown you love. It took losing you to realize you’re the most important thing in my life.” She clutched his hand and went into a crying fit.

Bloom was right that she hadn’t come here to take him. She was a defeated creature desperately seeking exoneration. And he had changed. Too broken to argue, he sighed. “Mother, I’m glad to hear you care about me. I only wish you’d said it when I was growing up.” He unclasped her hand and, holding his tender ribs, he rose from the cot.

She looked up teary-eyed. “Alexander, I’ll give you anything you want to make up for the past.”

“I want respect and that must be earned. It can’t be bought.”

Monica’s face contorted. “I’m a big, ugly, stupid woman. Tell me what I need to do so you don’t hate me?”

Alex smiled. “You’ve made me very angry, but I’ve never hated you. Someday we might patch things up, but not now. I first need to figure out who I am. Just go home, Mom.”

“You could come with me or I’ll live here. I promise not to interfere with your life.”

Alex stepped to the tent opening, pushed back the flap, and gazed out at the harpy gathering. “I’m not sure I’m staying on Dora. I believe I’ve worn out my welcome.”

Monica came to him. “Come back to Oden with me until you decide. We could start fresh.”

“I’m done with Oden too.” He turned from the opening to face her and had a strange feeling he would never see her again. “Mom, I’ve always known your pain, the past that made you cold and hard. I understand why you withheld affection, and I forgive you.” He kissed her forehead, stepped outside, and turned to her. “And, Mom, I never thought you were ugly. For me, you were always beautiful.” He spread his wings and flew north.

* * *

Alex traveled out of the valley and away from the harpies. His spirit was as battered as his body. He had no more high-minded thoughts of grandeur, and had only enough determination to flap his wings. After several miles, he set down near a brook. Normally, he would wade in and wash off the dirt and dry blood, but he didn’t bother. He knelt and sipped water with barely the energy to quench his thirst. Sensing another harpy, he lifted his head. Will landed beside him.

“I saw you leave,” Will said. “I wanted to make sure you are okay.”

Alex stood. “Why should you care, Will? I’ve been nothing but trouble.”

“That is true.” Will said with a slight grin. “But I was worried. Those, who soar the highest fall the hardest.”

Alex huffed. “Christ, you sound like Dad with his poetic crap.”

Will tilted his head. “You met him?”

“On top of the sacred mountain after the first challenge,” Alex said. “The crazy old fool basically said I was great and would rule the harpies.”

"Father is no fool, and with more time and the right training, you might have won. I have never fought longer or harder."

"I didn't have the right training, so Bloom let me down."

"Bloom taught you what he knew. Dark-winged harpies hold airspace and fight off the attack, but a golden takes the offensive. He attacks until his rival goes down or he dies. Our father taught me, and also about honor."

"Something else I apparently lack."

"Yes, trying to control my mind was not worthy of a golden."

"Shit, you were beating the crap out of me, Will. I was desperate. Besides, it didn't work. I should have known you were thickheaded."

"No more than you. But Alex, you have so many other qualities. You are the smartest, most tenacious, and fearless harpy I know. I could teach you like Father taught me, and I could learn a lot from you. We are brothers, and close to being equals. I still believe we could be friends."

Alex leered and puffed up his shabby feathers. "Forget it, Will. I might be beaten and down, but I'll never submit to being your pet flying partner."

"So cynical, Alex; always looking for the worst in others," Will said, spreading his wings to leave.

"Wait a minute, Will," Alex said, and looked skyward. Disclosing his feelings, especially to this brother, was difficult. "I *am* skeptical and have a problem with trust, but understand where I'm coming from. You've had everything; loving parents, the respect of the flocks, the freedom of the sky, and now you rule and have Sherry." Alex's eyes watered. "Don't you see? I've had nothing. You are my brother, and I would gladly die defending you, but we can't be friends. My resentment would eat me alive."

Will nodded. "Our grandmother and now father believe you will become a great harpy. I'm starting to think it's true. You are so different from us. Take care, Alex." He lifted off and disappeared.

CHAPTER TWENTY-EIGHT

Days after the harpy gathering, Alex soared to the base of the sacred mountain and found the valley deserted. The flocks had gone to their various nesting grounds, and the only evidence that thousands had been here was a few brown feathers and small pieces of charred wood from campfires. With a foot, he stirred up the ash and watched the wind carry it away. Like his dreams, the cold, dead cinders had once blazed brightly.

He had faced obstacles and setbacks throughout his life but had always overcome them and bounced back. This loss to Will was something else. He felt too disillusioned, too drained to rally and figure out his next step. He passed a thicket of berries but lacked the will to eat them.

He flew up into towering trees and found an abandoned harpy nest. A brook flowed below, and the clear water beckoned to his grimy body and wings, but instead, he curled up in the moss, catlike, and covered himself with his dingy feathers.

For the next several days, he stayed in the tree and slept. The nest became an inescapable rut. He couldn't climb out and knew he would die here. Though, it was strangely comforting.

"Get up," Bloom said, shaking Alex's shoulder.

"Go away, Bloom," Alex muttered under his feathers. "We're no longer friends, remember?"

"That was your decision, not mine. And you need help."

Alex shook off his grogginess. "First, Will and now you. I don't want your help. I'm tired and want to be left alone."

"You are not tired but depressed. It robs you of energy and hope." He extended one of Alex's wings. "Despair also takes your pride. Your feathers are filthy."

"I don't care."

"I know you do not. That is the problem." Bloom lifted Alex's wing to expose his body. "You grow thin. When was the last time you ate?"

Alex scratched his head. "I don't recall."

Bloom bent over him. "My beautiful young golden, you truly have given up on life, but I refuse to allow this." He straightened. "I shall bring you a new sash and food. While I am gone, go down to that stream and bathe. It shall restore some dignity."

"Suppose I don't want to."

"Alex, you are too weak and battered to resist me. I shall throw you in the water and hold you there until clean and then force the food down your throat. Do not defy me." His unwavering green eyes meant business.

"All right," Alex said, slowly rising. "Bloom, I don't know why you bother. No one cares."

"That is untrue. I and our queen worried about you. She sent me to find you, and it was wise I did. Tomorrow Will accepts the Outback rule in Terrance, and we shall fly to the ceremony. All shall see you are gracious and not a poor loser."

"But I am a sore loser," Alex said. "And seeing Will in all his glory sure won't help my depression. Besides, no one wants to see me."

"The harpies long to see you. They witnessed your bravery, how hard you fought Will, and the many times you were knocked down and kept rising. You are admired, Alex. We shall talk more when I return." He flew from the nest into the forest.

Alex wasn't in any shape to fight off the big harpy over a bath so he sailed down into the knee-deep stream, doused his feathers, and lay down to soak his body. "I'll get clean and eat," he grumbled, "but I'll be damned if I'm flying to Terrance to watch Will get his crown." The realization hit him that tomorrow Will officially ruled. "My father's vow!" he said, leaping from the water. Shail had sworn to give the flocks a great ruler. Once one of his sons reigned, his promise was fulfilled, and he would kill himself.

Leaping skyward, he flew rapidly south to the Turner estate, a one-hundred-fifty-mile journey. Shail should be there. Alex's motivation to save Shail was selfish, basically. He had been cheated out of a being with his father and felt entitled to have his turn.

He made the coastal trip in record time. Reaching Westend Harbor, he headed inland to the Turner estate and landed at the large white house. On the porch, he banged frantically on the front door, yelling, "Kari, Kari, is anyone in there?" No one answered. He realized the household was in Terrance for tomorrow's ceremony. At the small jungle clearing where Summer and Matt were married, he stumbled to a landing.

"Father, Father," he called, walking around the edge of the forest. "Please come. It's your son, Alexander." His hopes rose, detecting the presence of a harpy but were dashed when Bloom set down near him. "You followed me."

"You lost the will to live. I would not let you stray. Why are you here, Alex?"

"I'm looking for my father."

"He is usually here or at a nearby lake, but he may have flown to Terrance."

"Never. He wouldn't face those huge crowds. Where is this lake?"

Bloom pointed to the east. Alex took off and soon landed at the lake. "Father, Father, it's your son, Alexander," he called, walked up and down a grassy bank. Bloom arrived and leaned against a tree trunk, curiously watching him. "Bloom, is this the right lake?" he asked anxiously.

Bloom nodded. "All harpies know the story of how your parents met here. A giant mogel had snatched Kari off the bank, and though only a teenager, Shail fought it and saved her. Mogels are eelish water creatures and live a long time. The one your father encountered is probably still here. You look to the trees for your father but should be watching the murky water."

"This goddamn planet," Alex said, backing away from the water's edge. He continued to call for his dad while circling the lake. Finally, he returned to Bloom, still standing under the tree. Alex plunked down on the grass, giving up. "Maybe I'm too late."

"Perhaps you should tell me why you search for him."

"During the challenges, I met Dad on the sacred mountain and he spoke about his vow to give the harpies their next ruler. Once he fulfills his promise and Will rules, dad had no reason to live. He's going to commit suicide tomorrow, Bloom. I can't let it happen."

Bloom sat down next to Alex. "That is painful to learn. All harpies shall mourn his passing but they understand that Shail has suffered a long time. For a son, the loss is harder to accept. I know too well. But, Alex, you should respect his wishes and let him have his peace."

"No," Alex stormed, bounding to his feet. Not willing to tell Bloom the truth; that he wanted what Will had had, he came up with a half-baked reason. "Bloom, I can heal him. I could use my telepathy, go into his mind, and fix him. Please help me find him."

"No one, even you, can mend Shail's mind," Bloom said. "I have heard he does not even know Kari anymore. He shall not know or trust you."

Alex's eyes watered. "I have to try. Don't you see? I have nothing else."

Bloom sighed, "You have my loyalty. I shall help. Come."

They flew across the lake to a grove of towering trisom trees that grew near the shore, the massive roots half submerged. They landed on a high branch and Bloom relayed, *we hide in these trees and wait, making no sound. The human voice frightens Shail, so if he comes, do not speak aloud. Communicate with him silently in the old harpy way.*

Do you really think he'll come?

That is unknown, but searching for him is useless if he does not wish to found.

While waiting, Alex ate a few trisom fruits to restore his energy. After several hours, Bloom touched Alex's arm and nodded toward Shail, who had emerged from the jungle and sniffed the air.

He senses us, Bloom relayed, *He smells to find our location and shall soon spot us in these branches. Quietly and slowly go to him. But Alex, be submissive. Remember, he is the most dominant male to ever live and very dangerous. If he does not see you as a son, you must flee at once. He shall not tolerate a younger male invading his territory.*

Alex slipped from the tree limb, glided down, and landed several yards away from Shail. *I am Alexander, your son, and must speak to you.* He tiptoed toward him.

Flinging his locks back, Shail hissed, motioning Alex to leave.

Ignoring Bloom's advice and his father's threat, Alex moved closer, staring into Shail's eyes. *Don't you remember me, Father? We met on the sacred mountain.*

Shail responded with an angry hiss and arched his wings.

Bloom fluttered down, landing several feet beyond Alex. *Alex, you are challenging him! Lower your head and gaze and drop your wings on the ground. Slowly back away. He sees you as an intruder.*

Alex dropped his head and wings, but did not move. *I'm not leaving him, Bloom.*

Shail ruffled his feathers in aggravation and paced a few steps in front of Alex.

His reasoning is gone! Bloom exclaimed. *He readies to attack. Fly before it is too late.*

Shail shifted his glare to Bloom, the bigger mature male beyond Alex. He seethed, even more livid with two trespassing males. Without the warning signs of the pacing and fluttering in a typical challenge, he flew straight into Alex.

Hurled backwards, Alex hit the ground. Instantly Shail was on top of him, clutching for his throat. The assault was so fast that Alex had no time to think, and unlike Will, Shail aimed to kill. Lying on his back, Alex punched and kicked to get him off, but his father was unrelenting, choking the life out of him.

Bloom jumped behind Shail and tugged at his wing to pull him off Alex, but a well-placed whack from Shail's other wing flung him into the dirt. Bloom held his stomach and clamored to rise.

Alex saw Bloom couldn't help him, and his only option was to fake death. He stopped struggling, closed his eyes, and went limp. Shail released him and turned his aggression on Bloom.

Seeing he was next, Bloom flapped his wings and leaped clear of Shail's charge, but not wanting to desert Alex, he landed a short distance away. Bloom and Shail now faced off.

Alex coughed and lifted his head. Bloom's arched black wings opposite his father's deep gold as they strutted in a small circle. Bloom noticed Alex and relayed, *Go, Alex. I shall distract him!*

Alex scrambled to his feet, flew to a tree, and stared down. Although Bloom was younger, heavier, and taller than Shail, the outcome of this fight was obvious. Bloom didn't have a chance. Alex huffed with anxiety, knowing his best friend would die for defending him. While being choked, Alex had sensed that Shail had lost all harpy emotion and sensitivity, and was like a ruthless predator, lusting for the kill.

Cornered, Bloom dared not turn his back and retreat. Shail would grab him from behind and break his neck. Bloom's only choice was to stand and fight. Shail made a low, deadly seething sound and advanced toward his foe. Bloom hissed nervously and backed away. They fluttered simultaneously. Bloom kicked Shail's chest, but it didn't faze him. He flew into Bloom, ramming his stomach and ribs. Bloom struck the ground, and Shail pinned him on his back and choked him. Bloom thrashed wildly but could not escape.

To interfere, Alex would share Bloom's fate. "Get away from him," he screamed, but the human voice didn't frighten or deter him.

After a few agonizing minutes, Bloom lost consciousness and lay as limp as a doll. Shail stood over his lifeless victim and urinated on him, marking Bloom as a possession. He then knelt, bit Bloom's neck, and sucked the blood.

Alex had read that the gentle harpies had a savage past. This rare vampire behavior mainly affected full-blooded harpies. After a stressful fight, the winning male reverted to his animal ancestry, the loca eagles, and feasted on his victim to regain his strength. Alex knew Bloom's fate. Shail would drain Bloom of blood, break his wings, and possibly rip off his testicles. Weak, flightless, docile from castration, he would become a rich source of nourishment until his death.

Alex couldn't let this happen. Rallying his courage, he jetted off the branch and crashed into his father, knocking him off Bloom. Both Alex and Shail rolled quickly to their feet with wings spread. Shail hissed, shook the sand from his wings, and approached. Alex ruffled his feathers, hoping to hide his trembling. He hadn't recovered from Will's beating and was in no condition to take on the most lethal harpy on Dora. He couldn't survive this fight, but then again, could he?

Alex folded his wings and focused on his father's mind. He had failed to hypnotize Will, and it was probably useless on his strong-minded father, but it was his only hope. *Sleep, Shail, sleep,* he relayed with extreme concentration.

Shail shook his head and took a step closer.

Sleep, I said!

Dizzy, Shail staggered and collapsed. Alex breathed hard from fright, wiped the anxious sweat from his brow, and stared down at his comatose father. He turned to the crumpled mass of lifeless black feathers. "Bloom?"

Alex cringed with the lack of response and movement. Rushing to him, he dropped to his knees and cradled the harpy's head in his lap. "Please, Bloom, don't leave me," he whimpered.

He had been here before, repeating these words over another dead loved one. "Please, Bloom, you can't die like Mollie." He felt the lump in his throat that came with being too late. Too late to tell Mollie he loved her, too late to say the same to this big, faithful harpy who had died protecting him.

He rocked Bloom back and forth. "You were my only true friend. I loved you, Bloom." An eternity seemed to pass as he held Bloom and wept.

Suddenly Bloom gasped.

"You're alive!" Alex exclaimed and hugged him.

"Barely," Bloom said, coughing. He lifted his head and rubbed the bloody bite wound on his neck. "Where is he?"

"Over there." Alex pointed. "I hypnotized him and he's out cold." He helped Bloom rise.

"Alex, you are a troublesome harpy, but I also love you."

Bloom had heard his babbling, but Alex only chuckled, too relieved to care. "I was a little frantic, but it's true. I love you, Bloom."

"I know," Bloom said as they walked to Shail. "For the second time, your powers saved me. If not for you, I still would be in the mining camp or someplace worse."

"Hell, if you're keeping score, we're even," Alex said, "You rescued me on Oden and now from my own father."

Bloom gazed down at the dozing golden. "I have heard about his deadly skills, but never thought I would become his target."

Alex squatted and stroked his father's head. "He is truly something. No wonder, everyone was scared of him." He looked up with the realization. "Bloom, he's vulnerable. The hypnosis worked. I can help him." He stood. "Stay here and protect him from wild animals. I'll return this evening."

"Wait, Alex. Where do you go?"

"To Terrance for *Dream Weaver*, I'm taking Dad off Dora."

"I cannot allow you to steal him."

"How is it stealing? He's my father. For this to work, I have to remove him from the jungle, his comfort zone. Besides, no one trusts me, especially Will. He'd never let me have him."

Bloom shook his head. "I do not know, Alex. This might not be wise."

"What's the alternative? Dad is dangerous, and when he kills someone, Will and harpies will be forced to hunt him down, his father and the harpy who everyone worships. If dad regains reason, he'll commit suicide. His only hope is with me."

"I was thinking it might not be wise for you. You shall be alone and shut up on the small ship with him. You have seen he strikes with lightning speed. You might be unable to stop him in time."

"When you found me earlier, you knew I wanted to die. Dad also doesn't want to live. Alone we're both doomed, but together we could make it. It's worth the risk."

Bloom looked at Alex, then at Shail, and nodded. "I shall hope you save each other."

Alex looked around at the heavily wooded jungle. "Landing the ship at the Turner estate might attract attention. The only place else is the beach. Can you bring Dad there, and we'll hook up?"

"It shall be a great honor to carry Shail, but suppose he wakes while you are gone?"

"He won't. He's under my spell until I free him. I'll see you tonight." Alex leaped into the sky and began the four-hour journey to Terrance.

* * *

In the early evening, Alex arrived in Terrance and flew north along the river to where Matt had parked his ship in the jungle. He landed by the leaf-covered vessel, and two brown-winged harpies stepped from the trees.

You do not need to guard the star vehicle anymore, Alex relayed. *I am taking this foul thing out of our jungle to the stars, but first I wish to see my sister and Matt. Do you know where they live?*

Their home is in a large blue tree, relayed one harpy. *It is not far, but master, they and the rest of the golden family are at our queen's home, preparing for tomorrow's celebration of your brother's reign.*

Take me to Summer's home, anyway.

Alex followed the harpy to a massive blue tree with solar panels in its top branches. Closer to the ground and nestled in the trunk was a gingerbread-style tree house. They landed on the wrap-around deck and Alex said. "You can go." He entered the quaint dwelling, and on a rough wooden desk, he found the ship's remote, needed to open *Dream Weaver*'s door hatch. Grabbing the remote, he turned to leave but noticed the notepad.

He picked up a pen and wrote, "Sorry, Matt, for taking *Dream Weaver*. Show this note to my mother, and she'll pay you for the ship. I've only been trouble on Dora and don't belong here. Thanks for everything, and please tell the family I'm sorry. Sincerely..."

He stopped writing and stared at the last two words, "sorry and sincerely." It was a lie. He wasn't sorry that he was about to deprive the family of their great hero. His mind drifted to Will and his offer to teach Alex about fighting and the jungle. "Brother, I'll teach you what I know," he mumbled, "Teach you about loss." He scribbled his name and left.

He flew back to the ship and surveyed the trees that were tightly wedged against its hull. Unless they were chopped down, liftoff would take skill and a lot of luck. He entered the ship and sat down in the pilot seat. Directions in the ship manual came to mind, and he flipped some switches. The engines fired with a roar, and the vessel's shudder shook off the covering of fan branches.

"Okay, *Weaver*, you've been in tighter spots." He touched the lift controls and heard shearing metal against the trunks and branches when the ship rose straight up. After clearing the foliage, he swung the ship west and punched the throttle. It jetted over the jungle, and the distance that had taken him hours to wing was over in fifteen minutes.

Alex throttled down over the little town of Westend and the Turner estate. On the coast, he slowed the ship to a hover. The low tide had created a wide stretch of beach, but he landed *Dream Weaver* partly in shallow water and shore. Any evidence of a ship landing would wash away with the incoming tide.

He opened the door but didn't lower the ramp. He inhaled the moist breeze, a mix of sea and earthy aromas. The emerald ocean shimmered under the twin moons, and he viewed the thousands of colorful seabirds that rested on the rocky cliffs. Over the sound of the lapping waves, he heard the jungle; the music, chatter, hoots, and roars of its animals. Experiencing Dora for the last time, he knew he would miss this beautiful home of his people.

Bloom, cradling Shail in his arms, landed on the beach below the ship. Folding his wings, he said, "You came, so I assume you have not changed your mind."

"Not about this," Alex said. "Fly him up here. I don't want to waste time with the ramp."

Bloom flew to the ship door, stepped into the cabin, and gently placed the notorious golden harpy on the familiar couch that he had once occupied. Gazing at Shail, he said, "Waiting for you, I am having doubts, Alex. What we do is madness."

"You care about me and admire him." Alex patted Bloom's shoulder. "You are rescuing us. Feel good about that."

"I know, but it seems like a betrayal. I shall have difficulty explaining to Will that I helped you take his father. He shall not be pleased."

"Don't tell him," Alex said. "Don't tell anyone I took Dad. They'll only worry. And knowing Will, he would mount a fleet of spaceships and hunt me to the ends of the galaxy to get his father." He reached down to Shail and jerked out a handful of his yellow feathers. Stepping to the door, he tossed them into the surf. "When they search for Shail, they'll find his feathers and believe he flew out to sea and drowned himself. That is a dignified death. The harpies will forever remember him as the greatest harpy of all time, rather than an insane, bloodthirsty killer."

The sun slipped below the horizon as Bloom looked out at the floating feathers and a few others that the wind carried up the beach. "Alex, I am a harpy. I cannot lie."

"It's not a lie, if no one questions you about Shail. As for my disappearance, I left Matt a note explaining I took his ship and have left Dora for good."

"Are you leaving forever?"

"I think so. I've made too many mistakes, and I'm an asshole, lousy at sucking up and apologizing. I'm hoping to find a place for me and Dad, and with any luck, we'll settle down and be happy."

"You are a strange harpy, content to live in buildings, deserts, and starships." Bloom glanced at Shail. "But what about him? Dora is his home. If he heals, he shall wish to return."

"One thing at a time, Bloom," Alex said with a smile. "I'll worry about what Dad wants when it comes up. Well, I need to get going. Everyone is in Terrance, so I doubt anyone saw the ship land here, but why stick around and up the chance? Bloom, I'm sorry I caused you so much grief."

"Trust and affection come hard to one who has known the hurt of betrayal. I understood that about you. But I sensed much good in you. Someday you shall be the best of us."

Alex chuckled. “I keep hearing that shit and still don’t believe it. Guess this is goodbye, my friend. I’m sure going to miss you.”

They hugged and Bloom whispered, “I, too.” He gazed out at the dark horizon. “When I look to those stars, I shall think of you, a shining ray of light.” He soared down to the shadowy, empty beach.

Alex fired up the ship and blasted off into the night.

CHAPTER TWENTY-NINE

Matt climbed up the ladder to his tree house. Summer had already flown inside. "I'm beat, doll," he said, entering their little home. "Getting ready for tomorrow's party, Jim and I must have barbequed two-hundred pounds of ribs and roasts."

"Those poor cows," said Summer.

"Please, no badgering. Those out-of-towners won't be happy with your berries and nuts."

Summer wrapped her arms around his neck and kissed him. "I won't badger you tonight. Would you like a cold beer?"

"That'd be great. I love Jim, but it's no fun drinking around a recovering alcoholic." He wandered to the desk.

"Grandma sent Bloom to find Alex and bring him to celebration," she called from the kitchen. "Do you think he will have the nerve to show up?"

Matt read the note. "No, he won't be there. He's gone, Summer."

Summer walked into the living room with a bottle. "What do you mean gone?"

"The little asshole stole my ship and skipped town." He took a swig from the bottle. "He didn't even say where he was headed."

She read the note. "I cannot believe this, but it shouldn't be surprising. He did not have much of a future here. At least he said he was sorry."

Matt eased into a comfortable chair. "The funny thing when cooking, I heard a spaceship take off and told Jim it sounded like *Weaver*. He said it probably a big shot's ship from Hampton. You better call Will and let him know."

"He has enough worries, and Alex shouldn't be another one. I'll tell him after the ceremony."

"Alex's mother is supposed to pay me for *Weaver*, but it still burns me. All we've been through with that kid, and he couldn't even say goodbye."

"He was probably afraid you wouldn't let him have your ship."

Matt leaned forward in the chair. "Alex saved my life. I would have given him the damn ship."

* * *

Will stood on the tallest building in Terrance and gazed down at bustling street. Crowds strolled on the sidewalks and overwhelmed the small restaurants and hotels. Bumper to bumper traffic extended through the city, over the bridge, and down the Eastern highway. Beyond, the airport was equally packed with hovercrafts and ships of all kinds. Nearly every person in the Outback had come to Terrance and thousands had arrived from the East. The numbers, including the harpies, expected to top fifty thousand. They came to witness the rare royal event, the crowning of a new harpy ruler. Decades might pass before it happened again.

Yellow flowers that symbolized the golden reign adorned the windows, doors, and light poles. No building could accommodate such a crowd, so the ceremony would take place in a large park, west of the city. Food vendors set up in the park to feed the hungry masses. The city organizers had been built a stage to hold the dignitaries and Will. He sighed, not looking forward to being on display.

At noon, the massive crowd had gathered in the park, and Windy stepped to the microphone on the platform and addressed them. Humans covered the grounds, and harpies filled the trees. She gave a brief farewell speech and then expressed her confidence that her grandson, Will, would be a fair and wise leader. When she finished, a loud cheer rose. They truly loved her.

Will approached her, went down on one knee, and lowered his head. Windy placed a wreath of creamy-white flowers on his head that matched his low-slung hip sash. He rose and faced the hordes as a light breeze blew the locks off his tan shoulders and stirred his yellow feathers.

Windy smiled and relayed, *you look as dazzling as a fairy prince.* She turned to the crowd. "People of Dora and my harpies, I give you our new ruler."

The people went wild; clapping, hollering, and whistling. Most had never seen him, but they overwhelmingly approved. The harpies were silent, only lowering their heads to show him respect.

Will stepped to the microphone and said softly, "Thank you." Hearing his voice, a pack of teenage girls screamed and cried, idolizing him. The local and intergalactic media pressed against the platform to take his picture. He swallowed uncomfortably and glanced at his grandmother.

Windy relayed, *you look like your father, and they love you as much as him.*

They love what they see, but not for long. He lifted his hands to ask for quiet. After several long minutes, they settled down so he could speak. He took a breath. "Thank you for the warm reception and coming to Terence to celebrate with me and my family. I hope to follow my father's principles of integrity and wisdom. We live in peace on this beautiful land, but over the seasons, I have seen a growing threat. The jungle and its wildlife are disappearing because of human expansion. With my reign, this ends."

Many people clapped as others glared silently, already learning months earlier at the city council meeting about his plans.

"Some of you are displeased," he said, "but better you know me now. I am a harpy, and we speak true. The jungle is our home. With my last breath, I shall preserve it."

The speech was short, Will having no desire to yap on like a politician. Feeling like a prize-winning dog on exhibit, he couldn't wait to leave the stage. He shook hands with the dignitaries, kissed his grandmother, and fled to the sky. Musical bands took over the stage while the people ate and drank in the park. The festivity would continue into the night on the packed, littered streets of Terrance.

For Will, the event wasn't over. He flew to his grandmother's home for a private party. The yard, porch, and house were soon filled with various politicians, friends, and family. Will had to greet and speak to all of them.

The Dora governor and several senators cornered him on the porch, wanting to know more about his new policies.

The governor said, "Word is you plan to close the Outback borders to newcomers and shut down construction. Don't you realize that is bad for business?"

"If the beauty of this planet is lost, there shall be no business, governor," Will responded.

Will grew weary of explaining his plans to these men. He ruffled his feathers with irritation and snapped, "Sir, the Outback is not your land nor is it your concern."

Sam Waters stepped into the circle of men surrounding Will. "Gentlemen, Will knows what he's doing," he said. "Now if you'll excuse me, I need to borrow him for a minute. I suggest you have another drink and enjoy the barbeque." He took Will's arm and led him out of the pack of politicians.

Will and Sam walked across the lawn. "Thank you, Sam, for saving me. I try to be polite with them, but..." He shuddered. "It is very hard."

Sam chuckled. "I was saving them, not you. When Shail tussled his feathers, it meant watch out, he had enough. I would hate for those city boys to learn the hard way about a golden's temperament on your first day."

"I would not have thrown them off the porch, but merely ordered them to leave." He stopped walking. "I lack my grandmother's patience."

"Those politicians were testing you, but they'll soon learn that a golden male can't be bullied. Saving the jungle is a harpy's priority. You're on the right path and will do great."

At midnight the party ended and the last of the guests left Windy's home. Will and the harpies retreated to the trees. On the porch swing, Windy and Jim surveyed the clutter of dirty plates, cups, and leftover food that littered the tables and yard.

"I'm too tired to deal with the mess," she said. "Tomorrow the harpies will help me clean up."

"That's good because I'll be busy in Terrance. The garbage is ankle deep, and the jail is packed with the drunk and disorderly. It'll take a few days before things are back to normal."

Windy rested her head on his chest. "I think all went well. Most were pleased with Will."

"Pleased? Those women loved him." Jim smiled. "When he took the stage, I thought ambulances would be needed for those hysterical girls. Some even fainted."

"Yes, he is as alluring as his father, but humans see his pretty face and do not take him seriously."

"Ah, the curse of beauty, not being appreciated for your talent or intelligence," Jim said, laughing. "I've never had that problem."

Out of the dark, Will fluttered down and landed on the porch. "I am glad you are still awake."

"We were just talking about you," Jim said.

Windy pulled away from Jim and abruptly rose. "What is upsetting you, Will?"

"I am on my way to the Turner estate, but stopped to tell you, Grandma." He sniffled and wiped his nose. "I just spoke with my mother, and she believes Father is dead. I have sent Freely and the river flock ahead to find him. All harpies will search soon."

Windy put her arms around him. "Oh, Will, I'm so sorry. What did she say?"

"Dad had promise to give the flocks a good ruler. But mother failed to tell me that once I ruled and Dad fulfilled his vow, he would kill himself. He also told her that if the day came when he didn't know her, his life was over. Two days ago, he did not recognize Mom and I now rule. Both have come to past."

"That doesn't mean he's dead," Windy said.

Will shook his head "Last night Mom could not sense his presence in her dreams. That means he's gone. She knew all this and didn't tell me. I am so angry with her. Had I'd known I could have stopped him, saved him."

Windy hugged him and whispered, "She didn't tell you because she knew you would stop him. Shail has been in torment for a long time. Kari loved him enough to let him go and have peace. Do not be angry with her."

Will jerked free of her and glared. "You knew," he stammered, "also knew he planned to kill himself and didn't tell me."

"If I or Kari had told you, what would you do, lock him up until his mind was completely gone? That is selfish, Will. You are a ruler now and should consider the many others who care about him. Would you keep him alive and kill his reputation and legacy?"

"But, Grandma, I did not tell him how I felt, didn't say goodbye."

* * *

Over the following days, thousands of harpies searched the Outback for Shail. Despite his mother and grandmother's beliefs that his father should be allowed to die in peace, Will was not ready to let go. He still hoped his father was alive and could be found. He was further encouraged that his body had not been discovered.

A week later on the ocean near Westend, several fledglings played tag on the beach. The smallest female, outmaneuvered by her older siblings, strolled down the shoreline in search of shells for her collection. She caught a glimpse of yellow and picked up a tiny feather that had been half-covered with blowing sand. That night she showed the feather to her father, asking what bird had this type of feather. "It is the down feathering from a golden harpy, not a bird," he said. "But Shail's offspring rarely visit that beach." The next day the father took the precious yellow fluff to the Turner estate.

On the front porch, Kari held the feather to her nose. Her eyes watered, and she asked the male harpy, "Where did your daughter find it?"

He told her and she thanked him. Stepping inside the house, she called Will's portable com. "A harpy brought me a yellow feather, found on the beach, north of Westend harbor. The scent is fresh and unmistakable. It belonged to your father."

The following day the land quest for Shail switched to one of the sea. Will and his harpies scrutinized hundreds of miles of ocean and coastline for more evidence of Shail.

On a small island, the furthest west in the chain, Will bent over, resting his hands on his knees and panted. Other harpies set down to recover from the exhausting flight. For days they had been flying nonstop since Shail disappeared. Will straightened and gazed out at the endless western ocean, a place no harpy dare venture.

Aron, out of loyalty to Shail, had also taken part in the hunt for his adopted golden brother. He fluttered and landed beside Will. "To go further out is dangerous," Aron said, and placed his hand on Will's wing. "If Shail flew beyond this island and out to sea, he is surely dead. Perhaps it is time you let him go."

Shaking his head, Will said, "I cannot give up, not yet. I have to know what happened to him."

"You are determined, much like the brother you fought. I have heard he no longer dwells with us."

"Yes, Alex took a spaceship and left Dora while everyone was preparing for the Terrance celebration. All we did for him, and he snubbed us. I don't know where he is or care. Besides, I have been too busy looking for Dad."

"He was a very strange and bewildered harpy. He knew he could not win but refused to yield. Many thought him brave. I believe stubbornness, ego, and a lack of sense drove him."

"That was Alex."

In the distance, a lone harpy appeared on the horizon, gliding toward them. Coming closer, his wingspan was shorter than Will's, and he was in trouble maintaining his flight. His wings flapped and then drooped. Will turned to two large males. "Help him." The males took off as the young male crashed into a wave and floundered on the surface. They scooped him up, and one carried him back and placed him on the sand near Will and Aron.

Will knelt over him and growled, "What were you doing out there alone?"

So fatigued and out of breath, the young male couldn't answer but held up a yellow feather. Aron took the feather and sniffed it. "I lived most my life with this scent. It is Shail's."

The young male later relayed he had found the feather over a hundred miles beyond the island. The evidence was conclusive. Shail had flown west over the ocean until his wings gave out and he drowned.

One week later, the harpies gathered once more. On the beach where Shail had left them, they gazed at a golden sunset to honor him. No words were spoken or needed. All mourned the prince of dawn, as Shail had been affectionately called after liberating the flocks. Like the brilliant sun sinking into the dark horizon of waves, the greatest harpy of all time had slipped away.

* * *

That night, Bloom left his sleeping family in the nest and stood on a branch, reflecting on Alex and Shail. Because Alex had no relationship with his father, no one had made the connection that father and son had disappeared at the same time. To Bloom's relief, he was never questioned about Alex so he did not have to lie or betray Alex's trust. He looked up at a gleaming star. "I think of you, Alex."

CHAPTER THIRTY

In the ship cockpit, Alex tapped his balled fist against his mouth while studying the star chart on the screen. Ahead lay countless solar systems in the galaxy with life-supporting planets. He zeroed in on a small star and its fourth planet. Like its star, the planet was tiny, probably half the size of Dora and consisted of mostly ocean, but forests covered the landmass. The population was sparse, and it only had one spaceship port that could recharge *Dream Weaver*. More importantly, its location was off the frequently traveled channels so the feds were unlikely to hear about two harpies on the run.

"Paradise Haven," he said. "Sounds perfect and it's the right distance."

After leaving Dora, he had taken inventory on food supplies and calculated the ship maintenance. They were good to go for several months. He punched in the coordinates to a small wormhole leading to the planet and switched on the autopilot.

He entered the cabin. His father still lay on the couch where Bloom had placed him. In a deep hypnotic trance, his eyes held a blank stare, focused on the ceiling.

Alex sat down on the edge of the couch. "Now what am I going to do with you?"

Alex had lied to Bloom about his noble cause to heal his father. Self-interest was the objective along with jealousy. He smiled, reflecting that Will was probably heartbroken about now. His father's yellow feathers had surely been discovered on the beach. The explanation: Shail had intentionally flown out to sea to die.

Alex pushed the blond locks from his father's eyes. "There's not much left of you, but you're mine." He bit his lip and stared at his mentally ill father. "But can you give me what I want? Give me what you gave my brother?"

Shail, of course, couldn't respond.

Alex convinced himself of the reasons he took Shail, but deep down he knew it was about survival. When Bloom found him, he was beyond depressed and ready to die. Rather than floundering in agony for weeks, he had planned to eat poison berries on the following day. It was the only alternative. He had too much pride to crawl back into good graces of the harpies and his family. To return to Oden with his mother was a nonstarter. But saving his father gave him the willpower to go on.

"Aren't we a pair?" He sighed. "We're both fucked up. It's like the blind leading the blind."

He studied his father, a full-blooded harpy. He had a slighter, almost delicate frame, but in a flash, he had overwhelmed Bloom and himself, both taller and beefier. Alex was scared of him and reluctant to end the trance.

Alex tilted his head. "Can I really fix you?"

* * *

Over the next few weeks aboard ship, Alex kept his father under his spell and told him when to rise, eat, sleep, and urinate. Like a mindless robot, Shail obeyed. Alex struggled with his fears of ending the hypnosis. The consequences could be like freeing a Dora red dragon that could swiftly pounce and kill him. The concern, he might become too flustered to concentrate and end the attack. On the other hand, he was growing lonely. Daily the decision to release his father had plagued him.

On the cabin floor Alex sat alongside his father and preened his deep honey-colored feathers. The dark gold was a sign of age, different from Alex's pale yellow wings. He ran his fingers down a flight feather and forced the natural oils from the shaft into the vanes and sealed the split barbs. He recalled the night on the sacred mountain when these same feathers were wrapped around him and kept him warm. In those brief moments, Alex had felt the unconditional love of a parent.

"Are you still in there, Father?" Alex asked while folding Shail's wing back into place. "Does that harpy still exist?"

Like a zombie, Shail lay quietly.

Alex heaved a sigh and stood. The boring space travel and the monotonous routine of daily care for his father were wearing thin. Patience wasn't his strong suit. He had spent hours on the computer, studying his father's condition. The post-traumatic stress disorder had caused the suicidal depression. Humans could be cured with an operation that removed the damaged brain cells, holding memory, but the patient suffered from permanent amnesia. Drugs reduced the stress, but a patient might become lethargic, forgetful, or develop a host of other problems that included suicide.

After days of the research, Alex concluded that the treatments and their side effects were worse than the disorder. There was no fast, safe, or sure remedy. Furthermore, the studies were based on humans who suffered from PTSD and turned to alcohol, drugs, and even crime. Shail was a harpy with a different mentality and problems. Who knew the outcome or if the treatments would work? His dad's only hope rested in Alex's hands.

He looked down at his dozing father and decided. "You might kill me, but it doesn't matter anymore." He stepped out of strike range of a wing and closed his eyes. *Wake, Shail, I release you,* he relayed into Shail's subconscious. *Your mind is your own.*

Shail blinked and lifted his head. Seeing the solid walls and hearing the ship engines, he curled into a tight ball and covered himself with his quivering wings. Instead of a deadly, angry response, his father was terrified.

"It's all right," Alex said, and rushed to hold and calm him.

From under his feathers, Shail hissed and snapped at Alex's hand, nearly inflicting a nasty bite. He was behaving like a trapped animal, defending itself out of fear. He seethed and retreated under his shaking wings while his petrified eyes shifted back and forth between Alex and a possible escape. Each breath created a nervous, shushing sound. So frightened, he seemed on the verge of a heart attack.

Alex cringed with worry and considered re-hypnotizing him, but that would mean going backward. He sat down several feet away from Shail, and realizing his voice had made matters worse, he relayed silently, *No one shall hurt you, Father. There are no humans here, just me, your son, Alexander. I wish to help you, but you must trust me.*

After hours of gentle coaxing, Shail's trembling was reduced to an occasional shudder. Alex inched closer and slowly held out his hand. *Smell me, Father. I am your offspring. I'm your third oldest son.*

Shail lifted a wing high enough to expose his face and sniffed toward Alex.

Good, you are listening to me, Alex relayed. *Use your instincts and know I am your son. We are on a star vehicle, but there is nothing to fear. We are here so I can help end your terror and make you whole. Touch my hand and you shall know I speak true.*

Shail swallowed and pulled his wing back to survey the cabin. While worried, he reached out and clasped Alex's extended hand.

That's it. Alex's smile quickly evaporated when Shail uncurled his body and lunged for him. Shail's move was so quick that Alex couldn't hypnotize and stop him. "Wait," he yelled as his father wrapped his arms around him. So startled and frightened, Alex froze, unable to fend off the attack. His hard breathing slowly subsided, realizing his father's intentions. "You…you don't want to hurt me."

With his embrace, Shail nuzzled Alex's neck and cloaked him in his wings. Alex hugged his waist, consoled.

* * *

With a computer in his lap, Alex lounged in the large stuffed chair and studied a book about the physiology of a wild animal. He knew everything about intelligent, civilized mortals, but had little experience with creatures, never even owning a pet, up until now. A few weeks earlier, he had a breakthrough with his father. Shail had perceived him as a son rather than a threat and eventually adjusted to the ship. That's where the progress ended.

Mentally, Shail was stuck. He behaved like the same wild creature that Alex had removed from Dora. He couldn't communicate, silently or orally, and functioned instinctively. He used his eyes and gestures like head tossing, hissing, and feather ruffling to display his likes and dislikes.

Alex had probed Shail's mind and found it so damaged that no memory existed. He wasn't even aware of who he was. The question remained: was his memory shut down or had it been erased? Alex was growing desperate, dealing with him while looking for answers and a cure.

Shail rose from the couch and tiptoed into the galley. He sniffed the cabinet holding food and turned to hiss at Alex.

"All right, I guess it is time to eat." Alex closed the computer and rose. "That book says to change your ways, I've got to show you who's in charge." He opened the cabinet and removed a sealed bag of dried fruit. As Shail reached for the bag, Alex jerked it away and said, "Wait, I'll put it on a plate and you can eat it at the booth." He took a breath. "Dad, you have to start learning some manners."

At first, Shail seemed puzzled, and then with a glare, he snatched the bag from Alex's hand and ripped it open with his teeth. Half the berries landed on the floor. He returned to the couch with the torn bag and popped the food into his mouth. Shail didn't know his name, but was well aware he was the dominant male and no youngster gave him orders.

"Damn it, look at the mess you made," Alex growled. "You think you're the boss, but if you want to eat, we're doing things my way." He stepped to the couch and reached for the bag. Shail harshly slapped his hand and made a low, reprimanding hiss.

"Ouch, that really hurt," Alex barked, holding his smarting wrist. "You pull that shit again, and I'll hypnotize you. I'll turn you into a fucking dog that eats out of a bowl." He leaned over to clean up the spilled berries, unaware his hostile voice had triggered an aggressive response.

Shail flew off the couch and with a solid kick to Alex's ribs, he sent him sprawling on his back. Shail leaped on his chest and choked him.

Alex's initial fears were realized, too frazzled to hypnotize and stop him. Gasping, he cried out, "Daddy, please! Don't kill me!"

Shail suddenly stopped strangling Alex and released his deadly hold. With a stunned expression, he gazed at Alex and slid off his chest, and relayed sadly, *I must be mad to try and kill my own son.*

Alex grasped his throat and cautiously sat up. Since leaving Dora, this was Shail's first communication. The traumatic attack and Alex's panicked cries must have sparked something.

I'm all right, Dad. Do you remember me? I'm Alexander. We met on the sacred mountain.

Alexander is a strange name. Your mother must be human. I have no memory of you or our meeting on the mountain. Shail looked around the cabin. *I do not recall how I came to be here. Where am I?*

Alex grinned with relief. *We're on a spaceship in the stars.*

Shail shuddered. *I sense I have suffered greatly in these stars.*

This ship journey is one of hope, not fear or suffering. I'm going to try to remove your terrible experiences from your memory and make you well. You must have faith in me.

* * *

Alex was delighted with his father's breakthrough. Shail no longer functioned like an animal, relying only on instinct. His dignity returned, and he communicated with the old fashion silent talk of the harpies. For the next several days, Alex telepathically probed Shail's mind, but his past was a blur. Only during sleep did he experience terrible flashbacks, and he woke shaking and covered with sweat.

Shail's nightmares were disturbing, but they gave Alex optimism. They proved that Shail's memories, although damaged, still existed. The old Shail was in there and only needed to be drawn out. Alex had studied psychology in college, and on the ship he had read everything about the post-traumatic stress disorder. Taking what he knew, he devised his own method to heal his father. First using hypnosis and then his telepathy, he'd invade Shail's subconscious. Together in the dream state, he and his father would find, face, and hopefully overcome the horrendous memories.

As an amateur, Alex worried about dabbling with his father's subconscious. Besides memory, the nerve center held perception, feeling, will, and imagination, and they could be damaged. The other risk, Shail could become so petrified that he could go into shock or end up in a vegetative state. But there was no other choice.

Alex thought about his life; his lonely, miserable upbringing that gave him the incentive to develop his gifts. He had studied and trained hard, but after Will defeated him, the work had been done for nothing. He was a loser. He now realized that maybe all was worthwhile. He was the only one alive capable of healing his father.

He turned to Shail who rested on the couch. *Are you ready to start, Father?*

A willing patient, Shail nodded but had no idea what lie ahead. Alex had told him that the therapy would end his fatigue, aching muscles, and sleepless nights.

Alex sat nearby and placed his hand on his father's forehead. *Like I explained with the fruit, we shall slowly peel away the skin, starting at the beginning of your life and steadily work toward the core where your problems lie. Close your eyes and relax.*

Alex also shut his eyes. *Good, you are calm. See yourself inside a dark cave with a light at the end. Do you see it?*

I am in the cave and sense you are with me.

That's right. No matter what you see, I am here to protect you. Now let's walk toward the light and cave open. When you reach the opening outside, picture that you are a small fledgling in a warm secure nest.

The process began, and in the weeks ahead, Alex witnessed his father's life. Like the start of a long movie, he saw Shail's beautiful, adoring parents, his preliminary flight from of the nest, and his playful wrestling with an older, brown-winged fledgling named Aron, but at age five, Shail's carefree world came crashing down. A man killed his father, the ruler of the harpies. His mother, Alex's grandmother Windy, suffered from depression and vanished into the jungle. All thought she was dead.

Aron's father adopted Shail and raised him on the Western Islands to protect him from hunters. When Shail became a teenager, he was the last of the golden males, all exterminated while defending their flocks. Losing parents could make a harpy fearful and unsound, but the grief had the opposite effect on Shail. He became tough with unwavering grit to end the slaughter and save the harpies. Alex could relate. A broken heart can create gumption.

Alex kept the therapy sessions to a few hours a day, not wanting to overwhelm Shail. After releasing him from the hypnotism, they talked at length about the episodes to reinforce his memories. Recalling who he had been, Shail grew more confident and he started to vocally speak. He realized that retreating into the soothing jungle and becoming reclusive had increased his inner fears and was his ruin. He lost his memory along with his character and became a tormented animal.

Alex also learned that Shail's family had unwittingly aided his father's downfall. They refused to discuss his past and urge him to forget it, believing the brutal events would cause him more harm. And perhaps, they didn't want to know about his suffering. Alex, however, lacked their concern and charged headlong into Shail's memories. When the therapy was over, Shail's mind would either be healed or shattered.

Under psychotherapy, Shail's story continued. At fifteen he returned to the mainland but discovered harpy culture had changed. With the demise of the golden harpies, the brown-winged males became the flock leaders and each sought their own path of survival. Further, they had no respect for a scrawny teen with pale-yellow wings. Shail had told Aron, "For us to defeat humans, we must unite under one ruler." To fulfill this objective, he sought out each flock and challenged the large, older leader. With sheer tenacity, he won every fight and their admiration. At sixteen, he became the youngest harpy to ever rule. The great pressure to save the harpies from extinction fell upon his wings.

Dredging up these extraordinary circumstances that molded his father into a powerful leader also affected Alex. He once considered his father a has-been, but began to cherish him.

* * *

In the ship's back berths, Shail woke on the soft cushions and gazed at his sleeping son resting nearby. Alexander had said that only his mother used that name, and he preferred to be called Alex. Shail rose and stroked his son's locks in the dim lighting that simulated night. "You are an amazing creature, Alex," he whispered. "Unlike any harpy I have ever known."

Alex stirred, tucked his head under his wing out of reach, and continued to doze. Shail sighed. Even in sleep, Alex withdrew from a tender touch.

Shail walked into the shadowy cabin and curled up on the couch. Gazing out the window into space, he thought about the therapy, as his son called it. For weeks, he had allowed Alex to treat him and was seeing the results.

The achy and beaten-down feeling disappeared. His nightmares persisted but were less frequent, sometimes allowing him to sleep undisturbed through the night. His thoughts became clearer and his telepathy improved. For the first time in years, he felt self-assured.

This amazing son with his powerful telepathy, phenomenal mind control, and knowledge had accomplished the impossible. Alex had given him back his identity and spirit. Although, stirring up memories could be a blessing and a curse. After a session, he jokingly told Alex about how Kari had taught him to smile and appreciate humor. Sadly, he missed her.

His concerns turned to Alex. They had revisited the first twenty-something years of Shail's life, but were approaching the dark years. Shail didn't remember them, but caught hellish glimpses of those torturous events in his dreams. To expose Alex to them could be detrimental to his already disturbed son.

Initially, Shail was proud and impressed with his alien son, born of another world. Alex was extremely bright, capable of piloting a ship, fixing and working human gadgets, and his education surpassed harpies and most humans, apparently because of his gift of total recall. He was handsome, but his tall, muscular frame was uncommon for a golden male. At only eighteen years, he towered over Shail.

Alex seemed perfect but he had developed a talent of blocking his thoughts and feelings from other harpies. He also hadn't realized that Shail's senses had improved to catch glimpses of his issues. Besides, his refusal to discuss his upbringing and his avoidance of physical contact, Shail sensed that trust and affection were hard for Alex, and his charming behavior was an act to conceal his cynical nature. Shail felt his gloom and resentment. What had happened to him?

Alex strolled into the cabin. "Hey, Dad, you're up early. Want some breakfast before we start?" He opened the cabinet and grabbed a few food packets.

Shail stood. "Alex, I think we should end the therapy."

Stunned, Alex dropped the packets on the counter and wheeled around. "We can't stop. We have to reach the source of your problems to make you whole. If you're afraid, I'll be there."

"I am afraid, but my fear is for you. To travel my terrible past, you might be damaged."

"I'll be fine, Dad. I can handle anything."

"If you were fine, you would not block me from your thoughts. You wish me whole. I wish the same for you."

"There's nothing wrong so I'm not letting you dig around in my head."

Shail nodded. "That is your decision. Mine is no more therapy."

Alex sneered, snatched a bag off the counter and stormed to the back berths.

Shail lifted an eyebrow with his temperamental son and settled on the couch to eat. Hours later, Alex wandered back to the cabin.

"You deceived me," Alex said. "Didn't let me know your telepathy returned."

"I did no more than you. You asked me to trust you. I now ask the same of you. Let me help you."

"Open up so you'll learn I'm a sick bastard, a freak who is more human than harpy." Alex sniffled. "I didn't want to disappoint you."

"Alex, I am proud of you. Nothing in your mind and past shall remove my love for you." Shail stepped to Alex and hugged him. "You sense my feelings and know we must do this."

Alex nodded.

CHAPTER THIRTY-ONE

The role reversal took place. Shail became the therapist and Alex, the patient. Shail rested on the couch and placed his hand on Alex's forehead to probe his mind. What he saw made him sad. His son had not been physically hurt but suffered a crueler fate of emotional abuse. Shail knew too well that flesh wounds healed, but a scarred soul could last a lifetime.

Shail reviewed Alex's formative years. As a small fledgling, he had no father and his mother showed him no love, treating him more like a possession. She pushed him away and criticized his animal nature. By the time a loving nanny came into his life, he already had anxiety issues. The nanny took pity and spoiled him, not knowing golden males require a firm hand.

Growing up, Alex studied hard, hoping to win his mother's love and the respect from others. Neither of which happened. With his uncharacteristic wings and the ability to interpret thoughts, he frightened humans. He grew into a lonely and disillusioned teenager. He turned to his harpy telepathy and learned about hypnosis. That led to his imprisonment and the struggle with depression. When his nanny was killed in the rescue, it was the final blow. He lost compassion and became dangerous. He arrived on Dora confused, suspicious, and bitter.

Most harpies could not have survived Alex's life, but he had the golden resilience and was Shail's son. To gain acceptance and respect, he threw himself into the harpy challenges for leadership, only to have his spirit completely crushed. Shail saw that his son had given up and contemplated suicide.

Shail realized he and Alex were each other's last hope. Beneath his son's flaws lay a noble harpy. He only needed love and stern guidance to bring him out. But was it too late? Shail removed his hand from Alex and glanced out at the stars. A star that shines too bright burns out quickly. That was Alex. Helping his father was only a temporary fix from the inevitable. His starlight flickered on the verge of going out.

Shail was concerned with Alex learning more about his life. Kari, Aron, and Windy were aware of Shail's hardships, but they never experienced them. With his intense telepathy, his son would see, hear, smell, and feel his father's pain and horror. Alex was already in trouble, but exposed to the terrible events might push him over the edge.

Alex sat up and said, "Now you know everything; my shitty life, my killing spree, my screw-ups with your family. What do you think, Dad? Still love me?"

"I do. Learning what you have suffered, I understand you better."

"Really?" Alex questioned, surprised. "That means we can continue with your therapy."

Shail rose and paced in the cabin. He stopped in front of Alex. "I am grateful you healed me but have decided to end these treatments."

Alex leaped off the sofa. "We can't stop. We're only halfway there. You could relapse and turn back into a mindless fool."

"For your sake, I do not wish to continue."

"You...you saw who I was and don't trust me." Alex stomped into the kitchen and slammed the cupboard door shut. The force rattled the dishes inside.

"Alexander, settle down," Shail scolded.

Alex flopped on the floor and fumed. "I'm Alex. I told you to call me Alex. Only my fucking mother calls me Alexander." Looking up, his eyes burned with defiance, but he knew better than to disobey.

"It is true. I do not trust you. You are full of rage as you have just proven. When we approach the bad years of my life, your anger shall grow. I would rather be a mindless fool than have an angry son who never feels joy. You are an extraordinary harpy with great horizons in your future."

"I don't see horizons. I only see you." Alex gulped down a breath. "Dad, I've dreamed of being with you all my life. We can't stop now. Sure, I'll get mad, watching assholes abuse you, but it can't compare to my outrage if you slipped backward, and I lost you again. Nothing could be worse."

For several long minutes, Shail stared at him. "All right, we shall go on and hope for the best."

* * *

In the ship cabin, Alex continued his father's therapy. They approached the next two years in Shail's life, the most important for the harpies but devastating for Shail. All knew that hunters had tortured him and inflicted the trauma that destroyed his mind, but Shail hadn't revealed all the ghastly details to anyone. Alex would be the first to know what had happened.

To cure his father, he would find his father's terrible memories and then use hypnotism to remove them, but it could be a temporary fix. The memories were still there. A stressful event might trigger them, and the PTSD would return. Relying on his degree in psychology, Alex decided his father needed to face his terrors. Afterward, they would discuss them for hours, even days, until they lost their effect and became meaningless. It was the only proven cure.

Alex saw the vision. Shail was twenty-six and anxious. He hadn't seen Kari in ten years but learned she was returning to Dora. However, the happy reunion was shrouded in misery. In his attempt to save a fledgling, Shail was shot down and captured. This was his first ordeal with hunters. Kari found him with a broken wing, a laser blast to his side, beaten, and dying in a pool of his blood. She purchased him from the hunters and saved his life.

Alex sniffled, breaking the hypnotic trance.

Shail opened his eyes. "That is enough for today."

Alex jumped up. "Those fucking monsters," he cursed. "I'll find them. I'll kill those men for what they did. I'll…"

"Stop, Alex. They are dead. Aron and the harpies took revenge." He stepped into the kitchen and filled a cup with water. "Drink," he said, handing it to Alex. "It shall wash away the stress."

Alex finished the water and frowned. "I've never read about this...that water can calm you."

"It does not, but the time to drink it distracts the mind and creates quiet." He sighed. "What lies ahead is very bad. We should stop. Your anger increases, and you become disenchanted with life."

"I said I'd probably get angry with this stuff. That's normal, Dad."

"It is not normal for a harpy to lack compassion, and this therapy is not helping."

"You're worried I'm not compassionate?" Alex chuckled. "That's a joke."

"I see no humor," Shail said, his eyes deadpan serious.

Alex massaged his forehead, "Dad, you're afraid I'll grow worse if we continue, and I'm afraid you'll relapse if we stop. I promise your past won't affect me."

"You make a promise you cannot keep," Shail said. "When you see how men defeated me…"

"Defeated you?" Alex lashed out. "Men didn't defeat you. You accomplished your goals and saved the harpies. You hid in the jungle and defeated yourself." He closed his eyes and took a moment to cool off. "Look, I've failed at everything. I can't fail at this. I'll make a deal. After I heal you, we'll work on me. I'll do anything, kiss kittens and help old ladies cross the street. You can turn me into a really nice, compassionate guy. Okay?"

Reluctantly, Shail agreed to the deal. They plunged ahead into his dad's terrible past. After Kari rescued and healed Shail, the last golden pair bonded and enjoyed a brief time on the sacred mountain. It ended when Kari's human father was outraged with the match. He stunned Shail and reclaimed his daughter. Unconscious, Shail fell into the hands of Gus, a murderous criminal.

Alex was determined to stay calm, watching this cruel man and his sidekicks torture his father. Then the three drunk and depraved men chained Shail down and took turns raping him. After hours of the brutal sexual assault, Shail stopped struggling and was in shock.

Alex couldn't watch anymore and removed his hand from his father's forehead, breaking the trance. He was past rage and filled with heartbreak. "How could they?" he sobbed.

Shail sat up and stroked Alex's head. "Do not cry, Son. I have shed enough tears over that night for both of us. I learned some men have no heart, only a hollow space filled with vile."

Alex wiped his eyes and looked up. "What happened to those men?"

"I killed them. I recall the uncontrollable hate that unleashed my wrath. They had disgraced my body and destroyed my soul. I no longer believed that life was sacred."

"But later you saved thousands of humans from the swarms. I couldn't have done that. I would have let the beetles eat all of them."

"I was the harpy ruler and had to put vengeance aside for the sake of my flock. More humans would eventually come from the stars and blame us for these deaths. Saving them brought peace."

"You were smart, took the chance, and it all worked out, but I'm not you, Dad. I'm more like my mother."

"Stop, Alex!" Shail growled "Cease from using her and your upbringing like a crutch. You are a golden harpy. Take responsibility for your decisions."

With his father's angry outburst, he hung his head to avoid eye contact. "I'll try," he mumbled.

"Alex, you think you know everything, but do not understand yourself. You know there are good and evil people. For this reason, you would not have let all die. Deep inside you is a noble, caring harpy. He only must be drawn out." Shail rose and embraced Alex. "Feel me, son. Take my empathy and make it your own."

Clutching his father, Alex closed his eyes and sensed his father's unwavering devotion to him. He had felt this from Mollie, but that seemed so long ago. No matter what Alex was or did, his father loved him, and his sole purpose for living was to help him. It was a defining moment.

* * *

The therapy continued and Alex saw the following year in Shail's life. After nearly two hundred years of terror, the harpies finally lived in harmony. Shail appeared to recover from the abuse, content with his reign, and happy with his pregnant mate, Kari. However, Alex, deep within Shail's psyche, knew better. He'd been forever damaged.

Upon Will's birth, the peace ended. Wanting to reclaim the Outback and make the flocks leaderless, the Dora senators kidnapped Shail and his family and shipped them to Earth. Alex had learned from Bloom about the war that raged in Shail's absence. Under Windy's rule and led by Aron, the flocks and sympathetic humans fought and defeated the senators' mercenary army.

On the spaceship to Earth, Shail again was cruelly mistreated. A prostitute took possession of him and she drugged and sexually exploited him for the female passengers. One large callous woman choked and raped him. Ashamed, Alex hid from his father that the woman was his mother.

In the Earth zoo, Shail endured more horrific hardships, but then Alex finally came to his father's breaking point, the deep-rooted cause for his PTSD and suicidal longing. Surprisingly, men were not to blame for the final blow. In a lowlife bar, Shail's owner pitted him against five brown-winged harpies who had been driven insane with captivity and drugs. In self-defense, his father killed Seth, their flock leader. The unspeakable tortures inflicted by men, had broken Shail, but the grief of slaying a fellow harpy finished him.

After ending the telepathic connection and hypnotism, Alex said, "Seth, that's Bloom's father, isn't he?"

"Yes."

"Bloom had said he was captured and sent to Earth, and he later learned from Aron that his dad was dead, but didn't know how he died or why." Alex lifted an eyebrow. "I guess I can't blame you for keeping it a secret."

"Aron knew I killed Seth, but we kept it secret for Bloom's sake. At the time he was an impressionable, young harpy, still mourning the loss of his father. What good would come, knowing his father had tried to kill me, the harpy ruler? Bloom did not need the humiliation."

Alex nodded. "Bloom is one cool customer and my best friend. You and Aron did the right thing, not telling him."

Shail stepped in the kitchen, drank some water, and turned to Alex. "Now you know all of my bleak past, the pain, humiliation, and lastly my regret."

"I saw your pain, but nothing else. Men disgraced your body, but you never lost your dignity, and faced a tough choice: kill Seth and survive to save your family and the flock. You shouldn't regret that decision. You were afraid I'd change after seeing your life. I have. Bloom preached about honor, but I never got it. I do now, what it means, what it takes."

Shail cupped Alex's cheek, probing his thoughts. "Yes, but your hatred has grown."

Alex pulled away and walked to the window. "Is that really bad? Hating evil and injustice can bring about change. I want to be like you, Dad, a true golden harpy. That's my goal."

* * *

Throughout the therapy, Alex had noticed the difference in his father. He had gone from a wild animal to a reasonable, intelligent mortal. Now that the sessions were over, Shail had completely regained his identity before the abuse. He was self-assured and fearless. Alex had gone from the expert to a student and was happy about it. He was so proud of his dad and loved him like Will.

He walked into the cockpit and checked the ship coordinates on the star chart. They'd soon reach the planet of Paradise Haven where the ship could be recharged and the food restocked. After Shail's recovery, Alex had feared the one question: Would his father stay with Alex or want to go home? He had been somewhat relieved with his dad's answer. "You have healed me, but I am not done with you." What did that mean? Alex felt fine, never better, but apparently, his father thought differently.

Shail walked into the cockpit, and asked, "How much longer?"

"We're a few days out from our destination," Alex said, smiling. "I bet you can't wait to spread your wings. I got to readjust our course, but why don't you dig out breakfast for us? The fruit and nuts are gone, but there're still some veggie chips."

After Shail left, Alex lifted his wings to sit in the pilot seat and punched in the new coordinates. He turned on the com for a call to Oden. His mother appeared on the screen.

"Oh, my God, Alexander," Monica screeched. "I've been so worried. Are you all right?"

"I'm fine, Mother, but I need some money. Could you send a fifty thousand credit voucher to the port on Paradise Haven? I'll pay you back."

"It's your money. When you turned eighteen, you inherited it from your grandfather. Are you still on that man's ship?"

"Speaking of that man, did you pay Matt?"

"After seeing your note, I tried, but that smuggler said his ship was a gift, something about a mining colony and that you two were even. Alexander, you shouldn't be alone out there."

"I'm not alone."

"Who is with you?"

"It's not your concern, but thanks for sending the money. I got to go."

"Wait, I love you, Alexander," Monica said, tearing up. "I miss you."

Alex nodded. "Take care, Mom. I'll try and stay in touch." As he disconnected, he sensed a presence and turned. His father stood in the doorway. "You saw her?"

"Alex, I saw her in your mind, and then again when I regained my memory of the Earth voyage."

Alex lowered his head. "So you know my mother was the bitch who abused you on the voyage. I wasn't trying to deceive you, but was ashamed for what she did, and that there was no bond between my parents. I'm a bastard, a mistake."

"Nature makes no mistakes. Sometimes our choices are removed for a greater good. Your mother was cruel to both of us but look what our suffering created. You are a very special harpy."

CHAPTER THIRTY-TWO

"This is *Dream Weaver,*" Alex said into the com as the ship traveled toward Paradise Haven. "We're five clips out and seeking permission to land."

An old, white-haired man with a skinny weathered frame appeared. "This is Paradise. Been expectin' ya, *Dreamer*. You gotta a wire transfer here. When you reach orbit follow the electronic to Oceanside. It's the only port with spaceship hook-ups."

"Roger that, Paradise," Alex said, switching off. He glanced up at Shail. "It won't be long now." The ship approached the planet, and Alex frowned, seeing the brown surface. Instead of lush forests, Paradise was a barren wasteland with pockets of low vegetation. "This can't be right." He brought up the data on the planet."

"What is wrong?" Shail asked.

Alex pointed at the displayed screen. "The place is supposed to look like this, full of trees, but they're gone. It's nothing but ocean, desert, and mountains." He hit the computer keys again, rechecking the date on the stats. "The damn information hasn't been updated in decades. I'm sorry, Dad. I'd hoped this planet was like Dora, and you'd enjoy it."

"Never apologize when you are blameless. That is the way of insincere humans."

“Good point. I’m thinking they conveniently didn’t revise the info to attract visitors. We’ve been scammed but have to put down for supplies and pick up my money.”

The ship entered the atmosphere and across the ocean surface, the small coastal town of Oceanside and its port came into view. Alex landed the ship on the desert sand alongside a few paint-chipped, hovercrafts parked near the meager airport building. He opened the ship door, and he and Shail stared out at the one-street village made up of two dusty dome buildings and broken-down shacks. Their eyes squinted from the glare off the sparkling ocean and bright white sand. “What a shithole,” Alex said when they descended the ship ramp. “This place looks abandoned.”

The old man who was on the transmission trotted to them. “Which of you is Alexander Carlton?”

“I’m Alexander.”

“In my office there’s a twenty-five million credit voucher waiting ya, I ain’t never seen that kinda money.”

“Me neither,” Alex mumbled to Shail. “I guess Mom was feeling guilty and got generous.”

With the strong ocean breeze whipping at their long hair, he and Shail followed the man to the weathered building.

With a toothless grin, the man said, “I never seen men with wings.”

“We’re not men,” Alex said. “We are harpies.”

“Harpies, huh, never heard of ya,’ the man said. “Mr. Carlton, once we get inside and have your voucher squared away, is there anythin’ else I can do for ya?”

“My ship needs to be recharged, and our food restocked; dried fruits, vegetables, nuts, and froze bakery goods, but no meat. We’re vegetarians.”

“I’ll get right on it. My wife can put the food together. I’m Jasper. You need anythin’ on Paradise, I’m your man.”

They entered the building, and at a small cluttered counter, Alex signed the voucher.

Jasper chuckled, handing Alex the receipt. "When my wife sees you two pretty near-naked brothers, she'll faint."

"We are not brothers," Alex said. "He's my dad."

"Well, your dad sure kept his looks," Jasper said.

Shail stepped to the open door and gazed out at the desert, dotted with low scrubs. "Jasper, my son says this place once held trees."

"Yes, your info was deceptive," Alex grumbled, folding the printout. "This is hardly a paradise."

"Guess the name is kinda a joke now," said Jasper, "but I grew up here, and the big white cosha forests were as far as the eye could see and full of wildlife, and the ocean had plenty of fish. But it's all gone."

Shail turned from the doorway. "What happened?"

"Them big damn timber companies moved in and bought up the trees for a few lousy credits. They convinced us that with the forests gone between the mountains and sea, we'd make a killing in agriculture. After buying their song and dance, we learned the hard way that those trees had kept Paradise stable. The following year the first big rains washed away the topsoil and that caused our ocean to have one hell of an algae bloom. It suffocated the fish and wiped out the coral reefs. With loss of habitat, most of the wildlife was starved out. People packed up and left, but the stubborn ones like me stayed. We eke out a livin', supplying stray ships and exporting seashells, and what-nots."

"Why do the trees not grow back?" Shail asked.

"Without trees, the weather became erratic with longer and longer periods of drought. Young shoots don't have the deep root system to survive the first few years."

"This is all very interesting, but I'm hungry," Alex said. "Do you have a restaurant here?"

"Sally's just up the street."

Alex started to leave, but Shail stopped him. "I am not finished speaking to this man." He turned to Jasper, "Can this land be fixed?"

"Sure, but it'd take a lot of money and work," Jasper said. "The ocean is salt, so a huge conversion refinery would have to be built to supply fresh water to the trees. Heavy equipment would be needed to plant the seedlings and create irrigation ditches. Once the trees got a foothold, the rain runoff would stop and the ocean would recover. The remaining fish should multiply. That's what it would take, but nobody wants to invest here."

"Would your people protect or sell the trees again?" asked Shail.

"Them trees come back, anyone trying to cut one will have to do it over my dead body. I guarantee we'd protect them."

Alex massaged his forehead, bored. He had spent his life in a city and had no interest in nature and conservation like his jungle-raised father. "Dad, can we go?"

Shail ignored him. "With such a vow, may I shake your hand?" With a puzzled expression, Jasper shook Shail's hand. "My son shall bring back your trees. He is smart and has the money."

The uninteresting conversation suddenly captured Alex's full attention. "Wait a minute, Dad. What are you talking about? I'm not going to fix this lousy planet."

"You shall."

Alex said to Jasper. "Look, my father hasn't been well and says crazy things. Don't believe him." He ushered Shail outside. "Dad, what are you doing, telling his old dude I'll fix his planet? First off, we're not staying, and I'll be damned if I blow my inheritance on a dump. Even if I did, these people are dirt poor. They'd chop down the trees before half-grown."

"I sensed Jasper and he spoke truth." Shail walked past the building to the ocean. He stepped into shallow, rippling waves and gazed out at the horizon.

Alex watched and shook his head. "Goddamn it," he grumbled and wandered out to Shail. "Why, Dad?"

"I have my reasons. I want you to restore this land for me."

Alex rolled his eyes."Dad, you don't realize what you're asking. Just to get the equipment, engineers, scientists, and workers here will take months, and it will eat up a good portion of my money." He huffed. "I studied business in college, and this planet is a bad investment. Besides, I don't plan to live here, so why should I care about this place?"

Shail arched his wings and whirled around. "You should care." He seethed. "You are a harpy, a guardian of nature, and that is what makes us different from men, not wings. I shall not ask you again."

"Okay, okay." Alex apprehensively stepped away from him. On the beach he shuffled the sand with a foot. "If it makes you happy, I'll do it. But it's ridiculous."

* * *

On a small desk at the airport, Alex mapped out the planet's transformation. Cursing, he shoved aside stacks of dusty papers and used the tired com for intergalactic calls. Using the ship's com for numerous contacts might attract attention and be unwise. He priced the water refinery and big equipment needed to plant seedlings and irrigate them. He contacted the Federation Science Lab on Earth where all animal DNA was stored from newly colonized planets. Paradise Haven once had a fast array of unique creatures, but without the trees, ninety percent became extinct. Once the trees were established, the animals could be cloned and brought back. The planet was small, but the restoration was enormous.

After a few days, he had enough information to put a plan in place, but before ordering anything and throwing away money, he had to tell the inhabitants. Without their cooperation, the refurbishment won't last.

Jasper contacted the scattered settlements and asked them to come to Oceanside and hear the proposal to bring back the trees. At sunset a few thousand people stood near *Dream Weaver* at the port. Their weathered faces and ragged clothing illustrated their meager lives, but their hard, unflinching stares suggested they were a tough, suspicious bunch.

Alex stood near the port doorway and said to Jasper, "They don't seem happy to see me."

Jasper chuckled. "They're thinking you're another con artist, trying to cheat them out of what little they have. Your offer sounds too good to be true."

"Yeah, I can't believe it myself. So, are they all here?"

"Pretty much," Jasper said. "The Rivers Falls people didn't show, but that's no surprise. Those Asians are a mean bunch and keep to themselves. They move from planet to planet and harvest the wildlife so they don't care about our trees, anyway."

"What wildlife? I thought most of it was gone."

"Moliths are still around. The algae bloom doesn't bother those big seagoing reptiles but with the hunting, they're disappearing. Their meat is a delicacy and in demand. That's why the Asians are here." Jasper looked around. "Where's your dad?"

"He's up the coast, enjoying the scenery, but now that everyone has arrived, I'll go get him." Alex bounded into the sky and heard the gasps below from the crowd. He flew along the shoreline to a small cave in the cliffs. Shail stood at the entrance and gazed out at the ocean horizon.

"It's time, Dad," Alex said, landing. "All the people are waiting for you at the port."

"I am not coming."

"What do you mean you're not coming?" Alex put his hand on his hips. "This was your idea, your damn project, and you should cope with these pathetic people."

"They are your first flock, Alex, and shall teach you about leadership."

"They're morons and can't teach me anything," Alex growled, "The only thing they'll do is piss me off."

"Then you must learn patience. Now go."

Heatedly, Alex flew back to the port and landed on a rusty hovercraft overlooking the crowd. Upset with his father, annoyed with the stupid task, and now having to work these dimwits, he took a breath to calm down. He rubbed his lips, deciding what to say without revealing how he felt.

"My name is Alexander. I am a harpy," he began. Rather than talking about his restoration plan for Paradise Haven, he spoke to the crowd about the Outback on Dora. The harpies protected their jungle and wildlife while tourism supplied an income for the residents. "I believe we can do this here."

One man shouted, "You want us to give up our land tracks to create a park? What makes you think tourists will come?"

"Because throughout the galaxy, humans have been ravaged most planets for their resources," Alex said. "People live in dome cities, space stations, or desolate landscapes. To enjoy, even for a short time, the beauty and wonder of nature, they will travel to Paradise."

Another asked, "What are we supposed to do in the meantime, waiting for the trees to grow?"

"Prepare," Alex said. "Build your inns, restaurants, and gift shops where you can sell your shells. I will help you."

"What are you getting out of this?" yelled a third man.

"Nothing," Alex said.

"It's a trick," said the man. "I'm not turning over my land to a half-naked guy with wings. He's probably trying to get the mining rights for nothing. Let's go."

Alex noticed that many believed him and were encouraged with his plans for the planet, while others doubted him and would never get on board. For the restoration to be successful and last, all had to get behind it.

"Assholes," Alex grumbled under his breath. No matter what he said, some would never trust him and be convinced. He thought, so much for patience. "Wait," he called to the departing men. "I have one last thing to say." He shut his eyes and focused his telepathy on the crowd. Using hypnotism, he said softly, "Quiet now. Relax, forget your troubles, and listen to me. I am only here to help you. Envision this land whole again and realize we must cherish it for all time. Together, we can make a difference and do this for your children and their children." He opened his eyes, ending the spell.

The man who had called Alex *a half-naked winged guy* and his plan a trick, did an about-face. "Alexander, we'll do this. We'll turn our planet into a true paradise again."

Alex fluttered off the hover to the ground, and the enthusiastic crowd merged on him. Men shook his hand and women kissed his cheek and hugged him. He'd gone from an oddity and mistrusted stranger to a friend, a hero, a redeemer. Their passion was contagious. Gazing into their grateful eyes, Alex felt good. He was doing something worthwhile.

The next morning, Alex left Oceanside and flew down the isolated beach to the cave. His father stood in the lapping knee-high waves. When Alex landed near him, he held up some seaweed kelp. "Would you like some? It is very tasty, salty and sweet."

Alex shook his head, smiling. "No thanks, you can keep the wild food. It doesn't look appetizing."

"You shall never know if something is good unless you try it," Shail said. "Speaking of, how was your meeting yesterday?"

"It was good, actually great. You should've come. Everyone is excited about bringing back the forests." He lowered his head. "You were right about restoring this planet and then making me deal with the people. It was nice being appreciated, and I feel different, like I'm accomplishing something important for the first time."

"Restoring nature to this land and helping its people is a worthy cause, but we are here to mend you. It has begun."

* * *

In the little seaside cave, Shail woke at dawn and gazed at his sleeping son, curled up in his soft feathers. By all appearances, Alex resembled a handsome young harpy, but looks were misleading. His mind and soul belonged to a different creature. Shail's goal to transform Alex into a true harpy had him wondering if he could or should.

Leaving the cave, Shail fluttered from the cliff to the beach. The ocean was like a still pond that mirrored the gold and purple hues of the rising sun. The watery horizon could have been Dora's, and Shail felt the gut wincing from homesickness. Alex had given him the option to return, but what purpose would Shail serve? He would be missed but wasn't needed. His only obligation was rendering guidance to his extraordinary but damaged son.

He wandered down the shoreline and reflected on Alex's life, envisioned on the ship during the telepathic connection. Shail had witnessed Mollie's death on Oden and understood, even could relate to Alex's uncontrollable rage. Fearing disapproval, his son concealed the aftermath, but Shail had seen the killing of the police officers in Alex's dreams. Shail had also killed men, but there was a difference. The policemen were only doing their job when Mollie was accidentally shot, yet Alex felt no remorse or regret. Shail had killed evil men who deserved to die, but he had felt the sickening remorse for breaking his harpy vow to protect all life.

Summer had shunned Alex, not for killing but because of his heartless behavior. He felt sorry for himself and used arrogance to hide his insecurity, anger, and depression. His instability made him a danger to himself and others. Like a smoldering volcano, he would blow with the slightest provocation. No wonder the flocks and his harpy family distrusted him.

However, Shail was Alex's father, making him more tolerant and forgiving of his son's flaws and he saw the great qualities and possibilities in Alex. Unlike other harpies, Alex didn't look at a forest and see trees. He gazed past them to the sky and asked what if? His son was capable of amazing things, but would they be honorable or tragic? Shail looked at his hands. The outcome rested in them.

He waded into the ocean and dove in. Surfacing, he gazed at the vast empty beach. The memories he had lost were now as clear as air. He recalled Kari sitting on a similar shore and watching him swim. He yearned for her and her guidance with this son.

A shadow of wings flew overhead, and Alex nose-dived into the ocean. He emerged, smiling. "Good morning, Dad," he called, and swam to Shail. Standing in the waist-deep water next to Shail, Alex tilted his head. "I'm sensing you're sad and miss home and Kari."

"I was thinking of her."

Alex nodded sadly. "Okay. Once I finish with this planet, I'll take you back to Dora."

"I long for her and my family but they do not need me like you do."

Alex chuckled sarcastically. "I'm glad we're together, but I don't need you. I'm okay alone."

"Why do you speak to me as though I was human and would believe your lies? We both know you are troubled. On the ship you agreed to my help."

"I said that so you'd continue the therapy. I didn't mean it. Dad, I'm all right."

"A harpy is never insincere, like you. Proof your nature is not what it should be and needs improvement."

"You sound like my damn mother, wanting to change me." His eyes watered and he ruffled his feathers. "You want the truth?" he ranted in Shail's face. "Here it is, Daddy. Neither you nor her can call yourselves parents. She was a coldhearted bitch, and you…you were a mentally challenged has-been and a sorry-excuse of a father. You have no right to criticize me."

Shail smacked Alex's face so hard that he fell backward with a splash. "Ruffle your wings and insult me again, and you shall die."

Alex crouched in the water and rubbed his smarting cheek. His large, shocked eyes shifted to glaring hostility. "You hit me again, and I'll take you out."

Shail raised his wings. “You threaten instead of apologizing? I did not strike you harsh enough.” He stepped toward Alex and detected his son’s attempt to hypnotize him. “You cannot control a golden’s mind unless he allows it. Now stand and fight or beg forgiveness for being an unworthy son.” He knew Alex’s pride would overcome his fear, and the time had come he learned to respect others.

Alex swallowed hard and straightened. He fluttered out of the water and kicked at Shail’s head. Remaining stationary, Shail dodged the blow and caught Alex’s feet. He jerked him out of the air and flung him into the waves. Before Alex could recover, Shail leaped behind him, grabbed his hair, and held him underwater. Alex flailed wildly, but his striking fists and wings could not reach Shail, and being held down on his back, he couldn’t get his legs under him to surface. After several long minutes, Alex stopped struggling. The drowning had sapped his strength and fight. Shail pulled his hair up and allowed him to take a breath.

“You are my fledgling and shall treat me with honor,” Shail said.

Alex gasped and choked, “Let me go!”

“That is not what I wish to hear.” Shail shoved him back under the water and held him down again. After few minutes, Alex was as limp as a corpse. Shail let him rise and asked, “Are you ready to end your obstinate ways?”

Alex spit out water, gagging, but managed to cough out, “No.”

“Then I have no choice but to kill you, but know I have loved you.”

When Shail started to push him under for the last time, Alex cried out, “Wait! Wait. You…you really are going to drown me.”

“It is an act of mercy, but not my first,” Shail said. “Seth suffered in torment after losing his soul. You never had a soul. My seed created you, so I must end you before you inflict pain on others.”

Alex’s eyes filled with terror, sensing his father wasn’t bluffing. “No, Dad! Please, I’m sorry. I’m really sorry. I’ll change. I’ll do anything you want.”

Shail looked down, studying him. “I shall give you one more chance, but if you disrespect me or lie, you know the outcome.” He released his grasp on Alex’s hair. “I rather grieve your death than bear the shame of a graceless, vile son.”

Shail left Alex floundering in the ocean and strolled to the beach. Sitting down in the sand, he watched Alex slowly crawl ashore, coughing with his teary eyes filled with disbelief. Shail didn’t enjoy the radical approach, but mentoring words would not change Alex. He was stubborn and had been spoiled, believing he was superior to all. For him to listen and learn, he had to be terrified with his death. A harpy must value life, and this son did not.

CHAPTER THIRTY-THREE

After nearly drowning, Alex lay on the beach, choking up the water from his lungs and trying to recover while his mind raced with confusion. Admittedly, Alex had slipped up and angrily offended his father, but that hardly warranted the lethal, sudden attack. Or maybe it did? He breathed hard and questioned his father's love. He staggered to his feet, realizing both his parents had tried to harm him. It had to be his fault.

He wandered up to Shail and collapsed in the sand. "Why, Dad?" he asked. "I've tried so hard to be good and not disappoint you, but with one mistake, you're willing to kill me."

"Yes, you have tried to impress me so you are loved, the same reasons for seeking the harpy rule. Your motives are misguided. Your brother, Will, was already loved, respected, and powerful, so why did he fight you?"

Alex knew better than to come up with a half-baked answer. "Will knew that I'd be a lousy ruler. He was protecting the harpies. He saved my life, and I didn't even thank him. He is better than me."

Shail turned to him. "Yes, Alex, but he grew up with harpies and learned what is important."

"And I grew up with humans and became a monster. You probably should kill me." He covered his face and sniffled.

Shail massaged his shoulder. “You are no monster. Your values are only misplaced, and they are leading you down a destructive path. You question my love for you. I care more about you than my life. If I had drowned you, I, too, would die for failing you.”

“Oh, Dad,” Alex said and hugged him. “Can you fix me? Can you make me like Will and you?”

“Asking for help is the first step. It is like opening your wings to let new air lift you higher. You have believed seeking council from others was shameful and made you look weak. That is untrue. I accepted advice and grew stronger and wiser.”

Alex looked up. “What I said about you, I was hurt and didn’t mean it. You’re my hero.”

Shail kissed his forehead. “And I have no doubt you shall become mine.”

* * *

Alex flew back to Oceanside in the afternoon and ordered the equipment for the planet restoration. The morning had been first frightening with his near-drowning and then became emotionally draining with long talks between him and his father. His eyes were puffy from crying, and he felt exhausted, but oddly cleansed and content. His father had spoken with profound elegance, but used simplistic examples to convey his message. He had cupped some water in his hands and said that the water was like Alex’s ambitions. “The tighter you grasp the water, the faster it slips away. A dip in the ocean with open hands allows your hopes to float to you.” The more Shail talked, the more Alex saw the errors of his ways and was committed to changing. It had only taken nearly dying to open his eyes.

After calling the experts and ordering the machinery for the water refinery and the heavy digging equipment, Alex stepped out of the port office, and Jasper rushed to him.

“Mr. Carlton, sorry I wasn’t here. I was up the street having lunch. The settlements have been calling here, wondering about our plans.”

"Tell them that I've ordered everything but some of it will take months to get here. They should start getting ready. Figure out a place for the water refinery near the ocean and map out an area to plant the first trees." He lifted his wings to fly.

"Hey, where're you going?"

"My father wants to go on a journey and explore this land. We'll be back before the shipments and experts arrive."

Alex flew to the cave but his father wasn't there. Preparing for their trip, Alex attached the portable com to his hip sash and stuffed food, water, a blanket, and locator in a canvas bag. His father walked inside, and Alex hoisted the bag over his shoulder. "I'm ready. I have everything we need."

"This is a harpy journey of wing, wind, and flight, a bonding of father and son. Bring nothing."

Uneasily, Alex lowered his bag to the cave floor and removed the com, wondering how they would subsist without the human supplies, and if they met trouble, they couldn't call for help. He was skeptical of his father's decision, but knew not to argue.

"All shall be fine, Alex."

They left the cave and flew south along a narrow strip of white beach that separated the brilliant blue ocean from the stark golden landscape.

After thirty miles, Alex asked, "How will we eat, Dad? There's nothing out here."

Shail glanced across his wing. "I am sad you see nothing. Open your eyes and behold the wonder of this land. Forget who you were and embrace your animal side."

At noon Alex began to relax. All his life he had been conditioned to be somewhere and accomplish the next task, but that pressure vanished. He flapped his wings and felt liberated. The lesson and journey were the same. He smiled. "This is fun. I wish I'd done this on Dora."

“Did none of my harpies take you under their wings and show you the way?”

“Bloom tried, but I was stupid and brushed him off. As you know, I’m rather inflexible. I was only focused on fighting Will. Even on the sacred mountain with you, I couldn’t see past my nose and appreciate Dora. But I have the control to change.”

“Claiming control and claiming change cancel each other out.” Shail pointed ahead at an area of pink dotted with green. “I think we shall find food there.”

Alex glided along, considering his father’s words. Shail was known for his tenacious nature and had the determination to save his harpies, but Alex began to realize that his father’s unsophisticated wisdom had been the difference between him and past golden rulers. Alex’s chest pounded with admiration and the longing to be like him.

Approaching the pink and green vegetation, they saw it was a vast marsh. The tall pink blades of grass were half-submerged in clear water and swayed in the breeze while low green shrubs dotted the wetland. A wide meandering river flowed through the center and emptied into the ocean. On a peninsula near the river mouth, scattered wooden shacks sat on the bank, and several large vessels were moored offshore or tied to a long dock.

“That must be River Falls,” Alex said. “Jasper said these people were a nasty bunch, and we better stay away from them.”

“Men lack our instincts so they distrust strangers. This clannish behavior has caused death and wars. I pity humans.”

“For someone who suffered from their cruelty, you’re certainly tolerant.”

“Tolerance and understanding comes with age, but in my youth, I was not. You remind me of myself.” Shail smiled. “I was once foolish and hot-tempered. My poor friend, Aron, struggled to keep me alive.” Looking at the village, he bent his wings to the east. “Come, Alex, We shall not ignore Jasper’s warning and avoid these people.”

The village disappeared from view, and they descended into the marshes, landing on the thick green shrubs with stilted root systems that rose out of the water. "Do you recall my memory of Earth when I lived in a swamp to avoid capture? Shail asked. "Does this place seem similar?"

"It does. After that session, I got curious and researched that place. You were in the Florida Everglades. These shrubs resemble the mangroves, but the cattails here are pink."

"Your quest for such information is uncommon for a harpy, but I approve. Knowledge is powerful." Shail picked a plum-size fruit off the shrub and sniffed and licked it before taking a bite. "Earlier, you worried about food. Here it is."

Alex tasted one. "It's a little sour but okay. How'd you know we'd find food out here?"

"Animals once dwelled here." Shail leaped off the bush into the hip-deep water and pulled a clump of the pink grass. Stripping away the outer tough layer of the root, he sampled the bulb. "Try this," he said, tossing it to Alex.

Alex ate a bite. "Wow, it's like asparagus. Bet it would be great cooked."

"Asparagus, yes, Rachel fed me some on the ship to Earth," Shail dug up more bulbs. They gathered the food in their sashes and flew to rock outcrop beyond the marsh. Alex watched in fascination while his father struck two stones together for spark and created a small fire. Alex cleaned and roasted the root bulbs, admitting he'd never before cooked. As the sun disappeared into the horizon, they feasted and talked before snuggling into their feathers. Closing his eyes, Alex couldn't recall a finer day.

* * *

Over the coming weeks, Alex and Shail remained near the enormous marsh that was a few hundred miles across and lay between a northern mountain range and the ocean to the south. At the base of the mountains, small forests grew with more edible plants and some small wildlife. Alex came across a hand-size, red and yellow lizard and reached for it, but his father stopped him.

"His bright colors warn of danger, and his puffy neck probably holds poison for a deadly bite," Shail said. "He is also not afraid. That one you leave alone."

Alex backed away from the lizard. Every day was an adventure and a new learning experience. Leaving Oceanside, he thought the trip would be boring, but he woke every morning excited. From the sidelines, he watched his father stroke an ugly, large amphibian-type creature and coax a huge stork-like bird to eat from his hand. He was truly at home in the wild. Mesmerized, Alex followed him around like wide-eyed child.

Living and learning about nature, he started to appreciate it and regretted not doing this on Dora. But more importantly, he was discovering his long-lost and unknown father. Alex sensed the feeling was mutual. With a rocky start, his father had become an advisor and best friend, and Alex felt the growing bond of a father and son.

After an afternoon nap on the beach, Alex woke and realized he had changed. His uptight, sarcastic attitude was gone along with the resentment and insecurity. Smiling, joking, and laughing, he felt happy and loved. The tug-of-war within was over. He accepted he would never be perfect or have it all, but somehow, that was okay. His father was really fixing him.

He curled up next to his dozing father and whispered, "Thank you, Dad. You are making me whole."

Shail didn't respond, but clutched him and nuzzled his neck.

* * *

With the approach of fall, nights on the planet turned nippy so Alex and Shail sought shelter from the crisp wind inside a mountain cave. Crouching over a small pile of dried twigs, Shail used the stones to start a small fire.

Alex picked up the two stones and sighed. "I busted a knuckle and have gotten calluses using these stones and still can't make a fire. That proves I'm a retarded city dweller."

"It is not your nature to give up." Shail settled on a soft shrub nest and gazed at the low flames. "Tomorrow night you shall start the fire."

"Sure, but be ready for a cold night." Alex grinned and stepped to the cave opening. Wrapping his wings close in the blustery howling wind, he gazed out at the dark landscape and stars.

Shail lifted his head. "You are troubled."

Alex returned to the fire. "I've been wanted to tell you something but…"

"You were afraid I would frown on you. Alex, nothing shall end my love for you."

Alex crouched by the flames. "It's pretty bad, Dad. My sister, Summer, never forgave me." He exhaled deeply. "On the ship when I let you probe my mind, I hid it. You were worried about my anger issues, and rightfully so. After Mollie was killed on Oden, I went into a rage and used my telepathy and hypnotism for revenge."

Shail nodded. "You forced those policemen to crash their hovercrafts, and would have killed more if Summer had not stopped you."

Alex's jaw fell open and his eyes widened. "You know? All this time you've known what I did and said nothing? Did Summer or Will tell you, tell Aron and he told you?"

"You have a powerful mind and can conceal your secrets, but not in sleep. Many times I have seen this dream, the nightmare on the rooftop when the men died, but you had to trust me before telling of it."

Alex hung his head. "The cops shot Mollie, so I killed them."

"One man shot Mollie. And probing his mind, you saw he was horrified that his weapon fired accidentally. He did not wish her death. You know this to be true."

Alex jumped and huffed. “Fine, I made a mistake but I don’t care. I was angry.”

“Blind rage is a poor excuse, but understandable. I am troubled as was Summer that you feel no sorrow for the dead and no regret for your actions.”

“Bloom fed me the same crap...that I don’t have empathy,” he ranted. “Well, I’m different. I still don’t care about those damn cops!”

“Sit and be calm, Alex,” Shail said quietly.

Alex plopped down by the fire with annoyance and expected a tiring, long lecture on his flaws.

Shail rubbed his chin. “You are different. Throughout your life, you have learned to block painful feelings, but to be a harpy, to be free, you must face this past. Visualize those innocent policemen who you killed.”

Alex held up his palms. “I don’t want to do this. You don’t understand how much I loved Mollie, and those cops took her from me. I’ll never feel bad about killing them.”

“And Mollie loved you, but she would be unhappy, knowing you choose hatred over reason. You wish to be like me? You must open your heart and mind.”

In the golden glow of the fire, Alex stared at his father who was equally thick-headed and would not let this go. “All right, you win.”

“Envision the policeman who shot Mollie. You felt his guilt before the hover crashed. I wish you to go further and see his final thoughts.”

Alex swallowed and shut his eyes, revisiting the night. “He was thinking about his little boy. How he would not be there to greet him in the morning. He was worried about his family.”

“Yes, hardly the mindset of an evil man, only one who made a terrible mistake. Now see the pilot in that same hover when you took control of his mind and made him force his hover toward the street. What were his thoughts?”

“At first he was checking the instruments and screaming. When realizing he’d die, he thought about an unfinished cradle and then on his pregnant wife. That he’d never kiss her again.”

“Now another,” Shail said, “the men in the second hover.”

Alex rose. “You made your point. I don’t want to do anymore.”

“I have peered into the minds of bad men before I took their lives. Their thoughts were of fear, hatred, and revenge, always about themselves, not others. I grieved their deaths because I had lowered myself to be like them. The men you killed did not deserve to die.”

Alex nodded. “I keep thinking about that cop’s little boy, never seeing see his dad again. You succeeded. I feel lousy about it.”

“You feel awful because you and the little boy shared the same pain, both losing a loved one on that night. That is the compassion that you had buried.”

“I didn’t mean to go so far.” Alex collapsed on the nest and concealed his face in his arms.

Shail massaged his head. “I know you regret it.”

* * *

The following morning Shail woke alongside his sleeping son and stepped to the smoldering remains of the campfire. Crouching, he stirred the ashes, reflecting on last night.

For over a month, he and Alex had lived in the wilderness, and Shail noticed the improvement in his son’s attitude. Exposed to nature and isolation from humans, Alex grew less stressed, defensive, and bitter. He discovered that the little things in life brought joy. He was extremely intelligent, far more learned than Shail, but Alex had failed to know himself. Last night was an example.

Shail had hoped to turn Alex into a true harpy, but realized that was impossible. His son was too much like himself. Shail had been a trailblazer with uncharacteristic harpy behavior. Abandoning his gentle nature, he became the first harpy to kill a human. He ended the old sheepish policy of fleeing and hiding and declared war on mankind. The flocks feared him, unsure if he was a savior or demon.

Alex, too, was an independent thinker and cursed with a fiery, stubborn nature. Every decision would be a struggle for him, but at least he had been shown the right path.

He stepped to Alex and tapped his wing. “It is time to wake.”

Alex lifted his head and squinted. “It’s bright out.”

“It was a long night, and I let you sleep. How do you feel?”

“Tired,” said Alex, sitting up. “But better. Somehow I feel relieved.”

“Guilt is a heavy burden to carry.”

“Yeah but it is tough, facing up to my mistakes.”

“Life is full of missteps and you shall face others, but they are necessary. Without them, you would not appreciate happiness.”

“Dad, you’re so cool, always saying profound things.”

Shail tilted his head. “I am not cold.”

Alex chuckled. “Being cool means I like you. Matt used to say that. He was a good buddy, always calling me the kid. I wish I’d been a better friend.”

“More misgivings and honesty, you are growing wiser.”

Alex smiled, realizing that his education didn’t give him wisdom. In the distance a siren blared, and he and Shail stepped to the cave entrance. “It’s a warning alarm. There must be trouble in River Falls. We should go.”

In unison, he and his father flew over the marsh to the river. Following the waterway to the ocean, they came upon the small village. The people rushed around in a panic, some scrambled down the dock to the fishing boats. Several vessels had left the basin and were motoring at full speed out to sea. Two hovercrafts lifted off and flew rapidly in the same direction.

With a questioning glance at his father, Alex asked, “What do you think?”

“We shall help and seek the destination of the hovers.”

Flying high above and fast, they overtook the boats and then the hovers. After several miles, they heard a faint trumpeting roar. Zeroing in on the sound, they came upon the disaster. A forty-foot vessel heaved on its side on the verge of sinking. Ramming its hull with a vengeance was a mammoth creature, twice the size of the boat. Its reptilian head and long spindly neck were attached to a wide bulky body with flippers. The creature was savagely biting into the boat deck, railings, and crates.

"It must be a molith," Alex said, looking down. "Jasper said these people hunt them."

On the other side of the vessel, a smaller molith was tangled in nets and bellowed. "She attacks to save her baby," Shail said. "You help the humans. I shall free the little one."

"But, Dad, they're dangerous."

"Then be careful, son," Shail said, and dove toward the ship.

"But I wasn't talking about the men," Alex mumbled to himself. Jetting down, he noticed the female Molith disappear below the surface. He landed on the lopsided deck and said to frantic crew of six, "I'm here to help you."

The men were short in stature with black braided hair and dark almond-shaped eyes. At first, they were stunned, seeing Alex. A young man finally spoke up, "Our captain was hit with a loose crate and fell overboard." He pointed to the choppy waves off the bow. "He hasn't surfaced."

The mother molith charged the vessel again, and the impact jarred it further on its side. The men lost their footing and grasped the broken railings to prevent them from sliding into the choppy water. An old man cried out, "She's not going to stop until we're dead."

With extended wings, Alex kept him balance and stood. The molith submerged again, and Alex left the vessel to find the captain. Fluttering over the waves, he caught a glimpse of orange, possibly clothing, in the deep clear water. He flew higher to gain momentum, tightly folding his wings, he dove into the surf.

As in the contest against Will, he propelled through the water, using his wings as flippers. Thirty feet down, he saw the lifeless man in his orange jacket. He grabbed the man's arm, swam upward, and broke the surface. Holding the captain's head above water, he found himself directly in front of the ship. On one side his father stroked the baby molith's neck while trying to unravel the net.

"Dad," Alex yelled. "This man is too heavy for me to lift out alone."

"Keep his head afloat until I can help you. I must first free this baby, or all shall perish."

Alex wrapped his arm around the man's neck, holding his chin up, and swam on his side toward the ship.

"Here, catch this," the young man called, and tossed a rope out to Alex.

Alex tied the rope around the man's waist and yelled, "Okay, pull him." He then noticed the large shadow approaching underwater.

"She's coming right at you!" a crewman yelled. The men heaved on the rope, hoping to hoist their captain onboard before the next attack.

Seeing the massive silhouette below, Alex froze. "Stop pulling him," he called to the men, but in a panic, they ignored him.

The Molith's head broke the surface, and she eyed the captain's body that was being dragged across the surface like bait. She swooped in, bit into the doomed captain's girth, and lifted him like a doll. When she savagely shook the body, snapping him in half, the blood turned the blue water red. She arched her head and triumphantly roared, rippling the surface with the vibration.

Alex floated nearby like a cork. With her long neck, the molith could snap him up before he could escape. He felt and smelled her warm fishy breath on his backside when she opened her mouth to devour him. Remaining still had failed, and he desperately flapped his wings to lift off while turning to fend her off with his feet. Puffing with fright, he realized his life was over, but then saw a flash of yellow wings over the creature.

His father hovered above the molith, punching and kicking her large green eyes. Distracted from Alex, the molith lunged from the water and snapped at the harpy buzzing her head. Shail hissed and struck the animal's snout, hell-bent on defending his son and ignoring the danger to himself.

Alex managed to swim out of reach and leave the ocean. Fluttering and awestruck, he watched his dad combat the huge creature. The molith's aggression faded, ducking and blinking to protect her eyes. She launched one final attack before paddling away from the ship and submerging. Alex landed on the half-sunk ship, and Shail followed.

"Are you hurt?" Shail asked, gripping Alex's shoulders and looked up and down his body.

"No, only petrified. I can't believe you fought that thing off."

"Her fright is temporary, and she shall return soon," Shail said, "We must free her baby."

Alex turned to the crew. "I need a knife."

The old man pulled a blade from his belt sheath and handed it to Alex. "Be careful. Those calves are quicker and more dangerous than the big ones. It can take a leg before you blink."

"I shall handle the baby," Shail said. "You cut the mess."

Alex and Shail flew to the thrashing baby and stood knee-deep in water on the floating net that was buoyant enough to support their weight.

"Shhh, little one," Shail whispered, stroking the baby's head. "Do not fear. I am a friend and here to help you." Amazingly, the baby stopped flaying and grew calm.

Alex hacked at the nylon mesh that cut into the baby's flesh. The mother surfaced fifty yards out and bellowed. The baby wiggled and whined excitedly.

Shail stood and hissed at her. Instead of charging, she stayed stationary. “Hurry, Alex, my threats shall not keep her away long.”

“I almost have it.” Alex sliced the nets off the baby’s back flippers and tail, and the net drifted away. “Okay, it’s free.”

Shail sniffled and caressed the baby’s neck. He fluttered above the creature and continued the sound that encouraged the little Molith to follow him away from the ship and nets.

Still intimidated, the mother remained idle until her baby reached her. Once united, mother and young intertwined their long necks and rubbed each other with their heads before disappearing beneath the waves.

Standing on the uneven ship deck, Alex grasped what his father had already known. moliths weren’t mindless monsters. They were devoted, intelligent creatures with the instincts to relate to a harpy. The vessel lurched with the rapid intake of water into its hull. It would soon sink.

The young man approached. “You’re the winged men we heard about in Oceanside. Thank you for saving us.”

“We are harpies, not men,” Alex said. “And you are far from saved. Your ship will be gone within the hour and land is a long way. Do you have a raft?”

Shail landed beside him and the crew gathered around. The old man said, “There’s never been money for a lifeboat.”

Alex turned to his father. “Between the two of us, we can only carry one man to land.”

Shail lifted his head. “We might not be needed. I hear the hovers.”

Since the men couldn’t hear them, Alex pointed to the tiny dots on the horizon. “There they are.”

The young man said, “Those hovers are miles off, but you heard them. You harpies are incredible.”

Alex smiled with pride. He was no longer a freak.

CHAPTER THIRTY-FOUR

Shail stood with Alex and the crew on the sinking vessel and watched the two hovercraft approach. "My son and I shall stay until you are safely removed."

The old man mumbled, "Yeah, we're saved but hardly out of trouble. Mr. Chang won't be happy about losing this boat and his favorite captain, not to mention having no catch to make up the cost."

"He sounds like an asshole," Alex said. "Who is this Chang?"

"The owner," said the old man. "He has several seafood operations on other planets, but happens to be in River Falls now. He's probably on one of those hovers." With a sigh, he addressed the small crew. "Better go grab your valuables."

Shail sensed the crew and relayed to Alex, *I detect fear in these men. We freed the baby and shall be blamed. Perhaps we should go.*

I'm not afraid of Chang or any son-of-a-bitch, Alex relayed. *We'll stay until everyone is off the ship.*

Alex, you have strong telepathy but never developed the instincts of a hunted harpy. Men are unpredictable, and staying is risk.

"Dad, you worry too much," Alex said. "Besides, I've got a few things to say to this guy."

The first hover to arrive was shiny, new and expensive. Clean cut and well dressed, a man stepped off and stood out from his ragged Asian counterparts holding their meager belongings. He obviously was Chang. "What happened?" he ranted.

The old crewman stepped forward. “I am sorry, sir. We had a cow and her calf in sight and managed to net the baby. When the cow charged the ship, the harpoon jammed. She rammed us and killed the captain.”

Chang eyed Shail and Alex. “And what are these things?”

“They’re called harpies,” said the old man. “Luckily, they came along and freed the calf. That stopped the cow’s attack and saved us.”

“I don’t care if they saved your miserable lives,” Chang growled. “That calf was worth a fortune. It should’ve stayed netted until another ship could take it.”

Alex ruffled his feathers. “Mr. Chang, you are violating interplanetary laws, hunting moliths. I’ve checked, and they’re consisted an endangered species and are protected. You face fines and prison.”

Chang glared at Alex. “I’m exempt. Hunting molith is research.”

“That’s bullshit!” Alex fired back.

Shail nudged him. *Alex, you pick a fight that cannot be won. This man has no respect for laws or nature.* With a hard glare, he said, “We go now, Alex.”

Alex huffed, obviously not wanting to back down but knew he better not disobey. “I’m going but I’m not done with you, Chang. The Federal authorities will be notified about your fishing practices.”

He and Alex soared off the deck, but seconds into the flight, Shail heard a man yell, “Don’t shoot them!”

Laser blasts zipping past him and Alex. Shail dipped his wings and rolled in midair to prevent being an easy target, but Alex had never been a hunted and didn’t know to alter his straight flight. Before he could be warned, two blasts hit his side and wing. He spiralled out of control and splashed down in the ocean. Shail circled back and dove to retrieve him, but then felt the sting on his back. He tumbled end over end into the waves and blacked out.

* * *

Under a starry sky, Shail woke on straw and shook his head to clear his mind from the laser stunning. Concerned about Alex, he attempted to rise, but couldn't because ropes bound his wrists behind his back and tethered his ankles. Further, he was confined in a low metal cage. He twisted his neck and saw Alex lying behind him, also tied, but still unconscious from receiving two blasts.

Several feet away, two men acting as guards sat on crates, holding weapons with a small lantern between them. The cage was at the end of a narrow, dark alley. Beyond, were the dimly lit shacks that lined the dirt road of River Falls. One of the men noticed Shail's movement. "Hey, one of those creatures is awake." The men stepped to him and held the lantern over the cage.

Detecting their nature, Shail hissed at them, rolled over, and defensively covered Alex with his wing.

They chuckled. "He's trying to protect his chick like a damn bird," one said. "These harpies give me the creeps."

"The wife likes them," said the other guard, "She saw them unloaded and hasn't shut up about their looks. The sooner they're gone, the better."

"I heard Chang plans to kill them at sun-up." The men returned to the crates and sat down.

Shail hung his head and felt the familiar gnawing anxiety in his gut. Too often he had been a captive of cruel men and faced this grave situation. He was ready to accept his death, but he had parental obligations. He would fight to his last breath to save his precious son. Nuzzling Alex's cheek, he was relieved. His son's breathing and heart-rate were normal. Several stun blasts often killed a weaker, brown-winged harpy. He raised his head, hearing the approaching voices of more men.

The two guards stood when Chang and several others strolled into the alley. In the lantern light, Chang gazed down at Shail. "I see one is awake."

"Yes, sir, Mr. Chang," said a guard with a chuckle. "When we stepped to the cage, he hissed at us and covered the other one with his wing."

"The crew said this one is the father. I want you men to stay clear of their cage. These scrawny harpies don't look dangerous, but I've learned if they get their hands on a man, he's dead."

The young man from the ship jogged toward them. "Mr. Chang, the harpies didn't know that releasing the molith was wrong. They saved us, just like they're going to bring back the trees and help the planet."

Chang glared at the young man. "If they didn't know it was wrong, why didn't you tell them? Perhaps you and the crew should also be punished." Without a word, the young man shrank into the shadows and slipped away. Chang rubbed his jaw and faced a big man. "That boy brought up a concern. The other inhabitants might get upset if they learned we killed their winged saviors."

"No one in River Falls would tell an outsider," said the big man.

"True but no sense leaving proof," Chang said. "Once they're dead, load the bodies in a hover and dump them out at sea." He grinned. "The moliths will take care of the evidence."

Shail gripped the bars. "If you harm my son, I shall kill you."

Chang chuckled. "You and your boy like to make threats. No one does that and lives. I did some research on harpies. Your wings are worth plenty on the black market. That should make up my losses on the calf."

Chang lit up a cigarette. "While I was reading about your species, I found an old hunt manual on how harpies were once dressed out. Apparently they should be hung by their wrists. They thrash a little but then spread their wings, go into a trance, and don't move when their wings are cut off. The feathers aren't ruined and soaked with blood. I also learned that their testicle skin makes a fine wallet, and there was even a recipe for grilled harpy. I believe in tradition, and the large gaff hook on the dock for hanging moliths should also work for these harpies." He glanced at Shail. "I'll see you in the morning." He and his small group left the alley, and only the two guards remained.

One guard pulled his jacket close and said, "It's going to be cold tonight."

A strong bitter wind blew off the ocean and across the peninsula. Using his mouth, Shail pulled in Alex's extended wings in place so they shielded his body. For extra warmth, he huddled close to his son and added his own wings. He shut his eyes but was too worried for sleep.

In the past, Shail had escaped death when captured. Men considered him a rare, game trophy, more valuable alive than his taxidermy wings. This was not the case now. Few sportsmen would pay to kill a harpy and risk murder charges, but owning harpy wings was a minor infraction. He listened to Alex's slow, steady breath and felt responsible for his coming end. Despite his son's complaints, Shail had chosen to stay on this planet, go on the journey, and save the Molith and men regardless of the warnings. In trying to teach Alex, he had killed him.

* * *

A soft, lavender light crept into the dark horizon. Shail cherished sunrises, but this one, possibly his last, he watched with dread. One of the guards stood and urinated near the cage. Fastening his pants, he grinned. "It is almost time to hang. The whole town is looking forward to it."

The other guard yawned and stretched. "Not sure everyone will be happy, my wife for example. I say blast them in the head and be done with these feathered beasts."

"Chang is looking forward to lynching them. I wouldn't deprive him."

Shail lowered his head and nuzzled his sleeping son's face, so handsomely chiseled in the morning light. He pondered the lifelong question of why some men were so cruel and destroyed beauty.

Alex stirred and opened his eyes. "Dad, where are we?"

Shail relayed, *Silence, Alex. We were captured and are in River Falls. These men shall soon come and kill us. When they take me from the cage, I shall fight them. With the distraction, you must slip out and escape.*

Alex struggled in his bonds, but managed to sit up. *How will you fight them? You're tied up like me.*

But they did not tie my wings, not knowing they are a weapon. Shail lifted his head. *I hear them coming. Now, do as I say. Wiggle out of the cage and fly.*

Alex frowned and shook his head. *I'm groggy and can't think straight.*

Do not think but do. Shail saw Chang along with ten men approaching from the street. He sighed. Along with the guards, his wings were up against thirteen armed men. He turned to Alex. *When you leave the cage, do not fly for the sky. Soar low to the ground around the buildings. The walls should shield you from their blasts.*

Alex's mouth hung open, still not grasping their dire predicament. *But, Dad...*

I love you, son. Shail kissed Alex's forehead and slid to the cage door to ensure the men removed him first. *Be ready.*

Chang and his group encircled the cage. "I see the mouthy younger one is finally awake," Chang said, and turned to the big man. "When you get them to the dock and hang them, fasten their ankles down to the piling."

"Chang, you'll regret this," Alex said.

Chang laughed, 'Just like your dad, making useless threats. You wanted to report me to the feds for hunting moliths, and that has sealed your fate. I'm going to enjoy slicing you up."

The big guy spoke up. "Mr. Chang, I still think cutting their throats here will be faster and easier."

"And the blood will be hard to remove from those yellow feathers," Chang said. "Besides, slicing off their balls and watching them squirm will be entertaining."

Hearing Chang, Alex's eyes grew huge, and he turned to Shail. *Alex, do not think it,* Shail relayed. *You must flee. There are too many for you to stay and help me. I want you to go.*

A guard unlocked the cage, and Shail lowered his head, avoiding eye contact, and his wings drooped in defeat, giving the impression of submissiveness. Two men grabbed his arms, dragged him out of the cage, and forced him to stand. Face to face with Chang, he breathed a little hard and his feathers shuddered with fright. Chang smiled. "You truly are a good-looking creature. Too bad you became a problem."

Now, Alex! Go! Shail shifted his stance, and his untethered wings whacked the faces of the men holding him, knocking them down. He whirled around and with precision his wings struck Chang and another man in their throats. He fluttered a few feet off the ground, and his bound legs became an additional weapon, kicking one man in the groin and another in the gut. So shocked, the remaining men scrambled away from him.

Holding his throat, Chang croaked out orders, "Grab him, you fools, before he flies off!"

Withstanding Shail's wing blows, the big man lunged for Shail's legs and tossed him on the ground. Shail struggled to sit up but his bound wrists and ankles made it difficult. He flapped wildly, trying to lift off without standing. The men pounced on him and held down his flailing wings. Pinned under a crush of bodies, Shail looked to the cage, hoping to see it empty.

Alex had left the cage, but had not flown away. He stood calmly with his wings folded as one of Chang's men mindlessly freed his bonds. "Get off my father and untie him," Alex ordered. The men seemed dazed and followed his commands. They crawled off Shail, and the big man untied his bonds. Shail rose totally shocked.

Alex stepped to him. "Dad, I'm sorry you had to fight them. My head was messed up, and I couldn't use my hypnotism right away. Are you all right?"

Shail nodded, still amazed that Alex's mind controlled the men. Shail had witnessed his son's power in the visions when forcing the suicide of the Oden police, but seeing it firsthand was phenomenal.

Alex meandered to Chang. "You wanted to be entertained with a hanging?" he asked, looming over the smaller man. "I won't disappoint you. Let's go to this dock." Alex and the men walked up the alley to the street and disappeared around a building corner.

Shail didn't need instincts to know that Alex was filled with rage and sought revenge. He was going to kill Chang. Spreading his wings, Shai flew to catch up with Alex and the men. He landed beside his son and asked, "What are you going to do?"

"I think you know," Alex said, marching down the street with the men trailing like dogs. At the large main dock with a view of the ocean, several hundred people had gathered and milled near two heavy cross beams with a grappling hook used to hang and gut the massive moliths. Two ropes dangled from the hook, intended for Shail and Alex.

Shail flew to a fishing boat and settled on its cabin to oversee all. Alex walked through the parted crowd, leaving Chang and his men with the silent spectators, all appearing to be under his son's spell. Alex fluttered and landed on the dock near the hook. With a hard stare, he eyed the ropes and ruffled his feathers.

Shail knew that what happened next would be a test. Had Alex learned the values of a harpy or would he behave like a vengeful human? Shail didn't care about the men, but worried for Alex's nature, forever on a dark path.

"Come join me, Dad," Alex called. "Help me decide if I should I hang their leader and his boys or have this whole bloodthirsty village walk into the sea and drown?"

Shail landed beside Alex. "Let them go. To kill a few or all makes no difference. It is you who shall be harmed."

"But…but they wanted kill you," Alex stuttered. "If I hadn't woken up and regained my senses, you'd be…" He shook his head. "They must die."

"A harpy kills when he has no choice and is defending himself or others. You have a choice. Revenge is not our way."

"But it's my way," Alex said. "These sick bastards don't deserve to live."

"They are evil, but you asked what I wish," Shail said. "I wish my son had compassion even when it is hard. I wish he behaves like a noble golden harpy instead of a vindictive human." He gazed out at the crowd. "And I wish these cruel people would change, stop destroying nature and cherish it like the harpies. But I long for the impossible."

Alex gazed down at the dock in thought. With a deep sigh, he said, "I really would like these pricks to suffer, but I love and respect you. I'll grant your wishes." He closed his eyes and tilted his head back for a few minutes. He slowly opened his eyes to the crowd.

The people, no longer under Alex's control, began to stir and whisper to each other. Chang rushed down the dock to Alex and fell to his knees. "Please forgive me for wanting to hurt you. I promise we'll stop hunting and help you restore this planet and its wildlife. I have a lot of money and will invest it here. You have my word." The crowd rumbled in agreement.

Shail was stunned with the human transformation. "You changed them. You removed the bad and replaced it with good. They think like harpies now. How long shall it last?"

"If I don't reverse the hypnotism, they'll stay this way."

CHAPTER THIRTY-FIVE

Alex spent the next few hours with River Falls people and explained their part in restoring the planet. Chang contacted his operations on other planets, halted the decimating fishing, and turned his business into a conservation organization. Replacing greed with a worthy cause, the little Asian couldn't stop smiling.

Once condemned prisoners, Alex and his father were treated like kings and feasted on pickled seaweed and the pink fronds mixed with nuts and curry seasoning. Alex did all the talking with the villagers and noticed Shail was unusually quiet, gazing with wonderment at him.

At noon Alex and Shail left the village and flew to the mountains overlooking the marsh. They landed on the cliff holding their rocky night shelter. Alex had detected the numerous questions that baffled his father's mind. It was time for answers.

Alex leaned against the stone wall while his father stood in the cave opening and looked at the landscape. "I'm sorry I didn't tell you everything. I had wanted respect and power and knew you'd frown on my ability, just like Bloom and Summer. Traveling to Dora, we had trouble with a town of deranged miners. I hypnotized them to get out of the scrap but didn't hurt them. I opened their minds and let them judge themselves." He shrugged. "Summer had heard laser blasts and thought I forced them to kill themselves like the cops on Oden."

"Why not tell her the truth?"

"Because I was angry she had assumed the worst," Alex said. "And probably because I was too proud to explain. I blocked the whole memory so you wouldn't know I could manipulate so many at one time. Everyone considers me a freak. I wanted you to think I was normal."

"I knew from the start you were no normal harpy but I understand your reluctance to tell me. Too often you have been misjudged." He sat down on the nest. "How did you get such power?"

"Spending too much time alone," Alex grinned. "I fine-tuned my telepathy and studied hypnotism. The initial goal was to get into human heads and understand why they didn't like me and change that. Turns out, I had to use my talents like a weapon to defend myself. I became disillusioned, and it was all downhill from there."

"But you see clearly now."

"I think so," Alex said. "I only need more patience and your wisdom. Actually, putting those River Falls people on the right track made me feel good, far better than punishing them with hate."

"How does this hypnotism work?"

"It's like the telepathic communication with the harpies except my mind goes blank so I can send and receive thoughts. Then I envision a blank screen on their foreheads and enter their minds. I tell them to relax, count to three, and transmit my suggestive message. Humans don't use their senses and telepathy, so they have impressionable minds and are helpless to resist, unlike you and Will."

Shail paced briefly. "Alex, I believe I have realized something you have not."

Alex frowned. "What?"

"Your destiny," said Shail. "You have used your power only when it affects you, but have not seen beyond. You can turn evil into good. Today is an example of what shall come."

Alex puckered his brow. “I didn’t kill those assholes because you stopped me, but make no mistake, I would’ve killed them. I’m not the guy in your bigger picture.”

“You are wrong. You still struggle with anger but are learning. You saw how killing destroyed me and are smart enough to not wish this suffering upon yourself. You have a good heart and would not have killed those people.”

“Jesus, you got more faith in me than I do. You think it’s my destiny to use my abilities and change humans, but you’re forgetting I’m a jerk with messed up human emotions. Fixing mankind is a job for the righteous, not me.”

“That is why you are perfect for this. Unlike other harpies, you understand man’s struggle to be better and do right. For those reasons you shall succeed.”

* * *

Alex and Shail flew back to the little seaside town of Oceanside. The equipment to refurbish the planet along with the experts would soon arrive. In Alex’s absences, Jasper and locals had been busy. The decrepit old buildings in town had been patched up and painted. Under an enormous tarp sat potted seedling trees, and they had mapped out the arid landscape for the first forest. Within a few days, the entire village of River Falls arrived on their boats, eager to assist with the restoration. Once suspicious strangers, Jasper and Chang became friends and worked together.

Alex realized his supervision wouldn’t be needed much longer. The inhabitants could successfully handle the project, and his concerns switched to his father’s foolish expectations. He was only eighteen, never had a girlfriend, much less gotten laid but he was supposed to save mankind.

As night approached, he placed a loaf of bread and some imported dried fruit in a bag and flew back to the small coastal cave and his father, who preferred being alone with nature than socializing with humans. A small campfire burned on the dark beach, and Shail stood beside it.

"Hey, Jasper's wife gave me some goodies for dinner," Alex said, landing in the sand.

"Tell her thank you for me," Shail said. "Is all going well in the town?"

Alex sat down in the sand. "Yeah, great," he said, handing a slice of the loaf to Shail. "I actually think they'll do fine without me, and we can leave soon. Um…that leaves your plans for me. Paradise Haven is a little planet with only a few thousand people. Altering their thinking wasn't a big problem, but you're suggesting I change billions all over the galaxy. It's impossible."

"My hardships taught me nothing that cannot be done. Focusing on the *all* is daunting and crushes confidence so you fail. Start each day like a seedling tree, celebrating each new leaf. This place is the first leaf. As the tree grows, it branches out, shades the weary and its fruit feeds the hungry. People are grateful for the tree, and like birds, they carry its seeds throughout the lands and more trees grow with your message. Eventually, the tree towers above the canopy and looks down at the wonderful home it created for all. So it shall be with you. One planet at a time, you shall change the humans until you have a forest."

Holding his knees, Alex buried his head in his arms, but then looked up. "You make it sound easy, but it's going to be a bitch, forcing all those people to think like harpies."

"Alex, you know most humans are good and would welcome peace and a chance to bring back trees and wildlife. Perhaps you should focus on the greedy and heartless."

"I could do that. Start with leadership and work down to prisons and high-crime areas, but Dad, restoring nature to these planets is a whole different problem. Overpopulation destroyed the environment and wildlife habitat. Any suggestions on fixing that, short of wiping out millions?"

"Humans are mixed up, believing it is their right to multiply, and their laws support this out of control breeding. With your hypnotism, you must make them adopt nature's rules."

Alex chuckled. "And what are those?"

"Nature allows only the most worthy to bear young. The strongest and most determined fish survive the treacherous journey upstream to spawn. The weak die. In a grogin pack, the alpha pair has the most speed, courage, and hunting skills, and they are the only ones to breed so their good traits are passed on to the young. In a zel herd, a stag must fight off his opponents before a female accepts him, ensuring her of a strong fawn."

Alex laughed. "It's prejudicial and unjust."

"Yes, nature is selective, unjust but wise, breeding out the undesirables. Harpies strive for honor, courage, loyalty, and only those harpies mate and bear young. Worthy people who work hard, provide a home for their family, and rear their children with integrity are also disgusted with those who are lazy, selfish, and do not take care about their families. A child is a sacred gift, not a right."

"I agree, but the data shows lousy parents have more kids than your so-called worthy humans. The governments have to step in and take care of the kids. But how am I going to reverse this trend?"

"You instill that humans have to earn the privilege to bear young. They must be decent, honorable, caring, and willing to work hard and sacrifice to provide a home before having young, and they cannot have too many. Even the poor can meet this challenge. With this goal, the population shall decline and improve to the benefit of all life."

Alex lifted an eyebrow. "That way of thinking will surely weed out the drug users and bums plus end unprotected sex. Okay. I'll do it."

* * *

A month later, the water refinery that converted saltwater into fresh was irrigating thousands of newly planted seedling trees, keeping them alive during the drought. Jasper and his group worked the forests and land. In River Falls, Chang and the villagers erected a huge warehouse to raise fish spawn and replenish the ocean. In a few years, Paradise Haven would match its name.

After placing a crate of food supplies aboard *Dream Weaver,* Alex walked down the ramp to Jasper. "That should do it. She's stocked and loaded."

"I wish you would stay."

"You guys don't need me anymore. You're off to an amazing start."

"We might not need you but we'll miss you, Alex."

Two days later, the entire population of Paradise Haven gathered at the Oceanside airport in front of *Dream Weaver* for a final farewell. Alex walked through the tearful crowd, receiving handshakes, kisses, and hugs. His father stood in the ship's doorway and watched. Although he was the behind-the-scenes one who helped the planet and people, Shail didn't need to be thanked. It was a harpy thing.

Chang bowed his head to Alex. "You changed my life. I am grateful, Alex."

Alex nodded and stepped to Jasper. "I guess this is goodbye, buddy," he said, offering his hand.

The crusty old man bypassed Alex's hand and embraced him. "I don't have the words to thank you," he cried openly. "I just don't got the words."

Alex smiled, and his eyes grew misty. Their devotion to him was true, not forced from hypnotism. "The thanks are mutual. Your planet helped me too." He ascended the ramp, and at the top, he addressed the cheering crowd. "Make me proud, Paradise." After sealing the ship hatch, he walked into the cabin to his father.

"You have always believed that love and respect would fulfill you," Shail said. "Now you have it. Are you content and happy?"

"I am, probably for the first time. I owe it all to you. You taught me I had to give of myself and earn it." Alex smiled. "I'm looking forward to more, bettering people and planets. Let's get out of here."

Shail followed him into the cockpit. “Where are we going?”

Alex slid into the pilot seat and flipped switches to prepare for takeoff. “We could travel back to Dora and drop you off. I’m sure that would make you happy. I can handle what’s up ahead.”

“I would love to go home, but what lies ahead is far more important than my needs. I want to be part of it.”

“Okay, I’m think our first stop should be Earth. It’s called the cradle of mankind and the worst of planets plus the Intergalactic Federation is there. If I can change those sons-of-bitches’ way of thinking, half the battle is over.”

“Yes, Earth is a terrible place. The oceans are dead, and most of the trees and animals are gone. Hopelessness, poverty, and crime cover the land. It is a wise place to start, and I was once friends with the president of Earth. If he still lives, he would help us.”

“President Jeb Larson,” Alex said. “He’s alive and still carries a lot of pull. After the therapy session involving your past with him, I checked him out. You prevented his assassination, so yeah. He’d be a perfect contact.” He glanced back. “You better strap in. We’re blasting off.”

With a roar and violent shudder, *Dream Weaver* lifted off from Oceanside port and cleared the atmosphere. Once in space Alex shut down the thrusters and punched in the coordinates to the wormhole for Earth. With his inheritance he could afford a new, smoother ship with up-to-date equipment and conveniences, but like Matt, he’d grown fond of *Dream Weaver* and would never replace the old girl. He put the ship on autopilot and wandered into the cabin. Shail sat on the couch and stared out the portal as Paradise Haven shrank to a small orb.

“Sorry about the rocky ride,” Alex said, “but after a few times, you should get used to it.”

Shail turned from the view of space. “After all I have been through I am not frightened of a noisy, shaking ship. I was thinking of you and the night we meet on the sacred mountain. Shivering in the cold, you said your name was Alexander, and you were my son. I wrapped my wings around you for warmth and sensed your anxiety, rage, confusion, the longing for change but not knowing how."

Alex raised an eyebrow. "I was a mess."

"Yes, but I also detected you would do great things. Now it begins."

"Like Alexander the Great," Alex said with a chuckle. "I grew up with an old gardener, and when I was down, he'd call me that."

"Who was this great Alexander?"

"He lived thousands of years ago on Earth and was a young Greek with blond hair. He was smart. His battle strategies are still used today, and the guy was determined, conquered the entire civilized world before thirty years old." Alex held his jaw. "I just realized something. Alexander's motive was to unite the kingdoms and enlighten the barbarians."

"Then the gardener foresaw your future. You shall be another Alexander the Great."

About the Author

Susan Klaus was born in Sarasota, Florida and had a lifelong career with animals, owning pet shops, grooming shops, and a cattery of show cats. She worked for veterinarians and bred and raced thoroughbred horses for 14 years. Currently, she resides on a 40-acre farm in Myakka City, Florida and raises rodeo bulls.

She is an author of fantasy and thrillers and has been in Amazon Top 100 authors of Mystery/Romance. Tor Books released her fantasy, *Flight of the Golden Harpy* in 2014. It won the Silver President Award for Best Fantasy. The sequel, *Flight of the Golden Harpy, Waylaid* was released in 2016. Both novels won the Royal Palm Literary Award for Best Fantasy and are Amazon Bestsellers for Epic Fantasy. The last novel in the trilogy, *Flight of the Golden Harpy III, Sons of Shail* comes out in 2020.

Secretariat Reborn, the first Florida thriller in the Christian Roberts Series, was released by Oceanview Publishing in 2013 and won the Silver President Award for Best Adult Fl Fiction and is an Amazon Bestseller. The sequel, *Shark Fin Soup* won the RPLA for Second Best Unpublished Thriller and the Silver Presidential Award for Best Action/Suspense. *Wolf in the Crosshairs,* the third novel, was released Oct. 2019. It won the

International Thrill Writers award for Best First Sentence and the Bronze President Award for Best Thriller.

Klaus is president/founder of Sarasota Authors Connection Club, 200 members. For nine years she was the radio host for the Authors Connection Show with 18 million listeners worldwide.

Website: susanklaus.com.
On Facebook: Susan C. Klaus
Twitter: Klaussue.

Made in the USA
Columbia, SC
12 August 2023

21509732R00230